BITE CLUB

HAL BODNER

BITE CLUB

A WEST HOLLYWOOD VAMPIRE NOVEL

alyson books
los angeles

Celebrating Twenty-Five Years

MANUFACTURED IN THE UNITED STATES OF AMERICA.

THIS TRADE PAPERBACK ORIGINAL IS PUBLISHED BY ALYSON BOOKS,
P.O. BOX 4371, LOS ANGELES, CALIFORNIA 90078-4371.
DISTRIBUTION IN THE UNITED KINGDOM BY TURNAROUND PUBLISHER SERVICES LTD.,
UNIT 3, OLYMPIA TRADING ESTATE, COBURG ROAD, WOOD GREEN,
LONDON N22 6TZ ENGLAND.

FIRST EDITION: JUNE 2005

05 06 07 08 09 **a** 10 9 8 7 6 5 4 3 2 1

ISBN 1-55583-903-7
ISBN-13 978-1-55583-903-1

LIBRARY OF CONGRESS CATALOGING-IN-PUBLICATION DATA
BODNER, HAL.
  BITE CLUB : A WEST HOLLYWOOD VAMPIRE TALE / HAL BODNER.—1ST ED.
    ISBN 1-55583-903-7; ISBN-13 978-1-55583-903-1
    1. GAY MEN—FICTION. 2. VAMPIRES—FICTION. 3. WEST HOLLYWOOD (CALIF.)—
FICTION. I. TITLE.
PS3602.O326B63 2005
813'.6—DC22   2005041100

CREDITS
COVER PHOTOGRAPHY FROM IDENTIKAL/PHOTODISC RED/GETTY IMAGES.
COVER DESIGN BY MATT SAMS.

Dedication, Acknowledgments, and Apologia

I'd make a rotten vampire. Vampires need to adapt over time to new things. I hate change, and I don't deal well with it. I'm a creature of the late 1970s and early 1980s. I don't understand why gasoline costs more than forty-seven cents a gallon, and I think paying more than thirty dollars for blue jeans is completely insane. But I'm not a curmudgeon by any means. I'm not bitter or resentful. I don't protest in the streets. I'm just wistful for times that have passed.

My love affair with West Hollywood goes back almost two decades. Though I was not around when we seceded from Los Angeles and became our own city, I arrived shortly thereafter. And to my chagrin, West Hollywood has changed. It's neither better nor worse than it was. But it is…different.

The West Hollywood of *Bite Club* does not exist. It is a compilation of the city as it was, could have been, and should be. It certainly reflects my habit of wanting things to stay the same but adds an element of wouldn't-it-be-nicer-if. Readers familiar with our city may recognize some of the locations in their various incarnations. Others will be baffled that the geography or the nature of various buildings has been changed. Still others may search in vain for locations they *think* they recognize but that are complete fabrications reminiscent of something similar. Our city hall is no longer in a mini mall. We have instead a glorious architectural marvel, styled in something I affectionately call "Retro IKEA," from which the city is run. The Athletic Club and the Sports Connection are long gone and appear here, in combination, as the Boys' Town Gym. Some of the bars visited by Chris and Troy still exist, others have closed, and still others are fictional. The Harper apartment is a real building but is located elsewhere. Those readers who feel that a Spanish Gothic edifice covered in pink neon strains credulity are invited to tour our city—we have one condominium entirely sheathed in stainless steel. At one time or another, I have seen all of the costumes described in my version of the Halloween parade—and I have seen some of them in months other than October!

West Hollywood does not have a city coroner. Nor do we have an elected mayor; council members rotate to fill the office every year. We do have a city manager, however, and a sheriff's captain. We also have a unique way of making our town work for us. The weird West Hollywood laws and ordinances cited in the book are very close to factual: If you happen to be a ficus tree, you may come here to find sanctuary. If you are a Styrofoam take-out container, however, you will be shot on sight. Municipally mandated death by slow torture also awaits any West Hollywood resident who has the temerity to declaw a cat. Our city council's commitment to fostering the arts does not extend to making aesthetic value judgments. Thus, undesirable sculptures installed on the median strip of Santa Monica Boulevard are never removed because they are unattractive, but may be banished if their sheer ugliness renders them a distraction to passing motorists, thereby becoming "dangerous" art. Lest anyone assume that the rules, regulations, and mores of our city are completely insane, I assure them that smoking cigarettes within one's apartment is not grounds for eviction—that proposed ordinance was defeated some time ago.

The characters of *Bite Club* are all fictional. In any small town, however, one will find certain "types"—many of which appear in these pages. I emphatically deny that Becky, Pamela, Clive, and Eversleigh are based on real people. As for Chris, Troy, and Rex, the only real bloodsuckers one is likely to meet around here are Hollywood agents. Ghouls, on the other hand, can be sighted at almost any film premiere.

There are some people whom I would like to thank for their support over the years, and to them this book is dedicated.

John Altschul and Nancy Greenstein first introduced me to West Hollywood politics. Though Nancy has moved on to bigger pastures, John still serves as a city commissioner.

Andrea Carrero, Dan Felix, Jack Freinhar, Robert McGarity, and Rob Stevens all read early versions of this novel and made suggestions and comments.

I would not be alive at the ripe old age of forty-something had it not been for Sharon Nesselle. She has my "undying" gratitude.

My editor, Angela Brown, told me to trust my heart. She also waded patiently through roughly seventy-five title suggestions. Any thanks to Angela come accompanied by warm fuzzy thoughts directed to Harry.

Alyss Dorese, my brother Dark Hoffman, and Alan Neilson have always tolerated my dramas and eccentricities. When I was completely broke, when the computer crashed, when I "went Hollywood," and when I was dating any of the "Davids," they were always there for me.

Finally and most of all, this work is dedicated to Ty: *A Good Dog*.

CHAPTER ONE

Anthony Balencini fumed with impatience. He'd been circling the same block for twenty minutes, searching in vain for a parking space. He squinted through his sunglasses, finding it difficult to see in the rapidly fading light, and finally yanked them from his face in frustration. The late-afternoon sun, which had been blazing brightly when he'd left his office forty-five minutes ago, had already vanished below the horizon. At this time of year in Southern California, dusk had a tendency to fall with amazing quickness.

Three times his mood had brightened upon seeing what looked like a free space; each time he'd become more irritable upon pulling over and seeing the postage stamp–size parking signs promising penalties tantamount to removing fingernails with hot pliers should he even *think* of parking there without a permit. As he passed the West Hollywood branch of the Los Angeles County Library for what seemed the fifteenth time, he stomped on his brakes as he saw, like a gift from heaven, an elderly woman climbing into an ancient Dodge.

He pulled off San Vicente into the library parking lot and waited, barely restraining himself from leaning on the horn—or better yet, leaping out of the car and battering the old broad to death with his briefcase—while the old lady got into the car, reset the rearview mirror, tested all her lights, and, he thought with pique, probably read the damn owner's manual to figure out how to put the key into the ignition.

Finally, her rear lights went on and she slowly began to back out, stopping short after having moved barely six inches. Anthony's temper worsened as the Dodge sat for almost a full minute, not moving. The old woman then rolled down her window and stuck her head out. Waving to attract Anthony's attention and smiling brightly she called, "Excuse me, young man. Am I clear?"

Anthony rolled down his own window and prepared to ream the old bitch up one side and down the other. But she was *very* old. And smiling sweetly. And looking a lot like his great-aunt Jane. He couldn't do it. He sighed then said, "Yeah, you're clear."

"Thank you *so* much!" she called back merrily. "Have a nice evening!"

"Yeah, you too, you old bat," he grumbled as he rolled up his window. "Am I clear?" he mimicked. "Christ, lady! I'm thirty feet away from you!"

Slowly the Dodge backed up, finally clearing the other cars, and eventually the old lady managed to get it into a forward gear and drove off. Anthony started to pull into the space and a small white sports car tried to cut him off. The driver, however, made the mistake of glancing at Anthony through the windshield. Anthony glared back, trying to show the other driver *exactly* what he was about to get himself into. The sports car had second thoughts and pulled around him.

Anthony parked and got out of the car. Setting the alarm, he glanced at his watch. He figured he'd have just enough time to cut through West Hollywood Park to Anawalt Lumber, buy what he needed, and get home to Studio City before his dinner plans with Christine were irreparably screwed up.

Why, oh why, had he ever married Christine in the first place? At twenty-one, she'd indeed been gorgeous, he reflected as he trotted down the street. But in the six years since their marriage, she'd put on weight—a lot of weight. *Face it, Tony,* he thought as he passed the tennis courts, *she's starting to look just like one of those fat Italian mamas—the type you swore you'd never end up with.*

To add insult to injury, since Peggy had been born, Christine's voice had changed. What used to be a soothing contralto had deepened and roughened until Tony felt like he was married to a drag queen trying to impersonate Brenda Vaccaro.

"Don't forget to stop by that store on Robertson and pick up a new faucet on your way home," she'd nagged that morning. Fortunately, Peggy's whining and gurgling—and the loud *plop* as she threw banana-colored muck against the kitchen walls—helped to mute his wife's abrasive tone. "And don't be late for dinner. We've got reservations at seven-thirty with my sister."

Christine's sister Sheila and her husband. Christ! All he needed was a night out with those two! Sheila had six-inch-long nauseating pink Lee Press-Ons and those phony boobs she never ceased bragging about. If Tony heard one more loving paean to Dr. "Feelgood" and the fantastic job he'd done restructuring Sheila's breasts, he swore he was going to give her the opportunity to spend a lot more time with the doctor by reaching across the table and tearing the implants right out of her chest. And if Sheila's breasts could be considered large, her hair was positively gargantuan. Hadn't anyone ever bothered to tell her teased beehives had gone out with Silly String? Her husband was, if possible, even worse. John was one of those alcoholics who firmly denied his disease. After all, he reasoned—loudly and often—he never had a drink before six in the evening. The fact that he was usually plastered by seven fifteen didn't seem to give him a clue that his drinking might be just a bit of a problem. The last time the two couples had gone out to dinner, John had finished his sixth brandy, belched loud enough to disturb the air traffic controllers down at LAX, and had promptly passed out, facedown, in his plate of chocolate mousse.

But God forbid Tony should make one unkind remark; he'd never hear the end of it from Christine. Between his bitch of a wife and her relatives and his snot-nosed daughter, was it any wonder he looked elsewhere for…well, for some relaxation?

He emerged from the cul-de-sac across from the hardware store and stopped. The store was dark, obviously closed.

"Fuck," he said, then added for good measure, "Shit!"

Tony debated chucking the whole thing and calling Christine. He'd cancel dinner and tell her he'd had to work late and just go over to one of the bars on Santa Monica Boulevard. Maybe, if he were lucky, he'd meet someone and be able to spend a few hours just...relaxing.

He took out his wallet and glanced inside. Good, he had enough for a motel room if he managed to score. He turned back toward the park and started walking, fantasizing about one of the young men he'd seen in a bar the last time he'd been in West Hollywood two weeks ago. He got hard as he thought about picking up some really hot hairy stranger and letting him fuck him.

At twenty-eight, although Tony had been involved with many men, he didn't consider himself to be gay. After all, he always rationalized, he was married. Then again, no matter how good the sex, he never engaged in a repeat performance with the same guy; that wouldn't be just relaxation—that would be queer. And Tony thought himself anything but queer.

He was macho, a real man's man. He worked out at the Family Gym in Encino at least twice a week and, sometimes, if he could make it out of the house before Christine and the kid woke up, on Saturday mornings. In the fall he played baseball with some of the guys from the office on Sunday afternoons, and he managed to get in a half-mile run before work fairly often. His chest was deep, his shoulders broad, and his belly flat as it had been in college. In recent years he'd noticed the hair at his temples seemed to be slightly grayer than on the rest of his head, but a quick trip to the hair care products aisle at the supermarket had fixed that! And so what if his hair was going a little gray, he thought, grinning in defiance, his ass and thighs were still tight enough to please any of the olive-skinned young men to whom he was partial.

He cut across the grass, entering the park, and headed toward Rage, a trendy Santa Monica Boulevard disco, ignoring the elderly man with bleached blond hair who smiled at him from a bench. *What the hell does he think I am?* thought Tony, *Some kind of fairy?* Tony preferred them young, under thirty, hairy-chested, well-built, and, if possible, Italian.

Like the one over there, near the bushes next to the public swimming pool. Tony slowed his pace to a casual walk and subtly glanced at the young man. He was shorter than Tony liked, but handsome, and he had a great body. Even from this distance, he could make out the division in the center of the guy's pecs where they emerged from the top of his black tank top.

The youth returned his look, very directly. *Italian?* Tony wondered, *Maybe Greek?* as the stranger smiled.

Tony moved closer and nodded, in a way calculated to seem friendly but not too encouraging. It wouldn't do to appear too forward.

"Hello," said the stranger. His voice was deep, deeper even than Christine's, but without that harsh nasal quality. "Are you in a hurry?"

Tony stopped. "Uh, no…I mean, I gotta get home to my wife." Tony stressed the last word slightly; it wouldn't do for the guy to think he was gay or anything. "But I've got some time," he added nonchalantly, wanting the other to make the first move, afraid he wouldn't. "Why?"

"Oh, I don't know. I was just looking for some company. How about you?"

"What kind of company?" Tony hoped his voice carried just the right quality of interest and suspicion.

"What kind of company were *you* looking for?" the young man asked.

"Who said I was looking for…" Tony's eyes met the stranger's. Suddenly, he felt himself grow fully erect and lost track of what he was about to say. His mind grew foggy; his vision locked in to the other's gaze. *Strange,* he thought in the back of his mind, *It's like looking down a tunnel. To his eyes… Those eyes…*

The young man moved closer. His right hand brushed Tony's

shoulder once, then he rested both palms on Tony's chest, gently squeezing the muscle. Tony felt himself flush at the other's touch. The stranger kneaded Tony's chest softly.

"Is the rest of you as strong?" he murmured.

Tony could only nod, unable to speak. He was adrift in a fog, anchored only by those eyes. *Brown*, he thought. *No, black*, he corrected. *With little specks of silver.*

"Shall we adjourn to the bushes?" asked the dark-haired youth. Without waiting for an answer, he pulled Tony off to the side into the bushes by the municipal swimming pool.

Dimly through his mental haze, Tony heard the splashing of the West Hollywood Aquatics Team as they practiced. Soon, as his shirt was opened and he felt the stranger's warm mouth on his chest, nuzzling at the hair, even the splashes faded away.

Tony unbuckled his belt and reached to unzip his fly, but his hands were gently moved away. With excruciating slowness, the stranger unzipped Tony's fly and pulled his slacks down past his hips, all the while licking at Tony's chest and belly.

Tony leaned back against a nearby tree and, without a thought for his clothing, slid down the trunk to rest, knees spread wide, pants around his ankles, shirt open, and head tilted against the base of the tree.

It's funny, he thought, *I'm looking at the sky, but I can still see...those eyes.*

He felt the young man's mouth close around the tip of his penis and shuddered in anticipation. A few seconds later he flinched in pain.

He bit me, for chrissake! thought Tony, and the fog cleared just enough so that he was able to look down.

But the young man was looking up, recapturing Tony's gaze with his own, and Tony never saw the blood welling from the lacerations along the shaft of his penis. Instead he saw the eyes again. And the two razor-sharp teeth as the stranger smiled. Tony tried to yell for help, to scream so that the swimmers, only yards away, would hear him. But he couldn't.

BITE CLUB

"Sometimes," said the stranger, "in this modern world..." He stood up and used one hand to gently tilt Tony's face up toward the sky once again. "we get more than we bargain for."

He bent his lips to Tony's throat. As Tony, still unable to make a sound, felt the first agony of those terrible teeth piercing his throat, he heard the stranger add in a whisper, "Much more."

The silver specks dancing before him grew brighter and, oddly enough, one of them shimmered and became Christine's face.

Shit, Tony had time to think, *I'm gonna miss dinner. Is she gonna be pissed!*

And then he thought nothing at all.

◊ ◊ ◊

Ivana Petrov was exhausted. Her sister's two sons were adorable, but so much work to keep track of them! Five and seven years old, they had a penchant for mischief. At first, bringing them to the park had seemed like a good idea; now she was having second thoughts. Mikhail, the oldest, had already torn a hole in his best shorts on a nail sticking out of the side of the wooden jungle gym; Yevgeny had taken a toy fire engine from another child and had been reduced to wails of anger when she'd forced him to return it.

As if they didn't have enough toys of their own at home, she thought. Sometimes, even after eight years, she shook her head in amazement at the wealth of this new country. Back in Russia the boys would have been happy with a few wooden cars and a rubber ball. Here it was always the latest they must have: PlayStations, digital cameras, and all the new Disney DVDs.

Ivana had quieted the screaming child with a soccer ball, newly purchased. Now the brothers were kicking it across the park, Mikhail trying to aim it to hit his younger sibling on the head.

"Yevgeny," she called in Russian, "stay away from those bushes. You'll ruin your shirt."

Yevgeny ignored his aunt and dropped down on his hands and knees in the dirt to retrieve the ball. He emerged a moment later, knees filthy, clutching the ball to his chest. He threw it to Mikhail, who promptly kicked it back into the bushes.

Ivana released her breath, loudly so the boys could both hear, and placed her hands on her hips as Yevgeny knelt to go back in after the ball.

"How many times must I tell you?" she said, stomping toward the child, "Stay out of the bushes!"

She grabbed the errant youngster by the back of his coat and hauled him backward.

"You will stay here. *I* will get the ball." She crouched down and, thrusting her arms into the foliage, felt around for the missing ball. Her hands came into contact with something round, strangely much harder than a soccer ball had any right to be.

When one of her hands tangled in Anthony Balencini's hair, she began to scream.

CHAPTER TWO

Three hours later the body was lying nude on an autopsy table in the West Hollywood Morgue. The city coroner, a charmingly plump Jewish woman in her early forties with the unlikely name of Rebecca O'Brien, was puzzled. And when Becky was puzzled, she ate. In fact, any strong emotion, and even a few of the more subtle ones, created an irresistible hankering—usually for something sweet. Right now, Becky was busily unwrapping her third Snickers bar of the day. Snickers was her candy of choice whenever deep thought was required in the morgue; the deep chill of the room prevented the chocolate from melting.

Becky knew deep down that her weight was a problem. She'd tried dieting, but Lean Cuisine, no matter how luscious-looking the photographs on the package, couldn't compare to a two-pound bag of Double Stuf Oreos and a hearty strawberry milk shake so thick she had to eat it with a spoon. The only lasting mementos she kept from her attempts at a slimmer Ms. O'Brien were a minor addiction to chocolate malt–flavored Slim-Fast shakes and the habit of polishing off at least a half dozen Weight Watchers éclairs and an Entenmann's nonfat brownie or two before bedtime.

"I have big bones," she'd told herself and any of her friends who kindly suggested that she might have better luck landing a husband if she could lose forty pounds or so and squeeze herself into a size eighteen. But in her heart she knew it was her irrepressible sweet tooth that had condemned her to look like a stunt-double for Shelley Winters in *The Poseidon Adventure*.

"It's mother's fault," was her second line of defense. "All those years hearing about starving children in India makes me feel guilty if I don't eat everything I see." But to tell the truth, Becky had never really listened to her mother. If she had, she'd never have gone to medical school and, by now, would probably be no slimmer and still living in Bucks County, Pennsylvania, with a blue-collar husband, an early-model station wagon, and somewhere between three and eight kids to add to her problems.

A husband! Wasn't *that* a lovely thought! Becky had been actively searching for a husband for the past twenty years—or at least she'd been talking about actively searching for one. Somehow her incessant charity work and the demands of her job never seemed to allow her quite enough time to roll up her sleeves and dive into the pursuit of matrimony. So instead she contented herself with dating.

Dating, however, had proved to be more complicated than at first it seemed. First of all, Becky had somewhere developed the insane idea that the process of dating involved more than one outing with the same man. Unfortunately, the men she chose seemed to have disabused themselves of sharing her notion—or at least they promptly abandoned the idea of a second date sometime between the moment they asked her out and the instant they dropped her off at her front door after their first evening together. Becky thus returned from each date depressed, wondering what she might have done wrong and chastising herself for everything from the outfit she'd chosen to the restaurant she'd picked. Inevitably, however, she'd latch on to the probability that her weight had been what had chased her date away and, consumed with guilt, she'd voraciously attack the nearest half gallon of macadamia-fudge-ripple ice cream.

The truth was that Becky's weight was only part of the problem. Although her facial features were not conventionally pretty, most

BITE CLUB

men—provided they could get past the idea that they were in the company of someone whose poundage was somewhere between that of a small Volkswagen and Shamu—would have described her as such. Many of her gay male friends had said that her cheekbones were "fabulous"; her hair was a glossy dark brown with only a hint of silvery gray, which added to rather than detracted from, its sheen. Her smile could be dazzling. Her lips were full and on a thinner woman would have been called "kissable." She had deep brown eyes peeping out from under long lashes that would have been the envy of any professional model. But while her eyes and lashes might prove irresistibly attractive to the opposite sex, the intelligence lurking behind those same eyes could be downright terrifying to most men.

Becky would have been horrified to know that her sharp wit and macabre sense of humor had proved more off-putting to her dates than all of her excess weight. Although she was absolutely without malice, barbed comments escaped her mouth before she thought about the impact they would have on her dinner companion and were swiftly forgotten as her mind shifted gears and raced off to a new topic of conversation. The simple fact was that Becky left most of her dates mentally exhausted and with the nagging suspicion that they had been roundly defeated in a verbal battle without ever having had the chance to arm themselves.

Then again, she'd found that the few men who persisted in asking her out for a second date were fascinated with her job as medical examiner rather than repelled by it—and usually in an extremely unhealthy fashion. On two occasions she'd been forced to change her telephone number when men of rather odd sexual predilections had insisted that she have sex with them at, respectively, the morgue and the Hollywood Forever Cemetery.

To that rare man who could overcome her excessive weight, her passionate obsession with discussing her most intimate cases over dinner, and her perceptive, incisive responses to her dinner companion's conversation—which to those who didn't know her well would seem downright sarcastic—her actual eating habits proved insurmountable. Ty, her morgue assistant, had once made an analogy between Becky's table manners and Elaine May's in *A New Leaf*. No matter how careful she tried to be while eating, Becky adored food and soon lost her determination to be neat and fastidious and dove into her repast with gusto. She invariably finished each meal covered with most of it.

Ty, a charming Asian of thirty-four, was really the only man Becky could say she dated with any regularity. But in all honesty, her mental use of the word *dating* was stretching the truth a bit much. Although Ty was one of the few attractive, eligible heterosexual men living in West Hollywood, he was inevitably and exclusively attracted to women who would euphemistically be described as "mature." While Becky was easily ten years older than he, she knew that Ty's preferences ran toward women who were at least two generations his senior. Since she wasn't yet eligible for Medicare, Becky wisely figured Ty was simply a lost cause as far as a husband was concerned.

Men who were romantically attracted to middle-aged, short, rotund coroners were few and far between. So Becky contented herself with a number of close friendships, almost all of them with gay men, increasing the amount of time she volunteered to charity, and becoming almost fanatically absorbed in her work. In at least one arena, her redirection of repressed sexual urges had paid off; Dr. Rebecca O'Brien was one of the finest forensic pathologists on the West Coast.

In the time she'd been employed in West Hollywood, Becky had seen her share of violent death. California law required that any person who died while not in the care of a physician or hospital must be autopsied. West Hollywood, with one third of its almost 40,000 inhabitants being gay males, many infected with HIV and AIDS, and another third consisting of the elderly, who suffer from a variety of illnesses, created the coroner's office shortly after its incorporation as a city in 1984.

Although in many ways WeHo was like any other city, Becky often found its logic to be slightly skewed, and often her dark humor was kicked into high gear. Walking into City Hall, in the early 1990s, for her first job interview with the city manager, she had made the mistake of asking the woman at the front desk to explain the purpose of the ponderous gray granite objects that were placed at almost every corner along Santa Monica Boulevard. The receptionist had proudly replied that they were the first examples of West Hollywood's commitment to the elderly—bus benches, installed so that the aged could await the arrival of public transportation in comfort. Becky stifled a snort of hilarity; her dark humor was tickled. She doubted that the elderly folk of the city would be quite so amused had any of them been able to read her mind at the moment. To Becky, the bus benches looked alarmingly like tombstones, bearing letters spelling out CITY OF WEST HOLLY-WOOD where the name of the deceased ought to be.

Since then, she'd curtailed her troublesome, irreverent sense of humor. In fact, before becoming the West Hollywood city coroner, Becky thought she'd seen everything—but nothing in her prior experience had prepared her for *this* town. At times she almost longed for her residency in Philadelphia, with its routine stabbings, shootings, and traffic accidents. West Hollywood's residents seemed to be committed to offing themselves in bizarre and unusual ways.

Her first case involved two Santa Monica Boulevard male prostitutes found smothered by plastic bags as a result of a rumor that partial asphyxiation increased the intensity of orgasms. Although the method of death wasn't all that unusual, Becky found herself thrust into the limelight when the gay press picked up the story and descended on the coroner's office for comments from WeHo's new medical examiner. Completely flummoxed by the media attention, Becky made several sarcastic suggestions that found their way into the next issue of the *Gay Gazette*. To alleviate the furor, the City Council took Becky's quips as official recommendations and, in a flurry of legislative activity, came up with a solution: Further smothering would be avoided by distributing pamphlets on the dangers of misusing Saran wrap to all hustlers along the boulevard. Moreover, local laundries would be forced, upon pain of hefty fines, to print WARNING! USE OF THIS BAG DOES **NOT** INCREASE INTENSITY OR DURATION OF ORGASM! in large letters on both sides of every dry cleaning bag.

The heterosexual community wasn't much better at mundanely offing themselves. A pair of newlyweds on their honeymoon at the Mondrian Hotel on Sunset Boulevard found their marriage to be, quite literally, short-lived. The young wife, in her girlish eagerness to consummate her wedding night, was playfully bouncing on the hotel bed. Her enthusiasm had gotten the best of her and, after a particularly energetic bounce, she'd lost control of her momentum, sailed out the hotel room window to crash to the street eight stories below. Becky's second "patient" that night had been the doorman who tried, unsuccessfully, to catch the plummeting bride and was flattened by her falling body.

Shortly thereafter, the son of a prominent California assemblyman had been found dead in his apartment after a debauched week of staying home from work with a head cold and overindulging in illegal substances. The victim's blood had been filled with a wide variety of drugs, but none were in sufficient quantities to have caused the youth to die. Three days later, she finally identified the culprit that had driven the young man's system over the line. She briefly ruminated over the blank space on the certificate where she was supposed to fill in the cause of death. Then, with not a little black humor, she neatly printed: DEATH BY NYQUIL.

"Yeah, we're the Creative City, all right!" Becky mused wryly and took another bite. She examined the last morsel of Snickers and popped it into her mouth. Actually, she confessed to herself, given her high level of consumption, the peanut taste was becoming rather overpowering. She longed for her favorite, Tastykake Butterscotch Krimpets, which she'd never tired of. Unfortunately, Tastykake had not yet expanded its market to include California, to Becky's unending sorrow.

Becky licked her fingers, drew on her rubber gloves with a brisk snap, and prepared for work. She drew back the sheet covering the remains of Anthony Balencini, checked to make sure there was a new roll of film in her camera, switched on her tape recorder, and started her protocol.

Ninety minutes later, she slid Balencini into one of the upper drawers of the refrigerator built into the wall at the far end of the morgue. Her brow was furrowed in puzzlement.

BITE CLUB

The cause of Balencini's demise was obvious: His throat had been cut so deeply that the spine was severed and he'd bled to death. The sheriff's report, however, stated that very little blood had been found at the crime scene. Furthermore, there were no signs of a struggle. Becky concluded therefore that the murder had taken place elsewhere and the body was dumped in the foliage to await subsequent discovery. What bothered her, however, was the almost total lack of blood in the corpse. Exsanguination of a human body was rarely so complete.

Becky was also concerned with the lacerations on the penis; there seemed to be no explanation that would connect them with the death. In addition, and this was the really strange part about the case, a flap of skin had been removed from the corpse's neck. A strip, six inches long and an inch wide, had been excised, the edges of the wound torn rather than cleanly cut, but Becky could not identify the object used. Further, neither the extensive damage to the throat area nor the lacerations nor the removal of the small piece of epidermis accounted sufficiently for the blood loss.

She wobbled down the hall toward her office, deep in thought, stopping only to toss the cassette tape of the autopsy onto Ty's desk so he could type it up whenever he returned from wherever he'd run off to. Entering the office, she grabbed a bottle of strawberry Yoo-hoo from the small refrigerator, twisted off the cap, and took a swig. The cloying, sweet fruity taste did not improve her thought processes as it usually did.

Dimly, she recalled a case similar to this one. Either she'd read about it or someone had mentioned it to her. Maybe she'd seen it on the news. For the life of her she couldn't remember where. She took another gulp from the bottle, hoping it would help her think. But it didn't.

CHAPTER THREE

Billy Boyd was hot. Not hot as in temperature, but hot as in buff, as in cool, as in sexy. Everything about him, from the smoothly shaven, tautly muscled chest to the carefully disheveled hairstyle, was calculated to achieve one end: money in Billy's pocket.

He'd dressed carefully tonight, as always, choosing skintight blue jeans, with the crotch sanded to make his basket look like it was about to burst through the denim, and a faded brown leather vest to show off his tanned skin and the lithe definition of his upper body. He'd even covered his chest, biceps, and shoulders with baby oil to make them gleam as he stood under the street lamp on the sidewalk near Genesee, across the street from the Pleasure Chest, a sex paraphernalia shop on Santa Monica Boulevard.

Yes, Billy was ready. Ready to trade a half hour with his tight, toned body for as much of the green stuff as he could get.

He shifted his weight slowly back and forth from one hip to the other, scratching seductively at his chest and belly. He'd worked hard for his body, especially since turning twenty-eight the year before, when he noticed an alarming softening of the muscles of his lower stomach, his back, and his waist.

"No love handles for me," he'd resolved and spent hours in the gym until everything tightened up again and the washboard configuration, so highly sought after by middle-aged men from Chatsworth and Encino, reappeared.

Billy propped one leg on the seat of the bus bench and leaned forward, allowing his vest to fall open to reveal more clearly the results of his dedication to physical fitness. He'd already had one score this evening, a tremendously fat guy from back east somewhere, probably New York, who'd paid him thirty dollars just so Billy would stand over him and allow him to stroke his naked thighs and jerk off for fifteen minutes. For the past hour, though, the trade had been sparse.

Billy had long mastered the guise of nonchalantly ignoring passing motorists while at the same time quickly sizing up the drivers as potential clients. He remembered a business course in high school, before he'd been kicked out, where a teacher had told the class that a good salesman always checked out the shoes and watch of a prospective customer. If they were of good quality, the reasoning went, the customer most likely had bucks to spend. This was the only item of knowledge gleaned from his formal education that Billy used on a regular basis.

For Billy, money was the key—to everything. Why should he spend all day carrying trays in a restaurant or peddling cheap shirts and ties for a lousy $400 a week when he could make as much or more for a few hours of minimal effort on a busy Friday or Saturday night? And, maybe, just maybe, if he were very lucky, he'd meet someone, a director or producer, who would be so taken with Billy's stunning body and handsome face that he would, overnight, be catapulted to stardom in the movies. Now, *that* would mean really big bucks!

A rusty brown Plymouth station wagon slowed, its driver eyeing Billy appraisingly. Billy took one look at the car and turned his back; the Plymouth drove off. He turned back around to survey the street and noticed a dark blue Jaguar sedan had slowed and the driver was peering out the window at him.

Billy recognized the look; it was hunger of a type with which Billy was infinitely familiar. Slowly, assessing the expensive car, he sauntered across the street and stopped near the passenger window. The window rolled down.

"How much?" the driver called.

"For what?" Billy answered, feigning disinterest.

"Blow job."

"You a cop?"

"No." The driver, a man in his late thirties, slightly balding, looked amused. "Accountant."

"You do me or I do you?"

The driver grinned. "I do you."

Billy considered the request. If he came, he'd have to wait at least an hour or two before his body recovered enough to make another score. Maybe during that time he'd be lucky enough to pick up someone who wouldn't be interested in seeing him shoot, but he didn't want to take the chance. Unless Mr. Jaguar would make it worth his while to take the time off.

"A buck," Billy quoted.

"A hundred dollars?" repeated the Jaguar's driver in disbelief.

"Yeah," Billy said. "I come buckets." He shrugged off the vest and slung it over his shoulder with one hand, placing the other in his right pocket and pressing down so that his jeans hung lower on that side of his hips.

"I'll give you forty."

"Eighty."

"Fifty. And that's final." The driver put the car into drive.

"Seventy," said Billy.

"Sorry," said the man, who drove off as Billy stood there by the curb, mouth hanging open in disbelief and feeling like a fool.

"Oh, yeah? Well, fuck you too!" Billy yelled after the departing car and flipped the driver the bird.

"Such an emphatic response," murmured a soft voice behind him.

Billy whirled around, ready to nail the newcomer with a right cross if the guy so much at snickered at Billy's humiliation.

But the guy wasn't laughing. Instead he wore a look of pleasant, interested curiosity, combined with just enough sympathy, as if he'd just happened to walk by and witness the incident and was empathetically on Billy's side.

At first, Billy took the guy for another hustler. He had the looks for it certainly, and even though he was a little on the short side he was in great shape with a physique that almost rivaled Billy's own. Yes, sir. Under that tight black turtleneck was what Billy called a good body, a really good body. When the guy turned, motioning Billy out of the street, he got a good look at the guy's rear; through the black jeans Billy saw the muscles of his upper thighs and ass bunch intriguingly.

There was something else Billy noticed: hunger, the kind of hunger he saw so often along the boulevard.

This could be fun, Billy thought and smiled. "Well, you know how it is sometimes," he said.

"I do indeed," said the guy with mock regret.

Billy laughed and the guy joined in. "So," said Billy casually, "you score yet?"

"Not yet." The words held a deeper meaning that Billy recognized instantly.

"You, uh, wanna go somewhere?" Billy said, a little more hesitantly than normal. If the guy was working, Billy knew his ego would suffer another beating. It was considered bad form for one hustler to proposition another; after all, both would be giving away what they could sell. But Billy was still a little pissed at the Jaguar and he figured, *What the hell?* The guy was hot. And Billy, if he was going to go for a freebie, liked it to be hot.

The stranger grinned. "I was thinking that perhaps it was a little warm out here for this." He indicated the long sleeves of his turtleneck. "I'd probably be more comfortable…wearing less. And you?"

Billy frowned briefly, a little uneasy. Did the guy have some kind of an accent? He couldn't tell. Billy didn't like foreigners; you couldn't really predict what they'd be like in the sack. He especially hated French tourists; they tended to treat hustlers like they treated their wives—in Billy's opinion, badly. Well, the stranger sure as hell wasn't a Frenchie, even if he *did* talk a little weird, kind of piss-elegant.

Billy looked at the guy's body again and the vague troubling thoughts vanished from his mind.

"Sure," he said. "Let's get naked."

"Naked?" asked the stranger, as if he were talking to himself. "What a novel idea."

"Huh?"

"Nothing," said the stranger as he looked up, directly into Billy's eyes.

Billy noticed the guy's eyes were dark, almost black, with little specks of silver. For some reason Billy trusted those eyes and all his minor suspicions vanished.

"Shall we?" asked the stranger, and with an odd little bow he indicated the Pleasure Chest parking lot across the street.

Billy led the way across Santa Monica and pointed to the apartment building backing the parking lot.

"We can go in there," he said, "One of them's still vacant, I think. A trick took me there last week."

"Good."

They crossed the parking lot in silence; Billy licked his lips in anticipation. He felt into the waistband of his jeans and shifted his hardening dick so that it was more comfortable.

They reached the building, and Billy led his new companion around the side to the vacant unit. He opened the door.

"After you," said the stranger with another little bow.

Billy went in. He turned, but the guy in black was still outside. "Aren't you coming?" he asked, with a little irritation. "C'mon."

"Certainly." And the stranger was inside, pushing Billy backward against the wall and pressing his body tightly against him.

Billy thought his erection would rip right through the denim. The guy's chest against his was very erotic. And when the guy gently squeezed his dick, Billy thought he would come right then. Billy reached for his zipper and the guy backed away slightly.

"Oh, yes," he said. "That's right. You were going to 'get naked.'"

"You too," said Billy as he skinned out of his jeans, his stiff cock leaping free.

"Oh, I think not yet," commented the stranger glibly.

"What?" exclaimed Billy, instantly angry. "What the fuck…?"

The stranger's gaze bore into his own. The anger drained from Billy in a flash. Suddenly, he felt strangely tired.

"You," said the stranger, taking Billy by the shoulders and forcing him to the floor, "are going to lie there." The dark young man laid Billy down on his back and stretched his arms over his head. "And not move."

Billy felt his legs being separated. He remembered tricking with a guy once who'd tied him to the bedposts in a similar position. He didn't relish the memory.

"In fact, you *can't* move."

And suddenly Billy couldn't.

"And I," he continued, "am going to have some fun."

Billy watched helplessly as the stranger removed his own garments and neatly folded them, placing them in a corner before standing above him, nude. The guy's body was better than he'd expected; Billy wanted to reach out and stroke the smooth, creamy skin, but somehow he couldn't.

He knelt over Billy's paralyzed body and, with one fingernail, cut deeply into the flesh over Billy's right thigh, just underneath the groin. Billy felt the brief sting of pain. How could the guy's nails be so fucking sharp? He drew in a breath to protest.

"Shh-h-h," said the other softly. "You cannot move unless I tell you. You cannot talk. And you cannot scream."

This time the cut started under Billy's right armpit and ran down along his side to the waist. He felt blood welling sluggishly. He made not a sound.

"Ah, such a beautiful boy," said the young man as he slowly licked Billy's blood from his finger. "So docile, so easily held." He leaned forward and looked deeply into Billy's eyes.

"A lamb to the slaughter." He smiled for a moment, then the smile became cruel, viciously cruel.

"So easily held that I might modify my earlier instructions."

Thank god, thought Billy. *He's letting me go!*

"Oh, no," was the reply, as if he'd read Billy's mind. "But I will let you *feel*," he cackled. "I'll let you feel more intensely than you've ever felt in your little life."

The nails flashed across Billy's stomach. It felt like hot irons were being laid across his skin. His muscles contracted with the pain.

"Wasn't that delicious?"

Again, this time on the inside of his thigh down to his upper calf. Billy began to sweat.

"And this…" The voice was a hiss.

Slowly the villain teased Billy's right nipple with the tip of his nails, reducing it to a bloody pulp. Then he started on the left. Then the thighs again. Then the soft flesh under his arms and along his sides. Billy's washboard stomach began to resemble a cutting board upon which a chef had sliced a few pounds of raw, bloody beef.

Billy was in agony. Just when he thought he would pass out, the bastard would stop and calmly lick up the dribbles of blood. Within an hour Billy's entire body was a bloody bunch of sensitized, pulsating nerves.

When the fiend started slicing into Billy's penis and testicles, he was sure his body was feeling as bad as it was possible to feel. He was wrong.

Baring his horrible fangs so that the helpless young man was sure to see, the monster bent his head toward Billy's throat. And the pain went on…

CHAPTER FOUR

Clive Anderson was determined to remain calm. He was unwilling to allow the events of the past few days to ruffle his otherwise placid demeanor and even temper. Wanting badly to throw the nearest breakable object at the farthest wall of his office, he settled instead for heaving a mighty sigh at the unfairness of life. He was surprised at how good it felt. He considered a moment, indulged himself, and sighed again.

Waiting for the forensic report on the latest murder victim, Clive longed for the good old days. For the first time he began to regret the promotion five years ago that had put him in his soon to be uncomfortable position as captain of the West Hollywood Sheriff's Station. His instincts told him the citizens of the Creative City had a budding serial killer in their midst.

Clive's promotion and transfer to West Hollywood were supposed to have been a sinecure—a reward for his long years as an efficient and devoted public servant and the beginning of an easy sail toward his eventual retirement. Clive had examined the job transfer carefully, hoping his race had had something to do with getting him the promotion—another step along the department's road to the elimination of discrimination. But no, he was forced to admit, he had only his own scrupulous efficiency to thank for placing him in the awkward position of having to deal with the current unpleasantness. Clive sighed again, this time with substantially less satisfaction than before, and wished he were still back in the valley.

West Hollywood was notoriously free of the more violent crimes, he considered, and usually a quiet, pleasant place in which to work. Occasionally a car was stolen, summer months brought the usual groups of young gay bashers into town, petty burglaries were routine, and the partiers on the Sunset Strip brought a certain amount of trouble on the weekends. But other than that, West Hollywood was an anomaly—a small town with a small-town mentality and a small-town crime rate, plopped down right in the center of one of the largest metropolises in the world.

Clive felt twin trickles of sweat as they gathered under his arms and began their journey down his sides. He shifted uncomfortably and wondered if he had enough time to change into a fresh shirt before the coroner's arrival. One thing he hated, more than anything else, was to present a less than pristine appearance to the world. "You are what you wear," Papa had once told him, and Clive swore by the homily. He was as obsessive with the details of his wardrobe as he was about everything else. So obsessive, in fact, that his neatly folded pocket squares had become not only his trademark but also something of an inside joke within the higher ranks of the Sheriff's Department. He grimaced though as he considered Becky's well-known indulgence in anything that was laden with sugar, covered in whipped cream, or wrapped in chocolate. Clive was actually very fond of Becky, but given her propensity to leave trails of crumbs and sticky handprints in her wake he abandoned the idea of a clean shirt, attractive though it might be, knowing he would only have to change it once again after she left.

But he wasn't happy about it. Normally an impeccable dresser, sporting crisp white shirts and handmade Italian suits, Clive disliked perspiration on principle; it served only to mar his carefully maintained, unruffled composure. Already he felt his control quickly slipping away as he thought that, with the discovery of the second body, the usual annual homicide statistics for West Hollywood had just doubled.

Unlike many of the other people in the Sheriff's Department, Clive hadn't chosen a career in law enforcement for any of the usual reasons. As a small boy he'd had no burning desire to rid the world of criminals; he possessed no hidden insecurities manifesting in macho behavior, nor did he achieve satisfaction in holding authority.

Born in Louisiana, the only son of a moderately well-to-do pediatrician, Clive was at heart a very gentle man. He followed Martin Luther King's philosophy of nonviolence and it had stood him in good stead time and time again. He'd frequently, in his days as a deputy, been able to disarm and apprehend criminals with quiet logic in situations where his fellow officers would have gone in shooting. Thus he was sometimes amazed he'd ever chosen a career in anything like police work, which when you came right down to it was really a rather militaristic discipline.

Oh, he'd had his choice of careers all right. Papa'd seen to that. He'd studied law for a while but rapidly became uncomfortable with the idea of interpreting precedents and the notion that any fact could be argued in more than one way. It offended his ingrained sense of order and another motto of Papa's that he was fond of quoting: "A place for everything, everything in its place." Medicine was no better; it had taken him years of police work before he could tolerate the sight of blood. Fortunately, as he advanced within the department, his direct contact with the battered, shot, and stabbed of Los Angeles County had lessened.

No, what appealed to Clive about law enforcement, to the unending amazement of everyone else in the department, was the paperwork. Even with a crime that would remain forever unsolved he took great personal satisfaction in knowing that each and every report had been carefully filled out and was resting, with all its supporting documentation, in a specific and unique place in the files of the Los Angeles County Sheriff's Department.

It was his passion for order and neatness that had gotten him where he was so easily. As a deputy, his careful attention to detail had resulted in quite a few arrests where others had given up. Upon his promotion to detective, his reports had been masterpieces of ordered, logical thought; he even had good handwriting. His superiors had noticed, and despite his objections that there were others more worthy, he'd received promotion upon promotion, rising through the ranks in record time. Then again, he thought with only a little bitterness, the Fourteenth Amendment had probably helped, at least in the early days.

As he reached his early forties, Clive discovered something else about himself. To his great puzzlement, people seemed to *want* to like him. With no effort on his part, he was frequently invited to attend exclusive parties hosted by the sheriff himself and he'd lost track of the number of times he'd had dinner at the homes of various mayors of various cities scattered throughout Los Angeles County.

But even now, with fifty looming scant months ahead and the gray hairs cropping up at his temples with increasing frequency, Clive still couldn't understand this odd attraction he was cursed with. He'd long given up on finding anyone with whom to share his life; he felt his penchant for neatness and order was sure to drive the poor woman crazy. He'd tried living with someone once several years ago: an artist, complete with the artist's traditional creative temperament and lackadaisical attitude toward maintaining her living quarters. She'd lasted barely six months.

Before she left she'd tried to explain that, though she found his picayune attitude impossible to live with, others found him "comforting." Since he rarely got upset about anything, she'd told him, people simply assumed that he held all the answers. Clive supposed she had been right. On the rare occasions when he lost his temper, usually when faced with sloppiness or inefficiency, those around him, rather than becoming resentful or defensive, were embarrassed and hurt and responded by striving to do better the next time. In short, for reasons he could never fathom, people enjoyed making Clive happy.

With great patience masking the turmoil he felt, he straightened the blotter on his desk, lining it up so that it was precisely centered.

He wondered again when Becky would arrive, checking to make sure he had enough spare handkerchiefs in preparation for the anticipated onslaught she was sure to perpetrate upon his clothing.

Clive waited, examining his desk critically. Ah, there was a pencil that had managed to find its way into his pen jar. He seized the offending writing implement and placed it in the proper spot; he would have gently scolded it had he been one of those people given to speaking to inanimate objects. Sighing again in satisfaction of a job well done, he leaned back in his chair.

His intercom buzzed. "Ms. O'Brien's here."

"Send her in, Claire," he said, and before he could release the intercom button Becky came barging in, clutching a manila file in one hand and something Clive surmised was cherry goo on a stick in the other.

"Well?" he asked.

"There's a pattern developing," Becky reported with annoying cheerfulness.

"Great," said Clive mournfully. "I don't suppose you could manage to at least *try* to look a little concerned about it?"

Becky flashed him a dazzling smile and plopped into her usual chair in front of his desk after dropping the file in the center of the blotter. Clive looked at it with distaste, not only for what he feared it was likely to contain but also due to the undoubtedly tacky fingerprints splayed across its cover.

"It won't bite, Clive," Becky said, encouraging him.

"No," he sighed, "I don't suppose it will."

He gingerly opened it using his fingertips, hoping he could remain untouched by the sugary residue. Needless to say, his hopes were soon dashed and he resignedly took out a handkerchief to wipe the mess from his fingers.

"The victim was tortured this time," Becky told him brightly.

Clive looked up hopefully. "Then it's not the same guy?"

"Unfortunately, it probably is." Becky's cheery smile belayed the somberness of her statement as she shoved the bright red candy into her mouth and continued, forming her words around it, not bothering to wipe her chin as the dissolving candy trickled down. "There's not enough blood in the body—again. And there's the same flap of skin missing from the throat. It's the same guy all right. Or girl. ERA and all that."

Clive smiled weakly at the coroner's feeble jest and turned to examine the first page of the report. "Lacerations again," he commented. Becky grunted affirmatively in reply.

"Any clues there? It says here they covered the entire front of the body. Not just the...uh...penis." Clive gulped uncomfortably.

"Kinda gets you guys where ya live, don't it?" she grinned. "Ty had the same reaction."

With almost morbid enthusiasm she continued, "The sides of this guy's torso were spaghetti too. But look here." She stood and came around the desk, pointing with one hand and resting the other on the shoulder of Clive's clean shirt. He winced at the thought of his dry cleaning bill.

"Look at the depth. Very shallow. Just like Balencini. Nowhere deep enough to cause the massive blood loss we're seeing. Except for the one on the throat. Now, *that's* deep," she said with seeming satisfaction. "Almost took the whole head off again."

She glanced hopefully toward the small refrigerator that Clive kept in one corner of his office. "Did I leave a coffee cake in there the other day?"

"Half," Clive replied. "A week ago. It went stale so I threw it out."

"Damn," Becky's voice held true regret. "I'll bet it was a Sara Lee, too, wasn't it?"

But Clive's attention was caught by the report. "Is this one enough to account for the blood?"

"Huh?" Becky was still looking longingly at the refrigerator.

"The throat laceration," Clive reminded her.

"That would be nice, wouldn't it?" she said wistfully. "But no." She shook her head. "The spinal cord was severed after he was already dead. When they brought him in I first thought the cause of death was obvious: decapitation resulting in massive blood loss. But the blood was already gone."

"So he was killed somewhere else and the killer dumped the body."

"Looks that way." She paused. "Are you sure you threw it out?"

"I'm sure," Clive replied patiently. "Could we please get back to business?"

"Yeah, sure," Becky replied, finally mentally dismissing the lost coffee cake. "I've got another one back at the office anyway."

"What you're telling me doesn't make sense," Clive protested.

Becky looked at him surprised. "Sure it does. They were on sale at Pavilions. I stocked up. If you freeze 'em, they stay fresh. They had two-for-ones on Weight Watchers desserts too. You should stop by for a snack on your way home."

"I'm talking about the corpse." Clive's patience was wearing a little thin. Although he found Becky's obsession with sweets rather endearing in a mildly eccentric way most of the time, with the autopsy report in front of him, complete with color photos, he was beginning to feel slightly nauseated.

"We found the clothes in the same place as the body," he reminded her. "Not a drop of blood on 'em. It takes a long time to do this to a person. Why would the killer move both the body *and* the clothing?"

"Strange, isn't it?" She took the candy from her mouth and used it as a pointer. Clive absently handed her the remaining clean hanky. "It gets worse. Read on, MacDuff. Next paragraph. *This* is what *really* bothers me. I can't figure out what the killer used to cut with. It doesn't look like a knife. Didn't slice quite cleanly enough. The edges are ragged, but there's not enough evidence of sawing or hacking. I'm tempted to say it was done with something flat and dull, but there'd be more tearing of the tissue. And if the weapon was, oh, let's say a carpet scraper, it would have taken tremendous, concentrated force to make incisions like this. I was hoping a piece of the weapon had broken off in the neck wound, but no luck."

She returned to her chair and plopped down. "I dunno. Maybe he's a kitchen-gadget freak and used some kind of über lemon zester from Williams-Sonoma." She chuckled at her own joke. "Whatever it was, I sure can't figure it out." She rummaged through her huge black bag and a second later triumphantly pulled out a small box of doughnuts. "Aha!" she exclaimed. "I knew these were around somewhere!"

"What about a sportsman's knife? You know, something specialized for hunting or fishing? They manufacture all sorts of things." Clive looked up in time to see Becky chomping into one of the doughnuts. "Try not to get sugar all over the carpet," he told her mildly, knowing it was hopeless.

"Sorry," Becky replied and promptly bit down on the doughnut again, inadvertently spraying sugar and crumbs everywhere.

"No traces of oil in the wound," she mumbled, chewing lustily. "Those babies need to be oiled to prevent rust."

"So where are we?" he asked.

"That's the million-dollar question, ain't it?" said Becky flippantly around another mouthful of doughnut.

"This is not funny," said Clive sternly.

Becky swallowed and became serious. "I know," she said gently. "Serial killers never are. But it looks like that's what we've got. One more and I'll be sure."

"*Now* I hope you're being funny."

"I'm not," she replied. "No matter what we do we're not gonna catch this guy until enough bodies pile up or he gets cocky and makes a mistake."

"Believe me. I know," he moaned. The trickles of sweat had just turned into a river.

"I have a scarier thought," Becky said.

"What's that?"

"How long are we going to be able to keep this quiet?"

"I have no idea," he said. "But for now, not a word to anyone. Not to the mayor, not to the city manager, God forbid! Not the city council and especially not the press. No one. Got that?"

Becky mimed zipping her lips shut, leaving in the powdered sugar remaining on her face a smear of cherry candy that, to Clive, looked alarmingly like blood.

◆ ◆ ◆

That afternoon, back at her office, Becky wracked her brains trying to recall where she'd heard about a similar series of murders. It had been while she was back in Philadelphia. But it wasn't anything with which she'd been directly involved. *That* she would have remembered instantly.

Wait a minute, she thought. Dimly, a mental image was coming to her. She'd read something that seemed familiar; she could almost see the page in her mind's eye. Something about blood. Something that happened in another country. Where the hell had she been when she read it? It was during her days in medical school—she knew that. But she didn't think it was anything she'd read for a class. She'd always been able to remember the contents of her textbooks with uncanny accuracy. No, this was from something else entirely.

She couldn't remember. But she knew someone who would. Momentarily forgetting Clive's demand for secrecy, she picked up the telephone and, dialing from memory, called a number in Philadelphia.

The phone rang three times and she heard the machine pick up, the familiar voice coming onto the line via microchip.

"Chris? It's me, Becky. God, how come you're never home when I call? Anyway, I've got a problem out here. Do you remember something from school about a serial killer? It might have been from that abnormal psych course we audited together. I think it was in Europe—the killer, not the course. Something about some psycho draining his victims' blood."

She paused for a gulp of pineapple soda and the act of lifting the bottle to her lips caused her mind to make the first connection. "Drinking!" she exclaimed. "The son of a bitch drank it! Boy," she continued happily, momentarily forgetting that she was still speaking into the telephone, "sometimes I amaze myself."

There was a polite knock on her office door, and after a second Ty walked in bearing a large steaming coffee mug full of something that caused Becky's nose to twitch with pleasure.

"Swiss mocha," he whispered, his almond eyes crinkling with good humor as he gently placed the mug next to Becky's elbow. "Sugar-free."

"You're a love," she told him. Eyes closed with pleasurable anticipation, she took her first sip. Her tingling taste buds brought to mind the memory of a luscious Austrian bittersweet torte she'd once had. She froze, blinking, as she made the final connection.

"Germany!" she exclaimed, startling Ty with her outburst. "Of course! Your book! That Dusseldorf guy!" She caught herself, waved Ty's questioning look aside, and turned back to the receiver.

"Never mind, I got it. But call me tonight. I'll be in." She hung up and grabbed Ty by the arm.

"Tell Sara to mind the phones. Let's go!" She rushed toward the door.

"Where to?" Ty asked. Although he was used to Becky's rather eccentric way of running the morgue, such a burst of hurried physical activity on the part of his boss was unusual.

"Next door," Becky told him. "To the library."

"What for?"

"*The Dusseldorf Vampire*," she said impatiently. "My copy is at home."

"The *what*?" Ty paled slightly. He glanced nervously over his shoulder in the direction of the autopsy room.

"Oh, for cryin' out loud," Becky said. "Aren't you shaming your samurai ancestors or something, being such a wimp? The guy's been dead for forty years."

Ty crossed his arms, hiding his hands in the sleeves of his lab coat. Bowing deeply from the waist and affecting a burlesque Chinese accent, he intoned, "Honorable ancestors not warriors. Honorable ancestors hide in cellars. Wait for war to pass. Honorable ancestors make sure they stay alive so humble assistant can be here today."

Becky couldn't help grinning. "C'mon. I'll buy you lunch at Chef Ming's after we're through."

A look of mock outrage crossed Ty's face. "Offering Chinese food to a Japanese-American is politically incorrect," he told her.

"Sorry."

Once again, Ty bowed. "Humble assistant will be taken to nice restaurant. American restaurant."

"Oh, God," Becky moaned. "Not IHOP again!" She paused and reconsidered. "On the other hand, their chocolate chip pancakes…" Her voice trailed off as a look of bliss washed across her face. Ty had to call her name twice before she snapped back to attention and pulled him out of the office and down the hall.

CHAPTER FIVE

Christopher Driscoll stood in the living room of his partially refur-bished Philadelphia town house, staring at his answering machine. Chris was a rather handsome although nondescript looking young man of about medium height, looking to be in his late twenties. His only really distinguishing feature was a head of thick, rich, chestnut-brown hair that he wore slightly longer than the cur-rent fashion and that he sometimes, when he was in one of his more nostalgic moods, gathered together in a small ponytail at the back with a short black ribbon.

Chris was attractive enough so that people didn't totally ignore him but not nearly so arresting that he'd stand out in a crowd. For the most part that suited Chris fine; he didn't particularly care to draw attention to himself. Of course, whenever he entered a room with his lover, Troy, heads would swivel, but that was something to which he'd long ago resigned himself.

Troy thought him the very incarnation of the god Apollo, but Chris had never understood why. His body was well muscled and toned, his shoulders broad, and his waist, thankfully, perpetually slim—he had the body of a natural athlete. Fortunately, as he'd often told himself, his ancestors had passed on to him some very good genes.

Over the years, he'd carefully developed the ability to go almost unnoticed in a room full of people, quietly watching. And strange as he could sometimes be, the only outward sign of his talent was his unusual trait of seeming to be always slightly distracted, mind miles off somewhere, no matter how intently he might be concentrating on something close at hand.

At the moment Chris was standing almost motionless, features marred by a frown of concern as he tapped the replay button and rewound the tape to listen to Becky's message once again. His hair, which normally glistened with a healthy shine, was dull and lifeless, probably due to the large amount of pale blue paint covering both it and a large portion of his forehead and cheeks. The only sound accompanying Becky's disembodied voice was the occasional plop of paint as it dripped from the brush, forgotten in his left hand, onto the polished hardwood of the living room floor.

Chris's gaze was firmly fixed somewhere in the distance, his lips pursed tightly together. The few people who knew him well would have instantly realized there was something about what he was hearing that he didn't like. No, he didn't like it at all. Even though he'd known Becky for almost two decades and she was one of the few people in the world who he could honestly call a friend, she was beginning to make mental connections that could become rather uncomfortable.

He recalled the first time he'd seen her. At regularly occurring periods of his life, more and more frequently as he grew older, Chris became bored. After moping about lethargically for a while, he would seize upon some new project and throw himself wholeheartedly into it until he'd inevitably reach another plateau of ennui and abandon his latest fad in favor of something that might prove more interesting. The current refurbishment obsession was a prime example—its only distinguishing feature being that it had lasted almost three years; his projects rarely broke the two-month mark. The last time he'd stayed with anything for so long was when, almost twenty years ago, he'd decided to enter medical school. That one had lasted slightly more than two years.

He recalled with a smile the first evening of his second-year histology class. The class was already under way; the ancient professor had been droning on for fifteen minutes, establishing the rules and regulations to which he demanded his pupils adhere, one of which concerned the instructor's intense dislike of tardiness.

The professor, one Dr. Gruenfeld, had then proceeded to randomly grill his new students on the information contained in the first two chapters of the textbook. Since it was the first day of class, no one had bothered to take seriously the posted roster sheets requiring that the material be read. Gruenfeld seemed to take great delight in forcing one after another terrified student to rise to his feet to be shamed by his ignorance as Gruenfeld fired question after question, unwilling to settle for an "I don't know" or an "I'm sorry, I didn't read it."

Gruenfeld had just completed the evisceration of the fourth or fifth embarrassed student, reducing the poor girl to tears, when the double doors at the rear of the lecture hall slammed open and a heavyset young woman with frizzy brown hair waddled in, both arms laden with books, a roomy leather purse slung over one shoulder, and a large cinnamon bun clenched between her teeth. Silence descended over the assembled class as the woman bumped into people while murmuring repeated apologies around her mouthful of pastry, forced her way down a row of seats past several students, and plopped heavily into the empty seat next to Chris.

She dropped the books on the table in front of her, thunked the purse on the floor with a sigh of relief, and took a bite of the cinnamon bun before depositing it next to her books, where a puddle of partially melted caramel, spice, and nuts began to form on the table. She pulled a notebook from her bag, took out a pen, and, oblivious to the eyes focused in her direction, looked up expectantly waiting for the lecture to proceed.

"You! Miss...?" called Gruenfeld from the front of the room.

The young woman looked around, making sure she was the one being addressed. "Me?"

"Yes, you," said Gruenfeld testily. "Do you have a name?"

The young woman looked uncomfortable, but only slightly so. Chris felt bad for her, anticipating the verbal bludgeoning she was about to receive, and smiled reassuringly, hoping to give her encouragement. She returned the smile with a dazzling one of her own.

"Uh, Rebecca O'Brien," she said, partially to Chris and partially to the professor. "But everyone calls me Becky."

"Very well, *Miss* O'Brien. I assume since you saw fit to attend my class late—"

"Oh, I'm terribly sorry," Becky interrupted, not seeming all that sorry at all. "I stopped to get something to eat. Not that I really need it," she said, patting her middle. The class giggled nervously and Gruenfeld turned beet-red with anger. The young woman, in turn, grabbed the cinnamon bun and took another bite.

"In *my* class, Ms. O'Brien," he began with undisguised venom, "we arrive on time, we do not eat during lectures, we do not interrupt, and *we rise to our feet when addressing the instructor*! Is that clear?"

"Oh, I suppose so," said Becky. She reached down to the floor and rummaged about in the purse, finally removing a tattered paper napkin. Thrusting the napkin and the partially eaten snack at Chris, who took them from her in surprise, she said, "Do me a favor and wrap this?" Then she hauled herself to her feet and stood waiting.

"Well, Miss O'Brien. As I was saying, since you found it unnecessary to arrive at my class on time, I assume that you find no need for explanation or discussion of the material contained in the first two chapters of the text."

Becky nodded. "That's right," she said innocently.

Gruenfeld's jaw dropped. He recovered quickly, and with a look of self-contentment he began to grill her mercilessly on obscure points contained in the reading material. With growing astonishment, Chris, Gruenfeld, and the rest of the class listened as Becky O'Brien effortlessly answered every one of Gruenfeld's queries.

Despite the professor's rising frustration at being thwarted in his attempts to embarrass the young woman, Becky's responses were always polite; she seemed to be oblivious to the waves of anger emanating from Gruenfeld. Chris was amazed; O'Brien managed to avoid appearing obnoxious or as if she were showing off. Instead, like a small child, each answer was delivered in a tone suggesting she was eager to please, to gain the professor's approval.

Her answers were phrased in such a guileless, offhand manner that Gruenfeld became even more determined to best her. At one point, after a particularly difficult query, Becky prefaced her answer with, "I thought you said the first two chapters, sir? I think that's in chapter five." She then proceeded to give him the information he wanted. Gruenfeld looked ready to explode.

After each answer, Chris noticed, Becky would turn her head slightly and give Chris a repeat view of her charming smile. He found himself unable not to return it with one of his own. Gruenfeld noticed too and, desperate to regain face with his class, he commented nastily, "Ms. O'Brien? Are we attending medical school to develop a career in medicine? Or are we actively seeking a husband by flirting with the young man seated next to you?"

For the first time, Becky seemed lost for words. An awkward silence descended over the class as Becky's face reddened.

Chris had had enough. In his lifetime he'd seen more than his share of bullies. He had an intense dislike for those in positions of power who were given to the abuse of others. His initial sympathy for Becky O'Brien had quickly changed during the interrogation to an admiration of the young lady. He'd refrained from intervening earlier because she seemed to be holding her own against the onslaught. However, now Gruenfeld was attacking the young woman personally, which Chris found to be ill-mannered and without cause. He stood.

"Excuse me, *Doctor* Gruenfeld," he began.

Gruenfeld stopped, taken aback that a student should be so bold as to speak without first being recognized.

"I just felt I had to compliment Miss O'Brien on her obvious understanding of the material." Becky blushed even deeper. "I'd also like to add, so there is no doubt as to the reason for Ms. O'Brien's

BITE CLUB

presence in medical school, that I am a homosexual and have no interest in marrying anyone other than my current boyfriend."

The color drained from Gruenfeld's face.

"I apologize for responding to your question by divulging such personal information about myself," Chris continued. "But since your attack on Ms. O'Brien had moved off the subject of histology and onto a personal level, I thought it appropriate."

Chris put a hand onto Becky's shoulder and gently pushed her back into her seat while resuming his own.

"I believe Ms. O'Brien has answered enough questions for one day, don't you?" he added casually.

Gruenfeld looked at Chris in a way designed to be intimidating, but Chris refused to be cowed. Meeting Gruenfeld's look with a steely gaze of his own, he suggested mildly, "Perhaps we've all answered enough questions for today?"

To the shock of those assembled, Gruenfeld, with a vacant expression, simply turned and walked out of the lecture hall. The other students looked at each other in confusion for a moment, not knowing whether to stay or go. Chris made the decision for them.

He stood up and, excusing himself, reached across Becky's area of the table and gathered up her books. Taking up his own possessions, he moved to the end of the row. He turned back to look at her.

"Are you coming?" he asked.

"Where?" she asked in confusion.

"To the registrar's office. We're dropping the class."

"But..." she began.

"You mean you *want* to stay here and listen to that pompous windbag for the next four months? Don't forget your...ah...thing," he added as Becky scurried to gather the rest of her belongings, snatching up the wrapped cinnamon bun at his reminder.

"But you *can't* just drop a course in med school," Becky had protested, waddling as fast as she could after Chris, who was striding up the center aisle of the lecture hall toward the door. "They'll flunk you for the year!"

Chris frowned in thought, looking, Becky had later told him in a

39

moment of candor, boyishly attractive. "Well," he began, "dropping medical school altogether is out of the question I suppose."

Becky nodded in enthusiastic agreement.

"I didn't mean for you," Chris told her and then smiled his odd little closemouthed smile. "You seem to be well on your way to becoming the next surgeon general."

"Coroner," Becky corrected.

Chris remembered being amused by her struggles to balance her purse in one hand, tear the soggy waxed paper from the remainder of the cinnamon bun, lick the honey icing from the wrapping, and cram the few remaining precious morsels of pastry into her mouth all at the same time. He also remembered Becky's outraged surprise when he'd thrown back his head and burst into laughter.

"What's so funny?" Becky demanded indignantly. "Why shouldn't I be a coroner? Chicago's had a lady coroner on staff for years!"

"Oh, it's not your sex," Chris chuckled, dismissing Becky's concerns.

"I sure hope not!" Chris could see she was only slightly mollified, still suspicious that this young man, so recently her champion, might have subtly insulted her. "I'll have you know," she continued, indignant, "that I happen to like dead people!"

Chris saw the realization of what she'd just said register in her face as he felt a slow grin start to spread across his own. She was obviously attracted to him and on the verge of being mortified at having chased him away forever with her bizarre remark. Then suddenly the humor of the situation struck her and Chris saw the beginnings of a severe case of the giggles starting. Once she started laughing it was contagious and the two of them stood there, cackling their fool heads off, while the rest of the class shuffled past them and out the door, giving the hysterical pair some strange looks and a wide berth.

"It's, well, a private thing," Chris told her once the giggles had finally died out. "Maybe if we get to know each other better..." His voice trailed off as his mood suddenly changed and he became lost in thought. Obviously he had to do something about that impossible professor. Otherwise the semester was going to be insufferable.

BITE CLUB

Becky stood by his side, watching him stare off into nowhere as the rest of the classroom emptied. A few minutes after the last student left Chris suddenly came to himself with a start. "Well, it seems there's only one thing left to do. I hope I can catch him. Wait here," he'd ordered.

Chris darted back down the aisle and disappeared through the door, hoping it led to Gruenfeld's office. Becky was left behind, standing openmouthed with awe, dropping crumbs on the carpet. Scarcely five minutes later, having accomplished what he'd set out to do, Chris was back with a self-satisfied smile on his face.

"That's done it," he announced triumphantly.

"Done what?" Becky asked.

"Oh, I just had a little chat with Professor Gruenfeld," Chris told her and, with the absentmindedness of years of habit, opened the door, allowing Becky to proceed in front of him out of the classroom.

"What'd you say?"

"That would be telling, wouldn't it?" Chris grinned. In the years that followed Becky had often teased Chris about his diplomatic skills. Whatever he had said to Gruenfeld, she'd said time and time again—and he was always careful not to tell her what it had been—had certainly done the trick. For the rest of the term the entire medical school was inflamed with curiosity as to how the notorious Professor Gruenfeld had gone from being Mr. Hyde to the leading contender for the title role in a remake of *Goodbye, Mr. Chips*.

The two of them left the building together. Outside on the pavement Becky stopped and turned shyly to Chris. "Thank you," she said.

"For what?" he asked, genuinely puzzled.

"For taking me seriously," she replied. "Most people don't realize...What I mean is, just because I'm...well...you know." She shrugged and waved a hand, indicating her ample girth.

"Forget it, I enjoy being a control queen. Now then, how about some coffee to wash that thing down?"

Becky brightened instantly. "There's a fabulous old-fashioned diner on Spruce Street. I'd like to buy you a milk shake or something. They're divine," she added coyly.

Chris chuckled. "I'll go with you, but no milk shakes for me—lactose intolerance."

"Oh," she said. "Listen, I feel kind of silly. I mean, I know all this personal stuff about you already, lactose intolerance and...well...the other thing. But I don't know your name."

"Christopher Driscoll," he said, holding out his hand in mock formality.

"Pleased to meet you," she grinned, and they turned to walk, side by side, down the street. "Uh, about what you said back there in class...?" she began shyly.

"About your command of the material?" Chris asked innocently.

"Oh, that," Becky waved the notion away. "I've got one of those memories. It's not photographic or anything, but if I read something once, and understand it, it stays with me for years. No. I meant, you know, the other thing."

As she waited for his answer, Chris could see the mental wheels turning in her head. Although the odd Ms. O'Brien would undoubtedly someday make a brilliant doctor, he half suspected that somewhere in the deep recesses of her mind she'd also considered the possibility of getting the letters *MRS* in front of her name equally as seriously as obtaining the letters *MD* to put behind it. He could have turned the conversation, he supposed, and avoided both her and her questions, but for some reason he'd taken a liking to her quirkiness.

"His name is Troy," Chris told her. "We've been together a long time. And, yes, I love him very much."

"Oh, well. I guess you win some, you lose some." Becky smiled, seemingly unconcerned at having her hopes nipped in the bud. "How long?"

"Very long."

"My God, you make it sound like forever! You can't be that old!"

"Appearances can be deceiving," Chris said as he took her arm and gently guided her around a large puddle she was about to step in.

Momentarily losing her train of thought, Becky said, "Thanks. What's he like?"

Chris grinned. "Well, he's certainly unique. What they call 'an original.' He's little and blond and cute, and he has a passion for old movies. I guess the best way to describe him would be to say he's not the most masculine woman in the world when he's drunk—which can be frequently. Oh," he added with a smile, "I almost forgot. He's from South Carolina. Sometimes it's just like living with Scarlett O'Hara."

"I see," said Becky.

"No," said Chris, wryly reflecting that Troy really had to be experienced to be believed. "I'm afraid you don't."

He took Becky's arm firmly and guided her down the stairs of the High Speed Line entrance. By the time they had gotten off the train and arrived at the diner ten minutes later the seeds of their friendship had taken root.

Chris predictably grew bored with medical school by the beginning of the third year. But by the time he left he and Becky had become best friends. They talked on the phone almost every night and went shopping together at least two weekends a month.

Troy had never really warmed up to her, Chris reflected. Maybe Troy sensed that, disguised by the warm affection between Becky and Chris, she secretly nourished a spark of hope that one day she might be able to introduce herself as Mrs. Christopher Driscoll. Chris had long ago decided that his homosexuality would have to serve as an excuse. Even though Becky had become his dearest friend, he didn't think he'd ever be able to tell her all the reasons why her hopes would be impossible to achieve.

Now, many years after she had moved to California, Becky and Chris still kept in close contact. In fact, for the past two or three years Becky had been gently urging him to make the move to the West Coast. But since they hadn't spoken face-to-face in more than a decade, Chris was reluctant to let her see him in person again.

As Chris rewound the tape yet again, a bewitching elfin blond boy, tightly muscled and clad only in a pair of electric green spandex shorts, entered from the next room and paused in the doorway, posing dramatically with the back of his hand raised against his forehead.

"Play that again and I shall go mad! Mad, I tell you! Mad!" he said in a feeble attempt at a British accent.

"Huh?" Chris looked up, his concentration broken. "Troy?" he said, a little confused. "When did you get home?"

"Long ago enough to change and listen to you play that back about a dozen times. Surely," he said seductively, coming over to rub his bare torso against Chris's paint-spattered arm, "you can think of better things to play with?"

Chris ruffled the shorter boy's hair affectionately and prepared to give him a chaste little kiss on the forehead. Troy tilted his head back and unexpectedly met Chris's lips with his own open mouth. With a shock of delight, Chris absorbed himself in teasing Troy's tongue with his own as Becky's message played, once again, in the background.

Finally, Troy broke the clinch. "One of us still has to breathe, darling," he said coquettishly. He twitched his tight little fanny as he walked across to a small pile of brown paper–wrapped boxes stacked on the couch.

"You know," Troy said, a glint of mischief in his eyes, "if I made little messes like that, you'd yell at me for days."

"I'm painting," Chris replied, distracted.

"You're also stuck to the floor," Troy told him, tossing the comment over his shoulder as he rummaged through the boxes.

Chris looked down and noticed with chagrin that the paint, dripping from the forgotten brush, had unerringly aimed for his left shoe. Now, almost twenty minutes after he'd first begun to play Becky's message, his sole had gotten tacky. Another ten or fifteen minutes and he'd have been glued to the living room floor.

"Shit," he said and moved his foot. It came loose with only a minimum of effort. Chris took a step farther into the living room, where the can of paint thinner, on a table fifteen feet away, awaited the rapidly drying brush. As soon as he did he realized that, with one foot entirely covered in paint, he'd be leaving a trail of pale blue footprints across the living room floor, and right now he was too preoccupied with the telephone call to waste time cleaning it up.

He paused for a second, a look of helplessness on his face as he hopped up and down on one foot, trying to maintain his balance. He hopped twice more and managed to travel another three feet toward the can of thinner, but so focused was his attention on his goal that he completely forgot about the dozen or so opened cans of paint he'd left scattered around the living room. As he prepared for a third hop, the handle of one of the paint cans snatched the toe of his paint-covered left sneaker. With a grunt, Chris realized that, instead of being any closer to his goal, he'd managed to complicate the situation with a half-empty can of paint dangling precariously from his foot.

He shook his foot once, gently, but the paint can stubbornly refused to relinquish its hold. He shook his foot again, but blue paint sloshed over the side and onto the floor. Exasperated, he bent almost double, trying with his free hand to reach the tenacious paint can. His arms weren't quite long enough and as he felt his balance begin to go he straightened abruptly.

"Troy," he said quietly.

"Yes, dear." Troy had been watching silently from his spot next to the couch, fascinated by his lover's antics.

"Would you please take this from me?" Chris held out the paintbrush.

Troy's face wrinkled with distaste. "It's all icky!" he protested.

"Damn it, Troy!" Chris hissed, finally out of patience and, quite frankly, embarrassed as hell.

"Oh, all right," Troy scooted past him and grabbed a handful of newspaper. Gingerly, the newspaper protecting his hands, he took the damp brush from Chris.

"Yuck," he said as he stood, holding the paintbrush as far away from his body as possible, waiting to see what Chris would do next.

The two of them stood for a moment, Chris poised on one foot, like some oversize flamingo, with the paint can dangling from the other, Troy holding the newspaper-wrapped brush at arm's length as if it would instantly attack him should he be so foolish as to let it go.

"Troy," Chris said patiently after a moment.

"Yes?"

"Put the brush down on the table and get rid of this infernal can."

"OK," Troy replied brightly and scurried to comply. "How's that?"

With a sigh, Chris reflected that destiny had indeed perfectly matched him up with his lover. While his own preoccupations sometimes caused him to not think ahead, Troy simply never thought at all.

Chris focused his attention back to the problem at hand. "Now take the sneaker off," he instructed Troy.

Troy did, with a running commentary consisting primarily of the words "gross" and "ick," and Chris, relieved, turned to go back to the answering machine. Unfortunately, as he finally lowered his left foot it landed right in the middle of the pool of spilled paint. Before he had time to even cry out, his legs skidded out from under him and he found himself lying flat on his back, looking up at Troy's concerned face.

"Are you all right?" Troy asked. "The floor's wood, you know."

"I know," Chris replied as soon as he managed to draw breath for speech. "I felt it."

"Well, be careful next time, OK?" Troy said as sternly as he could. Suddenly his face brightened into an irresistible smile. "Now! You just drag your tired old ass up off that floor and come over and see what we got today!" His childlike enthusiasm made it hard for Chris to keep himself from smiling.

Troy rushed across the room to the couch and brought back a half dozen of the brown paper–wrapped parcels, dumping them onto the floor at Chris's side. He squatted and ripped open one of the boxes and began to *ooh* and *ahh* over a series of antique brass doorknobs and other fittings, holding each of them up to the light, admiring.

"Aren't these delish?" Troy glanced at the address of one of the other packages. "I think these are the molding samples from London." He began tearing off the wrapping paper, flinging strips of it over his shoulder, where it lazily drifted to the floor, most of it coming to rest in puddles of paint. "Can it wait?" Chris asked, dragging himself to his feet, still blushing furiously. As Troy made ready to pout, he added, "I think we might have a problem. Listen to this."

He marched lopsidedly over to the machine, his single shoeless foot causing him to list slightly to port, and played the tape again.

"So?" asked Troy, pulling out several samples of crown moldings and looking at them critically. "I think these are the wrong period. Too early—again." He turned to Chris impatiently. "I still don't understand why you won't let me get that cute lil decorator from that shop on Spruce Street to do something creative." He rocked back on his heels and stared dreamily into space. "Dotted Swiss," he said to the room in general. "I see something *fabulous* in dotted Swiss. And satin drapes. Green would be nice."

"She's making connections I don't like," said Chris, shuddering at Troy's decorating notions, which would probably get them black-balled from *House Beautiful* forever, and turned his mind back to Becky's message.

"My dear," said Troy, haughtily tossing the moldings aside, "if she hasn't figured it out by now…." One of the molding samples landed in a can of opened paint, adding to the mélange on the floor.

"Perhaps," Chris paused, thinking. "Oh well, I'll talk to her tomorrow and find out what's on her mind," he said with false non-chalance.

"There's a dear," said Troy, rising and coming over to wrap his arms around him. "*Now,* will you help me choose the stuff for the other rooms? Shall we start with the bedroom?" He began tugging playfully at the buttons on Chris's shirt.

In less than a minute, Chris was as bare-chested as his lover. Troy pressed forward and, without thinking, Chris took a step backward. Once again his foot skidded in the paint. Only this time when he crashed to the floor, knocking one of the cans over entirely, his bare back landing in a pool of partially congealed semigloss, Troy was right on top.

"This could be kinda kinky," Troy said with a grin, and before Chris could stop him he dunked a hand into the spilled paint and started to trace a pale blue line from the hollow of Chris's throat down his chest to his belly button. Troy's head darted forward and, after nuzzling for a minute or two, he plastered his paint-smeared mouth to Chris's lips, twisting his body around and hauling Chris up on top so that now their bare backs were both an attractive shade of powder-blue.

This time, when they kissed, although Chris found it no less delightful than he ever did—even with the paint—he couldn't keep from wondering just what the hell was going on out in California to cause Becky to bring up a subject that, at the very least, could become *extremely* uncomfortable.

CHAPTER SIX

The next day, back at the sheriff's station, things were heating up. The third body had been discovered late that morning, stuffed in a Dumpster in the alley behind the Gold Coast bar, a notorious cruising spot. The sanitation engineer who'd found the corpse had gone into a fit of hysterics the moment he opened the top of the Dumpster, prepared to tip it into the garbage truck, and had come face-to-face with the pale, glassy stare of one Lance Blowman.

In life Blowman, a.k.a. Harold Lefkowitz, had been a video star of no little renown. Famous in certain circles for an uncanny limberness that allowed him to do things to his own anatomy that were not the subject of discussion in polite society, his films had included such intellectually stimulating titles as *Nine Inches Naked, Do Me Right, Bottoms Up, Boy Slave From Planet Prostate,* and the ever popular classic *Lusty Lads and Lassie.* Blowman's dead body was found shirtless, his trousers wrapped around his ankles—a condition with which it was not altogether unfamiliar in life. This time, however, its throat had been cut almost all the way through, and once again the corpse was practically bloodless.

Clive was baffled. Although Becky hadn't yet completed her autopsy, upon first seeing the body she'd immediately told him she was fairly certain Blowman would turn out to be the guest star in the latest episode of West Hollywood's currently running *True Crime* miniseries. Clive was ready to start pulling out his hair in frustration.

To add insult to injury, Blowman's lover, a young film producer known for his innovative use of the video camera to photograph previously unseen portions of the male anatomy, had appeared at the station that morning in a panic. He explained to the duty officer at the front desk that his "roommate" had vanished two days ago and had missed an important dinner party with some "investors" the previous evening. The producer was hysterical with worry and emphatically demanded that a full investigation be launched and the FBI, CIA, and a host of other organizations be enlisted to help.

The duty officer, although at first tempted to dismiss the producer's ravings as those of a jilted lover, in the spirit of "community-oriented policing" decided instead to take a full report. Two hours later he was in a spare office, busily taking down a description of the errant spouse from the increasingly distraught producer, when the two deputies who had responded to the sanitation worker's call paused outside the open doorway to discuss the morning's events. Unfortunately, one of the deputies had seen Blowman's face, along with other recognizable parts of his body, gracing the box cover of a tape in a local video store. Even more unfortunately, this particular deputy had a tendency to speak in a very loud voice.

The producer overheard and, to the chagrin of the duty officer taking the report, immediately began to wail, growing louder with every passing second. Acting instinctively, the two deputies outside the office door drew their guns and burst into the interview room. Confronted with the barrels of two revolvers, the producer's keening took on a new note and grew even more piercing.

Seeing the two drawn guns, the duty officer, thoroughly flustered by the chaos surrounding him, yelled over the shrieks of the producer, "Don't fire!"

Because of the tumult issuing from the interview room, one of the secretaries seated at a nearby desk misheard the shouted command.

Taking up the cry of "Fire! Fire!" she and her fellows grabbed their purses and briefcases and fled the station, taking care to pull the fire alarm on the way out. As the alarm bell shrilled wildly, employees began to evacuate the building. Bells ringing and sirens screaming, the fire crew arrived in record time.

During the commotion, Clive had burst from his office, ordered his secretary out of the building, glanced at the emergency board to find out which alarm had been pulled, and ran down the hall toward the interview room, where he grabbed a handy fire extinguisher. But there was no fire upon which to use it.

Exiting the building himself, he was approached by the shame-faced duty officer, a relatively bright young man who had figured out what happened. He filled his captain in apologetically and Clive, dreading the prospect, went to intercept Fire Chief Fred Delaney, who had appeared on the scene with his crew.

Certain the whole mess could be straightened out in no time, Clive hadn't reckoned on Delaney's belligerent opposition to anyone who appeared to threaten his authority.

"You worry about the criminals, Anderson," he'd told Clive brusquely, "I'll deal with the fires."

"There is no fire," Clive explained patiently for the third time.

"You let me be the judge of that!" Delaney said pompously, puffing out his chest and drawing himself up to his full height, which, incidentally, brought the top of his head up to a point just south of the knot in Clive's tie.

"But Fred..." Clive was left talking to the empty air as Delaney grabbed an ax from one of his men and marched into the station.

Clive didn't waste a minute before he followed the fire chief. He broke into a trot and finally caught up with Delaney inside the station just in time to watch, horrified, as Delaney, with all his might, brought the head of the ax smashing down into one of the walls of the interview room.

"What the hell are you doing?" Clive demanded, aghast.

"Looking for fire in the frame," he said with an almost malicious smile. "Could be something electrical."

"It was a false alarm, Delaney! That's what I've been trying to tell you!"

"Can't be too careful," Delaney replied. He swung the ax again, demolishing the opposite wall. "You ever see a burned body, Anderson?" he asked as, with a joyful look, he hefted the ax, aimed it toward a framed photograph of the county sheriff hanging on one wall, and obliterated both the photo and the wall beneath. "Ain't a pretty sight, lemme tell ya."

The ax descended again.

"I suppose the fire could have been hiding in the interview desk, right, Fred?" Clive said weakly, looking at the shattered remains.

"Never hurts to check," Delaney answered cheerily. "Where were we? Oh, yeah! Fire victims!"

There was a look of bliss on the fire chief's face as he continued to speak. "Skin gets all black and brittle. Kinda like Kentucky Fried extra crispy."

Clive felt himself becoming slightly nauseated.

"Eyeballs boil into jelly. Eyebrows and shit burn clear away. Sometimes fingers and toes are gone. I remember one time we pulled a guy from a blaze in a dressmaker's shop, only way we knew he wasn't one of the dummies was he had pieces of charred bone stickin' out of him."

Fred paused in his onslaught, which had now progressed out of the interview room and down the corridor. On the way, he'd casually reached up with the pointed end of the ax and pulled down ceiling tiles, battered the hallway walls beyond repair, and sent a water fountain to its watery grave. He eyed the wreckage with the satisfaction of a job well done, reversed the ax, and leaned on the handle.

"Now, Clive," he began companionably, "would you ever forgive me if I let you come back into this old firetrap and you ended up like that?"

"No, no," Clive said, his head spinning from the gruesome description. "Of course not."

He wandered dizzily outside, leaving the fire chief and his crew to their work. Finally, an hour later, after finding nothing, Delaney grudgingly left the battered station after first warning Clive to contact him immediately at the merest scent of smoke. Thereafter, while people returned to what remained of their desks, Clive sadly surveyed the wreckage of the station and the producer, now heavily sedated, was whisked off to the morgue across the street to identify Blowman's body.

Now, several hours later, Clive was sitting in the remnants of his office, trying to ignore the deep gashes and holes allowing him to see through the wall to where his secretary was sitting, reviewing a facsimile from the FBI listing similar serial killer patterns. Nothing was helpful. The closest series of murders to the current killings had taken place back in the '30s somewhere in Georgia. Clive had difficulty imagining a ninety-some-year-old mass murderer with a Southern accent rampaging through the back alleys of West Hollywood.

His office door opened and Becky walked in without knocking. She tossed a file at him and flopped into her usual chair.

"Heard a rumor you had some excitement here this morning." She glanced at the battered walls of Clive's office, where Delaney had been especially enthusiastic. "For once it looks like the rumor mill was right on."

"Same guy?" Clive asked, ignoring her last comment.

"Same guy," said Becky. "No torture this time. But the skin's missing from the neck again. Boy," she said, leaning her chair back on two legs and poking her finger into a foot-long gash in the plaster next to the door, "this place is gonna cost a fortune to fix."

"What about the blood?" Clive asked through gritted teeth.

"What blood?"

"I was afraid of that," he sighed. He pushed a copy of the FBI report across his desk toward her. "Don't worry about messing it up," he said. "This is your copy."

Becky looked at him blankly as she picked up the document.

"Never mind," he said.

Becky glanced through the report and tossed it back onto his desk blotter. "Well, this is no help. Wow!" Her eyes widened as she took in some of the damage to the back wall. "Looks like someone took an ax to this place."

"Don't remind me," Clive said. "Any suggestions?"

"Yeah, get a construction crew in here before the whole place comes down around your ears."

"Becky…" Clive warned.

"Oh, all right. Lemme think." She paused. "I have a friend from med school…"

"Good for you," Clive said, not following the transition but assuming Becky had some kind of point to make.

"His name is Chris Driscoll. We used to date—well, kind of, anyway—but," she sighed fatalistically, "he's gay, wouldn't you know. My luck, huh?"

"Becky, you know I find your love life fascinating, but…"

"Oh, stop it, Clive," she said, slightly irritated. "This kind of thing is right up his alley."

"What is he? A shrink?"

"No," she said slowly. "He never finished school…"

"Just great! An amateur!"

"If you'd let me finish," she said sternly and went on. "He's a writer now—or was for a while. Changes careers pretty often. Wrote historical stuff. Nonfiction. He's also really into the supernatural."

"This is too weird," Clive said as if to himself.

"Not really." Becky dug into her purse and pulled out a battered book. "Take a look."

She handed it to Clive, who surreptitiously checked it for potential chocolate smudges before examining the cover. "*Peter Kurten: The Dusseldorf Dracula,* by Christopher Driscoll," he read flatly. He looked up, confused.

"This nutcase," said Becky, "killed a whole bunch of people in the 1920s. He was some kind of perverted sex fiend and, get this, he *drank* the blood."

"All of it?" asked Clive, feeling himself becoming nauseated for the second time that day.

"Of course not," was the terse reply. "But there are certain similarities here. There's some kind of sexual thing going on with our guy. None of the bodies we found were fully clothed—the hustler was naked, remember?"

"True," Clive said thoughtfully. "And there was the mutilation of the genitals."

"Exactly. And there's this thing with the blood. It's not a perfect match, but it's too close for comfort."

"So what does this Driscoll guy have that we don't?"

"That book's a psychological study. Chris may be able to give us an idea of what kind of crazy we're looking for."

"You want to call him?" asked Clive.

"I want to call him."

"I don't like this," Clive told her.

"I know. Beggars can't be choosers, though." She got up and walked toward the door. "I'll give him another call tonight and let him know it's OK with you."

"You already called him?" Clive's tone was angrily flat. Becky at least had the good grace to look sheepish.

"I didn't know what else to do," she apologized. "Don't worry. He'll keep his mouth shut. See ya."

Becky turned and squeezed through the door, thrusting her hip into it to close it before Clive could call out. The door slammed with a crash and a huge chunk of loose plaster thudded to the floor, shattering and spewing clouds of white debris into the air.

Clive sneezed twice, pulled out his handkerchief, and dabbed futilely at the white dust on the sleeve of his jacket, succeeding only in rubbing it further into the fabric.

"Things can't get any worse," he moaned quietly, looking mournfully at his ruined suit.

But Clive Anderson was wrong. Things could get worse. A lot worse.

CHAPTER SEVEN

harlie Copperman stumbled out of the bar, closing the door behind him, and collapsed against the brick wall to rest for a moment. Frankly, he didn't think he'd had all that much to drink; he was usually very careful about his alcohol intake, limiting himself to five margaritas, and he'd only had three. He never liked to go to the gym in the morning with a hangover. Maybe it was the shots of tequila poppers that the barely passably attractive bartender kept slipping him on the sly. What was his name? Bo or Bob or something with a *b*.

Charlie had flashed the bartender his most dazzling smile when he entered Rage several hours earlier. He'd taken a quick cruise of the dance floor first, and after deciding there was no one in the place pretty enough to waste his time talking to he seized on the bartender at the back bar, a lanky, almost buff, brown-haired guy with bad skin, as the most likely candidate to buy him drinks. His instincts had been right, as usual, and the tequila flowed like a river all night.

About an hour ago, however, after the bar began to fill up, Charlie had spotted a really hot dark-haired guy in the corner wearing a black button-down shirt and dark jeans. Charlie went into cruise mode and was rewarded with a nod and a smile. He waited a few minutes, until he was certain the eye contact hadn't been just coincidental, then strolled toward the bathroom. As Charlie passed him the stranger smiled again, removing any doubt. Charlie nodded coolly, not wanting to show too much interest, but paused at the men's room door and looked back over his shoulder. Satisfied the interest was genuine, Charlie opened the door and proceeded into the bathroom.

As he unzipped his fly to take a pee, he overheard a conversation between two effeminate types at the other end of the room.

"The Rage mystery bathroom, I always call it!" one of the young men exclaimed. "It used to be *much* smaller, but then they knocked down the walls."

"So what's the mystery?" his friend wanted to know.

"They took out most of the urinals," came the reply. "Of course, they might have wanted to make it more cozy."

The two young men came over to the urinals on either side of Charlie, unzipped, and went about their business. Charlie saw the wisdom of the first speaker's words when he realized that the positioning of the urinals meant he was hemmed in on both sides. As he zipped up he felt a hand on his ass and pulled away from the urinal sharply, jostling the other two. One of them yelped as he spattered onto the front of his trousers, but Charlie didn't care.

"You gotta be kidding, queen," he sneered and left the bathroom.

He returned to his previous position at the bar after making eye contact with the black-clad young man again. The bartender kept feeding him shots of tequila poppers, but, hey, if Bo or Bob was too stupid to realize Charlie was more interested in the guy in the corner, it wasn't Charlie's problem, was it? It wasn't like Charlie had propositioned the guy or anything; he just sat and smiled and drank his tequila. Charlie couldn't understand why Bo/Bob got so offended when Charlie hesitated before giving him his number. Bo/Bob wasn't really gross or anything, except for the bad skin and his profuse sweating—and it wasn't the most pleasant-smelling sweat either. Charlie decided he'd done the right thing by reversing the last two digits of his phone number when he wrote it on the "trick tablet" and handed it to Bo/Bob. He could always claim he was drunk and screwed up if he ever needed to use the bartender to cadge free drinks again.

Charlie breathed the cool autumn air, trying to clear his head. He felt the moist bricks against his back vibrating with the heavy beat emanating from the DJ booth inside the bar. *Lord save me from Cher fans*, he thought. *They should screen 'em all first before they let any of 'em become DJs.*

He waited several minutes. He had kind of hoped the dark-haired guy would have followed him out of the bar by now. He'd made eye contact with the guy at least three times during the past hour, and he was sure he'd watched Charlie leave the bar. He hadn't actually gone over and talked to the guy. Oh, no! That would be admitting that he found him attractive, something that Charlie Copperman would never do.

Let him come over and talk to me first, Charlie had thought. Now he steeled his resolve to always be the pursued—never the pursuer—and mentally added, *If he doesn't come out in two minutes, I'm outta here. His loss.*

Two willowy Hispanic men approached the doorway where Charlie was standing. "Well, *excuse* us!" one of them said loudly. "What's the matter, honey? No luck?"

"Worthless queens," Charlie mumbled as he moved away from the door, hoping the two would just go into fucking Rage and leave him alone.

"Oh! Aren't *we* just *too* butch? Why don't you try a real woman, sweetie?" the taller of the two asked.

"Not with her dick," Charlie shot back, closing his eyes and leaning back against the wall. The two men disappeared into the bar and Charlie took a deep breath of cool autumn air, hoping it would help him sober up.

"Good evening." The voice was deep and melodious. "I saw you in the bar."

Charlie smiled lazily, eyes still closed. "And…?"

"I thought maybe you might be interested in our spending some time together. Alone. I find the noise in there… distracting."

Charlie at last opened his eyes to confront the guy in the black shirt standing in front of him. Charlie smiled.

"What did you have in mind?"

"Oh, I don't know. Maybe we could take a little walk and become better acquainted with each other?"

Charlie grinned and held out his hand. "I'm Charlie."

Taking his hand with seeming amusement, the guy responded with his own name. Unfortunately, Charlie belched at the precise moment the guy spoke and missed it. *Oh well,* he thought, *I can always take his driver's license out of his wallet while he's sleeping—if his name turns out to be that important.* Charlie dismissed the identity of the stranger with a shrug and the two walked together, away from the bar and toward the parking lot.

"You live around here?" Charlie asked with studied casualness.

"Nearby. In a manner of speaking." They walked under a street lamp with a burned-out bulb and rounded the corner into the parking lot. Charlie spotted his car parked next to a dark blue Jag near the back fence in a pool of darkness.

"Fucking city hall," Charlie said just to make conversation.

"Beg pardon?"

"Smashed streetlights all over the place. Fucking homeless guy broke into my car and stole the stereo last month. They caught the bastard, though. He's gonna be livin' down at county jail for a while."

"Ah," breathed the stranger, knowingly. "You believe in revenge, then?"

"Fuckin' right, I do!" Charlie agreed emphatically. "I spent two weeks' pay on that thing!" Charlie pointed. "My car's over there."

"How nice for you," replied the other.

Something's wrong, Charlie thought. The guy sounded strange; his voice was almost a hiss. Charlie would have called it sibilant if he'd known the word.

Charlie turned to look at him, thinking, *Oh, shit. Another weirdo,* when his glance caught the other man's eyes. They were dark, black in fact, and strangely fascinating, flecked with sparkles of silver. Charlie looked deeper and deeper into those dark pools of sparkling light. He heard a deep, droning sound that seemed to be coming from inside his own head. His jaw dropped as he relaxed further into the hypnotic gaze. He didn't realize it but his shirt was becoming plastered to his upper body as he broke into a cold sweat, his forehead suddenly gleaming with perspiration.

As a hand brushed his chest, the droning sound grew louder and Charlie realized that the guy had moved behind him. Charlie suddenly began to feel *very* horny. The hand moved slowly down across Charlie's stomach and he felt his abdominal muscles start to quiver. He had a tremendous hard-on, but no matter how much he wanted to he just didn't have the energy to reach down to his zipper to free it.

Charlie dimly realized he should turn around but didn't seem to be able to move. *Way too much tequila,* he thought as he felt a hand tangle in his hair, bending his head backward, the other hand groping Charlie's crotch as the droning sound grew even louder.

Sweating with discomfort as his hard-on became almost unendurable, Charlie wondered whether the guy was going to try and jerk him off right there in the parking lot. But a freezing pain stuck him suddenly in the side of his throat and, as Charlie Copperman leaned back into the strange man's embrace and closed his eyes, he imagined he was still looking into those disturbing eyes, watching the silver specks of light flicker and go dim, one after the other, until the last one died out.

0 0 0

Unaware of Charlie Copperman's rapidly cooling corpse, Becky waited until almost ten o'clock California time before calling Chris in Philly. He was rarely available during the day, and she wanted to avoid talking to Troy if possible. She'd never quite understood the attraction between them, although any fool could see they were devoted to each other. Troy's flamboyant mannerisms had always made her slightly uncomfortable; in her opinion he was exactly the type of effeminate twink who gave gay men a bad name. Furthermore, Chris had an annoying habit of following Troy with his eyes whenever they were together, a look of adoration plastered across his face; she'd always found it difficult to carry on an intelligent conversation with him while Troy was in the room.

Becky was smart enough to realize that, in large part, her dislike of Troy was due to residual jealousy. Although she'd long accepted that any kind of romance between she and Chris was impossible, she was still envious of the relationship between the two young men.

"Please, God," she had often prayed silently. "Just once let *me* be loved like that."

Steeling herself to be polite in case Troy answered, she picked up the phone and dialed.

◊ ◊ ◊

Chris was quite literally up to his ass in hot water when the telephone rang. Part of the reason their reconstruction of the town house, originally estimated to take eleven months, was now rapidly approaching its third anniversary was due to Chris's perfectionism. Troy had pleaded for months with Chris to allow him to redecorate. Chris had finally succumbed but, a burst of whimsical inspiration striking him at the time, he had done so with the provision that their home be totally restored to its original condition as authentically as possible. In addition, though not particularly gifted when working with tools or—as had been recently demonstrated to him—with paint, Chris had gotten the idea into his head that he could do much of the work himself.

In the face of Chris's restrictions, Troy had tried to backpedal, insisting that he really, truly liked living in surroundings that could be classified only as "neo-gingerbread." There was no reason at all for Chris to embark on one of his little "projects," and, if there were, wouldn't Chris be happier taking up needlepoint or watercolor paints or clay or something? But Chris had stubbornly made up his mind and was not to be dissuaded.

Troy, predictably, refused to live without electricity; the thought of being unable to use a blow dryer left him in complete panic. Though Chris tried to explain that throughout most of human history people had gotten along fine with candles and oil lamps, he finally gave in to Troy's tears. Tearing into the walls revealed a baffling collection of frayed cloth-covered wires that Chris had innocently started to rip out. After all, he reasoned, rewiring must be quite simple—all one had to do was pull out the old wires and install new ones in their place. Several nasty shocks and a small electrical fire later, Chris decided that he should probably call in an electrician.

He'd had similar difficulties with the bathroom. Though he was uncomfortable with the idea that the effect he'd been looking to achieve would be spoiled, Chris enjoyed the luxury of modern bathrooms—outhouses having never been his style. He'd compromised by updating the master bath and disguising it to look as it would have in colonial times. Over the tub he'd installed a large wooden cistern covering a steel tank containing hot water for showers. One pull on a hanging chain allowed the water to flow from the tank into the false cistern bottom so that the illusion was maintained. The plumbers who did the actual installation were paid very well and just shrugged at Chris's eccentricity and followed his designs without comment.

Maybe I carry things too far sometimes, he thought as he stood in the tub, the water from the overhead pipe cascading down around him. He'd been trying to fix a leaky joint with disastrous results.

Shit, he thought, *I hope the wood doesn't warp. I'll have to buy another barn after all.* He was thinking of a purchase he had made at the outset of the project, a dilapidated farmhouse circa 1793, to provide authentic wood of the proper age for the living room and dining room floors. As Troy had said several times during the past year,

"If we ever want to sell this place, it'll be worth a fortune. No one will want to live in it, but it *will* be worth a fortune."

He climbed, dripping, from the tub, kicked off his waterlogged sneakers, and stripped. Drying himself with a towel, he darted into the living room and picked up the telephone on the sixth ring.

"Hello," he said.

"Chris? It's Becky. I was just gonna hang up."

"Troy probably forgot to turn on the machine again," he said as he deftly caught a drop of water with the edge of the towel before it could splash onto the hardwood floor. "What's up?"

"Sorry about the cryptic message yesterday. I've got a problem out here."

"Yeah, well, while we were listening to it we had a problem out here." He glanced ruefully at the last few faint traces of blue on the floor that had resisted his most strenuous attack with paint thinner. "What's wrong?"

"We've had three murders in three days."

"So? You're in Los Angeles. I'm surprised you haven't had two dozen."

"I'm in West Hollywood," Becky corrected testily. "We don't have murders here. At least not where the killer practically cuts the victims' heads off and drains out all the blood."

Chris started to feel a little uncomfortable. "Oh, come on, Becky," he said and forced a laugh. "*All* the blood? Even I know you can't just drain *all* the blood from a corpse without some kind of pump or something. Just check the hospitals and medical labs. Your killer's probably some guy who flunked out of med school and went crazy. For Pete's sake, Becky, this is L.A. It could even be some kind of wacked-out artist who's decided that only human blood provides the proper shade of red for painting sunsets."

"Chris," she said quietly, "I don't think this guy drains the *corpses.*" There was silence.

Chris prayed that Troy would magically return from wherever he was in the next three seconds and give him an excuse to hang up. He didn't.

Chris took a deep breath and then asked, trying to put polite disbelief into his voice, "You mean he drains them while they're alive?"

"Yeah, I'm pretty sure. That's why I called you. You wrote that Kurten book. I just read it again. It's very good."

"And I wrote one on Peter Stubbs—the guy who thought he was a werewolf—and another on the Salem witch trial mass hysteria. So?"

"Stop being obtuse," Becky snapped. "I need information on this guy. A psychological profile, if you can. Anything to help us figure out what kind of a crazy we're looking for. I want you to come out here and help."

"Becky," he said patiently, "I'm not a psychologist. Los Angeles is fruit and nut city. There are plenty of people out there who specialize in..."

"But what about Kurten?" she protested.

"What about him? Kurten was an extremely complicated case. Just because your guy has one small similarity doesn't mean I'm gonna be able to contribute anything helpful. Besides, Kurten didn't drain all the blood. He merely—"

She cut him off. "OK! OK! No lectures. It's an excuse. I confess!" she cried dramatically. Then her voice softened. "I...I want to see you again." She became uncertain. "It's been ten years."

I know, Chris thought. *That's the problem.*

"Fill me in on the details," he said aloud. "Let's see how much like my old friend Peter Kurten this guy really is. Then, well, I'll think about it."

With ghoulish relish, Becky began to speak. As her story unfolded, Chris felt knots of tension form in his stomach as he grew more and more concerned. Although he was convinced Becky was wrong about West Hollywood's being visited by a modern version of the Dusseldorf Vampire, he was beginning to suspect she had been right in trying to enlist his help.

"Flaps of skin, you say? Always from the throat? Spine severed?" He took a pencil from the telephone table and, hunting through the mess of papers where Troy liked to leave him little notes, he began to write on a clean pad that he finally found hidden under the phone.

As he wrote, Becky continued speaking.

"What I can't figure out is how he does it. You don't just walk up to someone, stick a tube in their arm, and say, 'Excuse me, but I'm taking out all your blood, OK?' I mean, it'd hurt for one thing. And the second boy must've been in real pain. You should see what this lunatic did to him! But, get this, there was *no* evidence that he'd been restrained. Nothing! No rope burns, no embedded fibers, no chafing on the wrists or ankles—zip!"

By this time Chris was really worried. "How are the newspapers handling it?" he asked, feigning calm.

"Oh, that!" Becky said with a huff of exasperation. "The porn star's boyfriend had a little problem when he went in to file a missing persons report. It hit the evening papers. What a mess!"

The front door of the town house opened and Troy walked in—along with a stunning young man wearing tight slacks and a white cotton shirt open halfway to the navel to reveal a chest covered with thick hair and a profusion of dangling gold chains.

"Uh, Becky," Chris said, "Troy just came in. Let me think about this for a while and I'll get back to you. Call me tomorrow night if anything else happens." Over her shocked protests, he hung up and turned to face Troy, one eyebrow raised inquisitively.

Troy fussed over the young man as he led him into the guest bedroom. Closing the door, he turned to face Chris.

"He was so cute I couldn't resist."

"He *is* adorable," Chris conceded. "But couldn't you find something, I don't know, maybe a little less South Philly?"

"He's from Jersey," Troy said proudly.

"I see," Chris replied with a smile. The smile faded. "I'll deal with him in a minute. First, tell me something. How would you feel about going to California?"

Troy immediately began to beam. "You don't mean it!" he cried happily.

"I might," Chris said cautiously.

"Lana Turner," Troy breathed with ecstasy, "at Schwab's. Elizabeth Taylor! Julia Roberts! Oh, my God!"

"What?" Chris was alarmed at Troy's shriek.

"Brad Pitt!"

"Knock it off. This is serious." Chris's brow furrowed in thought. "I'd rather not see Becky again, but something's happening out there that we may have to check into."

"Oh, thank you, Missy Scarlett!" cried Troy in a passably good Hattie McDaniel imitation. He dropped to his knees and clasped Chris around the thighs with both arms. "Thank you for takin' me back to Tara!"

"Cut it out, monkey," said Chris, absently stroking the tousled blond curls as Troy obediently got to his feet. "It's not gonna be just Hollywood fun and games."

He shook his head, making a conscious effort to clear his mind of concern. "Well," he said, rubbing his hands together in anticipation, "let's see what you've brought me."

He walked toward the guest room door.

"You know, it's funny," Troy said, "Gustav wanted to know if you'd changed your mind about visiting them in L.A."

Chris whirled around. "What?"

Troy was startled by the outburst. "Gustav. He called tonight. Said it was real important."

"When?" demanded Chris.

"Oh, maybe six or so. You were still asleep. He sounded real worried so I left you a note." Troy went over to the telephone table and began to paw through the accumulation of papers.

"Here it is," he said and handed it to Chris.

Chris glanced at it, darted to the telephone, and began dialing.

"What about *him*?" Troy asked, indicating the guest room.

"I'm sure you can keep him occupied until I get off."

"Get off?" repeated Troy wickedly. "I *beg* your *humble* pardon!"

"C'mon, Troy, get serious," Chris said. "You go in and play with him for a while. I'll be there as soon as I finish with Gustav."

Troy hunched himself over, lifting one shoulder higher than the other. "Thank you, master," he rasped in a bad imitation of Peter Lorre. "I'll wait in the laboratory." And so saying he limped off into the guest room.

Someone picked up the telephone at the other end.

"*Ja?*"

"Hanna? Is Gustav around? It's Chris." An excited babble struck his ears. "I know, I know," he said soothingly, holding the receiver away from the side of his head to prevent his eardrums from rupturing.

"Slow down," he commanded. "Tell me everything you know. From the beginning…"

CHAPTER EIGHT

After speaking with Gustav and Hanna on the telephone, Chris quickly dispensed with Troy's gold-chained trick. He then immediately telephoned his travel agent and his banker, waking them both out of a sound sleep, issuing them terse instructions and promising cash bonuses if his wishes could be complied with before dawn. The two men, well aware of their client's eccentricity as well as his generosity, were only too happy to lose a couple of hours' sleep. Troy had been delighted when, four hours later, Chris handed him the airplane ticket, a cashier's check for $10,000, and a detailed list of instructions on what he'd need to do before Chris would be able to follow him out to California. Troy kept insisting he was perfectly capable of remembering everything from the last time they had moved, but Chris, knowing how easily his lover could be distracted by a pretty face or a tight pair of buns, was taking no chances. The next morning, Troy had boarded a 747 bound for Los Angeles, arriving several hours later with the cashier's check, the telephone number of every attractive male steward on the flight, and uncountable suitcases and bags of clothing, comprising a mere soupçon of what Troy insisted was his "essential wardrobe."

BITE CLUB

Originally Chris hadn't planned on telling Becky he would be coming to Los Angeles until after he'd come and gone. The murders, however, suddenly and mysteriously ceased, with the sole exception of the Copperman killing, which Becky estimated to have occurred at almost exactly the same time she had been on the telephone with Chris. Nevertheless, she continued to call him every night, certain the killings would resume and begging for his help.

It seemed like each call from his old friend was calculated to catch him at the most inconvenient time. When she called on Tuesday, he'd been attempting to strip the varnish from the baseboards in the front hallway and the remainder of the spilled paint from the living room floor. Lost in deep concentration, he'd been startled by the telephone's loud trill and pressed down on the paint scraper, digging into the wood and ending up with an extremely painful handful of splinters.

On Wednesday, her call had come while he was high on a ladder in the dining room, in the process of replacing the burned-out candles in the chandelier. Foolishly reluctant to release his grip on the last candle as he had almost managed to position them all so that the drippings wouldn't overflow, he'd stretched to reach the kitchen extension, overbalanced, and crashed to the floor in a pile of shattered wax and plaster as his weight ripped the fixture clean out of the ceiling.

He could have simply broken down and called her before she had a chance to call him, but Chris irrationally felt that to do so would be giving ground. By Thursday, therefore, he'd prepared. Resolving that this time he would answer the phone without disaster, he refrained from any substantive work on the town house and contented himself with waxing the newly stripped floors and dusting.

As of eight-thirty, however, the telephone had remained silent. Chris decided to go out and grab a bite. He left the town house and, walking down the street, almost immediately encountered a tall, lanky blond engineering student from Drexel. One thing led to another and the student eagerly accompanied Chris back home, where Chris rapidly had him writhing in erotic passion. Chris had just gotten the young engineer out of his shirt and was slowly unbuttoning his own fly when the telephone rang.

Chris ignored it. It rang again.

By the seventh ring, he could stand it no longer. With a silent curse against all those who manufactured cheap answering machines, he excused himself from the sweating young man and, irritated, rushed out of the bedroom and across the hallway to the telephone, completely forgetting about the newly waxed floor.

His feet suddenly began to move much faster than he had intended them to. He skittered across the hall, arms flailing futilely for balance, and crashed into the telephone table, showering the hall with scraps of paper, pencils, and the cursed answering machine. He grabbed the receiver as, in a flash of anger, he threw the machine into the living room, where it burst against the far wall, gouging the wood paneling, bits of its innards flying through the air.

"All right already!" he yelled into the telephone, without bothering to say hello. "I made the fucking reservations! I'll be there tomorrow!"

So saying, he hurled the telephone after the answering machine and listened in satisfaction as it shattered with a lovely crunching sound. Picking himself off the floor, he returned to his guest. The mood, however, had been spoiled.

◊ ◊ ◊

Clive Anderson was pissed. He was outwardly calm and composed, but his insides seethed as the frustration of the week hit home. They'd had three days of respite, and then, without warning, this morning the fifth body had been discovered.

The victim was a young Asian lad, with a classic V-shaped torso and heavily muscled arms and thighs. Clive had had ample opportunity to jealously examine the details of the corpse's magnificent physique as, like Billy Boyd before him, this young man was stark naked.

Looking down as Becky worked on the body sprawled before her amid a cluster of forensics experts, and listening to the chatter of the group of local residents gathered behind the police barricade, Clive began to wonder if the neighbors were more upset at the thought of a killer in their midst or at the unfortunate youth's lack of proper attire.

"Without a stitch!" he overheard the effeminate man who'd discovered the body say for what seemed the twentieth time in as many minutes. "Just lying there, bare-assed, in the bushes next to the rear door of the shop. At first I thought, my dear, someone's dropped off a present!" Clive turned away in disgust.

The speaker was Charles Partridge, owner of Partridge's Pomade-a-Dorium at the corner of Santa Monica Boulevard and the normally quiet residential block West Knoll Drive. He'd discovered the body shortly after opening up for business when he exited the back door of his shop to take out the garbage.

Fifty-eight and, by means of an impressively dyed pompadour hairstyle that Clive suspected was actually a wig, trying to look twenty-five, Partridge was a notorious publicity hound. Three years ago a Rolls Royce convertible had spun out of control and left Santa Monica Boulevard behind, leaping the curb and crashing through the front door of the salon. Partridge capitalized on the event by creating an advertising campaign, complete with photos of the car sticking out of the front of the shop, with the copy: PEOPLE JUST CAN'T WAIT TO GET POMADED AT PARTRIDGE'S! In Clive's opinion the ad had been tasteless.

Partridge had recently been making noise about getting involved in West Hollywood politics, maybe even running for mayor. Even though West Hollywood's current mayor, Daniel Eversleigh, was somewhat of a joke to practically anyone who knew him, the thought of this buttercup yellow–haired buffoon running for election made Clive shudder with distaste.

Partridge was notorious for holding himself above the law. In fact, at least two or three times a week, Clive was forced to take the hairdresser's telephone calls and patiently explain that, although he was well aware Charles Partridge was one of West Hollywood's leading citizens and a bastion of the business community, there was still no way Clive could "get him out of" his parking citations for parking on the curb, the sidewalk, the middle of the street, or on someone's front lawn—whichever locale was the subject of the particular ticket that prompted the call. Partridge's handling of a corpse on his back doorstep had been typical of the man's arrogance as far as law enforcement was concerned.

Upon the discovery of the body, Partridge had immediately called his friend Ed Larsen, editor of the *Gay Gazette*. The Sheriff's Department had been notified only after Larsen showed up with a photographer to snap exclusive photos. Clive had been furious and seriously considered having both Partridge and Larsen arrested.

Larsen was currently a particular thorn in Clive's side. The porn producer, still shaken up by the way he felt he'd been treated that horrible day of the false fire alarm at the station, had given an inflammatory interview to the *Gazette* immediately upon his return from the hospital. Accusing the city, the department, and everyone else who was even remotely connected with municipal government of institutionalized homophobia, emotional gay bashing, and insensitivity, he also used the opportunity to promote sales of his deceased lover's latest video.

Egged on by Larsen, he'd managed to create a stir in the gay press, which, with the absence of new corpses, had only just begun to abate slightly. In addition, the producer had launched a rambling, sixty-two-page, $3 million lawsuit against the city; the city attorney was still trying to make sense of the complaint and figure out just what West Hollywood was being sued for.

Clive groaned mentally at the thought of what Larsen would come up with for tomorrow's headline.

He jumped as a hand came clapping down on his shoulder and a voice brayed loudly into his ear.

"What the hell happened this time?" The speaker was Pamela Burman. Pamela was widely known in city government for two things, her efficiency as West Hollywood's city manager and her obvious irritation with everyone she had ever met in her entire life. Burman had also achieved a certain notoriety with her neighbors due to her propensity, even though she had recently been quoted in a local newspaper as admitting to being at least sixty, for jogging three miles each morning wearing a variety of fluorescent jogging suits. Local dog owners, out taking the family pooch for a morning stroll, had quickly learned to prominently display shovels, paper bags, and rubber gloves immediately upon catching sight of Burman's famous hot-pink and electric-blue costumes descending upon them as signs of their compliance with West Hollywood's "pooper-scooper" ordinance. Pamela was not above stopping strollers and their pets without warning and turning her full wrath upon them, including a series of citizen's arrests, if the hapless animal lovers could not immediately provide physical proof of their ability to remove the offending doggy deposits from West Hollywood's pristine curbsides.

Burman's escapades had made headlines on several occasions. In fact, she'd been carrying on a love-hate relationship with both of the local gay newspapers for several years. Burman was a news editor's dream; on the one hand, she often allowed her innate rancor to get the best of her and made disparaging remarks about the local gay community's activities, which, but for the fact that she was a violently outspoken Republican in a mostly Democratic town, would have been forgiven. On the other hand, she was indescribably campy, without intending to be, and the gay press gleefully reported on each and every one of her eccentric activities. She had sued both local papers countless times, losing each lawsuit. In one instance, her claim involved some extremely arch printed remarks made by Ed Larsen concerning a neon green suede pantsuit, several sizes too small, that Burman had once chosen to wear to one of Mayor Daniel Eversleigh's swearing-in ceremonies. Burman was infuriated by Larsen's criticism and publicly promised to "...sue that nelly little bitch for everything he's worth!"—following this comment with a stream of vituperation that covered, among other things, Larsen's probable parentage and his dubious claims to masculinity.

The papers seized the opportunity and photos of the "Nelly Green Suit" began appearing everywhere, comparing Burman's wardrobe to those of locally prominent drag queens and serving to hoist her to a new level of mindless ire. When asked if he truly

believed the accusations of homophobia that his reporters were busily hurling at the city manager, Larsen replied, "Are you kidding? We
love her! What queen wouldn't? She's the fashion risk of the decade!
Besides, she sells papers!"

So much for her gay constituency. As for West Hollywood's extensive elderly population—they adored her. Long a candidate for Social
Security herself, she refused to reveal her exact age, responding to all
inquires with a clipped snarl of "Sixty-teen." Yet she was indefatiga-
ble and had become somewhat of a role model for many, instituting
many seniors' programs geared toward elderly residents. She'd fought
long and hard against the construction of a new city hall building,
citing that its proposed site was almost half a block uphill from the
nearest bus stop, making it difficult for the elderly to access. She'd
championed a taxi coupon program with city-sponsored discounts
for senior citizens, and with the help of West Hollywood's business
community she created a homeless shelter after receiving complaints
from elderly residents about being panhandled and accosted by the
city's homeless. In fact, it was rumored that city council was considering naming the shelter in Burman's honor. Even though she was
irritating and aggravating and a sworn enemy of the mayor, the
council was not so foolish as to ignore her popularity with constituents: In any election year, Burman's support could make the difference between keeping and losing a council seat.

Right now, however, Burman appeared less than charitable. She'd
seen Ed Larsen taking statements from the gathered crowd when she
arrived; the thought of additional bad press was doing little to
improve her notorious ill temper.

"Good Christ! Another one?"

"Another one," Clive sighed. *My God, it's unseasonably warm for
October!* Clive thought. He wanted nothing more than to be out of
Pamela's presence and back at the station, where he thought longingly of the spare clean, dry dress shirt once again awaiting him in the
bottom drawer of his desk.

Drawing Clive aside for a moment, away from the corpse, and
facing him so closely that they were almost nose to nose, she hissed,

"What the hell are you going to do about this, Clive? You've seen what the goddamn gay papers are doing with this? I've had half a dozen gay rights groups outside of City Hall protesting since last Friday. When are you gonna find this lunatic?"

Clive gently extricated himself from Burman's death grip on his arm and, smoothing out his wrinkled sleeve, replied, "We're doing the best we can, Pam."

"Don't give me that crap! I don't want your best. I want the son of a bitch caught and locked up. We've got the Halloween parade coming up in a few weeks and city council's on my back about publicity." She grabbed for the captain's lapels to draw him closer; Clive narrowly avoided her grasp.

"Look, we *tried* to keep this out of the papers. With five unexplained corpses *someone* was bound to notice *something* sooner or later."

"Can't you get a restraining order or something against the *Gazette*?" said Burman venomously as she caught Larsen's eye, waved at him, and bared her teeth in a beatific smile. Larsen, out of earshot, waved back and snapped a picture of Burman and Clive standing next to the corpse. "God, I hate that bitch!" she said quietly, the smile still frozen on her face.

"Talk to the city attorney," Clive suggested.

Burman's phony smile vanished. "Yeah, right," she fumed. "That asshole has had it in for me ever since I nailed his kid for Rollerblading without a helmet last year." She looked around in frustration at the increasing number of onlookers as Becky, finished with her preliminary examination, was supervising the loading of the body into the coroner's van.

"Get outta here!" she yelled at the startled crowd. "Shoo! There's nothing to see! Go home! Get a life!" She launched herself at the people pressed up against the police barricade, her lemon-yellow purse lifted and prepared to swing down upon the unprotected heads of the crowd. Clive grabbed her by the collar of her red-and-white polka-dot woolen coat and dragged her back.

"Are you crazy?" he demanded. "Larsen's got a camera! The last thing you need is a lawsuit for assault."

"Then get 'em outta here!" she demanded. "They're making me crazy." She turned back to the crowd. "Don't any of you people have day jobs? What are you standing there for?"

Clive motioned to two nearby deputies, who began moving among the gathered onlookers and clearing them out. He saw Becky moving toward them with the awkward gait she'd recently developed from her continuing efforts to hide her pudgy thighs. Her look of concern gave way to a grin at his altercation with Burman.

"What're you smiling about?" he demanded when she came within hearing range. He nervously smoothed down his hair with his hands, wishing desperately for a comb, a mirror, and a nice tall relaxing glass of scotch and soda.

"Nothing. Good morning, Pam."

"What's good about it?" Burman fumed.

"What have you got?" Clive asked hopefully.

A look of uneasiness crossed Becky's fleshy, pleasant face, wiping away her grin. "It's bad, Clive. Very bad."

"Great!" Burman snorted.

"Young, pretty, well-built...and gay. Just like the others."

"We *all* saw what he looked like," said Burman, waving in the direction of the coroner's van. "Jesus Christ, the entire world saw *exactly* what he looked like! Down to his fucking religion!"

"Believe me, I know," said Clive. He indicated a small group of four women and a man holding up handmade signs on broom handles on the far side of the barricade. "You see them?"

"So what?" said Burman with irritation. "Goddamn morbid looky-loos!" she shouted at the startled group. "What do ya do, stop at traffic accidents and have *picnics*!"

"Pamela," Clive hissed. "Will you stop? They're from the League of Decency!"

"The born-again group?" asked Becky. Clive nodded miserably.

"Oh, yeah?" said Burman pensively. Then her face brightened. "Watch this!" she ordered.

She marched up to the barricade, yelling out, "You! Hey, you there! Decency people! I wanna tell you something!" She motioned them toward her.

Slowly, the one male member approached, the women following behind. "Yes?" he inquired politely.

Burman leaned forward across the barrier. Breathing into the man's face, she yelled, "Get fucked!" Leaving the startled Christians behind, she marched back to the white-faced Clive.

"I wish you hadn't done that," he gulped. "They've been writing letters to the governor for the past week protesting against indecent attire in their neighborhood. It probably doesn't even occur to them that a corpse can't help the state it's found in."

"Does anyone want to know what *I* found?" Becky asked before Burman could attack the Christians once more.

"What?" Burman demanded in anticipation. "A clue? Finally!"

"I'm not sure," Becky mused. "But the blood tests prove that the first four victims were all negative for VD, including HIV, hepatitis, syphilis, the works. Not even a single low-grade infection." Becky removed her rubber gloves and, with a slightly apologetic look, took a Twink out of her pocket and began to unwrap it.

"Infection? You checked to see if they had the *flu*?"

"Anal sex, Pamela," Becky sighed. "Over time, the rectum can get infected."

"I need to know this?" Burman demanded with a look of mild distaste. "Some pathologist you are!"

"Pam," Becky began patiently, her brow furrowed in concentration as she attempted to remove the plastic from her treat without getting cream filling on her hands, "this city has a population of 35,000 people, a third of them gay men. Most of *those* guys have *some* kind of medical condition. If this one's completely clean too, something strange could be going on. The statistics are against it." She began to take tiny little bites from the cake.

"So what, the killer takes a blood test before he murders them? I'm supposed to tell that to that idiot Eversleigh and the city council?"

"It all comes back to the blood. There's been too much blood lost from every one of the victims. But we haven't found more than a few drops in the vicinity of the bodies."

Clive thought for a minute. "Could the killer be someone with AIDS? Dementia's a tricky thing. Maybe he wants revenge on healthy gay men."

"No. For once, Pam's right."

Burman glared poisonously.

"The killer would have no way of telling without drawing blood professionally first. There's no more sign of that than there is of what he used to get the blood out in the first place. Or at least..." She trailed off in thought and finished her snack. Clive absentmindedly took a handkerchief from his suit pocket, wiped a bit of cream from Becky's lower lip and, folding it neatly, replaced the bit of cloth in his pocket, fussing with it so that it lay just right.

"Maybe it's just some sick asshole who hates gays," Burman said with some concern. Despite her ongoing battles with the gay press, she considered herself extremely liberal—for a Republican—and, in truth, hadn't a trace of prejudice in her body. She disliked everyone equally. Any accusation of homophobia was sure to drive her blood pressure through the roof in righteous outrage.

"Well, I think the gay connection is obvious," mused Becky. "We have another problem though, something Clive may not have told you about."

"Did you have to bring that up?" Clive groaned.

"What have you been keeping from me, you bastard?" asked Burman with her usual tact.

"Each of the victims," Becky began, taking out a Suzy Q this time, "had a chunk of flesh missing. Peeled off like an old price tag."

Burman, who was about to make another snide comment to Clive, stopped, her mouth gaping open like a fish, and slowly turned to face Becky. Swallowing several times and turning a faint shade of green, she finally managed, "That's sick."

"Nevertheless," Becky continued, "there's a ragged strip of flesh, three or four inches, missing from the throats of every one of them." Becky bit into the chocolate cake as cream filling oozed out the opposite end, a bit plopping to the ground dangerously close to Clive's highly polished right shoe.

"Would you stop with the junk food?" Burman all but shrieked, snatching the cream-filled dainty from Becky's grasp and thrusting it toward Clive, who instinctively held out his hand to receive a crushed mass of chocolate and cream. Clive winced and removed his handkerchief once again.

Burman managed to get her temper under control. "Sorry," she snapped, and then continued thoughtfully, "Why would anyone do something like that?"

"Well, before today I would have said you'd have to ask the killer," Becky said petulantly, her eyes fixed on the remains of her stolen cake. "But this time I think I can finally give you an answer."

She tore her glance away from the traces of cream and chocolate on Clive's hand and toddled off toward the van. Clive and Pamela followed her and, as another Suzy Q defiantly appeared, Becky opened the door and climbed in.

"Take a look at this," she said as she unzipped the body bag.

The Asian youth's lifeless face was still extraordinarily handsome in death. Donning one of her rubber gloves, Becky reached into the bag and tilted the almost severed head to the right, exposing the torn veins and arteries of the throat.

"See here," she pointed. "This time the killer didn't quite have time to finish the job." With the hand holding the cake, she traced an odd looking ragged cut in the dead flesh on the side of the throat. "It looks like he was in the middle of slicing out a hunk of skin. But he didn't get a chance to finish. Which gives us something else to worry about."

"What?" Clive asked.

"Here." Becky indicated two small round wounds, no more than large pinpricks, really, little red puncture wounds surrounded by puffy white skin in the middle of the piece of partially excised flesh. She looked at Burman and, as the city manager began to turn green once again, bit into her treat, smacking her lips loudly for maximum effect.

"Ah, Christ, she's makin' me sick." Burman turned away, trying to mask gagging noises. "Always with a Twinkie in one hand and a scalpel in the other!"

Clive looked at Becky blankly.

"Well, it would explain the missing blood," Becky offered.

Realization flooded Clive's features, followed by a look of shocked disbelief.

"That's crazy!" he exclaimed.

"Maybe so," Becky replied, rezipping the body bag and removing the glove, which she tossed into a corner of the van. "And I'm not saying anything for certain. If we find traces of saliva, we'll be sure."

"What the fuck are you two talking about?" asked Burman weakly.

"What the coroner is trying to tell us, Pam," said Clive stiffly, "is that somewhere in this town is a lunatic who thinks he's Count Dracula."

CHAPTER NINE

Several hours later, back at the station, the most recent victim had finally been identified and Becky and Clive were pouring over the autopsy report. Becky shook her head sadly.

"Poor Gary," she mused.

Clive looked up sharply. "Friend of yours?"

"Not really. He was dating a friend of mine for a while. You know him—Roger—the blond who answers the phones for the Rent Stabilization Department down at City Hall."

Clive grunted affirmatively and went to pour himself a cup of coffee. He returned to his desk and picked up the report once again.

The victim's name was Gary Takashi. In life, he'd been a character animator for Walt Disney. His apartment was located on West Knoll Drive, easily within walking distance of the Boys' Town Gym, where Takashi had last been seen alive.

Becky sat, staring expectantly at the top of Clive's head as he perused the document. Suddenly he slammed his fist against the top of his desk in frustration. Becky started with a little jump.

"If only somebody could find something!" he blurted. "I sent a request in to Sacramento for all known deviants with blood and vampire fetishes," he confessed sheepishly. "Not that I think you're right, but we should have something from their computer tomorrow." He looked back down at the report glumly.

"Well, we know the killer is probably very strong. Takashi was a big guy. Did you get a look at the body on that man? My God, his biceps were…" Becky looked at him, amused as he trailed off. "Oh, yeah, right," he finished. "We *all* got a look at him, didn't we?"

"We can also assume that the killer doesn't always pose as a hustler or an easy trick," Becky said.

"How do we know that?"

"Well, just before I came over, I called Roger to get the poop on Gary Takashi."

"And…?"

"Well, Roger tells me that after he and Gary broke up, Gary met this guy that he's been living with for about a year."

"I'm not following you."

"From what Roger tells me, and he's a pretty good judge, they were faithful. Like really faithful."

"I'm still lost."

"Don't you see?" said Becky in exasperation with Clive's obtuseness. "The first one, Balencini, was married. To a woman. The wife had no idea what he was doing. So it's possible he was looking for a trick. Probable in fact. The same thing with Charlie Copperman. I knew Charlie," she said distastefully. "Hell, everyone in town knew Charlie. He was always looking for something."

Understanding dawned in Clive's eyes. "The hustler was looking for a john…"

"As for Lance Blowman," Becky interrupted. "Even though he had a lover, he was a porn star. Fidelity? Get serious. How come," she continued, as a thought struck her, "they're always called porn *stars?* You'd think they'd call themselves porn *actors,* but no. Not them, God forbid. They're all *stars.*"

"Takashi would have had no reason to try and pick anyone up," Clive reminded her.

"Exactly!" Becky beamed. "I asked Roger to check around. To

see if he knows anyone who's slept with Gary in the last six months. But frankly I trust his judgement. I don't think he'll come up with anything."

"But that only widens the field of suspects," Clive realized in annoyance. "I was hoping we could limit our focus to hustlers and cruisers."

Becky shrugged. "Sorry." She fixed her gaze keenly on the captain. "My friend from Philadelphia is coming in tonight," she said.

"Oh, yeah. The bugaboo expert," said Clive sarcastically. "I skimmed that book you lent me. Becky, this guy is out in left field. You read that one crazy theory of his? Pure horror film."

"You mean about certain psychoses being triggered by racial memory? What about it?"

"I'm no doctor," said Clive, a vague discomfort stirring in his memory, "but it sounds to me like he's claiming those critters really exist."

"Only archetypally. Carl Jung wrote a book about—"

Clive held up his hand to stop her from going on. "Forget I said anything. If you *really* think we've got some crazy out there in a black cape, fine."

"I think it's more than that," Becky continued warily. "And Chris'll be able to tell us what to look for."

"Becky, we've been friends a long time, so I'm going to give you a little advice," Clive began. "If and when we catch this guy, we may find he's got a closet full of tuxedos. We may find crosses and garlic all over his apartment. We may even find that he sleeps in a coffin. But," he said sternly, "we are *not* gonna find some supernatural monster with foot-long fangs."

Becky covertly glanced at Clive's face out of the corner of her eye. His expression was slightly irritated and cautious but not openly hostile.

"Are you sure about that?" she asked quietly. "When we found the first body, the throat thing got me thinking. That and the lack of blood. How was it done, especially without a struggle? More important—*where* was it done?"

Clive felt the glimmer of an uncomfortable idea. "Where was it done?" he repeated. He looked confused. "We always figured it was done somewhere else, but...wait a minute." He grabbed a stack of papers and began riffling through them, finally pulling one out and quickly scanning it.

"The statements from Takashi's buddies at the gym say he left around eleven last night. One of them remembers him complaining that the showers were already closed down." He looked at the first page of Becky's report and his eyes widened.

"You couldn't have made a mistake about the time of death, could you?" he asked hopefully.

Becky merely smiled, looking like the cat that ate the cream-filled doughnut.

"Let me get this straight," Clive went on. "You're telling me this guy was kidnapped, killed, taken somewhere else where he was stripped and his blood was almost completely drained, and then brought back to the original crime site and dumped there—all in less than two hours."

"No," Becky said carefully. "I'm telling you the time between when he was last seen and the time of death was two hours max. And the *cause* of death was exsanguination—he wasn't killed first."

"Is that possible?"

"Sure. If the killer just happens to have a slab, some restraints, and a blood pump set up somewhere on West Knoll Drive."

"We'll check it out," said Clive as he reached for the phone.

"Forget it," Becky said as Clive looked at her, uncomprehending. "You may want to check the medical supply houses and see if you can track down the pump, but I think you'd be wasting your time."

"Why?"

"That's the next question I was getting to. Why would anyone remove the skin like that, except to hide something? At first I thought maybe the victims were injected with some kind of sedative, but I couldn't find any trace of it. By the third one I was fairly certain that eventually we were going to find teeth marks."

Clive exploded. "You're talking Hammer Films, Becky! Are you crazy?"

"I know!" she yelled back. "But look at this autopsy report. Third page, second paragraph. Read it."

Clive brought his temper under control and, turning the pages of the report, read silently for a minute. He looked up puzzled. "*Teeth* marks? Unidentified organic substance, similar to human saliva? This is insane."

"I had Ty check the chemical analysis three times. Then I ran it myself."

"Becky, I refuse to believe there's a gay vampire running around the streets of West Hollywood. Save that kind of crap for the Halloween parade, OK? I'll stick to the hidden lab theory."

"Don't be ridiculous," she conceded. "I'm not saying we've got Dracula on our hands. But we may be dealing with someone who *thinks* he's Dracula."

"How do you explain this unidentified saliva?"

"Oh, it could be dozens of things. With Takashi's throat mostly intact, I've got samples directly from the skin. The full tests will take a few days. But I think you should consider talking to my friend. He may be able to give us an idea of what type of lunatic we're looking for."

"Look Becky, this is a criminal investigation, not some opportunity for you to take up with some old crazy boyfriend whose being gay sounds like the least of your problems. The next thing you'll want me to do is post deputies at Hollywood Forever."

"Don't be flip," Becky cautioned. "It might not be a bad idea. What happens if this guy's really gone around the bend? What better place to catch him than a cemetery?"

"All right." Clive gave in. His discomfort had grown as Becky made point after point. His mind started to drift backward in time... But with effort he returned to the present. "At this point," he sighed, "I'll try anything. Call this old flame of yours and ask his opinion. Get him over here if you think he'll have any ideas. But do it unofficially. I don't want anyone knowing. I'm not gonna be the laughing-stock of the entire department."

Becky was delighted.

"I'm not happy about this," Clive said sternly. "And if Pamela finds out we did this without telling her, neither one of us is ever going to hear the end of it."

"So ask her what she thinks first. No wait, I'll talk to her. Maybe I can convince her that consulting an expert is her own idea. She doesn't have to know he flew out at my request."

"Good luck." He turned back to the strange paragraph in the autopsy report. "Vampires!" he said with disgust. "What next?"

◊ ◊ ◊

The drive into Los Angeles from Orange County had been grueling. Like most Easterners who had never visited the West Coast, he had held the quaint notion that no place in California was more than a half an hour's drive from Disneyland. He'd called United Airlines and thanked the ticket agent for booking him on a nonstop flight from Philadelphia International to Orange County's John Wayne Airport.

Upon arriving, he asked directions to West Hollywood and blanched at the answer given to him by the young man in the information booth. Grumbling about having to rent a car when his own had already been shipped out and was waiting for him somewhere on Harper Avenue, a scant sixty miles away, he left the airport and headed north. After two hours on the 405 freeway in heavy traffic, he was irritated, jet-lagged, and more tired than he had been in months. He'd been amazed that at nine-thirty on a weeknight the highway was filled with cars going in both directions, bumper-to-bumper, alternatively motionless or speeding along at eighty miles an hour.

California drivers are completely insane, he thought more than once. With no regard for safety, they cut each other off, zipped across multiple lanes of traffic to reach off-ramps, and sped up to ninety-five to merge onto the freeway. He was beginning to doubt the likelihood of his reaching West Hollywood in one piece. He watched aghast as a driver missed her turnoff, jammed on her brakes, and backed up against traffic while blithely talking on her cell phone.

Trying to avoid being incinerated in a fiery wreck, Chris struggled to decipher the chicken scratches that Troy had faxed to him as directions. He got off the freeway on something called La Cienega Boulevard, which for the next week he would pronounce "La Kanga" until some kind soul corrected him.

He was fairly certain he was on the right road when he passed a sign on a building Troy had identified as the new Film Institute but which looked to Chris like a Catholic church with attached tennis courts. Finally, with a sigh of relief, he turned onto Santa Monica Boulevard. He was peering out the window, searching for a sign telling him where to turn onto Harper Avenue, when he had his first experience with a California pedestrian. A bearded young man in a leather skirt and feather boa darted out into the street in the middle of the block and, when Chris screeched to a halt, saucily gave him the finger, and sashayed on his way.

Shaking his head, Chris turned north onto Harper and parked in front of a florescent pink Spanish-style building designed by someone who had obviously never been to Spain or Mexico. He double-checked the address in disbelief. Sighing, he got out of the car, grabbed his suitcase from the trunk, and trudged up the front stairs to the building.

Locating the button next to apartment number 113 on the intercom, he pressed it and jumped back with a start as a voice, vaguely reminiscent of Tallulah Bankhead's but several octaves higher, came blaring out of the speaker.

"Is that you, dahling?"

"Who the hell else would it be?" Chris grumbled back.

"Did we have a rough flight, dearie?" Troy was doing a very bad Bette Davis.

"Yes, we did," Chris shot back. "And if you'll buzz me in so the whole neighborhood doesn't have to hear the details, I'll tell you all about it."

"Did we get our period on the plane?" Troy quipped. Then, as the loudest buzzer Chris had ever heard sounded, he pulled open the door and entered the courtyard of the building.

Chris located apartment 113. While he fumbled to get the keys Troy had sent him into the lock, the door was jerked open, practically ripping his arm from its socket. In another of his ever-wretched imitations of Maria Ouspenskaya, Troy intoned, "Welcome to your castle, master."

"Knock it off, monkey," said Chris with tired affection. "Just let me in."

Troy, wearing some kind of spandex pants and shirtless, as usual, suddenly bowed deeply from the waist, one arm bent behind his back, the other sweeping the floor in a grand opera gesture. "Won't you come in?" he droned in an ominous tone.

The tension vanished as Chris put one foot across the threshold and was immediately assaulted.

"Darling!" Troy leapt into Chris's arms, upsetting the suitcase, and planted a big, wet, messy kiss smack on the end of Chris's nose. "Did you have any trouble getting here? I tried to be as clear as possible, but, my dear, you have no sense of direction. Here, let me take that."

Troy grabbed the suitcase, nearly tripping Chris in the process, flung it into the center of the living room where it landed with a crash, and hauled Chris through the front door.

He plastered his lips against Chris's mouth and, forcing his lips apart, began to try and give him a tonsillectomy with his tongue. Chris felt the final remnants of tension from the drive fade as he allowed himself to relax into Troy's delicate oral ministrations. Little shivers of pleasure ran up and down his spine as he wrapped his arms around Troy, slipping his hands underneath the rear waistband of Troy's skintight pants, and gently kneaded the tight little rear end underneath. Troy emitted moans of pleasure and alternately tightened and relaxed the muscles of his rear end teasingly.

"Let me look at you!" Troy backed away, squinting critically, and after a pause said admiringly, "Not bad for 240-plus. You don't look a day over forty-five."

"Twenty-eight, you bitch," Chris grinned tiredly.

Troy smiled and flounced down on the couch, fidgeted for a

moment, and finally became still, one arm resting along the back of the couch, legs spread, his left hand dangling invitingly over his crotch. He stretched, leaning his head back, obviously confident that his taut little body was being shown to its best advantage.

"Welcome to L.A.," Troy breathed throatily. "How about a drink to celebrate?" He moved his hand up from his crotch, over his belly and chest, and lightly across his throat. "Just a little nip before dinner, hmm?"

Chris glared at him briefly and debated on his ability to win an argument given his present state of fatigue. Deciding to ignore Troy for the moment, he closed his eyes, steeling himself for any eventuality before he began to examine the apartment.

Chris grimly recalled the last time he had sent Troy ahead to secure living accommodations; it had been in the early '80s, when Chris had decided to move from Boston to purchase the Philadelphia town house. On that occasion Troy had indulged his sense of humor and had furnished their living quarters with his own slightly twisted idea of what was appropriate. The current refurbishment was witness to the fact that their home had never quite recovered from the onslaught.

The upholstered sofa and chairs had been rather obviously new imitations of Victorian pieces, covered in a dark forest-green velvet shot through with a pattern of gold vines. The drapes, also velvet, had been a deep wine-red, tied back with heavy gold tassels. Chris remembered Troy's choice of artwork with a shudder; he loved the boy dearly but, honestly, Troy had no taste! The paintings had been restricted to several atrocious dark and forbidding oil landscapes in heavy gilt frames. The room had been cluttered with a variety of matching pairs of marble-topped ormolu end tables; the gilt trim on the coffee tables and breakfronts had been almost blinding. And everywhere, Troy had put candles, dozens of candles in black and various shades of red, not for light but merely for effect.

The little monkey had carried the Gothic motif even further, Chris recalled with fond annoyance. He'd almost suffered permanent damage to his eyesight the first time he'd tried to read *The Philadelphia Inquirer* in his new home. Troy had removed all the lighting fixtures and had replaced them with imitation candelabrum; each sconce bore a flame-shaped bulb, barely sufficient to illuminate a thimble, which flickered annoyingly. He'd twice retired to his bedroom with a blinding headache before he'd finally convinced Troy to go out and buy some real lamps. Troy had in turn thrown this incident up to him years later when Chris decided to restore their home to a pre-electricity state.

It had taken Chris months to find a buyer for all the pseudo-Gothic crap that Troy had installed. He'd finally helped a Mrs. Braverman, an elderly widow from Pennsauken, New Jersey, to achieve her lifelong ambition to reside in a splendor reminiscent of the Addams Family by selling the lot to her for less that a quarter of what Troy had initially paid. Prior to the move to California, Chris had, he thought, wisely limited Troy's furniture allowance in the hope that a similar decorating fiasco could be avoided.

Chris finally opened his eyes to look. The walls were painted stark white and the room was gently lit with a few dark red enameled torchère lamps. So far, so good. The sofa and two upholstered armchairs seemed innocuous enough, except that they were also blood-red—apparently to match the carpet. The tables, at least, all appeared to be devoid of froufrou and any hint of a baroque influence; they were, however, laminated with some sort of ruby-colored, plastic looking material. And Troy had been unable to resist hanging several paintings on the walls; one was a modern print depicting what Chris assumed was a scarlet lightning bolt slicing through a field of jet-black. Another showed Marilyn Monroe, desperately in need of a monthlong sojourn at a fat farm, squeezing her bulk into a cherry-red roadster.

As he walked into the kitchen, Chris's first thought was that the previous tenants had been axed to death and the landlord hadn't bothered to clean up the mess before re-letting the property. The appliances were deep scarlet; fire engine–red checked wallpaper added to the effect. Troy had purchased vermillion potholders with matching kitchen towels, and a set of perky crimson ceramic ducks were lined up on the counter. Chris was starting to get a headache.

Coming out of the kitchen into the pitifully small dining nook,

BITE CLUB

Chris finally discovered the major Troyism he'd been expecting. A huge butcher-block table was squeezed into the tiny space, eight upholstered chairs, also red, arranged around it, backs tightly crammed up against the sides of the table. Chris attempted to pull out one of the chairs in an effort to sit down. The dining room wall, however, seemed to be in the way, so he miserably hopped up onto the table and stretched out flat, sighing loudly.

"Don't tell me. The table. You saw it and just *had* to have it."

"I got it on sale. Consider it your daybed," Troy quipped with a winning smile. "It's not *my* fault someone was being just a teeny bit stingy with the checkbook." He scratched absently at an itch on his upper thigh and, suddenly catching himself, began sensuously stroking his crotch.

"I found a *lovely* place on the corner of Crescent Heights and Fountain," he whispered seductively. "The perfect little love nest for two. It's about seventy-five years old and has these lovely high ceilings." He paused then said flatly, "The old furniture would have looked fabulous there."

Chris made gagging noises from his prone position on the table. "I'm sorry, monkey. I never again want to live in something out of *Gas Light.*"

Troy harrumphed, annoyed. "They wanted something like $2,000 a month," he said, and filed the building away in the back of his mind. He'd pester his lover about it later.

Chris looked around the room again. "It's kind of bright in here, don't you think?"

"Well, since you *asked* for my opinion, I think we should start keeping up appearances for the neighbors."

Chris sighed patiently. "I asked you to try and be discreet. This place looks like the site of the Saint Valentine's Day massacre." He supposed, if he weren't so tired, that he would actually find Troy's attempt at decorating rather funny. *Oh, well,* he thought. *We won't be here that long. I guess it'll do.*

"Nobody in Los Angeles is discreet," Troy said warmly. "It would be considered ostentatious to even try."

"What are we going to do about those?" Chris waved his hand to indicate the louvered windows running the length of the back wall of the dining area.

"I covered the windows in the bedroom with a blackout cloth. You'll be fine." Troy got up from the couch. "Come on. It's still early. Get changed and I'll show you Boys' Town. You'll love it!"

"Please, monkey! I just got off the plane. I'm exhausted. We'll go tomorrow."

Troy's pixie face twisted into a moue of disappointment. "What kind of a homosexual are you? Here you are in West Hollywood, the gayest city in the world, and you're bitching about a little airplane ride." He began waltzing around the room in the arms of an imaginary partner, humming "Where the Boys Are."

Chris pointedly looked around the apartment. "What kind of a homosexual are *you*? Did you get a good look at this place? What decorators did you hire? Manson and Manson?"

"Look, girlfriend," Troy began snippily as he marched over to the table and stood, looming over Chris, "I have been busting my adorable little ass for over a week to set this place up for you. I don't know what the hell year you think this is, but nowadays it ain't so easy making living arrangements."

"I'm sorry for being so bitchy." Chris gave Troy a little peck on the cheek and, sitting up a bit, nipped him affectionately on his bare shoulder. "I just don't like apartment living. It makes me nervous. There's no privacy."

"It's only temporary. I met this cute little real estate person. He said he knows of a couple of places for sale. He'd be able to show them to us by tomorrow night."

"Did you ever think about *renting* a house?"

"A house? In Los Angeles? For what you gave me to spend?" Troy looked at Chris, one eyebrow raised hopefully. "I didn't think we'd be staying long enough to need a whole house," he said tentatively.

Troy silently prayed that Chris would decide to remain in Los Angeles. Los Angeles, with its celebrities, palatial homes, and beautiful people, was Troy's idea of heaven. And even better, they made movies here! It had taken them a long time to get out to California and Troy had every intention of convincing Chris to stay. But he knew Chris too well to try to convince him directly. If Chris made up his mind to go back to Pennsylvania, wild horses couldn't keep him in L.A.

"We *have* been in Philadelphia a long time, you know," Troy ventured gently. "I'm not saying I don't want to stay put," he continued. "After all, with all the moving we've done, I feel like Mother Courage with her cart." He slowly ran one finger around Chris's ear and down along the side of his jaw and throat in a way calculated to give him goose pimples of pleasure. "But if you're worried about what the neighbors might notice…" He trailed off.

Chris reached up and took Troy's hand from where it was playing idly with the collar of his shirt. Sitting up suddenly, he grabbed Troy's other arm and lifted him onto the table, flipping him over onto his back. He pinned Troy's arms above his head with one hand and began nibbling at his bare torso while stroking Troy's sides with the other.

Troy wriggled with delight. "Nine days. Almost two weeks," he murmured contentedly. "It seemed endless."

"Maybe I'll cable Europe tomorrow for more money," Chris said as his fingers moved lower to elicit a little shriek of pleasure from Troy. "It wouldn't hurt us to have a home out here—but only for emergencies. I don't think I could settle in a place where the state flower is the avocado."

Nine days apart isn't such a long time, is it? Chris asked himself as he began to play with Troy in earnest. Their years together had given him an intimate familiarity with every part of Troy's body; he knew exactly what his lover liked.

Amazing, Chris thought for the ten thousandth time. *No matter how long we're together, he never bores me.*

As Chris continued gently nipping, licking, and stroking, Troy, arms still pinned above him, started to thrash back and forth helplessly. Enjoying himself immensely, Chris refused to even allow him to moan or gasp; each time Troy opened his mouth to do so, Chris cut him off with a kiss. Finally, starting at his feet and moving up along his body to his tightly gripped hands, Troy's body was shaken with a series of little shudders, growing bigger and bigger until he was actually lifting himself from the table and slamming back against it with lightning speed. Chris could barely hold him down.

As Troy lay, panting on the table, torso slicked with sweat, Chris released him and stood up.

"Maybe we'll do it half in cash and take out a mortgage for the rest," he said with blithe innocence. "*If* he can find us something by the beginning of the week."

"Huh?" asked Troy, still slightly dazed.

"The house," Chris said with a grin.

Troy hoisted himself up onto his elbows and exhaled luxuriously. He shuddered once or twice more and then, only slightly recovered, panted, "This is Los Angeles, my darling. Here wearing shoes is considered formal attire. Half of the town's economy is based on selling maps to movie star's homes. Boy, that was fabulous!" His body twitched again. "The ones who aren't standing on the corner trying to convince you that Tom Cruise lives in the building next to their uncle's deli are in real estate. You have to give them enough time to scurry around for a few weeks, make 'deals,' and get six of their broker friends involved so they can all split the commission. Otherwise their children all go hungry."

"Good God!"

Troy leapt up, hands covering his ears in mock horror. "You said it! You said the word! My heart! My heart!" He clutched dramatically at his chest and plunged to the floor, writing spasmodically.

Chris couldn't help grinning. "I love you, you little shit."

Troy finished his impression of Cleopatra, gasped once, and was still for a moment.

"You die beautifully," Chris commented, sliding off the table.

"And don't you forget it, sister." Troy rolled over onto his stomach, wriggling his rear end. "Want another bite?" he asked coyly.

"Tomorrow. I promise."

With that, Chris stepped gingerly over Troy's prostrate form and walked toward the bedroom.

"Love 'em and leave 'em?" Troy asked mischievously.

Chris looked at him. "Never," he said tenderly.

"I may hold you to that," Troy warned.

"I hope you do. Unpack for me, will you, monkey?" he called over his shoulder as he went into his bedroom.

"Yes, Missy Scarlett!" Chris thought Troy was trying for Butterfly McQueen this time, but it was hard to tell.

Chris closed the bedroom door behind him and looked at the blackout curtains with satisfaction. He peeled his shirt over his head and skinned out of his jeans, folding everything neatly and placing it carefully in the corner. He opened the closet, intending to put on his favorite robe, and blinked in amazement. Along with his meager selection of favorite clothing, which he'd managed to sneak into Troy's luggage amid the profusion of multicolored T-shirts, spandex shorts, and leather vests, he discovered the results of one of Troy's gleefully wicked shopping sprees. There, in a neat row on the rack, like so many deflated penguins, were no less than five black tuxedos. Hanging next to them, like oversize dark moths, were three black satin opera capes, each of them lined with red silk.

Rolling his eyes heavenward, Chris took out his worn brown terry cloth robe, put it on, and, hoisting up the lid of his casket, slipped inside for some much-needed rest. With a wry grimace as he pulled the coffin lid closed and settled down into the rich, black Massachusetts earth, he reflected that Los Angeles and Troy had at least one thing in common: Both took quite a bit of getting used to.

CHAPTER TEN

Chris was awakened by the steady staccato sound of someone beating out an unidentifiable rhythm on the lid of his coffin. As his mind gradually cleared, he realized the tapping was accompanied by Troy's off-key rendition of "Good Morning" from *Singin' in the Rain.*

Chris groaned and sat up, opening the coffin lid.

Troy had already dressed. Chris's eyes opened in amazement as he surveyed the "vision" standing in front of him, a perky smile splitting Troy's face, poised to show off his fashion creation to best advantage.

"They're not really dressing like that, are they?" Chris felt a pang of longing for the conservative frock coats and vests of his youth. "I mean, you might want to wear something that actually covers part of your body."

"Why?" Troy asked disingenuously. He pirouetted slowly, show-ing off baggy cotton pants that only barely covered his behind, the knees halfway to the middle of his thighs. A seam of bright red underwear peeped out from the waistband, almost but not quite concealing the mounded globes of his butt. Covering his torso, Troy sported a blindingly bright multicolored vest that was at least a size too small, the fabric straining at the buttons. Two rainbow-colored handkerchiefs were tied around his right bicep. A bright pink baseball cap bearing the motto, BEND OVER, I'LL DRIVE was cocked at a jaunty angle, Troy's blond curls escaping from underneath in artful disarray.

"In that outfit, don't you think the cap should say 'Tunnel ahead. Lights on next ten miles'?" Chris irritably shucked his robe and went into the bathroom.

"I happen to *adore* this outfit," Troy said huffily. "It's what all the best people are wearing, you know," he informed Chris. "Very gangsta."

"In my day, gangsters wore pinstriped suits," Chris grumbled. "It was so much easier to dress you when they were still making Garanimals. As long as you stuck to all monkeys or all elephants, you looked OK."

"But I've matured," Troy insisted. Then he added with a dramatic flair Bernhardt would have envied, "I've *eschewed* that behavior!"

"Troy. Please. Spare me," Chris begged. "It's too early."

"Coffee's on," Troy called through the door.

"Great," Chris murmured as he turned on the shower. He felt the beginning rumblings of hunger in his belly. He'd eaten briefly on the plane the night before, but the airline steward he'd chosen, though attractive enough, had traces of marijuana in his system and Chris was forced to imbibe lightly, leaving with a dissatisfied, unfulfilled feeling.

Chris rarely killed in search of food—at least not intentionally. He supposed that, by most definitions, he'd probably be considered a murderer were he ever hauled into some hypothetical court to answer for the actions of his life. But he felt he'd be able to present a good defense; after all, how many normal humans, if given a lifetime spanning roughly two and a half centuries, would be able to list their capital crimes on the fingers of both hands? And on the few occasions where a death had been unavoidable, it had usually been as a result of accident or in self-defense.

No, Chris preferred light snacking as opposed to a filling repast. Thus, the increase in the use of recreational drugs during the latter part of the twentieth century was something upon which he frowned with selfish disapproval. And despite his firm resolution to put the past in the past and to allow himself to be swept along by the waters of the present and adapt to the future, Chris was not always successful in refraining from silently wishing for the return of earlier, simpler times.

In the early 1800s, right after the last of his immediate family had died, he'd gone to England for a while, hoping the experience of a new country in a new century would help him to put the familiar New England surroundings of his birth in their proper place in the past. He'd been right; London helped heal the pain of Chris's transition into the next generation.

There, it had been easy to avoid tainted companions; he merely steered clear of the opium dens and various institutionalized drug houses. On the few occasions when he wanted to get slightly stoned, he would merely join an after-theater or late-night supper crowd and surreptitiously take a little nip from one of the group who seemed to have had a bit more to drink than was wise. The effect of taking the alcohol into his system directly from another's bloodstream gave him an intensified high; drinking spirits, caffeine, or other liquids directly from a glass or bottle never seemed to enable him to achieve the same effect.

When he finally returned to the United States, forty-some years had passed. Walking down the streets of his hometown in Massachusetts, he'd been pleased to note that he recognized very little; the intervening changes in the streets, shops, and homes had almost eradicated all that had been familiar to him in his breathing days. With a pang of mingled regret for his life of the past and a feeling of satisfaction that, finally, he'd managed to put it behind himself, he left the Boston suburb and had yet to return.

In Virginia some years later, nourishment had also been easy to find. Chris had, for a short while, actually enlisted in the Confederate forces, thinking he could take what he needed from the seriously wounded and dying soldiers while mercifully easing their passage into the next world. He'd debated about going north and enlisting there, but with his deep-seated dislike of bullies, the

Southern forces held more attraction. As for the slavery issue, although he disliked it on principle, Chris, rejecting his Yankee roots, didn't seriously consider that it was anything more than an excuse for the Union to justify its economic stranglehold on the South. Slavery was simply a fact of life back then, and Chris was a product of his time; it wasn't until almost the turn of the twentieth century that he'd truly detested the concept.

He hadn't remained in the army long, he recalled with a shudder. In addition to the problems encountered by having to be awake during daylight hours, the War of Northern Aggression had provided Chris with new insight into man's ability to be senselessly cruel to his fellow man. The war had been violent and bloody; the carnage sickening—even to someone of Chris's race. Then again, there had been an unhappy ending to a love affair, cut short by a Union bayonet; the memory still pained him.

The Great War in Europe had been cleaner, as far as wars went. Although the political situation in Europe had been anything but stable since the uprising in Russia, Chris was caught by surprise, along with the rest of the European population, by the assassination of Archduke Ferdinand. Fleeing St. Petersburg and trekking uncomfortably toward France, Chris had ample opportunity to observe man's inhumanity to man.

Mystified at why normals insisted on creating, maintaining, and obliterating enemies, he was nonetheless impressed with the efficiency mortal man brought to slaughter. Although the Great War had its share of mindless bloodshed, technology had advanced to the point where it was no longer necessary to meet the enemy face-to-face in order to slay him with musket or bayonet. Chris reflected that man's entry into the twentieth century had enabled him to make organized killing easier and easier as the minimum distance required to effectively destroy those who did not agree with his politics became greater.

And as for the rise of the Socialist Party in Germany and the resulting Second World War, Chris considered it an abomination. In his opinion, that insane, mustached painter had been, at best, a pompous bully—one inspired by the devil, but a bully nonetheless.

Together with his friend Sylvia, Chris had fled to Denmark, foolishly unable to comprehend that the Nazi's could possibly win their way that far north. There they had established a safe house for others of their race, drawing upon Chris's earlier experiences with the underground railroads of the American South.

The Nazis terrified him. Unlike the Union soldiers of the prior century, Herr Hitler had managed to take torture, murder, and the other accoutrements of war and turn them into an organized, efficient bureaucracy in the name of an Aryan race. The thought that an individual could harbor such deep-seated hatred for others simply because of a perceived difference from an impossible idealization of humanity struck deep chords of fear in Chris's soul; Hitler's propaganda stirred Chris's unconscious discomfort with his own condition.

When rumors reached Denmark that somewhere in the high ranks of the German government a member of their own race existed, Chris and Sylvia, frightened but determined, traveled to Berlin to make certain that an eternal Third Reich would not come to pass. The rumors had proven false, thank heaven, but not before Chris had experienced Herr Hitler's "Master Plan" firsthand.

The encounter left him shattered. It was decades before the nightmares of being buried beneath piles of sticklike human corpses finally left him. Even now, at least twice a year or so, he would awake in the evening with the stench of burning human flesh lingering in his nostrils as a fortunately vague dream faded from his conscious mind.

Upon his return to America, he'd sought refuge in the South once again—the "New South" as he thought of it. Aimlessly wandering, confused and uncertain of a God who would instill morality in a race of creatures who thrived on drinking blood from living human throats and yet seemed to deny it from humans themselves, he'd contemplated suicide.

Two centuries, he reasoned, was more than enough life experience for anyone. War and strife were an inevitable part of the human world, and since Chris's life was inextricably linked with that human world, he'd undoubtedly see the horrors of Germany again and again, growing more and more terrible with each new conflict. For a few years, dreaming of self-extinction seemed ironically to be the only way he could manage to continue living. That the two were mutually exclusive only heightened his inner turmoil.

And then, that fateful day in 1953, in that dismal little South Carolina town, sitting in that dreary hotel, he'd met Troy. There had been such despair, such helplessness, in that beautiful face, such misery creasing the brow below the golden blond curls. And yet Chris had sensed a childlike wonder at the marvels of the day-to-day world within the grief-stricken countenance.

That first night had been incredible. Not the sex—especially not the sex! Troy had been surprisingly naive. Chris had to teach him all the basics of physical intimacy—basics that Troy had long since mastered. Nevertheless, the outpouring of need and love, even that early in their relationship, was something that Chris simply couldn't ignore.

With Troy, Chris had rediscovered his place in the universe; it was at Troy's side. Endearingly irritating, delightfully unpredictable, and enchantingly helpless when confronted with life's little problems, Troy had enabled Chris to feel young again while experiencing life anew through his eyes.

And then there had been trust. From the moment that Chris, startled, had wrapped his arms around the weeping youth who had without warning launched himself forward to bury his tearful face in Chris's shirtfront, Troy had emanated trust—trust that had not even briefly wavered upon his discovery of Chris's true nature.

The creation of another vampire was not something to be taken lightly. Although most members of Chris's race were territorial and would have preferred to lead rather solitary lives, they soon found that a total retreat from the world could prove fatal. Whether it was the vivacity of mortal life they missed or something even less tangible, isolation invariably resulted in ennui and, eventually, the true death.

Chris and Sylvia had discussed this strange dichotomy of their nature many times. Sylvia put forward the theory that the eventual drive toward company was a safety mechanism, provided to the vampiric race by nature. A truly reclusive vampire would soon starve. Chris, on the other hand, believed they were, at heart, inherently social creatures and that the desire to be alone was an evolutionary outgrowth of the necessity for keeping the location of one's lair secret, hidden from ignorant humans brandishing sharpened wooden stakes. Sharing a common stubbornness, each had listened to the other's reasoning and had quietly held to their own beliefs.

Whatever the reason, inevitably, vampires were drawn to their own kind for social comfort. Small cliques of five or ten individuals would form in a particular city. There had probably been little communication between the different groups at first. However, humans tended to notice if a neighbor or colleague whom they had known for thirty years still appeared to be the same age as when they'd first met. And so the vampire would be forced to move on to a new town, a new country, and a new life. Once relocated, he or she would invariably establish a new support group, at least until it was time to move on once again. The result of this constant forced migration, when combined with the limited number of vampires in the world, was that almost everyone, at one time or another, had spent at least a decade or two with almost everyone else. A global network had developed; it was not unusual, upon arriving in a new country, to encounter someone with whom you'd spent a lifetime, albeit several hundred years ago.

There was also a natural reluctance to create new members of the race. After all, just like mortal infants, a newly made vampire could not be returned to the store for credit or exchange if he or she didn't work out. One was stuck with one's mistakes, in a word—forever. Not to mention the more obvious problem of haphazardly depleting the larder. And so some, seeking company, created companions for themselves, beings existing in a sort of liminal state between vampirism and humanity. Chris had heard of Eastern vampires who had surrounded themselves with veritable harems of these creatures. But until Troy, Chris had never met anyone with whom he felt eternity would not soon grow boring.

He'd agonized for weeks. On the one hand, he wished Troy to experience all the things that life had to offer, things that Chris had himself been denied—physical maturity, the love of family and friends without subterfuge, the joy of becoming a parent, aging, and finally the sweet bliss of death. Through it all, Chris vowed, he would be there, guarding the youth and shielding him from the cruelties that life would undoubtedly throw in Troy's way.

On the other hand, if he refrained from acting, their time together would be short. What was it Lincoln had said? Four score and ten? Or was it two score and ten? Oh, well, maybe it hadn't been Lincoln after all. In any case, Troy would leave him all too quickly. The alternative, for Chris to leave Troy before it became impossible to do so, was unthinkable. Chris had finally succumbed.

He recalled fondly the rush of pleasure and love he'd felt when Troy, innocently trusting and still not fully understanding the consequences, lay naked on the hotel bed and, drained of blood almost to the point of death, handed Chris a sharp knife after announcing proudly that he'd sterilized it first so that Chris wouldn't get infected with germs. Chris had used his fingernail to open the skin of his own chest before pressing Troy's lips to the wound, but he'd saved the knife as a tender memento of the experience.

Nightly, for almost a week, Chris and Troy had exchanged blood until finally Chris was certain the aging process had stopped, Troy having entered that limbo between mortality and death. Chris had considered converting Troy fully, but he knew, though he had never before done it, that to create a vampiric Troy the initial draining and replenishing of the blood must be swift and the potential convert must die the mortal death very shortly afterward. Chris would have to kill him.

Chris couldn't do it. His own death, despite his commitment to it, had been terrifying and painful; he refused to subject Troy to similar agony. Although Chris had felt minimal discomfort while shedding his mortal waste, the physical process of his body changing and becoming more than human had been excruciating. It had taken him years to recover from the sickening feeling he'd had when, as he thrust the point of a sword through his own heart, he'd suddenly doubted that eternal life was anything but a myth. The disbelief at what he'd done washed over him in waves, along with the horrible pain in his chest; he'd been horrified by the inevitability of his own imminent death. No, even though he would have remained with his lover throughout the process of dying, he couldn't bring himself to put Troy through the agony of doubt and fear that Chris himself had suffered. Remembering the ineffably sweet taste of Troy's human blood, Chris felt his hunger pangs renewed and his thoughts returned to the airline steward. Chris had friends, mostly in Europe, who'd made a conscious choice to seek out those unfortunates who used alcohol and drugs as an escape from reality, but few of them had survived the years. Many of their victims were of a class who, before the advent of modern medicine, frequently suffered from various diseases. And although sporadic encounters with hepatitis, syphilis, and, in more modern times, AIDS, would merely make Chris and others like him extremely ill, repeated exposures over a short period of time had been known to prove fatal. Chris chose not to take the risk.

The 1960s took him by surprise. A conservative by nature, Chris had made the mistake of ignoring the budding "free love movement" as a short, aberrant mortal fad, doomed to quickly die out before he would need to devote it any attention. His first encounter with a young man who had partaken liberally of LSD quickly changed his mind. Wandering about in a psychedelic daze for several weeks, disoriented and sick, Chris made a mental vow to pay close attention to future developments in recreational mind-altering substances. The fairly recent trend of "cutting" cocaine, a drug about which he had fond memories dating from the turn of the last century, had caused him not a small amount of discomfort as a variety of the more common substances used to dilute the drug played havoc with his system. Thus his tastes had become more and more Catholic in recent years and, for the most part, heavy drinkers were the only vice in which he would indulge.

Pills were forbidden to him by his very nature, as was solid food. He could ingest small amounts, and had on many occasions as a way of passing as normal in various social situations, but no matter how talented the chef or how exotic the meal everything always tasted wooden and flat; he was forced to disgorge it within several hours or suffer disabling cramps in his belly. He had been thrilled when bulimia and anorexia became popular diseases as they provided him with an excuse. He found that he could, in false confidence, admit his "affliction" in such a manner that people rarely inquired further. In fact, for the past two years he'd been attending fairly regular meetings of and eating-disorders support group in Philadelphia to provide additional cover.

Stepping from the shower, he toweled himself dry. He examined his body critically; there was never any change, but Chris had been extremely vain in life and his custom of constant and repeated self-appraisal was one of the few conscious habits he retained from that time. Satisfied with the results, he once again thanked whatever gods existed that he'd had enough advance warning of his change to be able to get himself into the physical condition in which he wanted to spend eternity.

He dropped the towel to the floor and, entering the bedroom nude, opened the closet. Troy leaned against the doorjamb, arms crossed, and made kissy noises at Chris's naked body. Chris ignored him.

"Nice butt," Troy commented.

Slipping into worn jeans and pulling a white T-shirt over his head, Chris replied with a grin, "You should know."

Troy couldn't help smiling lasciviously while pretending he hadn't heard Chris's quip. "I thought we'd start out at the Mother Lode and see what's going on. We can go dancing at Mickey's later, then to Revolver and on to the Spike for a midnight snack. Can you hold out that long?"

"I'll manage. Hair, please, monkey." He sat down on the coffin lid so that Troy could easily run a comb through his tangled locks.

Concentrating on pulling the comb through a particularly difficult snarl, Troy commented absently, "Miss Thing called while you were asleep. You know, the ghoul?"

"Coroner," Chris corrected. "Did she say when we could meet her?"

"Anyone who plays with dead things is a ghoul in my book."

"Why do you always pick on her? She likes you."

"No, she doesn't," said Troy seriously. "She thinks I'm brainless and flighty and immature."

"But ya are in that wheelchair, Blanche! Ya are!" Chris responded.

Troy glared at him briefly and with great dignity said, "I do that *much* better. Besides," he added, "she's jealous."

"I think she's over that," Chris said. "So there's no reason for you to start playing a scene from *The Women,* OK?"

"All right! I'll behave!" Troy threw his arms up in an elaborate gesture of exasperation.

He patted an errant strand of Chris's chestnut-colored hair into place. "We need to cut this, dear. I know how you love them, but ponytails are out of style again."

"It'll just grow back to this length," Chris reminded him. "The way it was when I died."

"So? I'll gather the clippings," Troy said dramatically, "and wear my fingers to the bone weaving them into one long braid. Of course, we'd have to live on a higher floor."

"What are you talking about?"

"Rapunzel!" Troy said, amazed that Chris hadn't caught on. "It'd be romantic."

"Troy," Chris said, trying not to grin. "What did Becky want?"

"For us to meet her at some bar on Robertson at nine. I put new dirt in the bottoms of your sneakers." Troy grinned.

"You may need it. Get this: The place is called the Abbey."

CHAPTER ELEVEN

Troy and Chris arrived at the Abbey after a brief sortie into a bar called Hunters. Before Chris's arrival, Troy had met someone who suggested it as a place to find "action." Upon entering the bar, Chris began to seriously doubt Troy's judgment in the type of company he had been keeping since he'd arrived in Los Angeles. It was immediately apparent that the sexual favors of each and every one of the hard-looking but nubile young men leaning against the bar clutching their beers could be purchased for the evening for the price of a few drinks, five dollars, and a pack of cigarettes. The ones playing pool, with their shirts either open or removed entirely, were undoubtedly more expensive; Chris figured a pool player might cost a potential buyer an additional two or three packs of smokes.

The bar was dark, filled with a murky, depressing fog of smoke and sultriness. Half the inhabitants wore expressions of thinly disguised lust; the other half barely suppressed the flashes of greed in their eyes. Each pair of eyes surreptitiously roamed the room, glances flickering quickly from one prospective contact to another. Chris, who had spent time in many a brothel in his day, couldn't help feeling unsettled at the patrons' blatant behavior. The seediness of the place was overbearing, and Chris had the suspicion that, were he to touch anything, whether it was the scarred wooden bar top or one of the customers, his hands would come away feeling grimy and oily.

Troy, in his colorful vest and sagging pants, was doing a good job pretending to be oblivious to the sneers and nasty looks his normally less-than-subtle behavior was drawing from the bar's largely blue-jeans-and-T-shirt clientele. But from long experience, Chris could tell Troy wasn't entirely comfortable in the surroundings. Seeking to teach him a lesson concerning his choice of newfound friends, Chris deliberately delayed their departure.

It was a mistake. Troy, refusing to acknowledge that the place was anything other than what he'd expected it to be, began to drink—heavily. As he flitted about, wildly flirting with one hustler after another, becoming more outrageously campy with each one, the looks became nastier, the sneers more pronounced, until Chris feared that an "incident" was in the making.

After one exceptionally hirsute young man with bulging biceps backed Troy up against the bar and announced his intention of "getting a piece of some girlie butt," Chris decided it was time to leave. The young man, however, had reached such a point of combined inebriation and belligerence that he was not so easily dissuaded. Bending Troy backward over the bar, he began to remove the blond boy's vest and was making headway with the zipper of Troy's fly—not that he needed to make much effort as Troy's pants were practically falling of him already. Chris decided enough was enough.

"Excuse me," said Chris politely, tapping the youth on the shoulder.

"Get fucked," came the reply, and a bulging forearm caught Chris unexpectedly in the center of his chest, throwing him off balance, and he staggered backward a few feet.

At about this time, Troy realized that his new friend was not so friendly after all and had started to try to get up. Bent backward as he was, however, he had no leverage; his struggles were limited to his hands gripping futilely at the bar top while his feet vainly scrabbled for purchase against the floor.

"Perhaps you didn't hear me," Chris said mildly, approaching again. "I said 'excuse me.'"

The drunk turned away from Troy for a minute. "Whadda you want?"

"If he wants to take those off," said Chris, his pleasant tone barely hiding the steely determination underneath, "he's quite capable of doing it by himself."

Chris's words penetrated the man's alcoholic haze. Momentarily abandoning his assault on Troy, he turned so that he was facing Chris head-on.

"Oh, yeah?" he sneered. "What is this? Your boyfriend? Looks more like a *girl*friend!" He laughed and was joined by the rest of the bar's patrons, who were looming alarmingly close.

"As a matter of fact," said Chris, feeling his age-old dislike of people who took advantage of those weaker than themselves surfacing, "He is."

So saying, Chris reached out and, with a deceptively gentle touch, took hold of the bully's right hand, which was still clutching the shoulder of Troy's vest.

Troy did nothing to help the situation. Unable to see the gathering crowd from his prone position over the bar, he announced primly to the ceiling, "I think I'd like to leave now."

The bully found this quite funny and with a sweep of his free hand tried to break Chris's grip. His arm met Chris's with a sharp crack, a look of pain crossed his face, and he looked down to see that Chris had not budged an inch.

Surprised and no longer quite as amused, he tried again.

"Third time's the charm," Chris said, his tone not quite so pleasant.

The bully released Troy and rounded on Chris, both arms swinging. Chris deftly reached out and grabbed both of the youth's hands. As shock crossed his face, the young man felt his arms being slowly pushed together in front of him as Chris captured both of the bully's hands in one of his own.

Chris turned to Troy, who was trying to pull together his disheveled clothing and to regain some of his dignity, and grabbed him by the front of his vest with his free hand.

"Apologize to the man for leading him on," said Chris.

Troy attempted a look of indignant outrage; it was unsuccessful.

"Troy…" Chris began warningly.

"Oh, all right," said Troy grudgingly. He turned and, flashing his most gracious smile, said, "I'm sorry for being a tease." He turned to Chris. "OK?" he asked haughtily.

"It'll have to do." Chris released both Troy and the confused bully, who immediately lunged forward only to be stopped just as quickly by Chris's hand, the vampire grabbing his shirtfront and lifting him an inch or so off the floor.

"That will be quite enough," Chris said mildly.

The bully burbled something—undoubtedly obscene.

"Yes, I know," said Chris sympathetically. "Sometimes those are my sentiments exactly. But after all, he's mine. What can I do?"

The other hustlers in the bar kept their distance, unwilling to help their companion in his argument with these two young men, who were surprisingly not as helpless as they had first appeared.

"I'm going to put you down now," Chris continued. "And we are going to leave." He looked full into the other's eyes, catching his gaze with his own. "There will be no hard feelings. Will there?"

The hairy young man nodded, and Chris gently set him back on the floor. "That," Chris added, grabbing a nearly full glass of scotch from Troy's grasp, "will be quite enough for you too."

The bully, confused that someone who appeared so much smaller and less muscular had bested him, was not about to return to his companions to face their scornful sneers. Embarrassed and very drunk, he felt he had to do something to regain face. It was at this point that he made a potentially fatal mistake.

Reaching out past Chris, he grabbed Troy by the shoulder and yanked him backward, brutally slamming the blond boy against the side of the bar. Troy let out a small yelp as the edge of the bar top dug painfully into the center of his back.

BITE CLUB

"I'll give you *hard* feelings," he said. He pulled a switchblade from his rear jeans pocket and, clicking it open, held it up so Chris could get a close look at the light glinting off the blade.

The entire bar was silent as the man quickly brought the knife down toward Troy's throat, stopping with the blade poised less than an inch from the skin.

"*If* I give him back to you, he won't be so pretty after I'm done." He turned back to Troy, moving the tip of the knife in closer, just piercing the skin at the base of Troy's throat and drawing it slowly down the center of Troy's chest, stopping only when it reached the top button of the vest. A thin glistening line of blood began to well out from the shallow cut as Troy yelped again.

"Now you've done it," commented Troy quietly.

The bully simply looked at him, shocked that the overly feminine youth should be so calm with an open switchblade pointed at the center of his chest. Had he glanced at Chris instead, as the rest of the bar's customers were doing, his emotions would have been quite different.

Every muscle in Chris's body had tightened. His eyes, which had widened in surprise at the initial assault on Troy, had flashed anger and narrowed to mere slits when the knife appeared. Everyone in the bar watched to see what he would do. Although most of the rest of the patrons were more than a little money hungry, none would have agreed to take the bully's place at that moment for any price.

"You will take…" began Chris as his right hand shot out with lightning speed to grab the hand wrapped around the knife hilt, "your hands…" he continued as he slowly bent the assailant's wrist backward, "off him."

A loud moan escaped from the hairy man as his wrist was stretched beyond its range.

"Or you will lose them," Chris finished, and there was a loud snap as the stressed bones finally gave way.

The bully let out a bellow of pain as Chris released his hand. Troy quickly scrambled away and took up a position behind Chris, shielded against further assault.

111

The young man took a deep breath in preparation for another scream of pain; he never got a chance to utter it. Chris reached up with his hand and grabbed the bully by the throat, choking off any possibility of sound. Squeezing the man's throat hard enough to hurt, Chris lifted him off his feet once again and brought his face to within an inch or so of Chris's own.

"Do I make myself clear?" Chris hissed. He gave the bully no opportunity to answer. Instead, grabbing the young man painfully by the crotch with his free hand, he threw him with a seemingly effortless toss through the air across the room, where he landed flat on his back in the center of the pool table, totally spoiling the shot of the only person in the bar who was oblivious to what had been going on: The drunken hustler, overweight and past his prime, who had been trying to make an eleven-five bank shot into the side pocket. The other bar patrons blinked in disbelief.

Without giving Troy time to protest, Chris skillfully guided him past the gawking onlookers and out the front door of the bar onto the boulevard. Once outside, Chris took a deep breath and slowly counted to ten, hoping his rage would subside. It didn't. He repeated the process several more times until he'd managed to calm down. Troy was, for once, wisely silent during this procedure. Finally, Chris felt the last vestiges of anger vanish.

"So much for being discreet," he commented with forced humor and watched Troy's expression as the barb struck home.

Troy, embarrassed and defensive about his behavior in the bar, was not about to let Chris have the final say. Rather than reply, he determined to drive himself on to more and more flights of outrageous activities. Chris, realizing that it was hopeless to argue with him when he was in one of his Diana Rigg moods, decided it would be easier to let Troy work off the mood by indulging his spleen on others than to risk a knock-down, drag-out rumpus in the middle of the street.

Troy was in rare form. He sauntered drunkenly across the street, in the wrong direction, amusing himself by making loud, bitchily clever comments about everyone they passed. He yelled, "Work it,

BITE CLUB

girls!" to a couple of anemic looking male hustlers standing across the street in front of the Astro Burger diner. Chris, chasing after him, finally caught him and barely managed to keep him from running out into traffic, pointing at the two youths and screaming, "Blue Light Special!" at the oncoming cars.

Chris decided to walk to their rendezvous with Becky in the hope that the crisp autumn air would help clear Troy's fuddled head. He prayed to whatever gods there were that by the time they reached the Abbey, Troy would be sober enough to behave himself. In the interim, he would content himself with the pleasant anticipation of his hand smacking against Troy's bare bottom when Chris finally got him home.

Chris got him moving in the right direction once again. But the long walk dissipated Troy's alcoholic haze only slightly. As they passed a bar called Rafters, Chris glanced in and noted it was empty except for the lone bartender at the far end of the bar.

"Wait here," he told Troy sternly.

Troy blearily stationed himself at the door, leaning against the entrance and unbuttoning his vest to show his taut little torso to better advantage. "I'll keep anyone from coming in," he said.

"I'll bet you will," Chris sighed and went in.

He quickly checked the DJ booth and, seeing no one inside, was satisfied that the music was prerecorded. The bathrooms were both empty also. Confident that he shared the place only with the bartender, Chris approached him with a smile on his face.

"Hi," the bartender smiled, wiping his damp hands with a towel. "What can I get you?"

"I don't know. What do you suggest?" Chris put as much sensuality in his voice as his 200-plus years of experience allowed.

The bartender seemed taken aback for a moment and smiled uncertainly, giving Chris a moment to examine him. He was tall and blond-haired with a slightly darker mustache, and he wore a pair of dark blue shorts cut off to reveal the swell of his lower buttocks. His yellow shirt, open almost to the waist, revealed a slim but well-muscled chest, obviously shaved. Chris noted with satisfaction the nicely defined bare arms and broad shoulders. Chris leaned forward over the service bar area.

"I said, what do you suggest?" Chris murmured seductively.

The bartender, leaning forward himself to catch Chris's almost whispered comment, made the mistake of looking directly into Chris's eyes.

Farther and farther over the bar he leaned as Chris artfully slipped his left arm around the bartender's right shoulder, angling the mesmerized youth so that his throat was exposed.

Lapping gently at the flesh just below and behind the bartender's right ear, Chris closed his eyes, tasting the slightly sweet, salty flavor of the young man's sweat. Slowly, gently, he sank the very tips of his fangs into the soft flesh, barely piercing the skin. As the first drops of blood flowed into his mouth, Chris rolled them around his tongue like a connoisseur savoring a fine wine, testing for impurities. There were none; the blood would be rich and sweet.

Maintaining the almost orgasmic sense of anticipation for a moment longer, fully aware that at any second his privacy could be invaded, Chris sank his fangs deeply into the man's throat as a burst of warm fluid flowed into his mouth and down his throat.

Barely two minutes later, Chris shuddered as with a postcoital chill and, sated for the time being, withdrew slightly from his still transfixed victim. Slowly he allowed several drops of his "special" saliva to fall from the glands just behind his upper fangs onto the two small wounds he had left on the side of the bartender's neck. Drawing back, he watched as the small holes magically folded in upon themselves and scabbed over. Satisfied that within an hour or so there would be no trace of his stolen meal, he maneuvered the bartender from his almost prone position across the service bar back onto his feet and released him, both physically and mentally.

The bartender's glazed eyes cleared, replaced with a look of confusion. "Huh?" he asked.

"I asked if you have a telephone in here," Chris said patiently, hiding his amusement at the bartender's befuddled state.

"Uh, yeah…I mean, no…I mean, it's outside. By the…you know. Where you come in."

BITE CLUB

"Thanks," Chris said sincerely and made his way outside.

"Uh, wait!" the bartender called.

Chris turned and with polite interest asked, "Yes?"

The bartender seemed to struggle with his memory for a moment, bewilderment in his eyes. "I just thought, well…nothing, I guess."

"You have a good evening, OK?"

"Yeah. Right," replied the bartender, still puzzled and absently scratching at an itch on his neck.

Chris turned with a small, private smile and left the bar to rejoin Troy.

As the two continued their walk down Santa Monica, Chris managed to keep Troy out of subsequent bars, although he was certain to note the name, location, and type of clientele of each.

They arrived at the Abbey only forty-five minutes late. Chris had been prepared for the decor to be faux-Gothic. After all, California was famous for its hot dog–shaped frankfurter stands and flower shops constructed to look like daisies, but Chris was pleasantly surprised that the Abbey's architecture seemed almost normal. There were no crucifixes hanging on the walls, no gargoyles peeping from the eaves, nor were waiters dressed in the brown homespun robes tied with lengths of raw hemp that Chris had imagined.

Instead the Abbey was a pleasant patio-style bar and restaurant, with plastic chairs, wooden tables, and brightly colored umbrellas softly lit by hidden floodlights. The only oddity was that, at one time, the place seemed to have been part of the statuary shop still located next door. The courtyard surrounding the fenced-in patio was littered with cement planters and stone benches. A fountain, topped by an epic bronze Mercury stretching more than twelve feet from the top of his helmet to the tips of his winged sandals, dominated the area. Clasping a bronze laurel leaf in one of its outstretched arms, the statue was otherwise totally nude and had a magnificent physique.

Troy stopped short in the entryway, causing Chris to smack into him from the rear. Chris began to prepare a suitably testy remark when he noticed Troy eyeing the statue speculatively, his expression laced with a look that could be described as a cross between awe and hunger. Chris traced Troy's gaze with his own and sighed in exasperation, which quickly turned to pique.

"First of all," he hissed, "it's not real. And if it were, it'd tear you apart."

"I know," said Troy dreamily. "But it'd be a *marvelous* way to go, wouldn't it?"

Chris shoved him off balance and broke the mood. Grabbing Troy by the scruff of the neck, Chris guided him firmly toward the bar proper.

As they moved across the patio, Chris's eyes bugged slightly at the assortment of beautiful men lounging about in various stages of semidress, laughing, chatting, and enjoying their drinks. There was a short, muscular black-haired lad in the corner, alone at a table reading a magazine, whom Chris found particularly intriguing; he made a mental note to try and speak to him before they left. The young man was what Troy would call a "KTF," or "Kitchen Table Fuck," which, as near as Chris could determine, meant that upon bringing the lad home one should quickly bend him over the nearest piece of furniture capable of supporting his weight, have one's way with him, and immediately send him back from whence he came.

"Well, well, well," commented Troy loudly in his best Bette Davis voice. "If it isn't Miss Thing."

Almost every head on the patio turned inquisitively in response to Troy's comment, some with slight anger, others with various degrees of surprise and pleasure—all obviously assuming that they had been addressed. As one by one they realized they were not the subjects of Troy's greeting, they turned back to their business, except for those half dozen or so who found Troy attractive. These erstwhile gentlemen either continued to stare, with various degrees of obviousness or discretion depending on their natures, or smiled enchantingly, trying to catch Troy's attention. Troy regally ignored them all.

Becky O'Brien was seated at a patio table just outside the open French doors of the shop, a plate of chocolate chip cookies at her right and a half-finished pie overflowing with some sort of unidentifiable fruit filling at her left. As Chris approached her table, Troy in tow, her expectant smile transformed into a grimace of distaste as if she'd just found a large insect in her fruit pie.

Rising, both arms outstretched for a hug, she failed to mask her annoyance at Troy and smiled brightly at Chris.

"It's been a long time."

"Yes, it has, Becky," said Chris, taking her into his arms for a chaste hug.

Holding Chris at arm's length, she commented, "My God! It's been years and you haven't aged a day!"

"Oil of Olay," piped Troy, plopping down into a vacant seat. "You should go out and buy a jar. It'd do you good."

"Troy…" Chris began warningly, but Troy had already lost interest and turned away, trying to scope both the patio and the interior of the shop for likely companions for the evening.

"Just ignore him," Chris said.

Becky smiled uncomfortably. "That's sometimes difficult to do," she said as she slid her chubby frame back into the chair. "Really," she continued. "You must be, what? Forty-something?"

Chris shifted uncomfortably, afraid of where the conversation was leading. "I've always been older than I look."

"You look fantastic."

"Good genes," said Chris tersely, his tone indicating that he didn't want to continue the line of thought.

Becky looked at him keenly. Chris could see the wheels spinning in her quick mind. Her expression cleared and with a small shrug she asked, "Want something?" She indicated the sweets on the table.

Chris patted his stomach, shaking his head with mock sorrow.

"Karen Carpenter's still around, huh?" She sadly surveyed the spread before her. "Maybe I should try that."

"Maybe you should," piped Troy archly. He rose gracefully and began to nonchalantly make his way across the patio, without any apparent destination. From long experience, Chris estimated that his path would take him just within range of one of the customers whose eyes had remained fixed on Troy, a blondish bodybuilder wearing a striped tank top and shorts. As Troy bent over to adjust one of his socks, his tight little butt perkily thrust out in the general direction of the striped tank top, Chris turned back to Becky, certain that they wouldn't be disturbed by Troy's asides—for at least fifteen minutes.

"Well, I'm here."

"What do you think of L.A.?"

"To be honest," Chris mused, "I'm not very impressed. Everything looks like a set from an old Maria Montez movie, covered in neon."

Becky laughed. "You think West Hollywood's bad? I'll have to take you down to Olvera Street, the oldest street in Los Angeles. It dates from 1800-something and they've turned it into a tourist trap."

"Eighteen hundreds? They call that old?" Chris's eyebrows rose in amusement. "In Philadelphia I have silverware older than this entire state!"

Becky chuckled for a moment, then became more serious. "Our little problem's gotten worse."

"Another one?"

She nodded. "We found him yesterday. I knew him. Fortunately not well."

"Any clues?"

Becky pulled out a copy of the autopsy report and handed it across the table. As Chris opened it, she began digging into the pie. Around healthy mouthfuls, chewing daintily, she commented, "It looks like I was right. We found teeth marks this time. Some lunatic thinks he's Frank Langella."

Chris finished reading the report in silence and closed it, passing it back to Becky. He sighed heavily.

"Becky," he began slowly, "I know you wanted me out here on the coast..."

She started to interrupt, but Chris stopped her with a lifted hand and went on.

"Whatever your reasons are, I hope they don't have to do with the husband hunt." He turned to look at Troy, who had started up a conversation with the blond boy. From the confused look on the young man's face, Chris was certain Troy was dazzling him with his wit and vivaciousness.

"I took him for better or worse. Usually he manages to turn the 'better' part into the best. But he's quite capable of making the 'worse' part…well…into something worse still. It depends on his mood, I guess. As for you, my dear," Chris continued with a gentle smile, "you are rather persistent."

Becky looked at him, blushing slightly "Well, you can't blame a girl for trying, can you?" Her eyes narrowed as she examined him critically, while Chris squirmed slightly in his seat. Finally, she shook her head. "I really can't believe how fabulous you look."

"Could we *please* stop talking about my age?" Chris asked irritably.

Becky grinned mischievously. "In a minute."

Chris glared at her, but she couldn't resist needling.

She lifted a forkful of gluey fruit filling to her mouth and licked it from the spoon with as much lasciviousness as she could manage. Leaning forward, a smidgen of filling smearing her lower lip, she breathed huskily, "I never have had any self-control, you know. How do you two feel about three-ways?"

Chris stiffened and looked at her suspiciously, not entirely certain she was joking. "I thought you wanted marriage, not just a tumble."

"A tumble?" she snorted and patted her middle before attacking one of the cookies. "With my weight, it'd be more like a rock slide."

"Anyway," Chris continued, certain now there was a germ of truthfulness underneath Becky's banter, "it'd have to be a package deal."

"There is that," Becky said, the corners of her mouth wrinkling in distaste. She glanced over to where Troy was busily "entertaining" the blond boy. "He *is* stunning," she said wistfully, then turned back to face Chris. "I don't suppose we could stuff a sock in his mouth or something?" she asked absently.

"Where would we find one big enough?" Chris said with one of those closemouthed grins Becky found so irresistible.

She put down her fork and reached across the table to take one of Chris's hands in hers. "All right. All right. Enough already."

Chris sighed with mock relief. "Thank God. I was just getting ready to grab him and head back to Philly. Where it's safe. Where the men are men…and the women are too."

"I'd never forgive you," Becky said, grinning. Then her mood turned suddenly serious. "You know, if things were different, we could have been good together."

"How Jacqueline Susann," Chris said, arching an eyebrow.

"Oh, I know it's hopeless," she sighed. "Just like most things in my life."

"Becky—" he began, but she cut him off.

"Yes, I know you're going to say just the right thing, just like you always do, and make me feel better. But it's time we both faced reality. Look at me. I'm a fat, middle-aged woman living in a gay town, cutting up corpses for a living. What chance do I have of meeting any nice guys? Sure, I joined one of those Jewish singles groups for a while. I met this very nice guy, recently divorced. Unfortunately, when he asked me what I did for a living I told him." She threw up her hands in exasperation.

"It was like I had the plague or something. First he turned the color of one of my patients. Then he started wiping his hands on his pants. You know, like he was trying to get the dead smell off or something." She sighed. "I even considered dating only funeral directors for a while. There are a few straight ones, you know. But it's kind of incestuous, if you know what I mean."

It was Chris's turn to try to interrupt.

"Let me finish," she said. "I'm closing on fifty and single. I've been doing a lot of thinking lately. At my age, in my position, you stop looking for a white knight to come riding along and sweep you off your feet and start concentrating on friends. And even though I know there's no chance of you and me ever, well, you know…" Her voice trailed off. There was silence for a minute until the coroner resumed her attack on the pie and patted her bulging middle. "Anyway, any knight that's gonna try and carry me off into the sunset better have a lifetime gym membership and be riding a water buffalo!"

Chris said nothing.

"All kidding aside, what I need from you isn't matrimony, it's help. Nothing ever happens in this town. If it weren't for the fact that half our population is over retirement age and if they die without a doctor, you gotta do an autopsy, I'd probably be out of a job." She laughed briefly. "You wouldn't think the competition in the body biz was fierce, but it is."

Her eyes narrowed and she looked Chris directly in the eyes. "We've got a serial killer on the loose. And if the captain and I can't figure out how to catch the son of a bitch, we may both be out of jobs. Our city manager is not the most patient of people."

Her tone became almost pleading, "I've got no life, Chris. I go to work and come home. I spend most of my free time working for char-ity—Aid for AIDS, UNICEF, the animal shelter. I guess maybe I don't like being alone. In short, Chris, my job is really all I have. And I need you to help me keep it." There was silence for a few minutes.

"Are you quite finished?" Chris asked testily. Becky nodded. "I am sick to death of you coming down on yourself that way," he said harshly. "If you don't have any respect for yourself, for God's sake, have some for me. Do you really think I'd have let you drag me all the way out here to Broken Dreams City if I thought you were really the lonely-heart fat slob you paint yourself?"

Becky blinked in shock as Chris continued. "I don't see that there's much I can do that you can't. But I'll try. Under one con-dition."

Becky leaned forward expectantly.

"One more self-disparaging remark out of you, and Troy and I really will take the next flight back to Philly. Deal?"

Becky smiled, chagrined. "Deal."

"Good. Now tell me everything…"

CHAPTER TWELVE

Becky left the Abbey an hour later, leaving behind a copy of the case file and autopsy reports. Chris found it remarkably easy to collar Troy and drag him away from his new boyfriend. "Pretty but dull," was Troy's only comment.

Chris snorted and resumed his perusal of the autopsy report, a frown creasing his forehead, while Troy became more and more frustrated, trying to signal a waiter for a drink. Unfortunately for him, the Abbey was in the midst of a momentary rush and, though he smiled, blinked, giggled, and waved coquettishly, he couldn't seem to draw anyone's attention.

"Jesus!" he exclaimed with disgust. "You'd think they had enough blonds out here to go around!"

"Shh, monkey," Chris said absently. "I'm reading."

Troy turned in his seat and fixed a determined glare on a waiter taking orders at the next table. "The service around here is terrible!" he announced. "What does a person have to do to get a drink around here? Scream?"

The waiter turned to him haughtily and without hesitation replied, "Scream? Mary, for you, this is a stretch?" and loftily walked off into the restaurant proper.

Troy's mouth dropped open. Too affronted to reply, he sat for a moment, shocked. He recovered admirably, however, and was just about to follow the offender to give him a piece of his mind when Chris finally closed the file and leaned back in his chair, tapping one finger thoughtfully on the table.

A now completely sober and much more serious Troy was quick to put the offending incident behind him and concentrate on the matter at hand, especially since his lover had missed his momentary embarrassment. He turned to Chris and inquired, "She knows about you?"

Chris thought for a moment. "No, I don't think so."

"She suspects?" Troy pressed, taking the autopsy report and glancing at the contents.

"No," said Chris with more certainty. "I mean she thinks I'm eccentric, but she's probably not given it much thought." He mused some more. "As far as Becky's concerned, I'm independently wealthy, spending my time writing, teaching, getting degrees, or doing whatever else I want." He grinned. "Sort of a modern dilettante."

"She should try living with you and your little hobbies."

Chris glared at him.

"My dear," said Troy, patting his arm gently, "you can be rather compulsive at times." He turned a page and continued reading as, with a spare fork, he started to idly pick the chocolate chips out of half a cookie Becky had uncharacteristically left behind. "How did she handle the age thing?" he asked absently, concentrating on Becky's report. "You were worried about that."

"I do believe," said Chris with a smile, "that she thinks me foolish and rather vain for having already had a face-lift at my tender years."

"You're kidding!" Troy looked up from the file and started to giggle. "Just think, you and I could open up a surgical practice out here and put half the doctors in Beverly Hills out of business!"

"True." Chris's expression sobered. "I'll have to be careful. She believes the bulimia story, so at least I won't have to keep coming up with excuses not to eat. But it's going to be tough coming up with reasons for seeing her only at night. In Philly it's almost always over-cast, and we mostly went out after class. I don't want her putting two and two together. Then there's that age thing."

Troy had a mischievous glint in his eye. "We could always gray your hair and put lines in your face."

"Funny," Chris snapped. He stood up, grabbed the file from Troy, and started for the exit. Troy followed him out of the Abbey and they started to walk up the street. "Hopefully," Chris said sternly, "we're not going to be here long enough for that to matter. I want to help her catch this guy and get out."

"Back to Philadelphia?" Troy pouted. "But it's so *colonial* there! We've only got another five or ten years there anyway. Before some-one starts to notice how young—" Troy cut short his sentence in response to a glare from Chris. "I was only suggesting...I mean, we've never lived in California."

"We'll deal with that later," said Chris, dismissing the notion. "Right now I want to concentrate on what we know about the killer. Any ideas?"

Troy's brow furrowed in concentration. "Well, he's male, obvi-ously."

"Why?"

Troy rolled his eyes in mock exasperation. "I didn't get a chance to read everything because someone without *any* patience pulled me away, but..." Chris glared at him, and recognizing that he shouldn't push anymore of Chris's buttons, Troy became abruptly serious. "Look at the victims," he said. "Do you honestly think three tricks, a hustler, and a porn star would allow themselves to be alone with a woman? In West Hollywood?"

"She could have lured them away or something," Chris sug-gested.

"No way!" Troy snorted. "Gimme that!"

He grabbed the file from Chris and halted under a street lamp. "Look here. First stiff, West Hollywood Park; second, behind the Pleasure Chest *and* a hustler; number three, the alley behind the Gold Coast; four, behind Rage; and five, get this, coming home from

24-Hour Fitness. All of them with their weenies to the wind." He thrust the file back at Chris with a look of incredulity at his boyfriend's obtuseness. "Get serious, Maude. It doesn't take a *Damron Guide* to tell you they were looking for sex."

"All right. All right." Chris threw up his hands in surrender as they continued walking. "I happen to agree with you. I just wondered what conclusions you'd come to on your own."

Troy shot him a withering glare. "And the one behind Rage? I know his type—typical twink. Attitude city."

"How could you possibly know his type?" Chris asked impatiently. "You only skimmed the bloody file for two minutes."

"I looked at the pictures," Troy said proudly. "Even though the bodies were a little damaged, you can see the victims were all really cute—especially the Asian kid. Did you get a look at the size of—?" Troy brought his mind back to the subject at hand in response to another glare from Chris. "Anyway, I know the types. Trust me," he continued. "So your killer's got to be either very fast, physically, that is, or a total stud. Otherwise the Copperman kid wouldn't have given him the time of night. As for the hustler and the porn star, those kind of guys aren't in the habit of doing it for free unless it's really worthwhile."

They walked in silence for a moment.

"So?" asked Troy archly. "What do *you* think, your highness?"

"Well, I'd say the killer's legit. One of us. Gustav and Hanna agree with me."

Troy looked pained. "What *us?*" He hunched over, lifting one shoulder, and resurrected his bad Peter Lorre, limping along and dragging one foot behind himself. "Ah, no, master, please! You cannot grant me eternal life in this wretched condition. No, master! Do not doom me to spend eternity a vile and depraved hunchback!"

"Stop that!" Chris hissed. "Someone'll see!"

Troy straightened. "And do what? Arrest us? Get over it, Martha. This is L.A. We're practically *normal* here."

"Sorry."

At the corner, they caught the West Hollywood City Shuttle and

Chris plunked some change into the clear plastic box to pay their fares. The shuttle was empty and the driver was listening to rock music over her headphones. Chris felt it was safe to continue their discussion.

"I'm worried about her lab tests, though."

Troy arched an eyebrow in query.

"She's too good not to have found something. She's got a few notes that are troubling, but she's put it down to possible specimen contamination." Chris frowned and opened the report. "If she reruns the tests on this last one and gets the same results…" He held the report out so Troy could see.

"Saliva? Teeth marks? Mommy did not teach this guy good table manners."

They traveled the rest of the way without speaking, Chris absorbed in thought while Troy pressed his face against the windows and made kissy faces at anyone he thought was cute. The shuttle stopped several minutes later. They disembarked and walked up the street in silence.

They reached the apartment building and Troy opened the front gate. As they walked up the stairs, Troy broke Chris's concentration by commenting, "So the killer sucks, eh?"

"Yeah, I'm fairly sure."

"Think it's anyone we know?" Troy opened the door and turned on the lights. The rush of crimson made Chris momentarily dizzy.

As Troy locked up, Chris sank down on the couch. "No," he said tiredly. "At least I don't think so."

"You mean you hope not."

Chris nodded as he opened up the autopsy reports again. "No, my first guess is a newborn."

Troy flopped down next to Chris sideways, his legs crossing Chris's lap, one arm flung out on the back of the couch behind Chris's head.

"What makes you say that?"

Chris, trying to see the report through a lapful of Troy, shrugged him off the couch, dumping him onto the floor.

"Cut it out. You're too big to be a lapdog."

Troy panted and made puppy noises as he settled on the couch again, snuggled up at Chris's side.

"Sometimes younger vampires, especially if they were created by accident, don't realize they don't have to kill their victims to feed."

"OK, I'll buy that," Troy offered. "But what about that woman in Georgia that had to be put down? Sometime before the war, I think."

"Yeah? What about her?"

"Well, wouldn't the throats be all torn up? Blood everywhere? This guy was practically Emily Post."

"True," Chris replied thoughtfully. "The younger ones do that. Very messy sometimes."

"Are we bragging about our technique, dear?"

Chris ignored the comment and continued, "You're right. If the killer's young, between newborn and, oh, let's say fifty or so, and untrained, the murders would be more violent." He stared off into space.

"So?" Troy urged, "What do you think's going on?"

"Maybe," Chris began slowly, "the killer is old—very old."

"Why?" Troy's attention was focused now.

"Sometimes, when we get old, and I'm talking four or five centuries, boredom sets in."

"Boredom?" Troy commented, emotionless.

"It could be our killer has a distinct purpose he's unaware of."

"And that is…?"

"To leave clues."

"No one would do that!" Troy exclaimed. "We know people who are positively ancient. Sylvia can be tiresome sometimes with her Miss Ennui shit, and Max is *always* doing his I'm-so-tired-of-it-all bit, but there's no way either of them would go around leaving a trail of bodies behind them."

"Someone else might. A rogue, maybe," cut in Chris. "And what worries me even more is the cutting out of the skin."

"Why?"

"It may mean he's trying not to be caught."

Troy was puzzled. "Of course he doesn't want to get caught."

"Not necessarily. Some rogues are just tired of living. But they don't have the inner strength to kill themselves. The only alternative is to get the normals to do it for them. That's when you get the torn throats, the dead victims. It's an unconscious way of self-destructing. I remember once, in Paris, we had to put down a rogue. He'd killed an artist, a painter, and left so many clues that even the French didn't have any doubt about what he was. When a group of us caught up with him, only hours ahead of the police, we staked him."

Chris was silent until Troy prompted him gently. "And…?"

"When the stake was in, just before he died, he…well, he seemed almost relieved." Suddenly Chris slammed the autopsy report on the coffee table, stood up, and began pacing. "That's what bothers me. If this guy is old, he's intentionally covering up. He doesn't want to be caught. Consciously or unconsciously. But then, why do it?"

"Calm down," Troy cautioned. "You'll have a conniption or something." He thought for a moment while Chris continued to pace, running his hands through his hair in thought as he marched back and forth across the living room.

"I've never seen you like this," Troy said. "Scared."

"Damn right, I'm scared!" Chris exclaimed. "The other, final possibility terrifies me."

Troy said nothing. He just sat with an expectant look on his face.

"Look," said Chris, finally stopping and kneeling in front of the sofa to meet Troy's gaze, "I've never known this to happen, but I've heard stories. Once in a while, when someone's *really* old, like from before Christ, they get this god complex. They begin to think they *can't* die, that they're not only more than human but also more than vampire, and that they're *better* than both."

"No one is *that* old."

"Don't be silly. I've met one and I know of at least two others. They don't come out much, but they're there."

Troy was now very concerned. "So, what can we do? It isn't that easy to put someone like that down, is it?"

"I don't know. But if I'm right, we're going to have to try."

BITE CLUB

Chris moved over to the telephone and picked up the receiver, holding the scarlet plastic in his hand gingerly. "The last thing I need," he told Troy, "is this lurid decor. Anyone who walks in here'll be convinced *we* killed those kids and mixed their blood in with a couple of gallons of Sherwin-Williams."

"I like it," Troy said, miffed at Chris's criticism.

"I don't," Chris replied. He started to dial the telephone. "Change it."

"*Excuse* me, oh great and powerful Oz!" Troy sniffed. He considered pulling what Chris called his *Star Is Born* routine, complete with tears, an obvious display of hurt feelings, and thinly veiled threats to load his pocket with rocks and walk into Santa Monica Bay. However, his curiosity got the better of him. In any case, Chris's comments about his decorating skills were sure to be repeated; he'd save the James Mason bit until then.

"Who're you calling?" he asked.

"Sylvia. Who else?" Chris frowned as the telephone rang four times without being answered. "She must be out." He replaced the receiver and began pacing the room.

"Maybe, if my hunch is right, we can figure out who this guy is."

"And what if we can't?" Troy asked innocently

"Monkey," Chris began with great patience, "sometimes you say things that make even me want to strangle you!"

CHAPTER THIRTEEN

It was scarcely an hour past dawn in Manhattan when Sylvia Gabrelli stumbled from her bedroom into the living room, wincing at the faint traces of sunlight leaking through miniscule cracks in the shutters covering the windows over her writing desk. One part of her mind silently cursed modern communication systems, making an emergency call from Chris capable of interrupting her day's sleep at this ungodly hour, barely after she'd managed to drift off. Scarcely 200 years ago, the urgent message would have reached her only after several days on horseback, allowing her not only to sleep in peace but also providing a home-delivered meal in the form of the messenger himself. The other part of her mind firmly resisted panic at the news Chris had managed to drowsily impart as his own bedtime fast approached. She had helped "put down" rogue vampires several times during her long life; it was a task she did not relish undertaking again.

Sylvia's creamy pale-olive skin and long raven hair allowed strangers no doubt as to her Italian ancestry even before she spoke with the faint musical accent she'd been trying unsuccessfully to lose for more than four centuries. A statuesque woman who appeared to be in her early thirties, she could easily have become a successful matinee seductress, giving even Sophia Loren a run for her money. However, given that Sylvia's image on film, like that of most members of her race, appeared only as a blotchy smear, Ms. Loren was comfortably ensconced in some Bel Air estate, secure in the knowledge that her career on the silver screen was unthreatened.

An inherently social woman, over the past few centuries or so Sylvia had become the unofficial grande dame of the vampire community. Vampires from all over the world would inevitably make their way to New York, clutching an introduction from some old friend, to be welcomed with open arms into Sylvia's magnificent home and invited to partake of her famous hospitality. When the time came for the guest to leave, days—or sometimes years—later, his or her name would be added to Sylvia's voluminous address book, and since Sylvia had been a compulsive letter writer since her breathing days, a course of correspondence would ensue. By the time Chris's call had so rudely awakened her, Sylvia was on friendly, if not intimate, terms with practically every vampire still walking the earth.

She sat at her writing table, looking at the thick book in front of her, wishing she had restrained her love of company slightly but knowing that most of those listed in the book would have to be contacted sooner or later if they were to locate the rogue before the normals realized they shared the planet with several other species, almost all of which preyed on them in one form or another. Sylvia hoped the search would not take long and she would come across someone, somewhere, who might have heard a rumor as to the rogue's identity. If Chris's theory about the rogue's advanced age was correct, it was probable he'd only recently arrived in America; someone in Europe or Asia might have witnessed an earlier murder that had been previously unreported.

Sylvia adored Chris, and the intensity of her feeling for him had through the years been returned. He was one of the few members of her race that she would quite willingly risk the true death for; in fact, she had done so several times. The two had met in London not long after the turn of the nineteenth century, although they had corresponded for several decades prior to their first face-to-face meeting. She had been there, providing emotional support, when his mother had died of consumption in 1812, and he, in turn, had always been the first with condolences, sagacious advice, or one of his wryly clever jokes to cheer her up whenever one of her numerous mortal lovers passed on to his higher reward, as they inevitably did.

As Sylvia leafed through her book, wondering where to begin, she reflected that Troy, his faults notwithstanding, had indeed proved through the years to be the perfect mate for Chris. She could not honestly admit that she liked Troy. She was frequently amused by him and found him often endearing, but his selfishness where anything but Chris was concerned and his uncanny ability to sense the exact inappropriate word, comment, or action that would send tempers flaring through the roof was sometimes difficult to take. No, she thought, although she loved the little imp as Chris's other half, had she met him independently she doubted that Troy Raleigh's name would be on the "must invite" list for any of her monthly social gatherings.

But, given her own failings in the amour department, she chided herself, she really couldn't be too judgmental about Chris's choice of a mate.

Fifteenth-century Florence had been a marvelous time and place. Sylvia had been born to poor parents of the peasant class, but her incredible beauty had helped her overcome not only the rigid social structures of the time but also the inevitability of death. Early in Sylvia's breathing life, she had developed a passion for beautiful things, things she had resigned herself to never being able to possess. Her change had opened up new opportunities for a substantially increased income and, posing as a middle-aged widow, she had purchased a small estate and had set about filling it with paintings, fine furniture, sculpture, and other objets d'art.

Her meeting with Botticelli was inevitable and the attraction had been both immediate and intense. Botticelli had an ardent love for life and an impassioned creative drive Sylvia had found irresistible. During the decade they had intermittently spent together, she had posed for him several times, regretting only that, since she had been changed at the fairly advanced age of thirty-two, Sandro refused to use her as a model for any of the mythological young virgins he was so fond of portraying. She contented herself with the knowledge that she would retain her looks and figure long after the sweet young things Sandro bedded on occasion had turned into withered crones.

Unfortunately, as the years passed and she grew more and more secure in her love for the artist, she became sloppy and began to skimp in her daily, artful application of face paint, which gave her the illusion of growing older. She failed to notice the rise of religious conservatism sweeping Florence until it was too late. Rumors surrounding Botticelli's perpetually youthful mistress were growing. Eventually, even Botticelli became suspicious and he finally confronted Sylvia with her "unnaturalness." Erroneously trusting in his love for her, she confessed her nature and invited him to share immortality with her. His response was as unexpected as it was emotionally devastating.

That very night, her former friends and neighbors burned her home to the ground. Sylvia barely escaped with her life and a few of her most precious possessions. Although she had managed to rescue them all, a century passed before she was once again able to gaze upon any of the gorgeous paintings that Botticelli had given her without bitterness and regret.

Her psyche was scarred for years, and despite decades of analysis Sylvia continued to find herself irresistibly attracted to men with artistic temperaments. Unfortunately for her, the more driven by his art the artist was, the deeper in love with him Sylvia inevitably fell. To her dismay, while artistic passion served to drive her lovers to make more beauty to add to the world, it also made them lousy vampires.

Sylvia tried converting several of the men whom she had most loved, but none survived even a mortal lifetime. Sorrowfully, she'd given up, contenting herself with a few, brief, stolen years of passion, followed by endless grief and vows that she would never fall in love again. But then she would chance across a work of art breathtaking in its beauty and, against her better judgement, contrive a meeting with the creative mind responsible for it. And voilà! The vicious cycle would begin again.

Sighing with mingled regret and amusement at her poor judgment in men, she continued idly flipping through the pages of her address book. Several of her past lovers had been vampires, but as far as she was concerned they hadn't had the stuff with which lasting relationships were made. The problem was that members of her own kind were all too much alike. Those who managed to survive the first century had common traits, necessary to enable them to continue existing but frequently irritating as hell to the vampire with whom they were emotionally involved.

Take Lucenzio Caravella, for example. In fact, Sylvia thought, she heartily wished someone *would* take him—preferably for an extended vacation to a place far away from New York. Lucenzio had been handsome in his youth, still was in fact. However, during the past few centuries he'd taken up homosexuality with a vengeance and had become enamored of the most god-awful effeminate trappings. He could frequently be recognized out on the town by his outré combination of brilliantly colored fifteenth-century brocades and silks and ornate eighteenth-century lace collars and cuffs. Sylvia had often voiced the opinion that Lucenzio would be considered a fashion risk in any century; the once attractive vampire had become a flamboyant caricature of his former self.

Well, she supposed, he *was* old enough. With only a slight grimace of distaste and reminding herself to be polite, she dialed Lucenzio's number. The answering machine came on after the fifth ring and she left a brief message. Several telephone calls later, she gathered that most of Manhattan's vampires had already retired for the day. Knowing that she would undoubtedly be forced to sell whatever soul she still possessed to Sprint to pay off the long-distance charges, she began to dial Europe, knowing that twilight would be falling and many of her kind would likely be already awake but not yet out for the evening. She reached several old friends and, after quickly explaining the situation, extracted promises that each would keep his or her eyes and ears open. In less time than she would have at first thought, she had managed to contact most of the vampires who had established informal salons and centers of social activity.

She hung up the telephone and leaned back in her chair to think. Sylvia Gabrelli hadn't managed to keep herself alive across the centuries by blindly marching ahead when her instincts told her to do otherwise. And right now her instincts told her that, if the rogue had been active at any time in the recent past, the word would have spread and one of the people to whom she had just spoken would have had, at the very least, an unfounded rumor to report.

She could wait until evening and try to call some of the other vampires she knew, but she was fairly certain the results would be no more promising. While members of her race possessed a certain curiosity, their inquisitiveness was usually directed more toward finding out who was currently sleeping with—or no longer sleeping with—whom and not of the type best suited for solving mysteries or tracking down murderers. Shuddering with distaste, she realized that, for a change, time was the one luxury she lacked and she would undoubtedly have to turn to acquaintances who, although they were not vampires, possessed skills and attributes unknown to mortal men. And although the earth was home to many species of intelligent beings who were not altogether human, she was afraid that she knew *exactly* which community would be best suited to hunting down a killer.

Hoping against hope that she'd come to the wrong conclusion, she mentally began to tally up the skills and attributes of the other groups, reluctant to make the telephone call to Queens that, if she were not mistaken, she would shortly have to make.

She quickly rejected calling friends amongst the "little people." Though terribly inquisitive, most leprechauns and elves flatly refused to venture into any of the larger cities where humans clustered in abundance. She also dismissed the idea of enlisting the aid of the goblins. Although they had established settlements beneath almost every city in the world that had a large underground transportation system, their malicious practical jokes had frequently been known to indiscriminately injure mortals and nonmortals alike—sometimes with fatal results. No, contacting the goblins was *definitely* out of the question.

As for the ghouls, they held only slightly greater promise. *If* Sylvia were willing to risk the utter ruin of whatever she happened to be wearing by tramping through the tunnels underneath Manhattan, and *if* she managed to locate a nest, the poor creatures would undoubtedly flee from her in terror. Furthermore, they lived in such a perpetual state of fear of outsiders that they rarely communicated with anyone outside their own families, not even with others of their own kind.

Sylvia sighed. This was getting her absolutely nowhere; she knew precisely what she had to do. Like it or not, there was only one person she knew who could provide her with access to the community that would be most likely to succeed in tracking down the killer. She spent an hour alternately steeling herself against the traditional narrow-minded lupine belligerence and trying to talk herself out of making the call and finally broke down and telephoned Hercule LeGrande to arrange a meeting.

One of the pups answered the phone, and Sylvia was rudely and unceremoniously put on hold for a frustrating ten minutes while the youngster went off in search of his grandfather. Finally, Sylvia heard Hercule's gruff voice come on the line, its lilting Cajun accent still familiar to her though she hadn't heard it since their last disagreement almost five years ago.

He masked his surprise at hearing from her remarkably well. She explained the situation in depth, stressing the danger that if one so-called supernatural creature was discovered by the humans, others would be sure to follow. Hercule heard her out without comment. When she was finished, the line remained silent for a full thirty seconds.

"So what?" he asked, unconcerned.

Sylvia managed to control her brief flash of temper. "So, I'm asking for your help."

"Why?" was his only response.

"You have packs located in every major city in the world. At least one near Los Angeles, if I remember correctly."

"The locations of our families have nothing to do with *your* problems."

The line fell silent as Hercule waited for her response. Sylvia cursed the well-known werewolf clannishness; she knew Hercule had no intention of making her entreaty for his help any less difficult than he could possibly make it. Her Italian accent grew slightly heavier from stress as she went on.

"It's easier for you to move around during the day. We'll gather as much information as we can. But who knows? If you keep your eyes open, you may see something. As far as we know, Chris, Hanna, and Gustav are the only vampires in Los Angeles. You can spot a stranger as quickly as I can."

"This is true."

Sylvia felt her frustration building. "Hercule, do I have to beg?"

"You could try."

Fighting the urge to curse him and all of his kind to whatever hell they believed in, she tried another tactic. "Could we at least meet somewhere and discuss this?"

"Why?"

She took a deep breath and then said through gritted teeth, "We could all be in terrible danger. Do you *want* peasants banging down your door, guns loaded with silver bullets? Threatening the safety of your family? Your children? Some things haven't changed in the last few centuries."

This time the pause on the other end was thoughtful.

"Why is it," Hercule began, "that each time *our* community is threatened it is always the fault of one of *your* people?"

Sylvia was silent, slightly ashamed, waiting for him to continue.

"That painter who was killed in Paris in the '30s, the woman in Georgia who went mad, each time it was *we* who found ourselves in danger. If you people can't control yourselves, why should we bother to try?... What? Excuse me a moment, Sylvia."

He'd evidently covered the receiver of the phone with his hand as his next words were muffled.

"Jacques!" he said sternly. "Grandmere told you not to chew on the couch!" There was the sharp crack of a hand contacting flesh and a high-pitched yelp of pained surprise. "Go to your room if you can't behave."

"I'm sorry," he said as he spoke into the telephone again. "What was I saying? Oh, yes, we were speaking of your kind's habit of running wild and endangering us all."

Sylvia allowed a hint of anger to creep into her voice. "Are you trying to tell me you've never known a werewolf to run rogue?"

"Not in my lifetime."

"Which hasn't been nearly as long as mine," she snapped. "If your kind lived for centuries, maybe you too would find aberrations cropping up."

"Aberrations? You speak as if this were an isolated incident. I find it occurs entirely too often for my taste."

"Three times since 1900?"

"My point exactly." He sighed heavily with disgust. "Well, I suppose I must at least hear you out, and the telephone is inappropriate. Where would you like to meet?"

There followed a ten-minute discussion while the two haggled out a neutral meeting place. Each time Sylvia suggested a location, Hercule vetoed it unilaterally; this place was too openly public; that one was too secluded; the other was too difficult to get to; the next was too close to a home den. Each time, Hercule steadfastly refused to suggest a spot of his own.

Finally, in a burst of thinly disguised sarcasm, Sylvia said, "I'll tell you what. My building has a recreation room in the basement. No one uses it except for Wednesdays, when the Hadassah ladies play bingo. I'll reserve it for Friday night."

Surprisingly, Hercule agreed.

Really! she thought as she bid him goodbye and hung up. *Those creatures are infuriating!*

The friction between the two species was long-standing and inevitable given their differing natures. Where vampires tended to be loquacious, chattering endlessly amongst themselves about their inevitable hobbies or reminiscing about the past, werewolves limited their verbiage to what was strictly necessary to get their point across. Vampires, due to their potentially infinite lifespans, had to be incredibly adaptable to changing societies and social conventions; their furry relatives, on the other hand, were extremely conservative, inflexible, and tended to be scornfully disapproving of change. Physically, a vampire could move much faster than a lycanthrope, even in wolfen form, and when walking on two legs the werewolves tended to be slow and ponderous in their movements. A vampire could, like Chris, look with wonder at the development of human society, or could, like Gustav, be amazed by modern technological advances, or could be, like Sylvia, emotionally moved by the beauty of human art. A werewolf could only wonder with dour fatalism about what new dangers man's development would pose for his pack or shake his head in sad disgust at the splash of brilliant colors in a Van Gogh painting, complaining that since his living room was brown the painting wouldn't match. It was no wonder that individuals of the two species, when forced into each other's company, could only be miserable with their mutual incompatibility.

It was no comfort to Sylvia that it was physiologically impossible for a vampire to suffer from headache. At the thought of having to endure the upcoming meeting with Hercule LeGrande, Sylvia could swear she felt a whopper of a migraine coming on.

CHAPTER FOURTEEN

Three stories beneath the ground, with the traffic on Fairfax Avenue muffled by the earth until it was a barely discernable hum, Rex Castillian slept. An observer, had one been able to witness Rex's slumber and survive, would have seen no gentle rise and fall of the chest, no wisp of breath across the cheek, no soft throbbing of pulse at the temples or wrists, no stirring of the eyeballs as they twitched following the images of a dream.

Even Becky O'Brien, had she happened across Rex's inert form, would have immediately declared him dead—and she would not have been far from wrong. Had she the foresight to attach the electrodes of an EEG to the corpse's temples, she would have been puzzled to note a tiny flicker of brain wave, high in the Alpha range, so small and so unusual that she would have probably dismissed it as a malfunction of her diagnostic equipment.

Of course, had the hypothetical intruder possessed both the knowledge and the courage to place the sharp point of a wooden stake at a particular spot on the chest, above the heart, the quality of their observation would have been greatly enhanced as Rex Castillian, disturbed briefly from his sleep, instinctively tore out the intruder's throat and sank back into slumber, unaware of what he had done.

Chris and Troy had been correct in their suppositions; Rex was old—incredibly old. Even he did not recall the exact time of his birth. His early memories had already begun to fade by the time a certain carpenter's son was breathing his last upon a wooden cross. He was a creature without roots, without a past, railing out in anger against a universe in which his very identity was slowly being distorted and stolen by the passage of time. He knew his advanced age was to blame. While his body was immortal, his mind could only absorb new experiences by letting slip the old. His memories of the time prior to the beginning of the Common Era were but brief snapshots of moments, much as if a short clip of motion picture film had been ripped from a larger movie and presented to an audience with no introduction and no resolution. The images had only one element in common: blood—blood resulting from pain and death.

During daylight hours, fast asleep in his lair, Rex's mind wandered, futilely attempting to dream and trying to bring his past alive once again. Visions of human suffering and misery swam through his subconscious. Sometimes the bloodstained images swarmed over him faster than his mind could cope; he was overwhelmed with moment after moment of sharp, crystal clarity, each vanishing as quickly as it had come, leaving behind a frustrated sense of hunger and sexual arousal.

Today, in the early dawn hours, Rex was just beginning to dream. The dim remembrance of an early incident in which he was amused by a young human's death agonies began to take form. Rex was familiar with this particular dream. A favorite, it recurred on a fairly frequent basis. Its duration was longer than most, spanning almost two minutes. Rex clutched at it, hoping that with mental repetition he could recapture some of his lost past.

The setting was a clearing in a dark wood, the moon gleaming ominously through the thick canopy of tall pine trees. A small group of robed figures surrounded a large flat block of stone, stained almost black with dried blood. A young man was led out of the wood toward the stone altar. Clad only in a pair of soiled homespun trousers, the victim was tall and muscular, with long dark blond hair in which bits of twigs and leaves had been caught. His shirt had been torn into pieces and now served as a gag; his arms had been bound tightly with cord to a stout tree branch that had been passed across his shoulders and behind his neck to function as a yoke.

The robed men forced their prisoner to a halt next to the altar. Rex had a clear view of the young man's back; he'd been flogged. The victim was perspiring with terror, his sweat mingled with the rivulets of blood, keeping it liquid as it slowly dripped from the raw flesh of his shoulders down his back to stain the waist of the trousers. The remembered scent was maddening; Rex's fangs ached in his upper jaw at the smell.

The yoke was removed and the young man was forced backward, stretched out, and bound faceup on the altar. Rex could feel himself beginning to salivate. He moved closer until he could meet the youth's eyes with his own. Maliciously, Rex smiled and allowed the poor victim to get a good look at his fangs. The prisoner tried to scream through his gag but could manage only grunting noises.

One of the robed figures approached, clutching a sharp stone knife, cowl thrown back to reveal a white bearded face. He raised the knife high into the air, poising it over the young man's bare chest. Rex shivered with anticipation. Swiftly the bearded man brought the knife down, piercing the prisoner's flesh, and a jet of blood shot into the air. Rex almost swooned as the torturer deftly twisted and hacked with the knife, ignoring the writhing body beneath him. Rex had time only to delightedly recall the look of horror in the young man's eyes as he realized he was dying. Then, despite his attempts to prolong it, the image vanished. This was the only dream Rex remembered with any clarity.

Part of him wanted a more total recall of his past; another part wanted desperately to be able to sleep in peace. But this was impossible. Of his breathing days he remembered nothing at all. His native earth was a mystery to him, and thus he was unable to include some in his coffin. His sleep was rarely refreshing; the dreams and memories continued to plague him. If he stayed in any one place for more than a half century or so, he sometimes managed to achieve a modicum of comfort, but not much. He supposed his body finally began to adjust to the foreign soil; but he was never truly able to rest comfortably. This only increased his ire at a world that denied him a home. Rex was many things—vicious, hate-inspired, evil in many ways—but he was also an intelligent creature. He was a voracious reader, history naturally being his favorite subject. He'd eagerly devoured scholarly texts and had often been driven to a blinding rage when faces of people related to what he was reading swam clearly into his mind—faces he *should* have recognized but couldn't. Sometimes in the depths of a deserted library, the echoes of his laughter would ring from the high stone walls and ceilings of the building at the absurdity of some scholar's conjecture about a particular incident or artifact. But to his great distress, although he knew the learned writer was incorrect, he could not, if his unlife depended on it, remember how he knew.

Rex had always enjoyed the company of mortal men. They were so innocent, even the most evil of them, so unsuspecting of his true nature. He took pride in his cleverness at his ability to pass among them. It had been centuries since he was last able to retain consciousness without effort once the sun rose above the horizon, even longer since he had been able to tolerate the contact of its light on his skin without instantaneous painful blistering and burning. As the years passed and his limitations grew, he had been forced to discover more ingenious ways to explain his inability to be seen by mortals during daylight hours.

He preferred male victims—always young and strong. Warriors gave him particular delight as, like a cat, Rex enjoyed playing with his food. He adored their shocked screams as they found their prized strength insufficient to prevent the agonies Rex inflicted. He was aroused at the sight of their bunched muscles as they strained to avoid his teeth and nails. The scent of their sweat and blood was a fine bouquet to his senses. The taste of their adrenaline-rich blood, flooded with a rush of hormones as they sought futilely to escape him, was an almost orgasmic pleasure to his palate.

And the more beautiful the victim, the happier Rex was. He loved nothing more than to reduce a once beautiful face and body to a writhing mass of torn, blood-soaked tissue and bone. Rex hated the pleasure others derived from physical beauty. He sought to possess it in the only way he knew how—by destroying it utterly.

Women, though, had always tasted flat to him. He despised them as weak creatures, fit only as chattel, which they were considered throughout most of Rex's life. They had no power in society and were used to suffering physical abuse. Rex missed the feeling of stripping away their physical defenses to leave them shattered, quivering wrecks. It was simply too easy to break women, and thus their conquest gave him nothing to relish. No, his favorite meals were males, secure in their own strength and ability, whose fantasies of superiority he could slowly crush.

As for other vampires, he had no patience with them; he simply killed them on sight. They were simpering, spineless creatures, hiding from peasants in graveyards and catacombs, terrified of their own shadows. But by the thirteenth century it was difficult to reside in any major city where vampires were not present—in abundance. Encountering their little groups became an inevitable nuisance. And frequently there were too many of them in a single metropolis to risk ridding himself of them all; he found himself in the despised position of having either to hide himself or leave. When an encounter with another of his race was absolutely necessary, he did his business quickly and departed; he doubted if he'd spent more than a dozen or so hours in converse with one of his own kind since Julian had been emperor.

The Inquisition in Spain provided him with a welcome respite. For once, he was able to sit back and enjoy himself as the church did his dirty work for him; he merely observed the banquet of pain and blood, lapping up the leavings with satisfaction. The Inquisitors did their jobs well. By the second or third decade of the fifteenth century Rex realized with a shock of pleasant surprise that he was quite possibly the sole remaining member of his race left alive in Spain. Seizing the opportunity, Rex joined the ranks of the church as an Inquisitor.

BITE CLUB

Gleefully immersing himself in his tasks, he sang ironic praises to a god whom he neither acknowledged nor believed in while glorying in the torture and degradation of helpless mortals. His favorite game was to prolong the agony until his victim was on the brink of madness and then reveal his true nature as he sent his captive on to hell. He excelled at his job—he was too good, in fact.

He'd finally drawn the attention of Torquemada himself. He met the inquisitor general only twice, the meetings almost thirty years apart. Unfortunately, he'd not reckoned with the churchman's amazing recall of faces. Rex's perpetual youth and beauty had caught the sly old man's attention and he quickly found himself naked, shackled to a dungeon wall in chains so heavy even he could not break them. As the Inquisitor's men worked on his helpless body with their red-hot irons, pincers, and tongs, extorting him to renounce Satan, Rex roundly cursed them through his screams of agony.

His uncanny ability to heal himself at first terrorized his captors. Soon, however, they dug in with a new zeal, determined to exorcise the devils that so obviously possessed the young man's soul. Rex writhed in pain nightly, sinking into blissful oblivion with each dawn, only to awaken at sunset fully healed as his torturers renewed their assault. Finally, hanging in chains from a high ceiling, shoulders dislocated and starved almost to death, he gnawed through both his wrists and crashed to the floor twelve feet below, almost shattering his spine in the process and leaving his hands dangling above him.

That evening, he feasted on his former captors and escaped. Vowing revenge on Torquemada, he fled Spain, trudging overland in great pain, leaving a trail of drained corpses in his wake until he finally reached the Black Forest of Germany. There, digging deep into the moist dark soil, he buried himself and succumbed to a sleep lasting more than a century.

Emerging from his makeshift grave, hands fully healed, he entered a nearby village and learned the date. Realizing that his enemy had gone to his grave lifetimes before, his fury was almost unendurable. His revenge thwarted by time, Rex drained the entire village, leaving in his wake the bloodless, mutilated corpses of some 200 men, women, and children.

His anger turned inward and festered. Now unable to tolerate even the company of mortals, he retreated even further from the world. He found himself a series of secluded dens, usually deep caverns hidden in the wilderness surrounding major cities. He would emerge occasionally and invade the nearest metropolis, capturing several strong young men. Back in his lair, he derived almost as much sustenance from their anguish and terror as he obtained from their blood. Their deaths were slow, hard, and satisfying.

As human society grew and expanded, Rex found it harder to preserve his solitude. Grudgingly, he abandoned his depraved pleasures and contented himself with a quick kill to survive. Eventually, the New World beckoned with its unexplored wilderness and vast frontiers, and Rex was quick to explore America's possibilities.

By 1750, the forests and plains of the American West had become his new home. The Western savages were his first prey. However, Rex soon found that the term "savage" was inaccurate; they were inestimably more canny than their pale-skinned brothers. Baffled and enraged by the Indian ability to thwart his attacks by the burning of mysterious herbs, maddened by the inexplicable pain caused to him by certain of their religious ceremonies, Rex turned his attention to the wagons of Eastern whites who were slowly beginning their westward travels.

The pickings were leaner, but easier. Rex became less choosy about his menu. Many entire families, eager to homestead land in the virgin regions of the country, vanished long before reaching their destinations. Parties of explorers and surveyors disappeared during their treks. Once, to Rex's pleasure and gratification, a contingent of a half dozen soldiers was unable to rejoin the main body of its force.

And always his hatred grew. He resented having to be careful so that he would not awake one evening with a sharp wooden spar denting the flesh above his heart. He loathed his vampiric brothers and sisters who had learned to derive sustenance from their victims without killing—their timidity was anathema to him. He despised the various shape-changers whom he met in abundance in the New World. He considered their hunting techniques to be sloppy and unprofessional; quick, violent kills forgoing the added spice of terror and anguish. And though he would never have admitted it, he hated his own self-imposed loneliness most of all.

It had been a century since he'd first stood on the beaches of the Pacific Ocean along the California coastline. The creamy brown-skinned men of the southern regions had been delightful prey. The various young members of the clergy, come to convert the heathen to Christ with youthful exuberance, had made excellent playthings. The almond-eyed Asians of the northern regions, muscles hardened from months of backbreaking labor on the railroads, had been most inter-esting quarry.

By the early part of the twentieth century, Rex had been forced to reevaluate his eating habits. California became too developed for the remains of his prey to lie undetected for long. Yet he was loathe to leave his feeding grounds. Modern man was, in many ways, stronger than his ancestors—health care and the abundance of good food had seen to that. In addition, California had been, since the 1930s, the home of the most beautiful men in the world. Even with the temptation of a second world war beckoning from Europe, he was reluctant to leave the dashing young American sol-diers on leave in their crisp uniforms. He'd stayed and, by a fluke of fate, met with misfortune.

In 1958, he'd been making his home deep within a series of cav-erns and caves below the city of Los Angeles. From the cave entrance to his lair, a walk of twenty minutes was required through twisting, dank corridors of stone, airless and without light, past pools of black standing water, hoards of rodents gathered around the edges. Rex had never before seen crude oil; thus he had no idea that greedy mortal men were in the process of raping the countryside in search of it. The drilling that had been occurring in the Los Angeles basin for several years, combined with massive construction on the surface, weakened the strata of the rock surrounding Rex's lair. A relatively minor earth-quake, which disturbed the surface not one bit, was all that was needed to send the walls and ceiling crashing down upon him as he slept one day, burying him in the rubble and trapping him in a makeshift grave for more than thirty years.

Rex had not awakened from his involuntary sleep until the California Department of Transportation provided the alarm clock late one August. Excavations for the new Los Angeles subway project penetrated his tomb one evening and he awoke, his nostrils filled with the scent of fresh prey passing by on the streets above him. Clothing tattered and torn, he emerged ravenous onto the streets of Hollywood.

His first victims were the homeless. Rex was amazed at the sumptuous repast of humanity modern Los Angeles had seen fit to provide him in its doorways and alleys. Unfamiliar with the modern society in which he found himself, Rex was careful to make certain the bodies of his initial victims would never be found. Watching construction workers from the shadows of a tunnel early one morning just before dawn, he cleverly realized how simple the disposal of his corpses would be. Thereafter, he would scrape a shallow grave for his victim in the floor of a new excavation. By the next nightfall, the remains of his meal would be covered with a layer of cement as the subway platforms and floors were laid.

He grew stronger and his standard of living increased. He moved on to prostitutes and then to occasional small groups of leather-clad teenagers who were given to roaming the streets at all hours—dangerous, but not to Rex. He staked out his new territory carefully, both above and below ground. With delight, he discovered a library in the midst of his hunting grounds. Breaking in, he began to voraciously absorb local newspapers, getting a feel for the modern world.

One night he opened a sub-basement door below the streets of Hollywood and was again able to experience malicious glee. Imagine his joy at ascending the building's basement stairway to open a door revealing literally dozens of men, many of them handsome and young, all bare-chested, wrapped in nothing but towels, restlessly roaming the hallways, alcoves, and cubicles of the Hollywood Bathhouse.

But Rex had learned from his sojourn in the library that late-twentieth-century law enforcement officers were nothing if not efficient; the newspapers seemed almost exclusively dedicated to the mortals' undying attempts to stamp out what they considered crime. So Rex was careful. Stripping naked, Rex wandered the halls of the bathhouse, gaining appreciative stares from young men who, had he not already fed that evening, would have made deliciously intoxicating entrées. In the hours before dawn however, he was stricken with one particular youth, blond and smoothly muscled, and his impulses proved irresistible. Capturing the young man's gaze with his own, he'd lured him back down into the bowels of the sub-basement and had feasted on his agony as he had not done in years.

His passion for literature had also been assuaged that evening. Stacks of newspapers had been provided for the bathhouse's patrons and Rex had been quick to seize one copy of each. Leaving the drained corpse of the blond boy behind an unused piece of machinery in an ancient, rat-infested boiler room in the sub-basement, satisfied that the voracious rodents would make short work of the evidence, he retreated back to his lair clutching copies of *Frontiers, Edge*, the *Gay Gazette,* and *Planet Homo* in his bloodstained hands.

As dawn neared, he scanned the magazines and newspapers, marveling at the shirtless beauties displayed in the various advertisements and briefly absorbing bits of information from the articles and letters. The personal ads were particularly intriguing puzzles. What was a "bottom"? What was the significance of the letters "HIV"? What in the name of all the forgotten gods did "out only" mean?

But as he read on, one short phrase began to absorb his thoughts, pounding at his consciousness with a dull murmur that quickly became a roar with each printed repetition. He sank back into slumber, seeing its imprinted image on the inside of his closed eyelids again and again. West Hollywood...West Hollywood...West Hollywood...

CHAPTER FIFTEEN

"I don't see why we have to drive all the way out to the valley," Troy complained. "Don't you know they're going to make you turn in your American Express gold card and take a blood test before they let us past Mulholland?"

"I told you, Hanna and Gustav may know something new that'll help us out."

"Couldn't we just call them?" Troy grumbled. "She's always trying to pinch my cheeks."

"So am I," Chris grinned. "And you never seem to complain."

He shifted into third gear as he turned serious. "Anyway, it's not the kind of thing we want to talk about over the telephone. All we need is one nosy operator. You remember Rosalind Russell in *Auntie Mame*, don't you?"

"There is no San Francisco," Troy quoted absently, nodding his head. "It's not like you and Sylvia weren't Chatty Cathys about this for *hours* on the phone last night, you know," he added with irritation.

"It'll be good to see them again," Chris said firmly, putting an end to the argument. "It's been a while."

Chris had been only partially successful at ignoring Troy's continu-

150

BITE CLUB

al bitching. He'd given up trying to get Troy to stay quiet or wear a seat belt and was desperately trying to focus all of his attention on the road. Gripping the wheel tightly, the tip of his tongue emerging from between his front teeth in concentration, he was silently cursing whomever had the bright idea to construct a road through Laurel Canyon. Just when he'd finally hoped to have negotiated the last of the hairpin twists and turns, new ones appeared as if by magic.

Chris fought with the gearshift, thanking Providence for making him incapable of sweating; otherwise he'd have been drenched by the time he reached the top of the hill at Mulholland. As he gazed ahead he thought that a straight stretch of road must have been anathema to Californians. Figuring that fate had been on his side for two and a half centuries and was unlikely to desert him now, he gave up and, shifting into neutral, rode the brake all the way down to Ventura Boulevard. At the light, seeing the road stretch out before them on a more or less flat plane, Chris breathed a heavy sigh of relief and turned to face Troy, a look of satisfied accomplishment on his face.

Troy, however, was unwilling to compliment him on his successful negotiation of their hazardous path. He looked Chris straight in the eye. "I told you to let me drive," was his only comment.

Chris had never been quite comfortable with automobiles, and in the fifty-odd years since they'd become popular he'd often cursed the memory of Henry Ford. He'd been born during a time when most transportation was via horseback or carriage and had never really gotten used to being behind the wheel of a car. Even though he'd been driving automobiles for nearly a century, he had never been able to break his instinctive habit of pulling back on the steering wheel whenever he wanted to slow down or stop.

Troy, on the other hand, had been young at a time when Americans were just beginning their never-ending love affair with the automobile. He adored cars. He didn't know the first thing about their maintenance or upkeep, and he couldn't care less about the mysteries of the mechanics involved in keeping them running—but he adored them all the same. Oblivious to the idea that his nature made him considerably more frail than Chris, Troy delighted in driving with reckless abandon, using the horn more frequently than the gearshift.

Troy suddenly twisted in his seat and flung his outstretched arm across Chris's line of vision to indicate the left turn, which would bring them to their destination, and Chris made a mental note to trade in the VW for a small Volvo. He figured any car that could be driven off a high bridge and sustain minimal damage, as he had seen a Volvo do in a television commercial, would also be able to survive having Troy as a passenger.

Shoving Troy back into his seat with one hand and trying to both shift and steer with the other, Chris managed to make the turn and park in front of a small house, half timbered so as to look like the interior of an old English pub.

For someone who'd been so obstinate a mere moment ago about visiting, Troy seemed unable to restrain himself a single minute more without seeing Chris's two old friends. He was out of the car in a flash and ringing at the doorbell before Chris had managed to set the parking brake and lock the doors. Chris had only gotten halfway up the front walk, inhaling the pleasant scent of the fragrant night-blooming jasmine trailing up the fence, when the front door was opened by a pleasantly stout, matronly looking woman wearing a white apron.

"Good evening, Hanna," he called.

"*Ach*! Christopher! It is good to see you after all this time." Hanna spoke with a heavy European accent, pronouncing "good" as "goot."

She opened the door wider and said with a private smile, "I invite you in. Enter freely and of your own will."

Chris grinned at the old joke and, following her into the house, said, "You remember Troy, don't you?"

"As if one could forget," was her reply. She reached out and gently pinched Troy's right cheek, cooing, "Give Aunt Hanna a kiss, *liebshen*." Troy dutifully complied, shooting Chris an "I told you so" look.

She led them into the house and down a paneled hallway to a set of louvered doors leading into the den. "Gustav," she called, flinging open the doors with a dramatic flourish, "stop with the games. The children are here."

A bearlike man rose out of an overstuffed chair positioned in front of a computer monitor on an antique rolltop desk in the corner of the room. He tapped a button and a colorful maze disappeared from the screen, leaving it blank and glowing softly. Coming forward, he grasped Chris's hand in both of his own and shook it heartily.

"Welcome to California, my dear friend." Gustav's accent was not quite as heavy as his wife's, but it was still apparent that he'd been born on foreign soil.

Troy cleared his throat loudly, impatient at not being the center of attention.

"And dear Troy," Gustav said, turning to embrace him. "It has been, what? Forty years?"

"That long?" Hanna said with surprise. "But the war was only..." She paused for a moment, mentally calculating, then said with amazement, "*Mein Got,* you're right!"

"What is that delicious smell?" Chris asked as Gustav motioned he and Troy toward the couch.

"Old habits," said Gustav with a grin. "My wife, she continues to cook!"

"Cook?" asked Chris as Hanna blushed furiously.

"The food we give to charity. But a house is not a home without smells from the kitchen. Wait, I'll be right back." She disappeared into the kitchen and returned almost immediately, apronless, wiping her hands on a towel.

"Sit," said Gustav. "We must talk." They all settled in as he continued, "You received the information we're sending you?" Chris nodded.

Hanna leaned forward. "When we read in the newspapers about the murders, we didn't know what to do."

"We thought about calling Sylvia," Gustav confided, "but we've always felt closer to you."

"*Ach,* those poor children," Hanna commented, shaking her head sadly.

"But you were so long in coming. I called you three times."

"Two times," Hanna corrected.

Gustav shrugged. "Who am I to argue?" He paused. "Three times." Hanna shook her head, making good-natured clucking noises with her tongue.

"I'd hoped," began Chris, "that Colin and Dwayne could handle everything from San Francisco."

"They went back to New Orleans," said Gustav. "We keep in touch."

"So sad," added Hanna. "Poor Colin! Dwayne is a good boy. But *such* a temper! No self-control."

"Yes, I heard," Chris said. "In fact, my first thought was that Dwayne had gone rogue on us."

Gustav and Hanna looked shocked.

"It *was* a possibility," Chris said. "But Sylvia assured me they were already safe in Louisiana by the time the trouble started here. Will you please sit still and keep your fingers to yourself? You'll break something!" This last was to Troy, who had risen and plucked up two Dresden china figurines from the mantle over the fireplace and was, Chris could tell, about to begin playing with them as if they were plastic action figures.

"No, no. It's all right," said Hanna sweetly, rising and deftly removing the fine porcelains from Troy's busy hands. "Such a sweet child," she said, pinching the startled Troy's cheek once again. "Almost my age and still so much like a little boy."

She guided him toward the kitchen. "Come, we will leave them to talk and I will let you help me with the baking. We make strudel. I will teach you to roll the dough."

She ushered him, scowling, out of the room. But as they reached the doorway to the kitchen, Troy stopped and sniffed, his face slowly lighting up.

"Chocolate!" he exclaimed happily.

"*Ja,*" Hanna told him. "Is chocolate strudel." She pushed him through the doors and turned to smiled mischievously at Chris as she closed them behind herself.

BITE CLUB

"He has the attention span of breakfast cereal," Chris sighed. "Snap, crackle, pop, and he's on to something else.

"But you love him," said Gustav.

"Most of the time. Other times I want to strangle him. We've been together so long, sometimes it's hard to tell if it's love or just familiarity that gets us through the rough times."

Gustav tapped Chris firmly on the knee while making his point. "It is love." He leaned back into the couch with a heavy sigh. "After everything we have seen, we learn to recognize it when we see it. There is too much hate in the world, even today." He looked at Chris keenly through narrowed eyelids. "You have heard? In Orange County? Skinheads. Neo-Nazis, they call themselves, as if they should be proud of what they are."

"Yes, I know."

"Hanna and I have talked. We are Jews. We remember. We will not go through that again. If it gets worse, we will leave soon. We came to America after the war to be rid of it all."

"I remember."

"Thank you again, my friend. Without you and Sylvia, Hanna and I would not have had these years together."

"Just thank your lucky stars you weren't put into the ovens."

"I do, my friend. I do."

"It wasn't purely selfless on our part, you'll remember. Without your help, Sylvia and I could never have gotten back to Denmark."

"Well, enough of that," remarked Gustav. "Though there were good memories of that time, I would gladly forget them to put the bad things behind me."

He rose and went back over to the wooden rolltop desk. "We have other problems now." He sat down at the computer, stroking the keyboard with undisguised pride.

"This modern age!" he said in mild awe. "The things we have to play with now. Can you imagine what Hitler could have done with this? The mind shudders to think!" He patted the top of the computer monitor affectionately. "And the games!" he exclaimed with barely concealed joy. "When I was young we had only soccer and baseball and playing with

155

marbles," he said. "But now! Just imagine!" He opened the bottom drawer of the desk to reveal fifty or sixty computer game packages. "I can hunt dragons, fly airplanes, or kill aliens without leaving my den. What a wonderful time this is!" His expression grew serious. "It is a shame that the hate mongers of this world cannot content themselves with the Sims and their friends, yes?"

He signed and, closing the drawer, withdrew a printed piece of paper bearing a list of thirty or so names and addresses and examined it briefly. Finally, apparently satisfied, he handed it to Chris. "This is a list of all of our kind on the West Coast. All that we know of anyway."

As Chris began to read the names, Gustav asked, "What changed your mind about journeying here?"

"First I found out that Colin and Dwayne had gone back home. Then, well, I have a friend, a woman who's right in the middle of this mess. Do you have a pencil?"

Gustav handed him one. "She's one of us?"

"No, one of them. I know her from Philly. Coincidentally, she happens to be West Hollywood's city coroner."

Gustav frowned severely. "She doesn't know about you?"

"No." Chris looked up from the list. "I know most of these people. None of them are old enough to be who we're looking for."

"Old enough?" Gustav repeated.

"Yeah, Troy and I figured it has to be someone who's bored, taking risks."

"Could it be someone who's recently arrived. A rogue?"

"Possibly. Sylvia's already checking on that. But it's more likely to be someone none of us know." Chris looked down at the list again. "I don't recognize Gerald Commoner, Monique de la Fleur, or Harry and Agnes Piper."

"Gerald is from England," Gustav said. "He's been living in Seattle for the past fifteen years."

"When was he made?"

"During the influenza epidemic at the turn of the century. Monique, she is quite young. She lives downtown. Hanna and I see her frequently."

"And the Pipers?" asked Chris.

"A very charming young couple from somewhere in Kansas. Made in the early 1970s. They staged their own deaths and moved to San Bernardino in '81." Gustav considered the list for a moment and then thrust it aside. "Where is Lucenzio Caravella? He was born in the sixteenth century, *ja?*"

"Early 1400s, I think. But both Troy and I know him fairly well. We just saw him last Christmas in New York." Chris laughed. "That old queen is anything but tired of living."

Gustav held up his hands, an unvoiced question hanging in the air.

"I don't know." Chris folded the list and put it in his pocket. "I see that Maggie Trillum still lives in San Diego and Barbara Rice is still in Vegas. I'll get them to follow up on the people on the list. Maybe we'll find something."

"Hopeful you don't sound."

"I'm not. It's possible we're going to have to do a lot of research. I have a feeling we're dealing with someone who doesn't get out in society much. If you don't mind, ask Sylvia to send you copies of her records going back to, oh, let's say just before Julius Caesar. See if you can come up with someone we don't have a date of true death for."

"Hanna and I will gladly do what we can to help. But will we not have a problem? I'm told the records from the peasant uprisings in the fifteenth and seventeenth centuries are incomplete."

Chris grinned. "Wait'll you start dealing with our French cousins during the Revolution. The paperwork's a total mess." He clapped his hands to his thighs and stood up. "I didn't say it was going to be easy."

Gustav also rose and put one hand on Chris's shoulder, meeting his gaze evenly. "And if we are unable to find this madman?"

Chris looked uncomfortable. "Unless we want the modern equivalent of peasants with stakes, we'll have to. In the meantime, you and Hanna should be very careful. And warn your friends to do the same—especially the younger ones. We old folks can take care of ourselves." As an afterthought, he added, "Do you and Hanna have alternative identities ready to go?"

Gustav was concerned. "Do you think it will come to that?"

"If this guy keeps up at the rate he's going, it's only a matter of time before someone gets smart and starts combing old birth and death records. I don't know much about computers, but nowadays it won't be difficult to track down someone like Lucenzio. He's been his own grandson for so many centuries he suffers from inbreeding. And once they find one of us…"

"We can only hope." Gustav forced a smile. "Come, let us see what our wives are doing in the kitchen."

Chris returned his smile. "If I know mine, he'll have yours climbing the walls by now."

The two men turned and, Gustav's arm flung across Chris's shoulders, went to join their mates.

CHAPTER SIXTEEN

That very night, even before Chris had finished nervously navigating his way back across Laurel Canyon to West Hollywood, Gustav telephoned Sylvia to discuss how they should proceed. Gustav was eager to abandon his beloved computer games and, for the first time, use his hobby for a practical purpose. He argued strenuously that their search for the culprit could more easily be conducted via the Internet.

At first, Sylvia was resistant. Like Chris, she'd never been quite comfortable with computers. Although she'd spent a fortune on her own PC, purchasing a top-of-the-line model, she wasn't exactly sure how to use it. She could turn it on, and after she'd had it for almost a year she'd learned to write letters on it. But anything more advanced flummoxed her. She'd once spent a frustrating several hours trying to fax something through the machine. No matter how carefully she'd followed the directions in the manual, the computer would invariably refuse to do what she wanted and would respond to her pleas, threats, and tantrums with nothing more than a rude beeping sound. And for creatures who had to keep their existence secret in order to survive, a hacker could be fatal.

Gustav spent a frustrating several hours on the telephone, talking Sylvia through the process of accessing the Internet. With perseverance the two vampires were able to interface online, and moments later information was flowing back and forth.

Since Gustav and Hanna had died in middle age, it had been necessary for them to fabricate new identities once every other decade on average; otherwise neighbors and acquaintances became suspicious. Sylvia, on the other hand, was able to cleverly use makeup to prolong her stay in any one place. Thus, they were both very familiar with the processes vampires tended to use to create new lives for themselves and to avoid discovery. They accessed the relevant records and were amazed, if slightly uncomfortable, at how easily they were able to compile a list of names, which was largely comprised of vampires whom one or the other of them knew. They also came up with a long list of people who fit the vampire mold, individuals whose records lacked either a date of birth or death, and identified certain patterns of inheritance that looked suspiciously like one of their race had tried to will all of his property to himself.

Hanna, in turn, made her own rather unique contribution to the task at hand. Standing behind her husband and looking over his shoulder at the screen, she quickly realized there were some important gaps in the information Sylvia and Gustav had available that databases were incapable of filling. Without a word to her husband, she went into the kitchen and quickly prepared a basket laden with freshly baked breads, homemade sausages, spiced apple cider, boysenberry preserves that she'd prepared and canned herself, and a host of other goodies.

Early the next morning, while Gustav was still pounding away at his keyboard, Hanna left the house, closing the front door quietly behind her so as not to disturb Gustav at his work, and pulled her ancient station wagon out of the garage. A colorful scarf wrapped around her head to protect her from the autumn sun, she headed off to the Studio City branch of the Los Angeles County Library.

She entered the library, breathing a contented sigh as the cool darkness washed over her, and almost immediately found what she was looking for. She approached the desk of the reference librarian, where a plump man in his early sixties wearing spectacles was occupying himself with the *Los Angeles Times*. She stopped and coughed demurely.

The reference librarian looked up in irritation, but seeing Hanna his expression quickly changed to one of delight.

"Mrs. Bromberg!" he exclaimed. He rose and came around the desk, taking her unencumbered hand in both of his. "It's a pleasure to see you again." He took the basket from her gallantly and ushered her toward a nearby chair at an unoccupied reading table, where he fussed over her until he was sure she was comfortable.

"What can I do for you this morning? Perhaps a nice Louis L'Amour? Or," he inquired with a wink, "how about the latest Harlequin romance? I finished it yesterday." He sat beside her, trying to avoid closing his eyes in bliss at the tantalizing smells emanating from the basket.

He leaned forward and confided in a whisper, "I wasn't going to put it out on the shelves until tomorrow. I was saving it in case you came in."

"Such a nice man you are, Mr. Eisenstat," purred Hanna coyly. The librarian blushed. "No," she went on, "today I need some history information." At his look of surprise, she continued, "Very boring, I know. But…" She lowered her voice. "my husband sent me. One of his little projects." She spread her hands in feigned bewildered helplessness. "What could I do?" In a normal voice, she went on. "So I said to myself, Hanna, you must go to that nice Mr. Eisenstat at the library. You'll pass a few hours, schmooze a bit…" She returned his wink. "Maybe share a little nosh first?"

She indicated the basket and watched with hidden satisfaction as Eisenstat's face lit up with greedy anticipation. She drew the basket closer and, taking off the cloth cover, began to remove its contents.

"Let's see, hmm…What have we here? Some pumpernickel bread with….ah! Sausages!"

"Homemade?" asked Eisenstat with eagerness.

"Of course," she said with mock offense. Seeing the librarian open his mouth to apologize, she relented. "From turkey. Cholesterol, you know."

Eisenstat patted his ample belly. "I know," he said ruefully.

Hanna continued removing delicacy after delicacy from the basket as Eisenstat *ooh*ed and *aah*ed in appreciation. Within twenty minutes, flirting outrageously the entire time, Hanna had the reference librarian, quite literally, eating out of her hand. Several hours later, she left the library, basket empty of food but refilled with sheaves of paper—copies of the relevant texts Eisenstat had made for her, free of charge, on the office copier.

She returned home and proudly presented Gustav with the result of the morning's activities. Looking at the documents with undisguised surprise, Gustav asked, "Do I want to know how you got these?"

"Mr. Eisenstat at the library," Hanna replied offhandedly. "For the hours I spend slaving in the kitchen for that man, he should, for once, get me something more than romance books, *ja*?"

She pulled a handwritten list from her coat pocket. "This he's getting from downtown."

Gustav's eyes widened. "Some of this is very rare. Not for the public. How…?"

"Tomorrow, I promised him schnitzel." She turned and, removing her coat, walked toward the kitchen as Gustav watched her retreating back with an expression of combined love and admiration. Then, yawning, he turned back to his screen and within moments was so enmeshed in his research once again that he completely forgot his fatigue.

An hour later, emerging from the kitchen, Hanna found him, slumped over his keyboard, quite literally dead to the world. With a snort of annoyance tinged heavily with affection, Hanna wrapped her arms around her husband's corpse and, thanking her god for the increased strength of the undead, hauled Gustav's body off to its coffin in the bedroom.

By the time Gustav awoke that evening, aided by the documents provided by Hanna and the unwitting Mr. Eisenstat, Sylvia had managed to come up with a tentative list of seventy-three names. These were vampires, either once personally known to members of the community and not seen for a while or named in records and diaries throughout the ages and for whom the dates of true death were unable to be determined.

Proceeding on the theory that the culprit must have, at one time or another, come into contact with at least one surviving member of the community, Gustav and Sylvia realized how involved the task they had set for themselves really was. Using the information they'd amassed, they would now have to abandon the computer and rely on Sylvia's extensive social contacts to establish a network with two purposes in mind. First, they would have to track down every vampire Sylvia had ever known and instruct them to immediately contact her in New York if they had noticed any of their older friends or acquaintances exhibiting strange behavior. This could be a clue that someone had recently gone rogue. If this line of inquiry were ruled out, they hoped the murderer was someone who was once known but had dropped out of sight, as some vampires were periodically known to do, so that at least an identity could be established.

The search was under way.

CHAPTER SEVENTEEN

B y the following night, with Gustav's assistance, Sylvia's information network had already expanded. But it was becoming apparent that none of the vampires living in major cities had any clues
to offer as to the rogue's identity. Still desperately hoping someone
would come up with some positive lead, thus hoping to make her
upcoming meeting with the werewolves moot, Sylvia prevailed upon
some of her oldest friends to leave the comforts of their urban homes
and head for the hills and countrysides in an effort to discover something useful.

The tension in West Hollywood, on the other hand, had begun
to ease. The weekend had come and gone without any more drained
corpses popping up. Although the press continued to milk the "Boys'
Town Killer" for all it was worth, the lack of new bodies seemed to
inspire West Hollywood's nighttime denizens with new confidence in
their safety.

Slowly at first, and then in greater numbers as each corpseless
night passed, the hustlers began to resume their accustomed posts
along Santa Monica Boulevard. In the La Jolla district the residents
were being rapidly driven mad by the seemingly ceaseless revving of

engines and blaring of car stereos as drivers in search of anonymous sex drove repeatedly up and down the avenue, around and around the block, passing through the parking lot behind the Gold Coast Bar as they cruised.

The drag queens on the east side of town regained their confidence and small groups clustered on the street corners, gossiping and trading beauty tips until the wee morning hours. The foot traffic between the Eagle, the Spike, and Rafters increased as young men began to bounce from bar to bar in search of a better-looking crowd.

Clive and Becky, however, were veritable basket cases. They were both familiar with serial killer patterns; both were certain the murders would resume with a vengeance according to some unfathomable inner schedule of the killer's. It was only a matter of time before another bloodless corpse would make its startling appearance. The tension built as they read and reread the various reports, desperately searching for a clue that would allow them to stop the killer before he resumed his activities.

The night after their visit to the Brombergs, Chris and Troy began to comb the city on a nightly basis, hoping to catch a glimpse of the killer as he stalked a victim. Troy considered their little jaunts to be eminently successful, having broadened his circle of attractive acquaintances. Chris, for the most part, sat back and watched, shaking his head in puzzlement as he tried to figure out how each of Troy's new friends was able to finance expensive gym memberships, exorbitant wardrobes, and truly impressive bar tabs without ever admitting to having any gainful employment or viable means of support.

Then again, there were the inevitable catastrophes, all of which were directly attributable to Troy's failure to watch his tongue. Between extricating his lover from a series of potentially disastrous encounters and their lack of success in spotting the rogue vampire, Chris found himself growing more and more frantic while at the same time fighting a burgeoning depression.

Unbeknownst to any of the people trying to locate him, Rex had never intentionally stopped killing; he'd simply decided to vary his diet and was, once again, feasting on the homeless population of

Hollywood Boulevard. It was while reading one of the West Hollywood newspapers that he realized the normals were not only looking for him but were stymied by the dearth of clues as to his identity. Amused that the lack of obvious corpses was driving those searching for him crazy with worry, he decided to resume his hunting in West Hollywood.

Thursday night he wandered in and out of various bars and night-clubs along Santa Monica Boulevard and finally settled into the Mother Lode, eager to choose the evening's victim. He'd just caught the attention of a deeply tanned, blue-eyed little muscle stud and was mentally eviscerating the lad. He admired the definition of the boy's bared chest and shoulders and wondered idly if there might be a secluded spot nearby where he would be undisturbed as he slowly stripped the skin from the boy's body. But suddenly he was distracted by a commotion at the front door of the bar.

A harried young man with reddish, dark brown hair had just entered, accompanied by a short, slim blond boy wearing an outlandishly provocative outfit that seemed to be entirely constructed of narrow strips of plum-colored leather and zippers. The blond boy was smiling broadly and chattering ceaselessly as the darker youth bent his head in an effort to hear. Since the blond was apparently trying to cruise every single one of the bar's hundred or so patrons at the same time, his head was in constant motion, his neck craning to get a better glimpse of anyone who caught his attention. His flood of conversation, however, never stopped. He would speak, looking in the exact opposite direction from where his companion was standing, and then turn with irritation to repeat himself as the darker boy repeatedly demanded, "What? What?" with increasing frustration.

Recognition had been instantaneous. Rex immediately pegged the two as vampire and renfield. Obviously, word of Rex's sloppy eating habits had gotten back to the rest of the vampiric community. The only explanation for the sudden appearance of the vampire and his renfield, therefore, must be directly related to the "putting down" of one Rex Castillian. Rex had no intention of making their task easier.

BITE CLUB

Furious at the audacity of any other member of his race's attempts to instruct him on how to comport himself, Rex had quickly hidden himself in the men's room to avoid being spotted. But the bathroom was already occupied; a bleach-blond man of about forty-five was standing at the urinal. He turned in mild curiosity as Rex came bursting in and made the mistake of meeting Rex's eyes.

Rex had taken great pleasure in exercising his formidable mental control over the unfortunate gentleman, paralyzing him so that the flood of urine cut off painfully in midstream. Grabbing the man and thrusting him out the door, he released his control and grinned maliciously as the man suddenly began to urinate once again, splattering his shoes and the floor as a gentleman using the telephone looked on in alarm.

Alone now, Rex slammed the door and angrily brought his fist down on the worn marble of the lavatory sink. He grunted with satisfaction as the chipped stone split wide open, slivers of marble flying off in every direction. He began to pace back and forth across the stained tile floor.

First he had to get out of the bar without being seen; the dark-haired boy would recognize Rex's nature as easily as Rex had identified his. The renfield was also likely to be able to pick out another supernatural creature at a glance and, the way he was carefully perusing the bar, Rex was leery of being able to escape undetected. The front door was the only obvious exit, but he was certain a rear door must be hidden somewhere. After all, Rex had reasoned, the bartender couldn't very well cart the garbage out the front past the customers.

Escaping unseen, however, would do nothing to solve Rex's greater problem. He had no intention of curtailing his activities to protect his fellow vampires' misguided notions of secrecy and safety. Therefore, the offending creatures would have to be removed—permanently. Others might be sent to take their place, but Rex was fairly certain that, if he could make the destruction of the two in the bar violent and bloody enough, he could cow any other prospective hunters into fearfully avoiding the area until he had decided to move on.

Then again, he thought devilishly, both of the hunters were young, male, and attractive. The renfield wouldn't last much longer than a normal human under Rex's torturous ministrations. The vampire, however, posed some intriguing possibilities: Rex could slice, hack, and burn to his heart's content, prolonging the other's agony almost indefinitely. His fangs ached just thinking about it.

His thoughts returned to the suntanned, blue-eyed fellow he'd seen at the bar. Perhaps the boy had uses other than to simply provide Rex with momentary pleasure as he slowly relieved him of his skin. Rex grinned, baring his fangs slightly, and opened the bathroom door.

The bleach-blond queen was still standing by the telephone gazing at his soiled shoes in shock. He was so stunned that he hadn't yet bothered to zip his fly; his shriveled penis poked out of his pants like some pathetic white worm. He looked up as Rex cleared his throat casually and, fear blinding his features, fled into the bar trying to get far away from Rex as quickly as possible.

His flight caused a nearby group of young men, Rex's potential victim among them, to look up. Rex caught the youth's eye and smiled. The youth smiled back and, in so doing, permanently sealed his own fate.

Rex beckoned to the boy and, as if in a trance, the young man walked slowly toward the bathroom door. One by one, Rex caught the gaze of the young man's companions, planting a different image in the mind of each one of them so they would later be unable to identify him.

As he led the young man through a back storage room, past the boxes of beer and crates of glassware, toward the rear door, Rex smiled in anticipation of the treat he had in store for his two new "friends."

Several hours later, back in his lair beneath the street, Rex stretched in contentment. It was close to dawn and Rex had spent the evening enjoying himself. It was a pity, he thought, that his plan hadn't allowed him the luxury of spreading his most recent victim's torment over a period of several days. But Rex's hunger had been sated by the conversion process; the youth had writhed in agony quite nicely, and now the young man's frightened blue eyes stared from where his head had been placed on a nearby shelf. Across the room, spread out on the floor, was the rest of the corpse. Rex had had ample opportunity to admire the poor boy's fine musculature as his nails had slowly shredded the skin from his body.

Rex glanced at his watch; he didn't have much time left if he wanted his surprise to be delivered the following day. He briefly considered disposing of the remainder of the corpse before it started to stink, but the room was very cool. He decided that nature would probably take its course in a day or so and the corpse of the newly made vampire would disintegrate into ash long before the reek became offensive. He left it where it was and began searching for a cardboard box.

CHAPTER EIGHTEEN

Pamela Burman was having a good day—for her. During her morning constitutional, she'd managed to locate not one but *two* cars
parked illegally. At the 7-Eleven at Holloway and La Cienega, she'd
called in the violations to the Parking Department, pleased that she'd
increased the city's coffers by the price of two parking tickets. She hoped
desperately that at least one of the vehicles would have outstanding war-
rants. She'd called parking twice already, asking, and had been assured
they'd call her back before lunch.

As a result, she was in a remarkably good mood and had only
yelled at her secretary, a neurotic, willowy man named Carlos, twice.
The first time had been because he'd tried to—intentionally, in
Burman's opinion—bring her a cup of coffee that had been sitting on
the burner since the day before. She'd shrieked at him, thrown the
cup across her office, and demanded the first cup from a fresh pot.
She'd spattered a few drops of stale coffee on her hot-pink chenille
sweater, but the alacrity with which the new cup appeared on her
desk, along with the knowledge that she would be greeted with the
choicest from the pot every morning for at least the next two weeks,
made it well worth the dry cleaning bill.

BITE CLUB

Burman was never intentionally mean: She merely set great store by efficiency and strict compliance with rules and regulations. She was blissfully ignorant of Carlos's hasty retreat into the men's room to pop a Xanax and would have been horrified to know that she'd recently caused him to increase his therapy sessions to thrice weekly.

It amazed everyone at City Hall that Carlos had managed to last as long as he had. Burman was famous for going through secretaries and assistants in much the same way that a toddler goes through shoes. Carlos's reasons, however, were his own, and he held his cards very close to his chest. He'd angled for almost eleven months to get the position as Burman's number two. Born and raised in West Hollywood, the only child of an unmarried immigrant mother, Carlos had always regarded Burman as somewhat of a legend. He admired her dubious style, her undoubted campiness, unconscious of it as she might be, and her ability to alternately charm or bully her way into getting what she wanted.

Carlos worshiped Burman, although she reduced him to tears on many occasions, and hoped one day to be just like her. He had, in fact, modeled his drag persona, Ms. Shanda Leer, after her. Luckily, his best "girlfriend," a drag queen known as Trampolina, a name descriptive of both her boisterous nature in bed and the frequency with which she exercised it, was a sales clerk at Mister Fred's, the boutique where Burman purchased many of her outlandish outfits. It was scarcely an imposition at all for Trampolina to put aside copies of whatever Burman bought, in Carlos's size, so that Shanda could be sure to match the city manager's wardrobe.

Unbeknownst to him, Burman had caught a glimpse of Shanda during the previous year's Halloween parade and, although at first angry, had recognized the obvious care and time he had put into re-creating her. After making several subtle inquiries, Burman had uncovered Carlos's odd form of hero worship and was secretly pleased. Since that time, childless herself, she had begun to look upon him as the son, or daughter—depending on whether she happened to be thinking of Carlos or Shanda—she'd never had.

To compensate for the unaccustomed motherly feelings that grew steadily stronger, Burman was sometimes unduly harsh. She always made up for it, however, frequently taking Carlos to lunch or dinner at a restaurant he couldn't ordinarily afford, in her own way desperately trying to make him feel loved and appreciated. Burman was a smart enough woman to realize that should she ever push Carlos over the edge and make him quit, the gap that would result would have little to do with having to train a new secretary.

Burman also made it a point to find out whom Carlos was currently dating. With an almost proprietary vengeance, she would arrange to swoop down upon the unsuspecting potential Mr. Shanda and grill him to within an inch of his life. After her first several encounters with Carlos's future ex-husbands left each of them shattered in her wake, she dismissed Carlos's choice in men as self-destructive and counterproductive and skillfully arranged to place young men of suitable caliber in his path. Unfortunately, as yet she'd been unable to make an appropriate match, which did nothing but cause her to redouble her efforts to find an acceptable son-in-law.

There was a timid knock on her door.

"What?" she barked loudly.

Carlos peered cautiously around the door frame.

"Oh, for chrissake," she said. "I'm sorry about the goddamn coffee."

Carlos didn't move.

"I'm not gonna bite you. If you want something, get your ass in here."

Carlos angled into the room sideways and, avoiding looking at Burman, deposited a package wrapped in brown paper on her desk.

"What's this?" she demanded.

Carlos mumbled something.

Burman began tapping her pen against the side of her desk, a sure sign that her patience was going to begin to deteriorate momentarily. With a great show of even temper she asked, "Would it kill you to speak like a normal person?"

Carlos shook his head rapidly, panic in his eyes.

"Sit," she ordered.

Carlos all but fell into the chair, arms and legs stiff, perched as if prepared to run from the room at any moment.

Realizing she might have gone too far, Burman relented, throwing the pen to the center of her desk.

"Do you think I'm an ogre, Carlos?" she said calmly.

Carlos's eyes opened wider, like two saucers. Sweat appeared on his brow.

"I promise I won't yell at you. Just answer the goddamn…" She caught herself. "Just answer me."

"No ma'am," he squeaked.

"Carlos, I don't believe you."

"Yes, ma'am."

"Does that mean yes, you're not being honest with me, or yes, I'm the wicked witch of the west?"

"Yes, ma'am."

Burman sighed. "I'm truly sorry about the coffee. I'm under a lot of pressure right now. Do you understand that?"

"Yes, ma'am."

Burman sighed again. "No, you don't." She picked up the pen once again and swiveled her chair to look out her office window. She began tapping the pen against her front teeth, thinking. She finally turned back to Carlos.

"Look, I'll tell you what. Accept my apology and I'll take you to lunch. We haven't gone to lunch together for a few weeks. Would you like that?"

Carlos looked doubtful but eager.

Burman pressed her advantage. "I promise I will try, just try, mind you, not to yell. We'll go to Montage. The maître d' over there is very cute. We'll sit where you can cruise him all through lunch, OK?"

Carlos began to relax slightly. He adored publicly basking in the company of his heroine. He smiled timidly.

Burman smiled back. "Now, dear," she said pleasantly, "what's with the goddamn package?"

Encouraged by her reasonably jovial tone, he replied, "Someone

left it in front of the building last night. It has your name on it. See?"
He pointed and continued like an eager puppy. "We would have
found it earlier, but it was behind the little newsstands out front and
they delivered a stack of *Gazettes* this morning. One of the guys from
parks and services found it while he was sweeping."

"Well, how about if you and I see what's in it?" she whispered
conspiratorially.

Carlos was almost giddily ecstatic at the attention he was getting.
These shared playful moments between them were all too rare.

Burman opened her desk drawer and took out a pair of cuticle
scissors. She began clipping the string tying the parcel together.

Tossing the wrapping into the recycling bin by her desk, she
began to cut through the tape holding the box shut.

"What do you think it is?" Carlos asked.

"God knows," said Burman. "Probably something for the homeless shelter." She had frequently received parcels of old clothing and
kitchen items for her pet charity.

Finally, the box was free of tape. Opening the flaps, she commented, "Let's see what goodies we got."

She looked in.

She turned white.

She uttered a strangled scream.

She passed out.

Carlos jumped to his feet. Lunging across her desk, trying to grab
her before she slipped from her chair, his elbow struck the box, sending it flying into a corner of the office and spilling its contents out
onto the floor. Without thinking, he turned to look.

There, just rolling to a stop in the center of the floor, was a
human head.

Carlos's scream was anything but strangled.

CHAPTER NINETEEN

An hour later, City Hall was in chaos. The city's entire complement of seven on-duty sheriff's cars sat in the parking lot, their drivers bravely attempting to fend off the growing crowd of irate but buff young men who were accustomed to parking at City Hall and walking across the street to 24-Hour Fitness and the Boys' Town Gym to work out.

One of the spandex-clad youths had, upon being told that parking privileges were being temporarily denied, called the Gay, Lesbian, Bisexual, and Transgender Activists League hotline, charging discrimination by the Sheriff's Department. Shortly thereafter, the activists began to show up bearing signs and banners accusing the department, the city council, the owner of the parking franchise, and the Supreme Court of homophobia.

At first there was dissension within the ranks as the activists immediately began to shout disparaging remarks at the gym bunnies, accusing them of political inactivity. Slowly, however, the two groups merged into one as the activists, most wearing ripped blue jeans, leather jackets, and vests bearing a variety of political buttons, began to garner support from the boys in the tight tank tops and even tighter bicycle shorts. At one end of the parking lot an aerobics instructor had formed his class into a series of human pyramids, each topped by a gay, lesbian, bisexual, or transgender activist hoisting high his or her protest sign.

The West Hollywood Cheerleaders had also arrived—an even dozen mostly bearded and mustached men in red miniskirts and fluffy white cotton sweaters, trimmed to match. Each sweater bore a prominently displayed scarlet W, the bottom points of the letter calculated to terminate at the nipple of each false tit. These worthies, after having performed a variety of complicated gymnastic maneuvers, were organizing passersby into a cheering section. Bravely they stood, twelve dubious drag queens all above six foot one, in their bright tangerine, chartreuse, and turquoise beehive wigs, wildly shaking their pom-poms and urging their brothers and sisters on to new heights of righteous outrage.

West Hollywood's business community was also represented—at least in a manner of speaking. Two lesbians who owned a local graphic arts company had, upon seeing the massing crowd, stopped their Jeep Cherokee in the far right lane of Santa Monica Boulevard. Seizing the opportunity, one whipped out an expensive set of professional markers and several large sheets of cardboard and began artfully creating new signs for the swelling crowd, while the other moved among the masses passing out her business cards.

As traffic on Santa Monica came to a halt, blocked by the lesbians' Jeep, the traffic enforcement people were called out to assist. They vainly tried to tow the errant Cherokee. However, since the line of cars now stretched, bumper-to-bumper, from City Hall down to Santa Monica and Holloway, almost six blocks away, the tow truck was unable to get through. In fact, at the intersection of Santa Monica and La Cienega, the tow truck driver was brawling with an irate securities analyst from Beverly Hills who had failed to stop in enough time to avoid kissing the rear of the tow truck with the front bumper of his BMW. Other motorists had simply parked their cars in the gridlock, emerging from their vehicles to avidly urge the two pugilists further toward bloodshed. Traffic on La Cienega was halted, and the side streets began to back up.

Back at City Hall, the local press had gotten wind of what now could be called a riot. Several reporters from each of the local magazines and newspapers had managed to bully, con, or plead their way past the police barricade and were besieging the City Hall reception area. Eve, the receptionist on duty, returned from her quiet lunch in the conference room to be greeted with a scene right out of the horror novel she'd been reading while munching on her tuna fish sandwich. Aghast and frightened at the commotion, she hid in the ladies' room. The lead reporter from the *Gay Gazette,* a six-and-a-half-foot-tall lesbian with pink spiked hair and pierced nostrils, witnessed Eve's flight and, trying to get her attention, jumped the gate in the reception area. This provided the signal for the other reporters and they quickly seized the opportunity to follow the *Gazette* reporter over the gate, flooding down the hall to pound at the mayor's locked office door, demanding an interview.

In Burman's office, the cries and shouts from the mob below were starting to cause the windows to rattle. Two deputies were in the midst of trying to take a clear fingerprint from the brown paper wrapping. Clouds of fingerprint powder were billowing across the room as Burman had insisted the air conditioning be turned up full blast to try and dissipate the vile odors she was convinced would soon be emanating from the severed head.

The package's gruesome contents had been covered with someone's sweater to await Becky's arrival. Carlos had been escorted into an adjacent office, where, despite frequent bursts of hysterics, he was attempting to give a statement to one of Clive's sergeants. Clive himself was making a largely ineffective attempt to calm Burman down.

"Please, Pamela," he begged, "just relax. We'll get to the bottom of this."

"Relax?" Burman shouted. "Listen to this idiot! Someone drops a head, a fucking *head,* on my desk and he wants me to relax!"

Trying to replace a wet cloth on Burman's forehead, Clive spoke soothingly, "Becky's on her way. Here." He held out the glass of water and two aspirin he'd been unsuccessfully trying to get the city manager to take for the past half hour.

Burman grabbed the cloth from his hand and flung it at him, where it landed draped across his shoulder. She whirled and shouted at the two deputies. "Can't you morons stop with the frigging dust? You're giving me lung cancer!"

"Pam, if you would let us turn off the air conditioning…" Clive began, removing the wet cloth as he twisted his head to examine the resulting spot and wondered if it would leave a stain.

"I already had to *see* that thing. Now you want me to *smell* it?" She whirled about, knocking the proffered glass from Clive's hand and spattering his crotch with water. "Someone open a goddamn window!"

Clive sadly watched as the water spread across the lap of his gray woolen trousers. Taking out the ubiquitous handkerchief, he dabbed at the stain halfheartedly. Giving up on the odds of his suit surviving the rest of the day, he neatly folded the hanky and replaced it in his breast pocket. His attention still focused on his ruined trousers, he replied, "Those windows don't open, Pam."

He jumped and looked up sharply as a loud crash echoed through the office. Burman was standing in front of the shattered window, a metal wastepaper basket in her hands, smiling.

"They do now," she said, a wild look in her eye.

The door opened and a police photographer entered.

"Sorry, chief, the traffic," he apologized.

Clive wearily waved his hand toward the mound under the sweater. "It's under there."

Burman stalked across the room and grabbed the photographer by the knot of his tie. In a low, evil voice she said, "One photo, one fucking photo of me and that…that *thing* makes the press, and you are dog meat. You got that?"

Releasing the hapless photographer, she returned to stand by the window. She looked out and her eyes grew very wide. She tried to speak, first making only gasping noises, following them with several unintelligible grunts. She turned to Clive, helplessly pointing through the shattered glass to the streets below.

Moving next to her, Clive looked out and turned to her, puzzled. "What?"

Burman burbled something.

Clive sighed. "It's been going on for almost an hour, Pam. You were too busy yelling to notice."

Pamela Burman looked out over the masses of people and cars congealing in the middle of *her* city and, for the second time that day, fainted dead away.

◊ ◊ ◊

Becky O'Brien finally managed to shoulder her way past the teeming hoards and up the central stairs of City Hall. She'd left immediately upon receiving Clive's call, but the line of cars going north on San Vicente Boulevard had been so heavy she'd despaired of being able to pull out of the morgue driveway. Seizing a brief opening, she recklessly forced the van out onto the street and managed to make the left onto Santa Monica at the corner. She was unable to go farther. Giving up any thought of being able to make the U-turn to City Hall, she'd abandoned the coroner's van in the right-hand lane by the Boys' Town Gym and darted across the street to City Hall. Black bag clutched firmly in hand, she pushed open the front door and entered the reception area, tired, out of breath, and sweating.

She stopped for a moment, confused. Although she could hear shouting from somewhere deep inside the building and the echoes from the crowd penetrated the glass doors behind her, the reception area was strangely silent. It was also strangely, well, disheveled. The chairs had been overturned and the framed pictures were hanging at odd angles on the walls; the glass on one of them had been smashed. The floor was littered with pamphlets and announcement flyers. Becky knelt and picked several up, standing mutely, Animal Rights Task Force, Anti–Gay Bashing, and Senior Services leaflets clutched in her hand.

"Eve?" she began tentatively.

A small squeak came from behind the receptionist's desk.

"Eve?" she asked again as she bent over the desk to see a terrified Eve, glasses askew, huddled underneath the desk.

Becky quickly passed through the gate and squatted on the floor in front of the almost catatonic receptionist.

"Are you all right, honey?" Becky tentatively took Eve's hand and began to measure her pulse.

"There were thousands of them," said Eve dully. "Millions."

Becky dropped Eve's hand and straightened her tilted glasses, seating them firmly on the receptionist's face.

"They wanted to see the mayor. I got back from lunch and there they were, all wanting to see the mayor."

Digging through her bag, Becky removed a hypodermic and a mild tranquilizer. Eve clutched her arm.

"I hid. In the bathroom. Until they left. Then I came back here."

"I'm going to give you something to make you feel better, honey." Becky readied the needle.

Eve slowly stood up, awkwardly dragging Becky with her. She turned to the desk and picked up a shattered piece of plastic covered with red and clear plastic buttons.

"They stepped on my switchboard!" she wailed. "How can I answer the phone if they stepped on my switchboard?"

She sobbed as Becky deftly slipped the hypodermic into her arm. Eve didn't seem to notice.

Righting the overturned chair, Becky settled Eve into it gently.

"I've got to go see Pamela. You stay right here, OK? I promise I'll be right back."

"I have to answer the phone," Eve repeated blankly.

Becky searched until she found the smashed telephone receiver where it had come to rest at the base of one of the large potted plants. Handing it to Eve, who seized it happily and clutched it to her ear, she said, "Here dear, it's for you."

The front door opened and a harried deputy came into the building.

"You," Becky called. "Watch her."

The deputy crossed the wreckage of the room and looked quizzically at Eve.

"Is she OK?"

"She's just in shock. I gave her a sedative, but I don't want to leave her alone. Stay here. Don't go back outside."

"Thank you, ma'am!" the deputy said with relief.

Satisfied that Eve would be safe, Becky steeled herself for whatever she would have to face and marched down the hallway toward Burman's office.

Passing the mayor's door, she stopped for a moment and rapped sharply.

"Daniel," she called. "It's Becky O'Brien. You all right?"

The mayor's door slowly opened. An impeccably manicured hand appeared, followed by a face suitable for a movie star.

"Are they gone?" a rich baritone voice asked with more than a hint of timidity.

"Yes, Daniel, they're gone."

At this, West Hollywood's mayor, Daniel Eversleigh, straightened to his full height of six foot one and declared with false bravado, "Well! Storming the mayor's office! I've never heard of such a thing! I'll make certain Clive gets to the bottom of this! Tell him I want to see him. Right away!"

"Whatever you say, Daniel," Becky sighed.

The door slammed as Daniel Eversleigh returned to the depths of his office and to the perpetual state of blissful ignorance with which he governed the city.

Despite his well-known penchant for having absolutely no idea of what was going on around him, Daniel Eversleigh had managed to remain West Hollywood's mayor for the past three terms. This was in no small part due to the fact that, while he was incapable of making a decision on anything, he possessed a bright, affable manner and the ability to tell various supporters of opposing issues exactly what they most wanted to hear.

Daniel Eversleigh was an arresting man in his late fifties. He'd gained a few pounds since his days as a UCLA quarterback, but he still managed to keep a more or less svelte figure. The dashing bearing that he affected, with medium brown hair attractively gray at the temples, was faintly reminiscent of Errol Flynn, a resemblance Daniel was intelligent enough to exploit. For those voters who had no fondness for old Hollywood movies, Daniel reminded them of a favorite uncle, and Eversleigh was adept at cultivating an avuncular style. He was always the soul of gentility, pleasant yet with a slight air of distance that caused people to want his approval. In short, for the voters of West Hollywood, Daniel Eversleigh was a man they felt they could trust as mayor.

Eversleigh had developed the perfect formula for reelection: He abstained from every council vote and he always appeared at civic functions to congratulate whatever group was sponsoring it. In great demand for the openings of everything from supermarkets to pet hospitals, he freely granted civic commendations and plaques to community group leaders and to quite a few surprised private residents who had absolutely nothing to do with city politics. His office was covered with photographs of him holding cute little furry animals and kissing babies. Politically, he was neither a registered Democrat nor a Republican nor a Libertarian; thus, when speaking in front of any partisan group, he was always able to declare his imminent intentions of running out and joining the relevant party.

His civic accomplishments were dubious but never offensive; he took no risks. In response to the city's parking problem and the dissatisfaction with permit parking, he erected signs, alternately stating THIS IS A PERMIT PARKING NEIGHBORHOOD and THIS IS NOT A PARKING PERMIT NEIGHBORHOOD.

To show his support for the environmentalist concerns of his constituents, he issued a proclamation declaring West Hollywood a "Cruelty-Free Zone for Our Friends in the Plant Kingdom" and declared the first week in May as West Hollywood's "Be Kind to Palm Trees Week," personally tying the first green ribbon around the large king palm in front of City Hall as the kickoff to the arboreal celebration every year.

On his own initiative, startling the rest of the city council and causing Pamela Burman no end of grief, he managed to pass a municipal ordinance, designed to protect the environment, forbidding Styrofoam cups and plates from being sold anywhere within the city limits. The

BITE CLUB

proprietors of West Hollywood's fast-food restaurants were appalled at Eversleigh's audacity and immediately besieged Burman's office with telephone calls. After endless meetings at McDonald's, Burger King, and El Pollo Loco, Burman assuaged their outrage by convincing the chamber of commerce to extend short-term, low-interest loans, guaranteed by the city, to assist the restaurants in their conversion from Styrofoam to cardboard. Almost simultaneous with Burman's relief at a commercial disaster averted, Eversleigh, while being interviewed by the West Hollywood City Channel, announced proudly that his next proposed municipal ordinance would be one that would criminalize the sale of nonunion grapes "anywhere in our fair city, which is devoted to helping the underprivileged field-worker," a remark that caused Burman to throw up her hands in disgust as her phones began ringing off the hook with irate calls from the managers of West Hollywood's thirty or so supermarkets and produce stores.

For the city's gay and lesbian population, he denounced the Carl's Jr. at Santa Monica and La Brea as homophobic and ordered rainbow flags to be hung along Santa Monica Boulevard; for the Jewish population, he displayed a Star of David prominently in his office window overlooking the boulevard; for the Russian immigrants, he prevailed upon the Fine Arts Board to commission a large modern sculpture for the center of West Hollywood Park, depicting a woman wearing a babushka, stepping from a rowboat onto a multicolored map of America.

It logically followed that Eversleigh was affectionately known as "Uncle Dan" by his constituents and his fellow council-members. In fact, during his campaign every four years, life-size cardboard photographs of Eversleigh, complete with not-so-subtle MGM backgrounds, could be seen popping up in the front windows of many of the shops along Santa Monica Boulevard. The only text on the signs was the word VOTE!; he was known well enough that he needed no identification to ensure voter response.

Then again, it was well known in the community that Pamela Burman couldn't stand him. The citizens, wise enough to recognize how lost the city would be without Burman's skills as city manager, nevertheless took great joy in goading her slightly with every reelection of Eversleigh. The ratings on the first cable-televised city council meeting after every election climbed sharply as eager citizens tuned in to the West Hollywood City Channel to watch the sparks fly from Burman's gray hair.

Becky stood, nose within inches of Eversleigh's slammed door, and briefly debated opening it up and shouting "Boo!" into the office in hopes of reducing him, once again, to helpless terror. She reconsidered, however, figuring she was in enough trouble due to her inability to provide the Sheriff's Department with any clues to the identity of the murderer, and blew out an audible sigh of frustration before walking steadfastly down the hall to Pamela's office.

She knocked, opened the door without waiting for an answer— a cloud of fingerprint powder billowing out of the room—and went in.

"It's about time you showed up," said Clive as he knelt by Burman's prostrate form.

"My God, what happened to her?" Becky asked with concern.

"She finally calmed down enough to notice what's going on out there and fainted."

"Shit. I don't think I've got anything. Wait a sec." Becky took a small brown glass vial from her bag. Opening it, she thrust it under Burman's nose. Burman's face wrinkled with distaste and her eyes fluttered open.

"What the hell is that god-awful smell?" she demanded. "Goddamn it, Clive! I told you to keep the air on!"

"It's amyl," Becky replied, replacing the cap and tightening it.

"Poppers?" Burman said in disbelief. "You gave me poppers? At my age, you could give me a heart attack!"

"Look, Pamela," said Becky testily, "I don't carry smelling salts. One of the boys left it in the ladies' room at the morgue. You don't like it? You can just pass the hell out again. I had to sit in traffic all the way from the office and I am *not* in a good mood. Both of you can just cut the crap and let me do my job. Now, where's that fucking head?"

BITE CLUB

Clive and Burman both blinked in astonishment at Becky's uncharacteristic outburst. Clive pointed wordlessly.

Becky squatted by the sweater-covered lump and, after taking out her tape recorder and turning it on, put on her gloves. She gingerly removed the sweater and placed it in a large, clear plastic bag.

She whistled long and low and, taking a breath, began to speak into the recorder.

"September 29. Preliminary coroner's report. Dr. Rebecca O'Brien. City Hall."

"You're gonna do a protocol *here*?" Clive was aghast.

"I'm not sitting in traffic for an hour to drive him two blocks back to the office," Becky replied impatiently.

"I'm gonna throw up if she takes out a scalpel," Burman snarled.

"Or a Hershey bar," Clive agreed.

Becky ignored them, leaned back on her heels, and thought for a moment.

"The subject is male, Caucasian, late twenties. The head has been severed from the neck column just below the chin at about the seventh vertebra. The location of the rest of the body is currently unknown. There appears to be no bruising of the cranium or of the face. The head appears to have been..." Becky swallowed several times before continuing, "torn from the spinal column. There are no initial indications of any sharp instrument being used. The..." She stopped and turned off the recorder.

"What's wrong?"

Becky turned to Clive, sighing in disgust. "I'm gonna have to take this back to the lab after all. It's too strange. I want to run some tests and I don't have enough equipment here."

"No blood?" Clive inquired, cringing slightly.

Becky nodded.

"Did I hear you say *torn* from the neck?"

Becky nodded again. She turned to Burman. "You'd better have the city staff start raiding refrigerators. We're gonna need ice."

Two of the deputies rushed to comply as Burman turned pale at the coroner's words. Clive, as an African-American, couldn't quite match her pallor, but he gave it his best shot.

Burman's voice was quiet, scared. "What's going on?"

"I don't know," said Clive. "But it's really starting to get to me too. Can you stand to look at this for a minute?"

Burman apprehensively joined Clive as the three of them squatted on the floor next to the disembodied head.

"Are the photos done?" Becky asked. On Clive's affirmative nod she reached out and gently turned the grisly object so she could examine its other side.

"Do you notice anything weird?" asked Becky.

Burman looked at her and dryly commented, "You mean other than that the goddamn thing obviously didn't walk in here?"

Clive thought for a moment, then his eyes brightened with realization. "There's no trauma!"

"At least none we can see," Becky said. Burman looked confused.

"Heads just don't fall off bodies," Becky explained. "Something's got to take them off. You see here?" She pointed. "The edges are jagged. I can't be sure, but it doesn't look like the killer used any kind of knife or ax."

"Even with a knife, we're talking about someone who's *very* strong, aren't we?" Clive asked.

"That's right. But in this case it looks like it's been pulled, torn off."

"So?"

"There's no injury to the face or skull. You know how hard it is to do something like this? It's almost impossible without leaving some signs of what caused it. Obvious signs."

"You mean like paint from a car or something?" Burman asked.

"Right. Or windshield glass in the wound. But a car accident would have crushed the skull or at least damaged the vertebrae."

"What about some kind of heavy machinery?" Clive asked.

Becky sat back on her heels, tapping her teeth thoughtfully with the edge of her cassette recorder. "Maybe. But I'd still expect to see some trauma. A large animal might have done it. Something like a grizzly bear with a neatness fetish or something. A bear would have the strength, but again, the tear's too clean."

"Great! I can just imagine what Ed Larsen's gonna do with a press release about some fucking bear tearing off a head and wrapping it up like a frigging present." Burman fumed silently for a minute, thinking. "I got it," she said. "We'll tell 'em it *was* a car accident."

"Be reasonable, Pam," Clive said. "Becky just told you. No paint. No glass. Nada."

"Goddamn it, Clive!" Burman shouted. "The press doesn't have to know everything. Larsen doesn't give a shit about details if he's got a chance to rake me over the coals. We coulda found the front bumper of a 1963 Cadillac sticking out from between the fucking thing's front teeth for all he cares!"

"How are you gonna explain how it wound up in your office?" Becky asked irritably.

"I dunno!" Burman yelled, throwing her hands up into the air. "Maybe it *bounced* in!"

Becky ignored the city manager's hysterics and turned back to Clive. "Look, even if the victim's head had gotten caught in something somewhere and it was the body that was pulled off, we'd still have some signs on the skull, abraded skin, for example."

"All right, already! I give up!" Burman slumped into her chair. "So, you tell me. What's the answer?"

"Well," said Becky slowly, "don't quote me on this, but a human being, a very, very strong weight lifter maybe, like on the caliber of Superman, might, just might, be able to do this without a car, a machine, or a bear for that matter."

"With what then?" Burman asked, still not getting it.

Becky looked surprised that Pamela didn't understand. "That's what I've been trying to tell you. With his bare hands."

CHAPTER TWENTY

It was very late Friday night and Becky was frustrated. Her level of frustration could more or less be measured by the increase in her dietary consumption of sugars, animal fats, and heavy creams. Her office desk was littered with the remains of her most recent meal. The wrappers from two Fatburgers were crumpled up next to several empty bottles of Yoo-hoo. She'd also demolished two of the three chocolate cupcakes she'd bought in the Pavilions supermarket bakery. Considering biting into the sole surviving cupcake, she realized suddenly that she had no appetite for it. She swept the refuse into the wastebasket and carefully wrapped the cupcake in plastic, dropping it into her desk drawer to save for later. This done, she collapsed forward on her desk, head sunk into her arms in exhaustion.

She'd completed her preliminary autopsy report several hours earlier, while it was still daylight, only to have her worst fears confirmed; the victim's head had apparently been ripped from his body, quickly, by someone, or something, of enormous strength. In addition, from her analysis of what little blood remained in the cranium, she had discovered a series of unusual antibodies the likes of which she'd never seen before. She'd faxed the results of her preliminary blood tests to a friend at UCLA and was told that either she'd made a mistake or her samples had been contaminated.

She was also puzzled by the condition of the victim's mouth. Apparently with brute strength, every tooth had been removed from the skull. In some spots, the roof of the mouth had been severely lacerated and deeply gouged. Both the reason for and the mechanism of the mutilations remained a mystery.

The identity of the body also puzzled her. Without the teeth or the rest of the body, it would be difficult to determine. All she could say with certainty was that the victim had been male, young, attractive, and in reasonably good physical shape judging from the remains of the musculature in the neck. From the highlighted hair and the pierced left ear, she'd also be willing to bet a bucket of Popeyes fried chicken against a month of Jenny Craig that the young man had been gay: Very few straight men would wear a single pink triangle–shaped earring.

She'd tried to get Clive on the telephone at about four-thirty, but he was still involved in the aftermath of the City Hall riot, only having enough time to tell her that, thus far, there were no clear fingerprints on the package or its wrapping. Sheriff's deputies had made only one arrest, for lewd conduct, when one of the drag queens had squatted behind a bush next to the City Hall parking lot, lifting her skirt to answer a call of nature and relieving herself onto the boots of a deputy who had hidden in the bushes to sneak a cigarette while on duty.

Pamela Burman was, for once in her career, subdued and had refused to comment to the press—amazing the reporters by passing up what seemed the perfect opportunity to revile them. Daniel Eversleigh, however, had quickly taken the opportunity to call a press conference on the steps of City Hall, commending the rioters for their "citizens' involvement and concern in the face of the devastating crime wave that has recently swept our fair city." Even though the rioters had long since gone home and traffic had been clear for more than three hours, he'd urged the eleven reporters, the members of the Activists League still remaining in the parking lot, and a solitary puzzled homeless woman to "control their baser instincts and cease the wanton destruction of public property" and proceeded to pose for press photographs amid the wreckage of the reception area while tenderly holding a cocker spaniel.

Becky desperately wanted to talk to Chris, hoping he'd managed to come up with some ideas. She'd left two messages on his machine and was waiting for his call. She briefly debated stopping by his apartment and inviting him to dinner, but frankly she was too fatigued from the days' events to do anything but go home to her own bed.

Making a mental note to stop at Chris's first thing in the morning, she tidied up her desk, locked the office, and, exhausted, trudged out to her car.

◊ ◊ ◊

At about the same time Becky O'Brien reached home, Hercule Legrande arrived at Sylvia's apartment building in New York, accompanied by three limousines that discharged more than a dozen members of his pack. Sylvia was bewildered by the interminable introductions of children, grandchildren, uncles, aunts, nieces, nephews, and cousins. She already knew Hercule's immediate family, but could only fix in her mind the names of three or four others, wisely choosing to be able to identify at least the elders of the pack.

She'd asked two friends to accompany her to the meeting: Clarence Chou, a young Asian vampire who was a history professor at NYU, and a perky vampire named Sally Perkins who had been the motivating force behind her long-deceased husband's career as a British diplomat during the last century. She'd considered attending alone but knew that the werewolves would consider it a sign of weakness if she showed up without at least a small token "pack" of her own.

Thus, with three vampires and close to twenty wolves, the room was crowded. The bridge tables had been folded up and shoved against a far wall; the chairs, accustomed to the Slim-Fasted fannies of mesdames Goldberg, Horowitz, Greenspan, and Schwartz, now creaked alarmingly under the werewolves' heavier weight. The faint musky scent of so many lycanthropes in such close quarters was making Sylvia vaguely ill, and their constant shifting as they vainly tried to settle in served only to increase her discomfort. After much fidgeting, several of the younger members of the pack simply curled up on the floor, making the rest of the evening rather awkward at times as the vampires had to remember to keep stepping over them to avoid tripping.

The meeting started off on the wrong note. Without so much as a by-your-leave, Hercule granted his eldest son the honor of "marking territory" via a process known to anyone familiar with the habits of man's best friend.

"My God!" whispered Clarence to Sylvia. "What is he doing to the carpet?"

Sylvia blanched as she whispered back, "Please. I'm trying not to think about the cleaning bill," and she backed away from the activity to avoid having her Prada shoes irreparably spoiled.

Sylvia had taken extreme care in dressing for her company so as not to offend her highly sensitive guests. Lupine customs and mores were entirely too complicated for Sylvia's taste, but she nevertheless did her best. She wore a plain black silk floor-length dress that she'd purchased years ago, tried on once, instantly hated for its drabness, and shoved to the back of the closet. It had been designed by Coco Chanel herself and had cost her a small fortune.

The dress was open at the neck so that her throat would be bare; the rest of her body, from wrists to ankles, was demurely covered. She'd cautioned Sally and Clarence against wearing anything with a high collar; the werewolves would take a covered throat as a sign of defensiveness. And she told Sally to forget about sporting a short skirt, as was her custom; their guests would feel the sight of so much bare flesh was obscene. While the werewolves invariably went naked in the privacy of their dens, the easier to change forms, the nudity of others was considered indecent.

She'd even instructed Clarence to wear long sleeves, but when he showed up in a bright blue designer button-down shirt, she'd rushed out to purchase him a tan oxford. She explained that Hercule and others of his race shied away from bright colors as being garishly ostentatious and in poor taste. By the time she was finished with the dos and don'ts of werewolf etiquette, poor Clarence and Sally were totally confused and certain that, within two minutes of greeting their guests, they would commit some horrifying transgression that would haunt them for the next two or three centuries.

Sylvia took full advantage of the lupines' rather middle-class tendency to be easily impressed by displays of obvious wealth. She indulged her spleen with malicious glee by gracing herself with her best jewelry—some of it literally priceless. On a gold chain around her neck, she wore a five-carat teardrop-shaped diamond that had been given to her by Marie Antoinette. On one wrist she wore a stunning undocumented Faubourg bracelet set with gorgeous dark green emeralds; on the other was a cunningly crafted pink-gold serpent with a deep red ruby clutched in its jaw. Topping her look was a smart black cloche, held in place by a Victorian jet-and-diamond hat pin. Over her right breast she'd pinned a jeweled cameo porcelain brooch depicting a wolf baying at a ruby moon. It was with great regret that she decided to part with it, making it a gift to Hercule's wife, Lillian, in thanks for his agreement to meet.

Despite the gift, however, and despite Sylvia's having taken great pains to avoid offending anyone, the meeting was a disaster. What she hadn't counted on was the werewolves' insularity; since they were quite capable of taking care of themselves in isolation, they simply couldn't, or wouldn't, grasp the concept that they were part of a larger community that needed their help. Hercule was distantly polite throughout Sylvia's pleas. He listened attentively, but it was clear to all present that he had already made up his mind to let the vampires drown in their own blood, so to speak.

And to be quite honest, despite the seriousness of the occasion, Sylvia had difficulty concentrating sufficiently to summon up her most eloquent oratory style; there were simply too many distractions.

Jacques not only persisted in chewing on the furniture but also made a terrible nuisance of himself, delightedly running his claws up and down the walls of the recreation room, shredding the wallpaper. It had been specially designed and put up only six months before at a cost of $95 a square yard. Sylvia cringed at the thought of what replacing it would do to her condo assessment fees.

Several of the nieces were bored with the whole proceeding and amused themselves by grooming each other. As Hercule had strictly forbidden them to change form during the meeting, part of the gathering began to resemble a lesbian orgy as the young women alternately licked each other's hair or nipped gently at her neighbor's skin in search of fleas.

Jacques's mother finally corralled him by the scruff of the neck and deposited him at the foot of her chair, where he amused himself by digging into the carpet. Sylvia silently added the price of replacing the Berber carpet to her mental tally of the evening's mounting costs.

To Sylvia's initial relief, Jacques's father cuffed him roundly when he realized that his offspring seemed intent on destroying anything his eager little paws could come in contact with. But her relief turned to alarm as Jacques's mother objected strenuously to this treatment of her beloved pup. Soon, fangs bared and growling deeply in their throats, the two squared off to settle their differences in child rearing in traditional lupine fashion. The recreation room began to sound like a kennel during feeding time. Fortunately, in his one show of deference to the vampires' sensitivities, Hercule commanded them to stop before actual blood was shed.

Sylvia continued gamely onward, trying to make her point to Hercule, interrupted by a more or less steady stream of startled growls and pleas of "Excuse me" and "I'm terribly sorry" from Clarence and Sally as they moved around the crowded room, dispensing refreshments and treading on the tails of those who had arrived in lupine form.

In short, the meeting was a catastrophe. The werewolves remained unconvinced that the killings in Los Angeles could possibly have anything to do with them. And, in the unlikely event that they were affected in some way, they could take care of their own, thank you very kindly.

Several hours later the werewolves began to shuffle out as Sylvia sank, exhausted, into a chair to survey the final damage to the room. She'd managed to extract a reluctant promise from Hercule that he'd reconsider his position—if he were given irrefutable proof that humans were growing suspicious that they might be sharing the planet with several other intelligent species.

It would probably take a front-page article in the Times, thought Sylvia tiredly. *"Werewolf Stalks Mayor in Lincoln Center" or "Vampire Attack at the Met" might do it.*

The last to leave was Hercule's mate, Lillian. Sylvia had always liked her. A stout, plain woman, she possessed the habit of being addicted to gossip, rare in werewolves, and was remarkably talkative for a member of her race. Of all the guests, she had been the only one besides Hercule who had paid any attention to Sylvia's monologue, and at times Sylvia had almost sworn she'd seen expressions of concern and sympathy cross Lillian's frumpy features.

"My dear," said Lillian gently as she rested her hand briefly on Sylvia's bowed shoulders, "I cannot promise much. But I will speak to him." She knelt and briefly planted a kiss on both of Sylvia's cheeks in the French manner and quickly followed after her husband and family. She paused in the doorway and, with a shy backward glance, touched the brooch pinned to her blouse and added softly, "Thank you."

Well! thought Sylvia with surprise. *Perhaps something will come of this evening after all.*

CHAPTER TWENTY-ONE

As Barbra Streisand loudly bemoaned the loss of Nicky Arnstein from the CD player, and Barbara Stanwyck shrieked, "Why can't you just leave me alone?" from the television set, Troy considered that, all in all, his life was happy. As Troy and the talking pictures had been born within a decade or so of each other, his deep-seated love affair with Hollywood and the silver screen seemed almost inevitable. Now, more than sixty years later, he was proud of himself, figuring that his contribution in helping to convince Chris to relocate to the land that gave birth to Schwab's and the Brown Derby was not insubstantial. In short, Troy was blissfully happy. Now, if only he could think of some way to make Chris want to stay…

Troy's only regret was that the days of the musical movie extravaganzas he'd so loved in his youth were long gone. However, with the advent of videotape and DVD, Troy had amassed an impressive collection of Hollywood musicals and frequently spent his days sitting mesmerized in front of the TV screen, fantasizing that he was dancing with Fred Astaire or being crooned to by Gene Kelly.

Born in 1927 on a small farm just outside of the small town of Wetherby, nestled deep in the hills of South Carolina, Troy had been a

Depression baby. When he was six, his mother had taken him to the theater for the first time; the film was *42nd Street*. Troy had been entranced. From the instant the gold velvet curtain parted to reveal the huge screen, its white surface splashed with pink and blue spotlights, Troy had fallen in love with Hollywood. During the years that followed, on the rare occasions when he could afford to go see films, Troy could be found seated sixth row center at the Wetherby Palace Theatre, blissfully enraptured. At twelve, he'd begged his mother to take him to see *The Wizard of Oz* when it opened and doubled up on his chores for three weeks in anticipation of her promise to do so.

The movies provided his only escape from an otherwise dreary existence. His family was poor, as was most of the rest of the town. Shorter than any of his siblings and far prettier than a boy had any right to be, he was constantly the object of cruel practical jokes played upon him by his three older brothers, whose favorite game was to hog-tie him and leave him hidden in the hayloft of the barn overnight, cold, frightened, and hungry. His father barely tolerated him; Troy was never strong enough to do the heavier work around the farm. He was stricken with uncontrollable bouts of sneezing whenever the hay was mown; even cutting the sparse grass on the front lawn of the house reduced him to an attack of watery eyes and gasping for breath.

He couldn't help harvest the garden as the sight of a bug or worm reduced him to petrified hysterics; to this day, the thought of anything possessing more than four legs filled him with shudders of loathing. And, to be quite honest, he'd never been keen on four-legged animals either. The mere thought of being alone in the stall with Mabel, the gentle family cow who was three or four times Troy's size, put him into a state of terror. He even had difficulty with dogs and cats. A German shepherd had knocked him down once when he was a toddler and he was badly bruised; he'd been uncomfortable with anything larger than a Pomeranian ever since. As for cats, a nasty scratch from the farm's tabby, when Troy had once tried to get a closer look at a litter of kittens, put him off felines for good. In addition he was allergic to both dogs and cats.

BITE CLUB

Living on a farm, where everyone must pull his weight as a matter of survival, his father made the mistake of figuring that if his youngest son was no good with the livestock, maybe he could be trained with a more mechanical goal in mind. One day, when Troy was about twelve, Jeremiah Raleigh set him to painting the house. But after falling off the roof twice and covering himself with more paint than he'd been able to get onto the shingles, his father forbade him to ever touch a paintbrush again.

Mr. Raleigh bravely tried another tact. He carefully explained the use and purposes of each tool in his toolbox, certain that the look of intense concentration on Troy's face meant that some of the instruction was taking hold. But Troy's abilities with tools were even weaker than his skill with a paintbrush. His father set him to practice by pounding a dozen or so nails into a spare board and watched in chagrin as Troy managed to bend every one. They tried screws, but Troy's only talent seemed to be in stripping the threads. As for watching his son try to use a handsaw, Jeremiah's predominant emotion was shame.

After the oldest of his two sisters died suddenly of a summer chill, Troy's mother began to enlist his aid with the housekeeping. She quickly realized that unless she wanted her home to suffer the ravages of a fiery cataclysm, she needed to keep him away from the stove. If she wanted the few china heirlooms that she possessed to survive, she'd best not set him to dusting. In fact, the only thing he seemed to be able to do without causing a disaster was to help her with the dishes and mop the floors. On her forty-fifth birthday, however, she'd made an amazing discovery. Troy had invaded her ragbag and, with amazing adroitness, sewn her a beautiful set of new curtains for the kitchen windows. With a sigh of relief and the hope that her son was not a total walking disaster after all, she set him to work and he'd become invaluable, mending and repairing the family's clothing and reducing her workload.

Although she loved all of her children deeply, Charity Raleigh could never quite figure out what she and her husband had done wrong when it came to Troy. To their dying days, in 1949 and 1951, respectively, they were confused by their youngest son, who had an inexplicable penchant for trying on his sisters' crinolines and who was given to recurrent attacks of the vapors.

In 1940, Mr. Horace Grenham, the effete owner of Wetherby's sole dry-goods store, took pity on the increasingly attractive thirteen-year-old boy and offered him a job sweeping and dusting for a few dollars a week. At first content only to have the pleasure of surreptitious glances at the blond-haired youth as he performed his menial tasks, Grenham found that Troy's bright smile and affable sense of humor worked wonders with his female customers. He was also scrupulously honest, and Grenham began to place him behind the counter more and more frequently.

Grenham began to notice Troy's increasing gauntness as things became more financially desperate for his parents and his four remaining siblings. His initial physical admiration for the boy having become somewhat avuncular, Grenham made certain that the youngest Raleigh was well fed. His kindness transformed the formerly frail youth. In a matter of months, Troy grew several inches; for the first time in his life, he looked older than he was rather than younger. His shoulders broadened and his chest and arms became hard and muscled as a result of his stacking and carrying heavy bolts of cloth and large sacks of flour, sugar, and feed.

Grenham took silent pride in having the town's unanimously acclaimed handsomest young man as his number-one assistant. The single women in town began to spend more and more time in his store, flirting outrageously with the oblivious Troy, and sales continued to increase. Troy was given a series of small raises, the lion's portion of which was dutifully handed over to Jeremiah and Charity Raleigh, who had at last found some purpose in the existence of their strangest and most disconcertingly beautiful child.

In 1953, more than a decade after he went to work for Grenham, Troy's life was drastically and irrevocably changed by three events, all happening within several days of each other. The first was entirely unexpected: Horace Grenham died, passing away quietly in his sleep of heart failure. Troy's sorrow when his natural parents had passed on

BITE CLUB

a scant few years before had been mild compared to the almost debil-
itating grief he experienced at the loss of his surrogate father.

At the funeral, Troy was subjected to an even more severe emotional beating. Grenham's sister, a middle-aged bovine woman with
an equally bovine adult son, arrived from Mobile, Alabama, to
attend her late brother's interment, and even though she and her
brother had not spoken for more than twenty-five years, she
assumed ownership of the store. Meeting Troy at the graveside for
the first time, and accepting his offered handshake of condolence
with evident distaste, she loudly announced to all present that "this
nancy boy will continue working in my shop only over my dead
body" and fired him on the spot.

Returning home later after wandering in the rain for hours,
alone with his shock and grief, he was greeted at the door by his eldest brother, Jeremiah Jr., who informed him that he could not in
good conscience allow a pervert like Troy to continue living in a
house with his young nieces and nephews—especially since Troy
would no longer be able to contribute his fair share to the household
expenses. Troy's sister-in-law, teary eyed, had done him the favor of
packing his belongings, and two small suitcases and a large white
cloth bag sat lonesomely on the front porch, becoming steadily
drenched by the rain.

The next day saw a desolate Troy ensconced in one of the twelve
rooms of Wetherby's solitary hotel; the proprietors of both local
boarding houses had heard what was said at the funeral and refused
to allow him to stay. He grimly surveyed his meager savings and realized that he had, at best, two weeks before complete penury.

The Lord, however, works in mysterious ways.

Less than a week later, having exhausted what scant employment
opportunities Wetherby had to offer, Troy returned early one
evening to the hotel, head hanging low in abject despair. Passing
through the hotel's small lobby, he barely noticed the chestnut-
haired young man checking in and arguing with the ancient bellhop
about the difficulty of getting his luggage, an enormous trunk and
several smaller bags, up the stairs.

199

Sitting dejectedly at his table in the dining room later that evening, breakfast and dinner being included in the room rental, he looked up in response to a loudly cleared throat to behold the handsome young man standing beside his table.

"Hi," said the man. Troy felt an odd stirring in his chest as he met the youth's piercingly green eyes.

"Hi," he replied.

"My name is Christopher. Christopher Driscoll." The man smiled, showing blinding white teeth. "My friends call me Chris. I'm new in town. Just arrived tonight and, well…" he smiled again, shyly this time, "I'm afraid I don't know anyone here. Are you alone?"

Troy nodded, speechless, absorbed in the faint play of the light off the auburn highlights of the stranger's dark brown hair.

"May I join you? I'm not very hungry, but I could sure use the company." Without waiting for a response, he pulled out a chair and sat across from the startled Troy. He held out a hand in greeting. "Do you have a name?" he asked kindly.

"Troy. Raleigh." Troy took the offered palm in his own. "Pleased to meet…" Although Chris's hand was surprisingly cool, Troy felt a strange warmth traveling up from his right hand along his arm, down across his chest, and settling deep into the pit of his stomach.

"Do you live in town?" asked the stranger.

Tears welled up in Troy's eyes as the burden of the past week fell upon him with stunning force. His breath began to come in great heaving gulps as, panicked at the realization that he was about to embarrass himself in front of this attractive stranger, the dam broke and the sobs came.

Suddenly, Troy found himself crying desperately, supported by the surprising strength of the stranger's arms, face buried in the man's chest. The other occupants of the dining room looked on in various attitudes of disbelief, disgust, and shock, but the strange young man totally ignored them, soothing Troy's anguish with soft words and gently caressing his blond hair.

The two had remained together ever since, city after city, home after home, through good times and hard times, through bitter arguments and tender reconciliations, even through life and death.

Today, however, Troy's thoughts were far from Wetherby, South Carolina. He'd been looking forward to a double feature of *The Opposite Sex* and *On the Town,* an old favorite, passing the day away with Dolores Gray and friends. But upon returning from Hanna and Gustav's, Chris had spoiled his plans with snide comments about the deplorable state of Troy's housekeeping and his inability to find a clean shirt. Troy lamely argued that Chris had gone through more clean clothes in the week since he had arrived than the chorus of *No, No, Nanette,* but Chris was implacable, accusing Troy of a hefty contribution to the backlog of laundry with his irritating habit of trying on an outfit, wearing it for twenty minutes, and then tossing it into the hamper or onto the floor in favor of something more alluring. Realizing that Chris was under extreme tension, Troy felt he was trying to be cooperative in suggesting that Chris simply give him the credit cards to go shopping. After all, even in California the fashion designers persisted in launching a winter line.

Chris blew up and one of their rare fights ensued. Minutes later, after reducing Troy to tears, Chris stormed off to his bedroom, slamming and locking the door behind him. An hour afterward, however, Chris relented and apologized and the two had cuddled together in the coffin until Chris finally drifted off to sleep at around four-thirty.

Troy's condition required minimal sleep, so after two hours of snuggling with the catatonic Chris he'd risen slightly after daybreak and gone about the apartment collecting sheets, towels, and clothing, separating them into piles on the living room floor. Chris had always preferred that Troy do the laundry himself, eschewing the use of a dry cleaner, arguing that his shirts and trousers bore bloodstains too frequently to risk raising suspicions of foul play. So Chris had painstakingly shown him how to use vinegar, peroxide, and other household substances to remove blood from various types of fabrics; Troy was quite pleased with his acquired expertise and proud of his mastery of this odd process.

The telephone rang, shattering the early morning silence. Arms laden with dirty clothes, carefully balancing a large bottle of bleach atop the bundle, Troy ignored it and, leaving the door ajar behind him, left the apartment to go downstairs to try and find the laundry room.

Once there, he carefully piled the whites into one machine, the darks into another, and the dubious items into a third. He added detergent and bleach to all three loads, closed the lids, pushed the start button, and sat back and waited for the water to come.

It didn't.

He pushed the button again.

Nothing happened.

Confused, Troy scratched his head for a moment and then came up with a solution. Obviously, someone had simply forgotten to hook up the machines. Proud of his powers of deduction, he craned his neck in an effort to see behind the machines. But no, everything seemed to be just dandy.

He stood for a moment, frowning in thought. People did the laundry every day; surely there was something obvious he was missing. Dimly he remembered something about lint filters clogging; Chris had told him once that lint filters needed to be cleaned to prevent fires. He had absolutely no idea how the dryers could possibly be linked to the washing machines but, fire and water being connected in his mind by some inconceivably Troyesque thought process, he figured cleaning them couldn't hurt. The job was quickly done; still, no water.

He kicked the machines.

Nothing.

He kicked them again.

"What are you doing?"

A distinguished elderly gentleman in a bathrobe had entered the laundry room with his own pile of clothing, escaping Troy's notice.

"Hi!" Troy turned and smiled brightly.

"Hello," said the man. "Are we having problems, sugar?"

"I can't seem to get them to start," Troy said, airily waving at the washers.

BITE CLUB

"Let's see if I can help." The man put down his burden and went to examine the machine. "I'm Sheldon, by the way."

"Troy Raleigh."

Pushing the start button, Sheldon inquired, "You're the one that just moved into 113?" Troy nodded. "You have a roommate?" asked Sheldon, studiously nonchalant.

Troy noticed that Sheldon's attention seemed to be equally divided between the washing machine and Troy's partially bare midriff, alternately concealed and uncovered by the not-quite-long-enough purple T-shirt he'd chosen to wear.

"My lover, Chris," Troy said gently. After all, for his age, Sheldon was quite attractive.

"I see." Sheldon smiled, disappointment showing in his large brown eyes, and turned back to the machine. "Did you have a problem putting the quarters in? Sometimes they get stuck."

"Quarters?" Troy asked. "What quarters?"

Sheldon looked at him in amazement. "You got to put money in the machine. Haven't you ever done the wash before?"

"Well, yes," Troy said, feeling slightly foolish and not quite knowing why. "But we always had our own machine before. You mean you gotta *pay*?"

Sheldon smiled. "These belong to the building. How many loads you got?"

"Uh, three."

Sheldon examined the fistful of change he carried. "Sorry, sugar," he said, "I don't have enough to lend you. There's a mini-mart at the gas station down the block. They'll give you change."

"Thanks," said Troy as he moved toward the door.

"Uh, sugar?" Sheldon called.

"Yes?"

"Take dollar bills with you, OK?"

"Got five bucks right here," said Troy, patting the back pocket of his cutoff shorts. "Will that be enough?" he asked uncertainly.

"Should be," replied Sheldon, shaking his head in disbelief as Troy left the laundry room and skipped up the stairs and across the courtyard.

At the front door of the apartment building, Troy realized he'd left his keys in the apartment. He barely managed to grab the front gate before it swung shut behind him. Breathing a sigh of relief, he considered for a moment. Finally, he removed the pink hankie from his back pocket, tied it around the latch of the gate to keep it from locking shut, and flounced happily down the street toward the gas station.

CHAPTER TWENTY-TWO

roy returned to the apartment building less than ten minutes later, recovered the handkerchief, and with Sheldon's gracious help managed to get the machines started. Walking up the stairs to the apartment, inordinately pleased with his ability to overcome all obstacles thrown in his way by the trials and tribulations of modern life, he stopped short, aghast; the apartment door was swinging wide open. Cursing himself roundly for his stupidity, he bolted up the stairs and into the apartment. Bursting through the door, he was horrified to see Becky, grim-lipped and white-faced, sprawled out in one of the crimson armchairs. He glanced toward the bedroom and, with a low groan, noticed the door was more than slightly ajar.

Panicked, Troy stood motionless, stricken by a vision of his beloved Chris lying in his coffin, headless and with a blood-stained two-by-four sticking out of his chest. Instantly, Troy came to a decision. Although he'd never killed anyone before and Becky outweighed him by at least a hundred pounds, if she'd so much as laid a finger on his lover, Troy would kill her or die trying to.

But even though Troy was standing almost directly in front of her,

Becky didn't seem to see him. In fact, Troy discovered when he leaned cautiously forward to look into her face, Becky didn't seem to be capable of seeing anything. Her eyes had rolled back into her head until the whites were showing and her mouth hung slackly open, her ample bosom heaving as she gasped for breath.

Troy darted into the bedroom doorway and glanced inside. With a sigh of relief, he saw that the coffin lid was still closed and the room appeared placid. Had Becky tried to drive a hunk of baseboard through Chris's chest, he knew, the bedroom would have been subjected to a much more severe onslaught than the few piles of Troy's discarded clothes that were lying on the floor.

He came back out into the living room, relieved, and tried to force his mind to stop racing so he could deal with the problem of getting Becky out of the armchair and, hopefully as soon as possible thereafter, out of the apartment entirely. But from the looks of things, the coroner wasn't going to be going anywhere very quickly.

"Becky," he called softly. But there was no answer.

Puzzled, he approached her cautiously and waved his hand in front of her face. She didn't react. Slightly annoyed now, he gently slapped at her cheeks, but her only reaction was a soft groan as her eyeballs tried to retreat farther into her skull.

Dimly recalling something he'd read in a romance novel once, he went into the kitchen and filled a tumbler with cold water. He returned to the living room, dipped his fingers into the glass, and began to flick droplets of water onto Becky's face. When this provoked no response, he gave up with a snort of irritation and, allowing himself a small smile of sheer bitchiness, dashed the entire glass of water into Becky's face. The coroner coughed and her eyelids began to flutter. By the time she came to, her eyes finally focused, droplets of water dripping from the end of her nose, Troy had forced his features into a mask of concerned sympathy.

Becky opened her mouth to speak. Troy stood, desperately wondering how he was going to respond to whatever it was she was going to say. Fortunately, he was spared making any decision. Becky seemed to be unable to say anything intelligible. She just burbled and gagged for a minute, unable to catch her breath.

She looks, Troy thought with a shock of recognition, *just like the fat version of Goldie Hawn in* Death Becomes Her. *When they were dragging her away from the television set.* He snorted arrogantly to himself and patted his own flat little belly. *It's disgusting how some people let themselves go.*

Then, unable to resist, he grinned and leaned forward, twisting his face into a creepy leer, and whispered, "Boo."

Becky let out a strangled squawk and immediately passed out again.

"I've got to stop doing things like that!" Troy said aloud, irritated with himself this time.

He stood for a moment, thinking, when suddenly he was seized by an idea that was in his estimation nothing short of brilliant. He went back into the kitchen and opened the refrigerator. The pickings were rather lean, if typical. Although Troy's system needed nourishment on a regular basis, his heightened constitution enabled him to indulge himself in a diet that would have sent a normal human being straight to the Betty Ford Center. The refrigerator contained two bottles of Stoli, a six-pack of Evian water, a half gallon of margarita mix, a jar of maraschino cherries, and the remains of half a dozen McDonald's Happy Meals that Troy had purchased so that he could have the plastic toys inside. Tucked away neatly on the shelves lining the door was a selection of practically every condiment known to man, a bottle of Hershey's syrup, and a can of whipped cream he had picked up with the faint notion that, even though Chris couldn't indulge himself, the idea of whipped cream and sex in a coffin was kinky enough to be intriguing yet not quite warped enough to be considered truly depraved.

The yield of the freezer was similarly dismal. Aside from a few microwave dinners, there were only two items: a package of chicken breasts Troy had forgotten and left on the counter for almost two days and a lonely pint of Ben & Jerry's Rocky Road ice cream, Troy's favorite.

Sighing and telling himself that his noble sacrifice was just penance for having indulged himself by deliberately scaring Becky half to death, he pulled out the ice cream, the chocolate syrup, a spoon, and an exceedingly large ceramic bowl—scarlet, of course—and set to work. Five minutes later he had constructed an ice cream sundae which, he admitted modestly to himself, would do even Becky O'Brien justice.

Carrying the bowl back into the living room, having gotten almost as much whipped cream and chocolate sauce on himself as he'd managed to get into the bowl, he paused at the sink, debating with himself for a moment.

"If I have to give her my Rocky Road," he murmured aloud, "I think I'm entitled!"

So saying, he went back to the refrigerator and took one of the bottles of chilled Evian. Standing in front of Becky's chair once again, he unscrewed the plastic top and dumped the contents over her head. As she began to sputter into consciousness once again, Troy shoved the sundae under her nose.

Becky coughed again several times and her eyes unglazed for only a brief instant before they crossed as she tried to focus on the large scarlet object scarcely two inches from her face. Her nose twitched and, instinctively, she reached up and liberated the bowl from Troy. She grabbed the spoon and shoved a heaping load of ice cream into her mouth, swallowing it so quickly that Troy was miffed she hadn't taken time to savor his creation.

Troy was about to launch into a speech about the ingratitude of people who had just been waited on hand and foot, to the detriment of certain other people's supply of their favorite flavor, when Becky held up her hand, commanding silence. The two remained still for several moments, not speaking, merely looking at each other while Becky continued eating and finally managed to compose herself.

Finally, she spoke. "May I have a glass of water, please?"

"Another one?" Troy asked before he rushed to comply, bringing it to her in a red aluminum tumbler.

She grimaced at the color then sipped daintily, commenting absently, "Isn't it awfully...well, red in here?" Troy said nothing, merely watching her apprehensively as she continued sipping at the water. She looked up a moment later, surprised.

"I'm soaked!" she exclaimed.

"Well, I had to do something," Troy told her.

She continued alternately sipping the water and spooning ice cream into her mouth. A few minutes later, when the last smidgen of chocolate sauce had been consumed, she placed the bowl on the end table next to the empty Evian bottle, closed her eyes for a moment, and took a breath.

Opening her eyes, she fixed Troy with a remarkably level gaze and said, "I called first. There was no answer."

Troy nodded, afraid to speak. Becky was, after all, taking this quite well, he thought. She was still slightly pale, gripping the arms of the chair so tightly that the vinyl was going to rip any minute. And the dampness under her arms was obviously not a result of Troy's having drenched her, but the ice cream seemed to have done wonders.

"I hoped I could catch you at home. I thought maybe the two of you were still sleeping." She looked directly into Troy's eyes, steeled herself, and said very softly, "It looks like I was right."

"I can explain," Troy said desperately.

Becky stood. "Yes, I'm sure you can," she said primly. She walked over to the bedroom door and, with an obvious effort, forced herself to glance inside. "I guess I should have guessed," she commented rather distractedly. "I'm usually not this obtuse about things."

"Oh, that!" Troy began, forcing a light, airy tone and grasping at straws. "It's an antique. I'll admit it's strange, but Chris loves it so. I haven't got the heart to make him get rid of it." His tone became even more friendly, conspiratorial. "Actually," he confessed, "It gives me the willies, but—"

"I opened the lid." Becky still seemed to be struggling to speak coherently, but Troy had no intention of doing anything to help her out.

Desperate, Troy tried another tact. "Look, Becky," he said sternly with what he felt was just the proper touch of righteous outrage, "I don't ask about your sex life. Kindly keep your nose out of ours!"

She gave him a withering glare. "I am a doctor," she said. "I checked for a pulse." Her eyes went vacant again. "A pulse," she repeated, her voice slightly higher with tension. "I couldn't…find…a pulse." Now her tone was one of sheer disbelief.

"It happened last night." Troy was panicked. Maybe they could stage a quick funeral and return to Philadelphia for a fake burial. If Troy played his cards right, they could be out of Los Angeles before nightfall with the added benefit, in Troy's opinion, of having to sever their ties with Becky completely. Then again, in the event that there were delays, or if Becky insisted on an autopsy, or if Chris happened to wake up… Nevertheless, flawed as the plan was, Troy decided to go all out with it and worry about the details later.

"I was going to call a doctor, really I was." An artful, contrived tear came to his eye. He sniffed, making sure Becky noticed, and wiped it away. "I just wanted a few hours with him. Alone. To say goodbye." He collapsed dramatically into the chair Becky had vacated, throwing his arm across his eyes and sobbing with great realism. A moment later he peeked out and noted that Becky was unmoved. To add to his dismay, she seemed much steadier on her feet.

"When you're completely finished playing Camille…" she snapped, then suddenly burst out, "What do you think I am? A total moron?" She was practically screaming.

Frantically, Troy darted to the front door, slamming it closed.

"Will you puhl-e-e-eze keep your voice down!" he hissed. "There are some things you don't want the whole neighborhood to know!"

Becky began to giggle, quiet little giggles at first, giving way to louder and louder uncontrollable whoops of laughter. Shaking with mirth, she collapsed on the couch, clutching her sides. Troy struck an offended pose as she slowly regained her equilibrium, wiping tears from her eyes.

"I feel much better," she snorted, a few final chortles escaping

BITE CLUB

despite her attempt to stifle them. "Oh, God, what I wouldn't give for something sweet right now." She looked up pathetically.

"You ate all the ice cream," Troy told her, hoping that his tone would let her know how displeased he was by that fact. "What did you want? A catered spread from Sweet Lady Jane?"

"I don't suppose you'd have any…" she said hopefully and then stopped. "No, I guess you wouldn't, would you?" she finished wryly.

Troy gave up. Sinking to his knees before her, he begged, "Please, you won't do anything, will you? You can't tell anyone!"

Becky looked at him, surprised and slightly offended. "Why should I?"

"Jesus H. Christ! What the hell is going on out here?"

Troy's jaw dropped in horror as Chris appeared, nude, in the doorway to the bedroom.

Blinded and shielding his eyes from the sunlight streaming in through the dining room window he snapped, "Will you please close those infernal curtains?"

Troy sat frozen on the floor. Becky rose stiffly and silently and, moving to the windows, firmly pulled the shades closed.

"Now, if you don't mind, I'm going back to bed," Chris said irritably, rubbing his eyes with his fists. He turned, about to go back into the bedroom.

"You might at least say thank you," Becky murmured. She still stood facing the window, unable to bring herself to turn around and look at Chris.

Chris stiffened. Ever so slowly he turned and took two small steps into the living room. The tension was palpable.

"Becky!" he said brightly. "Why didn't you call?" He shot Troy a look of curious concern.

"She knows," said Troy helplessly.

Calmly but tentatively, almost in a singsong chant, Chris asked, "What do you mean, she knows?"

Troy began to cry, but this time the tears were real.

"What did you tell her?" Chris roared, serving only to increase the volume of water flowing from Troy's eyes.

211

"Knock it off!" Becky snapped, spinning around, her anger winning out over her fear. "*He* didn't tell me anything. I stopped by to tell *you* something. The door was open. I came in and nobody was here. So I went into the other room and saw…" The blood drained from her face again. "Well…you know."

Chris feigned embarrassment as best he could. "Look, I'm sorry. Some people are into leather, some are…"

"I tried that," Troy moaned petulantly through his tears. "She took a pulse, and probably a Breathalyzer test if I know her." He rose from his position on the floor and threw himself into Chris's arms, sobbing plaintively.

Over Troy's shoulder, Chris looked at Becky respectfully, eyes narrowed, measuring.

"I also tried the grieving widow act. She wouldn't go for it."

"Well, well, well." Chris put his hand on Troy's shoulder and kneaded the muscle gently. "I'm sorry I yelled, monkey."

Troy clutched at him even tighter. Chris hugged him back and kissed him gently on the forehead until he seemed to relax a bit. Gently moving Troy aside, he turned to Becky and asked conversationally, "So, what are we going to do about this…ah…situation?"

"I don't see that we should do anything, do you? I mean, I'm not in any danger, am I?"

She walked back to the vacant chair, her studied casual attitude betrayed by the action of grabbing onto the chair back to keep herself from falling into it. She finally managed to lower herself into the seat and clasped her hands tightly together, the whitened knuckles the only visible sign of tension.

"Danger?" Chris pondered her question, a grave expression on his face. "I hope not," he said finally. "But I guess that depends on you." He looked at her, an unvoiced question showing clearly on his face.

"Good," Becky said tersely. "Oh, I've got dozens of questions, and I'll expect answers to every one of them. But the murders started well before you got here. Even if they hadn't, I know you too well, or at least I thought I did. I can't imagine you doing something like that."

"No, you're right."

She smiled weakly. "I do think, though, that it's going to be tough to carry on an intelligent conversation with you right now." She indicated Chris's naked body. "Not that it wouldn't be fun to try," she added, an attempt at humor which predictably enough fell flat.

Chris blushed. "Excuse me for a minute." He disappeared into the bedroom.

"Imagine that," said Becky, as if she were unconscious of Troy's presence in the room. "Ten years I've wanted to see him like that, but I never thought... I had different circumstances in mind," she finished, blushing.

Troy glared at her. "Ten minutes ago you were catatonic," he said. "I'll thank you to remember that Chris's lover is the one responsible for making sure your carcass didn't just melt away into a puddle of mush on the floor."

"I appreciate that," Becky said so sincerely that Troy almost regretted, if not the first glass of water, at least the second.

Chris returned a moment later wrapped in his brown robe, forestalling any retort Troy could have made. "Do you mind?" he asked, indicating the bedroom door as he pulled it shut behind him. "I think I'd feel better about the conversation we're about to have if my, uh, bed weren't staring us in the face."

"Please," Becky said, relieved. "Seeing it once was more than enough."

Chris sat on the couch and arranged his robe around himself. "Where do we begin?"

"I'm so used to being politically correct around this town," Becky said with studied caution, desperately trying to keep her tone conversational. "Is *vampire* the correct term, or is it offensive? Or would you prefer something like, say, nutritionally challenged?"

"No, 'vampire' is accurate."

"And Troy...?"

Chris smiled affectionately at his mate, ruffling his curls as he hopped up onto the couch and snuggled next to him. "No, Troy is...something else entirely."

Becky grinned weakly. "People say that about him."

Troy sniffed indignantly. "I suppose this means I have to be nice to her from now on?"

Chris kissed him gently but otherwise ignored the comment. He turned back to Becky. "You're wet," he commented.

"I know," she said. "Do you want to fill me in, or do we play twenty questions?"

"Go ahead." Chris yawned. "You'll have to excuse me. I'm normally asleep at this hour."

"We'll get to that in a minute," Becky said dryly. She thought for a moment. "Just how old are you?" she ventured hesitantly.

"Let's just say I'm older than Olvera Street."

"Let's not," she snapped, slightly irritated at the evasion. "I told you I wanted answers."

"Why?" Chris asked, all wide-eyed innocence.

Becky was more than slightly angry now and let it show. "Listen to me, you smug bastard. If I'm right, and as of this morning, I'm sure I am, one of your relatives is going around killing people in my city and dropping their heads off on the city manager's desk."

"What?" Chris asked, alarmed.

"That's what I came over to tell you. We don't know whose it is yet, the head I mean, but the entire town's in an uproar. You promised to help me, and whatever the hell kind of ghoulie or ghost you may be, I'm gonna make you stick to your word. I need information and I need it pronto. I can't seem to get it from the killer, so I'm gonna get as much as I can from you. Got it?"

"Fair enough." Chris gathered his thoughts for a moment. He cleared his throat several times.

"When I was born," he began slowly, "King George III was sitting on the throne of England and people over here were beginning to get rather annoyed with him."

"It's why we never drink tea," Troy piped in.

Becky's eyes widened and her jaw dropped. She made a conscious effort to close it, but it just dropped again, so she sat gaping like a fish.

"Well, you wanted to know," Chris said defensively.

"But that means you're, uh…"

"Two hundred forty-three next month," Chris told her.

"Forty-five," Troy corrected.

Chris smiled and shrugged apologetically. "We didn't keep very good records in those days. I know the day but not the year. Sorry."

"But how….?" she trailed off.

"If you're asking how it happened, I'm afraid that's very personal and I won't go into it right now. It couldn't possibly have anything to do with your problem and the person who did it isn't here."

"Dead?"

"In a manner of speaking." A misty look entered Chris's eyes and he seemed to be thinking of something else for a moment.

Becky noticed a look of alarm on Troy's face and quickly changed lanes, bringing Chris back to the present. "What about Troy?"

At the mention of his name, Troy snuggled deeper into Chris's side as if to avoid unwanted attention.

"What about him?"

"You're avoiding the question. What is he?"

"Since the turn of the century, this past century that is, some of us would call Troy a 'renfield,' after Stoker's book."

"A name you should know is *not* politically correct," Troy announced snootily. "I find it extremely offensive being compared to a creature that eats…" he paused and shuddered with distaste, "bugs."

"He has a thing about insects," Chris explained. "Sort of a phobia."

Shaking his finger admonishingly at Becky, Troy continued, "If I ever hear that word come out of you, I will personally wash your mouth out with soap."

"Relax, monkey," said Chris, then explained further, "Troy doesn't have my strength and he'd be a lot easier to kill." He continued cautiously, "If anyone were inclined to try."

Becky waved the comment aside. "We've been through that. You're safe with me."

"I hope so," Chris said guardedly. "Well, let's see. He's not as sensitive to sunlight as I am, and he doesn't have my, ah, shall we say, dietary restrictions?"

"Karen Carpenter explained," Becky mused.

"Exactly." Chris couldn't help grinning again.

"Some of us, however," said Troy haughtily, "do not have problems entering peoples houses without an invitation."

"You're kidding?" Becky's curiosity was fully aroused. "What about mirrors?"

"They can be...disorienting."

"Crosses? Holy water?"

"Hail Mary, full of grace," Chris replied. "I can also recite kaddish if you like. I'm a Protestant, or at least I was. Church of England, actually. But I was also bar mitzvahed in 1917," he explained. "It's a long story."

"I'll bet. Garlic?"

"How should I know? I don't eat. I'm not fond of the smell on someone's breath, but I assume you aren't either."

"The stake through the heart?"

"Try it on yourself first and let me know how you feel."

"That's not an answer," Becky snapped.

"It's a sensitive subject," Chris retorted angrily.

Becky sighed. "Look, Chris, I'm not about to nail you with a piece of picket fence, if that's what you're worried about. But I've got some maniac out there who probably buys his bedroom furniture at the same mortuary you do. If I have to run him through with a hunk of palm tree to stop him, I will. *Capisce?* Now, back to business. Can you turn into a wolf? A bat?"

Troy collapsed in a fit of laughter. Even Chris chuckled.

"Pure nonsense," he said, then added, "It would be convenient, though, wouldn't it?" He grew serious for a moment. "Here, let me help you out." He began to tick items off, one by one, on his fingers. "One: I've crossed the Mississippi more times than I can count, although this is the first time I've been this far west, so the thing about running water is out. Two: Silver bullets are for werewolves."

"Werewolves?" Becky looked a little faint.

"Vile, smelly people," Troy put in.

Becky turned to look at him, unsure whether or not he was serious.

"Becky," Chris said warningly, regaining her attention, "you don't want to know. Trust me." Faced with her continued look of disbelief, he added grudgingly, "He's allergic."

"That has nothing to do with it!" Troy exclaimed, outraged that Chris should have exposed to Becky's view what Troy considered an extremely private failing.

"They tend to be very family oriented, if you know what I mean," Chris explained. "After all, they do live in packs."

"They don't approve of our lifestyle," Troy said haughtily.

"Your lifestyle?" Becky repeated.

Troy playfully slipped one hand inside the open neck of Chris's robe and stroked his bare chest. "We're both male," he explained.

"Stop it. No tickling while I'm trying to talk." He pushed Troy away gently. "They see themselves as the arbiters of morality in our world. Some of the younger ones are loosening up, though."

"Just tell me," Becky said faintly. "Do I have to worry about laying in an extra supply of Nair if I see a German shepherd during a full moon?"

"That's balderdash," Chris snorted. "It's genetic. Anyway, I think the nearest pack is somewhere out in Riverside."

"Where was I?" he continued. "Oh, yes! Three: As for demonic possession, I'm of the opinion that exorcisms are the Catholic Church's feeble contribution to bad performance art."

"I never met a demon I didn't like," Troy quipped.

"Cut it out, monkey. She'll think you're serious."

Troy began to devote undue attention to examining his cuticles, a wicked smirk on his face. "Well, what about that guy we met in Atlantic City a couple of years ago?"

"That was an incubus," Chris said sternly, "and I still haven't completely forgiven you for that. She'll think we're talking about horns, tails, and pitchforks. Can it."

Becky looked slightly dazed.

"Now the facts," Chris continued. "If someone were to cut my head off, I'd die. Same with fire. Anything that destroys the spinal column. That's why stakes are so effective. They usually fracture the spine."

Chris leaned back, crossing his arms behind his neck.

"So concludes your lesson in vampirism 101. Any questions, class?"

"Just one more thing," Becky said.

"Yes?" Chris was politely inquisitive.

"How do you, well, you know…ah…drink?"

Chris smiled broadly and leaned forward so that Becky could get a clear, unobstructed view. "Why, I've got fangs, of course!"

Becky O'Brien, doctor of medicine, forensic surgeon, pathologist and performer of hundreds of autopsies, simply and without making a sound, swooned.

◊ ◊ ◊

Chris and Troy sat looking silently at Becky's unconscious form.

"Is she dead?" Troy finally whispered.

"Good God, I hope not." Chris leaned forward and took the file folder containing the most recent autopsy report from the coffee table where Becky had dropped it. He opened it and began to read, commenting absently, "I'd forgotten how off-putting my dental work can be."

"Should we bring her round?"

"No, not just yet. She'll come to on her own in a few minutes."

"I just think it's kinda rude to leave her all spread out like that. I mean, she is a guest."

"If you must practice your 'hostess with the mostest' routine, just have a damp cloth for her when she comes out of it."

"Oh, shit!" Troy cried. "I forgot the wash!" He rushed out of the apartment, this time being certain to close the door behind him.

Chris read silently while Troy was gone. Occasionally he frowned, and once or twice he shook his head in dismay. Finally, he closed the file and placed it back on the table. He leaned back, head tilted as if he were staring at the ceiling, and closed his eyes to think.

Troy came tiptoeing in a few minutes later with a small armload of sodden cloth.

"Is she back yet?" he whispered.

"No," Chris replied, eyes still closed.

"I'm gonna hang these up to dry in the bathroom. Do you want me to make the bed?"

"No, I'll go back to sleep after Becky leaves." He opened his eyes to look at Troy. "Do me a favor? Could you stay in there for a while? I need time to talk to her alone." At Troy's look of dismayed disappointment, Chris kissed him consolingly and added, "You can eavesdrop if you want. Just don't come out for a bit, OK?"

Troy nodded, mollified, and left the room as Chris closed his eyes again and sank back into deep thought.

Several minutes passed, the silence broken only by the low murmur of the traffic on Harper. Becky groaned once, not loudly, and slowly came to.

"That's very alarming," she said hoarsely after a moment or two.

"What is?"

"You sitting there. Eyes closed. Not breathing."

Chris looked at her. "You'll get used to it," he promised.

She sighed. "I doubt it."

Chris took up the folder and tossed it into her lap. "I peeked while you were out," he said.

Becky blushed, her pudgy cheeks resembling red apples. "I'm sorry. I just didn't expect…" She stopped, flustered, and taking a deep breath continued as if paying Chris the sincerest of compliments, "Your teeth are very impressive."

"Two of them anyway," Chris chuckled. "The original tooth fairy, that's me! Well, now!" he continued, rubbing his thighs with his palms and clapping his hands sharply together. "Let's get down to business, shall we?"

Becky tried to look attentive.

"First, there's no doubt there's another one of us in town. I saw that right away from the stuff you showed me when we met at the Abbey the other night. We also know a couple of other things—I'll explain how later." He started to tick off the points on his fingers again, a habit Becky was beginning to find faintly annoying.

"One: The killer is male. Two: He's probably very good-looking. I'd guess he appears to be in his early twenties to mid thirties. Three: He's actually very old, certainly older than I am. Four: He's probably a little on the short side in height."

"Huh? How the heck do you know the guy's freaking *height?*"

"Easy. As you go further back in history, people get shorter and shorter. In my day, for example, I was considered to be fairly tall. Now, hush. Don't interrupt."

Chris physically ticked off the points on his fingers once again, his brow furrowed as he silently mouthed the salient facts he'd wanted to recite. He visibly brightened when he got to his pinkie.

"Ah, yes! Five: As far as we can tell so far, none of us know him, but we're still checking."

"None of us?" Becky began, and then asked tentatively, "How many of 'us' are there?"

"Quite a few," Chris replied. "I'm not going to tell you exactly who or where they are. I may be forced to trust you with my life. They'll have to make their own decisions about that if it's ever necessary. Think of it as being like coming out of the closet." He looked at her sternly. "I hope you'll respect that."

Becky nodded.

"There's a married couple who live near here. They owe me some favors." He smiled wryly. "They're Jewish. A friend and I helped them get away from the Nazis with something more than their lives. They're going to trace our records back and see if they can find any male vampires whose final fates weren't recorded. If the rest of us don't know him, there's a shot that he's still alive—a recluse or in hiding for some reason."

"Then we might be able to tell exactly who he is?"

"Probably not," Chris cautioned. "There have been several times in human history where your kind were more concerned with destroying my kind as a matter of principle than with bothering to keep track of who it was exactly they had killed."

Becky looked more than a little uncomfortable.

"Fortunately, the Catholic Church keeps scrupulous records of almost everything. We had someone at the Vatican for a while. He worked in the library there. So our records are more complete than if we had to start researching from scratch. We may even be able to get a description. That'll help if our killer's using another name."

"The Vatican?"

"Does that surprise you?" Chris asked. "I've known three vampire priests in my time. And one rabbi. In fact, one of the priests is still alive. He's a journalist now. Somewhere in Florida, I think."

"So, what can we expect?"

"A list of names. I'll send them off to my friend in New York. One of her hobbies is keeping track of our family tree, so to speak. She'll probably be able to narrow it down even more. Hopefully, we'll be able to tell who it is from that. And if I should happen to run into him around town, I'll know what he is right away, but he'll be able to tell what I am too. That is, if he doesn't know I'm here already."

"Then what?"

"That depends." Chris's brow furrowed with deep concern.

"On what?" Becky prompted.

"Ordinarily," Chris began slowly, "we'd deal with him ourselves. We call it 'putting someone down,' and I'm sorry to say that I've had more experience with it than most. But in this case, it may be more difficult."

"Why?"

"Your killer may have some very specific reasons for his recent actions."

"What are you talking about?"

"Did you read your own autopsy reports?"

"Of course I did," Becky snapped impatiently. "Stop asking me questions like I'm twelve. Get to the point."

"Sorry. I thought it was obvious." He motioned for her to pass him the file.

"Your last victim. The headless horseman. The head was intentionally delivered to City Hall. That's a pretty brazen thing to do."

"So?" she asked. "Most serial killers get overconfident at some point. They're convinced they can't be caught. That's usually when they make a mistake."

"This one won't make a mistake. That head he dropped off was a calculated challenge. I'll bet he's seen me already without my knowing it."

"What makes you say that?"

"That head on your city manager's desk was recently removed from the neck of a vampire. In fact, since it didn't disintegrate, I'd say he'd been newly made."

CHAPTER TWENTY-THREE

The Monday-night West Hollywood city council meeting proved, as usual, to be a debacle. After several hours of closed-session debate, the council had elected, over Pamela Burman's strenuously vocal objections, to proceed with the Halloween parade in slightly less than three weeks' time. Already, orange and black banners decorated Santa Monica Boulevard and signs were going up on telephone poles informing the community that parking would be prohibited on the main thoroughfare from dusk on Friday through the morning of Sunday, November 1.

Despite the murders, the chamber of commerce estimated that more than 150,000 people would flood West Hollywood's streets on Saturday night to watch the procession of costumed witches, ghosts, and bearded young men in ball gowns and high heels, showing off the fruits of their months of painstaking labor with sewing machines, staples, and glue. This year the chamber had managed to coordinate a series of carts, wagons, and stalls to sell food, drink, clothing, jewelry, and knickknacks to the gathered throngs along the median strip.

Pamela Burman had alternately spent her time reluctantly issuing orders in connection with the upcoming Halloween festivities and figuratively beating her head against the wall during fruitless meetings with Clive Anderson and Becky O'Brien.

She'd almost come to blows with Daniel Eversleigh. The idiot refused to listen to reason! It was typical of Eversleigh, Pam thought, to assume that since West Hollywood had momentarily withdrawn from the corpse-of-the-night club, the murderer had merely, in the words of Eversleigh, "gone away."

"Yeah, right," Burman had growled during the public portion of the meeting at West Hollywood Park Hall. "What'd he do, Daniel? Take a fucking trip to Tahiti?"

She'd stood up and slammed the council table as the attending reporters delightedly licked their pencils and readied their tape recorders and video cameras in preparation for a knock-down, drag-out fight between Burman and Eversleigh. The mayor stood in turn, one hand resting on the council table, the other thrust out, pointing accusingly at Burman. The pose was calculated to evoke one struck by Errol Flynn in a particularly dramatic moment from *Captain Blood*.

"What the hell's the matter with you?" Burman snapped. "You think a fucking serial killer gets two weeks' paid vacation?"

This prompted Eversleigh to launch into a fifteen-minute speech about the inappropriate use of foul language by city officials in front of the public and the media. He was a magnificent orator, his rich rounded tones carrying easily through the auditorium, his gestures expansive, dramatic, commanding. Burman slowly turned purple.

She was even more enraged by the fact that, although strong allusions were made as to the identity of "the perpetrator of public obscenity," Eversleigh never once mentioned Burman by name. She'd tried to interrupt several times, but Carlos, who was coincidentally subbing for the regular council staff person, had wisely pretended to trip over one of the many cables littering the floor between the council table and the audio system, thereby cutting off Burman's microphone.

Burman, realizing her mike was dead, had stormed off the stage and rooted about in the floor cables until she managed to reconnect herself. Then, in a burst of malicious spite, she pulled Eversleigh's plug. Clutching the connector firmly in hand, she remounted the steps to the stage and tapped her own microphone with one orange-lacquered nail.

"Is this on?" she demanded, and as Eversleigh attempted to shout her down, she leaned forward and yelled into the mike. "I said is this fucking thing on?"

The audience, including the assembled media, began to spontaneously applaud her. Their city manager was in rare form and they were certain this council meeting would go down in West Hollywood history. The three telephone booths in the hallway outside the council room were jammed as the spectators fought to call their friends, spouses, and neighbors with instructions to "Turn on City Channel! She's at it again and it's gonna be a good one!"

The rest of the four members of the city council, respectively (A) found fascinating moral and ethical implications in the suddenly intriguing minutes of last week's council meeting, (B) found fascinating moral and ethical implications in the suddenly intriguing patterns of the acoustic tiles on the ceiling, (C) wished fervently that certain other members of the municipal government could be convinced to take their next vacation in the company of the absent killer, and (D) found fascinating implications, neither moral nor ethical, in the intriguing bulge in the front of the slacks worn by the moderately attractive male reporter from the *Los Angeles Times*.

Burman continued, saying just loudly enough for the microphone to pick it up, "Why anyone would vote for a man who wanted to ban the Coppertone Baby as pornography, I'll never know." The audience cheered anew at this reference to one of Eversleigh's first failed attempts at municipal legislation.

Burman fixed the cheering crowd with an icily disgusted stare. "But looking at the other idiots gathered in this room," she continued, "I'd be willing to make a guess." Now the room was filled with good-natured boos and hisses. Burman was being true to form and the spectators were loving every minute of it.

"Can't you people see?" she shouted. "This lunatic is *still* out there! Do you have any idea what could happen if we don't cancel that goddamn parade?"

There were more boos from the homosexuals in the audience as the Halloween parade was generally considered a queer event and oft referred to as "Faggot Christmas" by the local gay and lesbian community.

"You all may not give a shit about your safety, but I do!" she snapped. The boos turned once again to cheers, which rose in volume as Burman spoke into the mike without meaning to. "We are the only goddamn city in the country with a peanut gallery at council meetings!"

Finally, the commotion died down and Burman went on, her tone fervent, pleading. "Look everyone," she said, "just give me one chance. One chance and I'd invite that murdering bastard over to my place for a one-on-one session. I'd let that son of a bitch know we don't tolerate that kind of crap in *my* town! Then I'd get in line to be the first to pull the goddamn switch on the fucking electric chair and fry the bastard!"

Shouts of "Way to go, Pam!" and "Let 'em have it!" rang through the auditorium.

"But I can't do that," she went on, her eyes filling with tears of anger. "And until someone can, our streets are not safe. We *must* cancel the parade. Don't you see the risk we're taking?"

"What risks?" This was from Edward Larsen of the *Gazette*. "National media coverage?"

"Oh, fuck the press," Pamela said, and as the reporters' pencils and pens suddenly increased their activity, she added wearily, "Don't forget to quote me on that one."

She turned back to Larsen. "Ed, I've known you for almost forty years. Couldn't stand you for almost thirty of 'em and barely tolerated you for the other ten. But I need your help. This town thrives on two industries: entertainment and tourism. You all know that. Since that moron porn producer opened his mouth about his lover's murder, hotel and restaurant grosses have dropped almost forty percent from last year."

BITE CLUB

"Why, Pam!" said Larsen from his seat in mock surprise. "You sound like the mayor in *Jaws* who wanted to hide the shark attacks from the summer swimmers."

"Cut the crap, you simpering bitch," Burman shot back as the audience began to raise a chant of "Pam-e-*la*, Pam-e-*la*!"

"You too!" she yelled, quieting the crowd. "Ed, if I wanted to hide this from the tourists, would I be trying to scratch Halloween? Come on. Try using what few brain cells God gave you." As she paused for thought, the room fell silent. "Ladies and gentlemen," she said, "I just don't know if we can withstand the effect of a murder being committed during Halloween weekend. If we *don't* catch this guy, and someone gets killed during the parade, do you think anyone's gonna show up for Gay Pride? How about Labor Day? The Street Festival? Maybe we could throw a free concert during Lesbian Visibility Week. The lesbians seem to be the only ones the killer's not interested in!"

"Neither am I!" shouted a male voice from the audience. There were some shocked gasps of outrage and not a few giggles.

Burman pointed toward the offender. "Clive? Get that asshole out of my council hall, will ya? I don't give a shit whether it's constitutional or not. Just do it."

Clive looked up from where he had been attempting to remain invisible at the foot of the stage.

"Uh, Pam?" he began, but she cut him off.

"And make sure you use a dyke cop to throw him out," she added. Once again cheers and whistles of approval filled the hall.

Clive reluctantly moved toward the offender, hoping he could diplomatically talk him into leaving quietly. As he approached, he noticed three or four rather muscular women moving in on the same target. They reached the heckler first, and Clive sighed in relief at not having to participate in the removal process. He quickened his pace and caught up with one of the women, whom he recognized, as the others escorted the man out through the door. Clive tapped her on the arm. "Gently, Darlene. OK?" he said.

The woman grinned. "We just want to give him a good scare. No violence. Scout's honor." She closed the door as she left.

The debate up on stage continued. Clive was later to reflect that the council meeting was a fitting beginning to an altogether miserable week.

On Wednesday, Clive had received the final FBI report detailing the habits of serial killers throughout the nation, but it was unhelpful. He had conjectured that the killer was a recent arrival to West Hollywood and hoped that the police of some other state might have some clues resulting from similar murders committed elsewhere. Nothing in the report confirmed his theory. The closest thing to the city's current problems had occurred in Georgia in 1937, and after four murders the killings had mysteriously ceased, never to resume.

The state reports from Sacramento were equally baffling. There had been a series of similar murders, sporadically spanning almost 150 years, suddenly ceasing around thirty years ago.

Clive's thought processes were beginning to meander down trails that he would prefer to remain unvisited. Disturbing memories from his Louisiana childhood were trying to surface, but Clive kept firmly pushing them back down. There were certain things which, for the purpose of his continued sanity as a rational man, he simply refused to think about.

Nevertheless, he'd been broad-minded enough to consult scores of experts in aberrant psychology and several specialists in the occult. Although all were most helpful in propounding theory after theory, none could offer any concrete course of action.

To add to his problems, the head that had been dropped at Burman's office had been accidentally left with the biological and infectious waste in Becky's lab. It was been carted off by the waste-disposal company and incinerated. Becky apologized shamefully and formally reprimanded her laboratory assistants, but the damage had been done.

Further complications arose on Thursday, when Clive's report to the city council included an admission that an autopsy file had mysteriously vanished. Becky assured him that it had probably only been misplaced and would be found in a matter of days. She had combed her office for it twice, but Clive had still been faced with the embarrassment of having to explain its absence to Eversleigh and the council. Amid murmurs of incompetence, Clive had bravely defended Becky and was relieved to report the fortuitous reappearance of the file on Friday morning. Unbeknownst to Clive, Becky had taken the time to quietly alter her report after first subtly checking to make sure that her friend at UCLA had not kept copies of her fax detailing the odd saliva samples.

Thursday was also the day when Becky managed to introduce Chris to both Burman and Clive under the guise of his being not only her closest friend from medical school but also the celebrated author of books dealing with the psychology of certain types of serial killers. At the meeting, Becky had watched, barely managing to disguise her amusement, as her two fellow public servants listened, disbelieving at first and then with growing interest, as Chris deftly pulled the proverbial wool over their eyes. He spoke intelligently and convincingly about hemoglobin and ferric deficiencies which, coupled with an aberrant psychosis and a latent schizophrenic disorder, could give rise to a homicidal mania based on infantile role-playing.

Burman and Clive listened, glassy-eyed, floored by the stream of technical jargon emanating from Chris and highly impressed with his seemingly endless store of knowledge. Even Becky was almost taken in at one point by the erudition of her friend and wondered if there were some aspects of psychology or medical knowledge, hitherto undiscovered by mortal man, that were known to the vampires. However, as Chris confessed to her later that evening, he'd simply been making it up as he went along.

Having listened carefully to Becky's reports of Clive's frustration with the other experts, Chris had carefully refrained from suggesting anything proactive. Thus, he was labeled a crackpot by Burman, albeit an interesting one, and Clive simply classified him as one more ivory-tower consultant.

But contrary to Clive's and Burman's opinions of him, Chris had been far from useless, even if his activities had yet to bear fruit. He'd called Hanna and Gustav's two friends in San Diego and Las Vegas and imposed upon them to try to locate and contact all known vampires on the West Coast. Barbara Rice, a young woman who'd been a slave prior to the American Civil War, panicked and fled to stay with friends in the Dominican Republic. Chris couldn't blame her. Though Barbara tried desperately to live unobtrusively and to remain innocuous, she'd had several bad experiences in the early 1960s. Having foolishly purchased a home in a white middle-class neighborhood in segregated Alabama, a series of run-ins with racist groups had finally forced her west to Las Vegas, causing her to abandon her home. Decades later she still hadn't recovered from the scars of her experiences, and the thought of discovery filled her with terror.

Maggie Trillum, however, was invaluable. A garrulous grandmotherly woman who still retained a slight British accent, she led a fairly solitary and exceedingly lonely life in San Diego, donating her time to various charities and desperately trying to fill her nights with constructive activity. She happily undertook the important duty of telephoning each of the people on Gustav's original list. Fortunately, every one of them was still living at their last reported addresses and each was cautioned to immediately report any newcomers to Sylvia in New York. Maggie took the opportunity to entertain them all with stories of her youth in India and excitedly made plans to exchange visits with several of her new friends.

The hunt for the rogue vampire continued as the net spread, the Halloween festivities grew nearer, the bodies that both Chris and Becky *knew* were accumulating refused to turn up, and the tension mounted.

CHAPTER TWENTY-FOUR

In New York, Sylvia had also had a busy week. The Manhattan vampire community was much more densely populated than any other and rivaled the vampires of Paris in their unending commitment to social intercourse. Sylvia, not one to remain long discouraged by her frustration with the werewolves, clearly remembered having helped to put down the vampires in Georgia and Paris; she wasn't looking forward to repeating the experience. She realized the increasing urgency of discovering the killer and put Clarence and Sally to work combing through records and tabulating the bits of information that were coming in from other species in Europe and Asia. Assisted by Gustav's research, the three of them managed not only to fill in some missing information in Sylvia's never-ending quest for the complete, ultimate vampire genealogy, but also to make some educated guesses and weed out an additional thirty-one names from their master list.

The rest of the community got busy on the telephones, calling old friends and acquaintances, some of whom they had not spoken to in lifetimes, in order to discover whether anyone had recently migrated to Los Angeles. No recent moves were reported, but for the first time in centuries members of the community from across the United States began to draw together, motivated by their rogue brother in California. Old acquaintances were renewed and new friendships formed.

Sylvia faxed the thirty-two remaining names to several older vampires she knew in Paris, Leningrad, Florence, Rome, London, and Hong Kong. The European community was mobilized and the hunt through history continued. Sylvia was saddened to note the fairly recent final passing of two old friends. But the list was further reduced to eighteen, and she and Chris both agreed they were getting closer to the killer's identity.

Finally, early Tuesday evening, Sylvia received a call from her old friend Max Ashcroft, a florid, pompous vampire born in Shakespeare's time and currently living again in England.

"Sylvia, old girl! Max here. Terribly sorry I haven't gotten back to you sooner, but I was on a brief tour. Chekhov, you know. Delightful notices. I must send them along to you. No matinees, you understand." And Max bulldozed on, regaling his friend with so many extraneous details of his magnificent performance in *Uncle Vanya* that Sylvia resolved never to see the play again.

After repeated tries, she was finally able to interrupt. "Max, darling, your play sounds fascinating and I'd adore hearing all about it. But I really do have to get back to this rogue thing. If you'd be a dear and come to the point...?" she suggested gently.

"The point?" Max said, confused, and then his tone brightened. "Ah, yes! The point!" He cleared his throat dramatically.

"I say," he said finally, "Have you thought about trying to find Katrine?"

"Katrine?" Sylvia's interest was piqued. The only person named Katrine she could think of was a legendary ancient vampiress, rumored to be still living in the ruins of a probably mythic castle somewhere in Hungary.

"Hasn't she been dead for years?" Sylvia asked cautiously, hardly daring to hope that Max had stumbled upon a previously unknown source of information.

afেিয

"Dead?" Max huffed. "Certainly not. At least not before the Revolution. Now, let me see…"

"Max, dear?"

"Wait a minute. I'm thinking…"

"Which revolution?"

"Why, in the Russias, of course! That's it! Must've been aught-eight or so."

"Did you know her?" asked Sylvia eagerly.

"Heavens no!" was Max's reply. "If the legends are true, we'd have to be much older than we are to have known *her*! Although," Max said with a chuckle, "I understand she was quite the thing in her day."

"Max." Sylvia was carefully patient. "What happened in aught-eight?"

"Someone saw her: a fellow thespian. Playing in Marlowe, I believe. She didn't see him, but I trust his word implicitly. Fellow did a marvelous Laertes in Stockholm in thirty-eight. Truly remarkable."

"Can you find her?" she asked eagerly.

"I can surely try. I'm booked on the eight-thirty in the A.M.—if you can believe it—out of Heathrow. Landing in Budapest late afternoon, God help me. I'll call you from there. That is if I can get a trunk call through on those bloody commie lines. Ta!" And, so saying, he hung up, leaving Sylvia holding the receiver in confusion.

Max arrived in Hungary as scheduled and spent the next three nights tramping about the countryside, cautiously interviewing peasants and baffling everyone he spoke to. Alive at a time when Britain ruled the world, Max was of the belief that since the queen spoke English *everyone* ought to. He took up residence in a small country inn where the owner, more amused than frustrated by Max's inability to communicate, took pity upon him and presented him with a battered Magyar-English dictionary. It helped, but not much. Fortunately, Max's genial affability caused most of the villagers to go out of their way to try to figure out what the Englishman wanted. Max's continued butchery of the language proved to be only a minor problem.

The *real* problem was his hobby: photography. Max was an inveterate shutterbug and looked upon his visit to Hungary as an opportunity not to be squandered. He shot several dozen rolls of film to capture what he informed the innkeeper was "the local color." Unfortunately for the other guests at the inn—not to mention the innkeeper's family—Max had never entered the digital age. He insisted on developing his photos of ruined castles and little scenarios of rustic life himself. By the end of his first night's stay, the entire premises reeked of developing fluid and toner, and Max was about to be tossed out into the elements.

Unfortunately, Max had never practiced the subtle manipulation of mortal minds, an ability possessed by many of his race, and lacked the talent. Thus, he was forced to resort to bribes to keep his room, the chief of which was providing the innkeeper with an entire roll of pictures of his wife.

"You will photograph her very sexy, yes?" the innkeeper insisted.

So Max spent four hours with his camera, a very large Hungarian woman, and a trunk of "lingerie" that would have put Victoria's Secret into immediate bankruptcy. Max considered it his penance for causing the smell.

On the third night, Max met a young gypsy lass who succumbed to his infectious charm and was able to steer him in the direction of an ancient crumbling chateau. The young lady proudly recited the local legend of the "White Lady" who was rumored to live there. When all the extraneous hyperbole was filtered out of the girl's description, Max was fairly certain he'd reached his goal.

The "White Lady" was indeed Katrine. Having retreated from the world in the early part of the sixteenth century, convinced she was one of the sole remaining vampires on earth, Katrine had carved a niche for herself with the help of the inhabitants of the small village near her home. She soon realized that country peasants would be more likely to stumble onto her vampirism than town folk. Thus, she used an artful bit of misdirection and set herself up as a reclusive wise woman. Rumors of "witch" trickled through the area. But Katrine had sensibly chosen a locale far enough out of the church's reach so that she would be reasonably safe. Besides, except for burning at the stake—generally the church's last resort—she figured she'd be impervious to most of the more popular witch-hunting techniques.

For centuries, she had provided the villagers with herbal remedies and potions. And if every few weeks one of her customers awoke slightly fatigued, a bit anemic, and with the details of the previous evening a little fuzzy, no one was the wiser. Her stock-in-trade was mostly benevolent; she refused to deal in curses. And more often than not her philters were naught but water flavored with bitter herbs—accompanied by a healthy dose of common sense and advice to the lovelorn.

Though uncivilized, the locals were far from stupid. As the years passed, many of them guessed her secret, especially after the twentieth century dawned. But by that time Katrine had become such an integral part of local life that few bore her any ill will. In fact, the villagers had become fiercely proud of her and even more fiercely protective of what they considered to be their very own pet vampire.

Katrine was delighted to once again establish communication with her own kind. Fortunately, she and Max both spoke German and French, and although their respective accents—especially in the latter tongue—made it difficult for them to understand each other at first, they were soon conversing like old friends.

Katrine was able to confirm some of Sylvia's deletions from the list and added five more of her own. She also provided verbal descriptions of an even half dozen of the remainder as she'd either known them personally in her youth or had known of them by reputation. In addition, Katrine's most prized possessions were a series of centuries-old oil paintings of various vampire acquaintances she had painted herself, frequently from memory.

Confronted with Katrine's fascination with his camera, Max spent almost a full night showing off, snapping and developing photo after photo of Katrine—none of which came out clearly—the chateau, the surrounding countryside, and the paintings. It was on Sunday, a full twenty-four hours after he and Katrine had first met, that Max, slapping himself for his absentmindedness, finally remembered to try and get a call through to Sylvia to share his success.

Unfortunately, the concept of a telephone was as alien to Katrine as it was to the surrounding village, the villagers having abandoned most forms of technological progress at about the same time that Katrine began her own seclusion. Borrowing a small oxcart, the two set off for a village several hours to the south where Max remembered seeing a single set of telephone wires two days earlier. Due to the incessant photo opportunities presented by their scenic surroundings, however, the journey, which should have taken a little over three hours, took almost eight. The ancient trunk lines and the necessity of gratifying Katrine's intense curiosity as to how he could speak to someone thousands of leagues away occasioned even further delay. Finally, however, he was able to get through to New York.

Sylvia was delighted at Max's success in finding Katrine and immediately extended to her an invitation to visit Manhattan. Katrine, who had only vaguely heard about the discovery of the New World, leapt at the chance to see it. Escorted by Max, she arrived in New York two days later, marveling at man's ability to travel by air in what she persisted in calling "a giant metal casket with wings." She quickly got over her culture shock at being thrust into the twenty-first century. At first slightly frightened, her fear quickly gave way to a childlike fascination with modern man's ingenuity.

On her first night in town, Sylvia took the pixielike woman shopping for clothing as Katrine's wardrobe was, to say the least, several hundred years out of style. Katrine was entranced at her ability to purchase clothing without having to hire seamstresses to make it. She became almost instantly addicted to Bergdorf Goodman and Barneys, and became slightly crazed upon being introduced to the concept of credit cards. Sylvia amusedly indulged her in gratitude for her help, and tens of thousands of dollars in new dresses, skirts, and blouses were the result. Fortunately, Katrine refused to wear pants, which she considered blasphemous, and Sylvia breathed a sigh of relief at not having to add another five or six thousand dollars to her American Express bill.

Unfortunately, they made the mistake of walking past Tiffany & Co. before retiring for the evening. Sylvia finally drew the line upon seeing the expression of unadulterated lust cross Katrine's features as she pressed her nose against the glass, seeking a closer view of the luscious jewels displayed in the window. It took twenty minutes of attempted persuasion and, finally, the combined strength of both Sylvia and Max to drag her away.

Sylvia faxed the thirteen remaining names to Chris along with copies of six of the photographs Max had taken and Katrine's descriptions of some of the others she had known but had never gotten around to painting. At first Chris was distressed that the list of possible suspects numbered thirteen. However, with the photos to assist them, he and Troy quickly managed to disqualify five of the thirteen as being either the wrong sex or appearing too old or too ugly to be attractive by modern standards.

"My God!" Troy had exclaimed upon seeing the photograph of one particular gentleman. "This guy has a face that looks like it should be served with a side of salsa!" He passed the photograph to Chris. "Maybe his nose caught fire and someone tried to put it out with a rake," Troy giggled.

"You know, monkey," Chris said, kissing him on the forehead so as to mute the force of his reproach. "Not everyone was lucky enough to be born as pretty as you."

"I'm not pretty," Troy quipped. "I'm *beautiful*." He stood and paraded across the room, one arm outstretched in front of himself in a parody of a Ziegfeld showgirl.

"Nevertheless," Chris scolded, "you should be thankful you're blessed and not make fun of others."

"You sound like my grandmother," Troy said with mild distaste.

"I'm serious. It's not nice."

"I know," Troy said with a sigh of sorrow. "But what can I do?" He threw himself onto the couch, arm covering his eyes, a veritable Bernhardt. "One day God will have someone pour acid on my face to teach me humility. Then where will I be?"

Chris couldn't help grinning at his lover's dramatics. "Oh, hush up and take a look at this one."

A moment later, Troy went into gales of laughter as Chris presented him with a photo of a painting depicting an extremely corpulent, luxuriously mustached and bearded vampire, lost since Attila's time. The image of this pompous-looking gentleman attempting to pick up the unfortunate Charlie Copperman after dancing at Rage proved too much for him and, over the next several days, he developed the annoying habit of periodically bursting into fits of giggles at the thought.

Thus the final count was eight. Eight vampires, some or all of whom could have been dead for centuries. Although Chris acknowledged that their records were far from complete, he thought it very unlikely that a vampire had been made at any time in recorded history that one of them hadn't known.

"One of these is our guy," Chris told Troy. "I'm almost certain of it."

"But which one?"

"That," Chris sighed, "is the million-dollar question."

"And even if we knew for certain which one it is," Troy asked, "how are we gonna track him down?"

"As to that question, monkey," Chris said with a sigh, "I have no idea."

CHAPTER TWENTY-FIVE

With Halloween less than two weeks away, Chris and Troy spent every waking moment out on the streets and in the bars, shops, and restaurants of Boys' Town, hoping to catch a glimpse of the rogue vampire. Although they had Katrine's descriptions and photographs of the paintings to help them, what they didn't have was luck. Night after night they continued their search until even Troy's exuberance had dimmed.

Back at City Hall, the current theory was that the murderer was suffering from a bizarre vampire fixation, and the hope was that he could be caught if law enforcement entered his psychology. At Becky's urging, Clive had finally broken down and enlisted the help of the Los Angeles Police Department, who reluctantly assigned two officers to patrol the Hollywood Forever Cemetery on Melrose Avenue between dusk and dawn. On his own initiative, and feeling rather foolish, Clive contacted a local blood bank and pleaded with them to recheck their inventory. Nothing was missing.

Becky made the rounds of the city's four funeral parlors, asking the directors if they might have sold any coffins outside the usual course of business. One, an elderly Jewish man of Russian ancestry, was visibly amused and assured her he was quite certain that all of his recent clients had been quite dead. Another huffily informed her that his establishment was not in the habit of selling caskets to private parties as "packaged goods."

Desperate for ideas, Becky ordered Ty and Sara to contact every interior designer who lived in or had a shop within the city, hoping one would remember a client with rather odd tastes in decor. They enlisted the help of the manager of the Pacific Design Center, a glass two-building complex of designer showrooms, known to the residents as "the blue whale" due to its distinctive color and enormous size. No one had anything unusual to report in the way of sales of large boxes or trunks suitable for the hiding of a body.

On a hunch, she telephoned the three local sex shops. Although the owner of one admitted that he did, in fact, carry coffins in his catalogue, it was an expensive item and the only one purchased in recent memory had been shipped to a heterosexual state senator from Wisconsin.

Becky even went so far as to visit the Silver Screen Costume Museum on Hollywood Boulevard and managed to get a look at the original coffin from Bela Lugosi's *Dracula*. It was empty.

When she reported on her ingenuity to Chris, he simply snorted in disgust and said, "I've seen it. No self-respecting vampire would ever sleep in that thing! It's got dry rot!"

"And the lining's torn," Troy added helpfully.

Chris urged her not to forget the churches and synagogues; if the culprit was as old as they suspected, he might be counting on a vampire's supposed inability to enter holy ground to protect his hiding place. And so she spent one morning, along with four deputies, prowling around the innards of West Hollywood's religious buildings, accomplishing nothing other than seriously injuring the rector of the West Hollywood Community Church on San Vicente Boulevard.

Two of the deputies exited the basement boiler room and inadvertently knocked against a stacked pile of old wooden school desks that were illegally stored. The desks collapsed with a crash, and the two men, anxious to be free of the dark, dank room, decided between themselves not to mention the incident and tiptoed quietly upstairs, pretending nothing was amiss.

Unbeknownst to the two officers, however, the rector had followed them downstairs to the basement, prepared to offer his assistance in the search, and became distracted by his discovery of a pile of discarded hymnals for which he'd been searching for some time. Arms laden with musty old books, the rector reached the door just in time to greet the leg of one of the falling chairs with the side of his head. As he passed silently into unconsciousness, he dimly heard the ominous click of the lock on the basement door as the deputies locked it behind them.

Awakening an hour or so later, confused and disoriented, the rector stumbled around in the dark, not quite able to remember where he was. Reduced to speechless terror as a result of imagined noises in the dark, he barked his shins painfully several times on the scattered furniture and finally tripped over a cluster of abandoned paint cans that had been stacked near the boiler. The lids of two of the cans popped free, and within ten minutes the rector was greeted by a leaping flame as the fumes, ignited by the open fire of the boiler, began to provide him with light.

He began pounding frantically on the basement door with a splintered chair leg, dangerously close to a heart attack. Fortunately, the janitor heard his screams for help at about the same time as the antiquated sprinkler system in the basement went off. Fred Delaney and his crew of firemen showed up in minutes, rescuing the unfortunate clergyman and depositing him into an ambulance. As the paramedics made their final preparations for rushing the rector off to Cedars-Sinai, Delaney took the opportunity to slip more than $2,000 worth of citations for illegal storage of combustible materials into the pocket of the hyperventilating man's cassock.

Happily, the rector survived his ordeal with few aftereffects, and the next day he sued the city. The city manager, predictably, hit the roof and threatened to hold Clive personally responsible for the outrage, vowing to make his life even more miserable for the next several weeks than it already was.

Burman was convinced to accept the "Dracula Complex" theory for lack of anything better. She alternately begged and bullied the various city council members until they passed a resolution authorizing Clive to conduct searches of the basements of all city buildings, reasoning that the lunatic, if his delusions held true, might have holed up in one of them during daytime hours. Ed Larsen gleefully picked up on Burman's resolution, and soon the *Gay Gazette* was running the story, complete with a full-page, full-color cartoon of Pamela dressed in a gold-and-blue polka-dot gown and bright green track shoes, holding a slavering, red-eyed monster at bay with a pink umbrella as a terrified city council, all carrying dogs and pooper-scoopers, hid behind City Hall in the background. *Gazette* sales skyrocketed, the murderer was redubbed the "Dracula Killer," and the city went into a quiet panic. Burman was less than amused.

The Coalition for Economic Survival, a local renters' rights group, sent a delegation to Daniel Eversleigh demanding that sheriff's deputies search the basements and storage areas of their apartment buildings to save them from the hideous beast who undoubtedly lurked within. As CES formed the single largest bloc of voters in the city, Eversleigh hastened to comply with their wishes and Clive Anderson was immediately summoned to the mayor's office and ordered to carry out this detail.

The debate on the cancellation of the Halloween parade continued; Burman was something of a bulldog on the issue. Nevertheless, the city council refused to be swayed by her arguments, bowing instead to pressure from West Hollywood's business community to permit the festivities to go on as planned.

Finally, on the Thursday evening just before Halloween, something was found.

◊ ◊ ◊

The West Hollywood Prop-a-teria was a small two-story gray building located on the west side of Fairfax Avenue between Willoughby and Santa Monica. Designed by a man who had been the art director on several of the old Universal horror films, the building was a well-

BITE CLUB

known West Hollywood landmark, easily recognized by the two imposing granite gargoyles mounted on either side of the front door. Run by a pair of older gentlemen named Biffy and Brucie, retired set dressers who were obsessed with movie memorabilia, a large part of the annual income of the business was earned during the months just prior to Halloween.

At about six-thirty that evening, working late, Biffy had gone into one of the storerooms in the basement to retrieve a just-remembered set of ancient candelabrum from *The Buccaneer,* which he felt were an absolute must for the finishing touches to the ambiance of Mrs. Beidersheim's very exclusive Halloween costume party to be held on Saturday night. Eagerly counting the additional income from the outrageous charges the twelve candelabra would warrant, Biffy failed to notice that the storeroom door, normally kept locked, had been opened.

All thoughts of Mrs. Beidersheim's nice fat checks vanished, however, as Biffy entered the room and noticed that not only had the inventory been shifted around but two of the candelabra showed signs of having been recently used. Not having been in the storeroom since just after last Halloween, Biffy was first puzzled by the half-melted candles and the matchbook from a restaurant that—he knew for a fact since he and Brucie had celebrated their fortieth anniversary at the restaurant's opening in late August—had only been open for two months.

Holding the matchbook in one hand and a used candle in the other, Biffy's realization was swift—a bloodcurdling scream the result. Brucie came running down the stairs to find the unconscious Biffy, sprawled artistically on the storeroom floor, having passed out from shock.

Less dramatically inclined than his mate, and much more conscious of his own instinct for self-preservation, Brucie immediately sized up the situation and, in a burst of frantic terror, ran screaming up the stairs and out of the shop. Fortunately for Brucie, moments later he saw two deputies from the West Hollywood bicycle patrol peddling down the boulevard. Running down the street after them as

243

fast as his varicose veins would allow, he drew their attention with his shrieks of anguished terror and practically castrated one of the unfortunate young deputies as he bodily pulled him from his bicycle and began to haul him back up the street to the shop. Clive was immediately summoned. Stopping only to order his secretary to call Burman and Becky and tell them to meet him at the Prop-a-teria, he dashed out to his car and raced down the boulevard to Fairfax, nearly killing a dozen pedestrians.

Entering the basement, accompanied by Brucie and the two deputies, Clive ignored the still prostrate Biffy, his attention immediately drawn to the coffin in the corner. The casket was partially hidden by a pile of half-rotted fabric draped across its lid, and Clive was faced with the startling possibility that, at last, the killer's lair had been found.

He ordered one of the deputies to remove the two men from the basement. Biffy had recovered and the two were now wrapped in each other's arms, Biffy clutching Brucie and Brucie clutching Biffy, alternatively moaning quietly and whimpering loudly.

Drawing his gun and trying to concentrate over the noise made by the two terrified civilians in the hallway, Clive motioned for the remaining deputy to cover him. He moved toward the coffin and used an old wooden walking stick that he found leaning against the wall to sweep the curtains and costumes from the casket's lid. He crouched next to it, carefully positioning the end of the walking stick underneath the lid's slight overhang. Then, using the stick as a lever, with a mighty shove he lifted the lid of the coffin and pushed it to one side, where it slid to the floor with a resounding crash.

At the sound, Clive could hear a renewed chorus of wails from the hallway and rolled his eyes in exasperation. The deputy covering him grinned nervously.

Clive stood and carefully looked into the casket's interior. At first, bitter disappointment struck him as he realized that the box was empty. After a moment however, his eyes widened in triumph as he saw that the coffin contained a pillow, dented in the middle as if someone's head had recently rested there. Further careful examination revealed a small bag at the casket's foot that contained some clothing and from which one sneaker protruded.

"Get forensics out here stat," he snapped at the deputy, who hurriedly pulled out his radio to make the call.

Clive's narrowed eyes carefully swept the rest of the room, searching the dark corners for the coffin's former occupant. The room was so tightly packed with a miscellany of objects that Clive could see no place for anyone to hide. He did, however, notice an oddly shaped pile of dust that had not been stirred by the crash of the coffin lid.

Puzzled, he holstered his gun and carefully wiped his sweat-covered hands with the ever-present handkerchief before donning the pair of lightweight leather gloves he always carried. He knelt on the floor, careful not to disturb the strange mound, and examined it closely. His eyes widened as he saw what appeared to be charred pieces of bone. Now, wavering between thorough confusion and the glimmerings of an extremely disquieting memory, he looked around the room again, praying silently he would find signs of fire. There were none.

By the time Becky arrived, the basement was swarming with forensics people and the police photographer had come and gone. She knelt with Clive as they both peered closely at the mysterious pile of dust.

"That's bone, isn't it?" asked Clive.

Becky removed a large pair of tweezers from her bag and, grasping a single sliver, held it up to the light of the single lightbulb that provided the basement's only illumination.

"Yep," she replied, placing the sliver into a plastic bag.

"Is it human?" Clive asked.

"Hard to tell." She used a small brush to carefully sweep the contents of the dust pile into a larger bag.

Over the past week or so, Clive had noticed her increasing reluctance to speculate. Coupled with the stirring of memories he would prefer to keep buried, his annoyance got the better of his normally restrained demeanor.

"Christ, Becky! Tell me something!"

She looked up at him calmly. "I'm sorry, Clive, but I don't know anything." She turned back to her work. "Assuming, for the moment, that these *are* fragments of human bone, I'd say this was a body once, wouldn't you?"

"It looks like it's been burned."

Becky sighed. "I know. And I have eyes too, Clive. There are no scorch marks in this room. Obviously it was done somewhere else. Don't ask me why, how, or where. I don't know. I may have a better idea after the tests."

"Try to keep hold of the results this time, will you?"

"*That* was uncalled for!" she snapped and then relented, feeling not a small twinge of guilt at the necessity of hiding the extent of her full knowledge from him. "Look, Clive, I'm as lost as you are. I know you're under a lot of tension, but so am I. I promise, as soon as I can give you answers, I will."

She closed her bag and, picking up the samples, trudged out of the basement and up the stairs. She emerged from the prop shop a moment later and, looking around to be certain she was unobserved, pulled out her cell phone and punched in Chris's number. She considered hanging up when the machine answered but decided to leave a message anyway.

"It's Becky. Remember that Peter Cushing film? Is there any truth to this turn-to-dust stuff? 'Cause I'd bet dollars to custard doughnuts we just found the remains of a body that matches up with Pamela's gift-head."

CHAPTER TWENTY-SIX

Much later that evening, in fact well into the next morning, Chris and Troy had their own stroke of luck. For more than ten nights they had dutifully made the rounds of every gay bar and disco in West Hollywood. Between them they had agreed that the most likely place to catch sight of their hitherto invisible nemesis was in one of the dance clubs—at least two victims had met their fates there. As many vampires had favorite hunting grounds, perhaps the rogue preferred to stalk his prey accompanied by a dance mix.

Against Chris's better judgement, they started their evening back at Hunter's. Fortunately, this time there were no difficulties with the clientele. They left the bar rather quickly and began to work their way westward along the boulevard. Troy had promised to keep his drinking at a minimum and had been remarkably true to his word. Aside from a narrow escape from a bitch-fight between Troy and a large drag queen brandishing a gold lamé spiked pump whom Troy had insulted at the corner of Santa Monica and Orange Grove, the early part of the evening was without incident.

The only other unpleasantness involved Troy and a piano bar. Chris blanched upon Troy's announcement that he would bestow his talents as a chanteuse upon the accumulated crowd of mostly middle-aged drunks by performing his own stylized rendition of "Moon River." Pulling Troy aside, he reminded him that, although he undoubtedly possessed many valuable talents, singing was not one of them. He assured Troy that his wit and acuity with a barbed comment were unsurpassed, that his figure was that of a proverbial Greek god, and that his face was tantamount to that of the handsomest matinee idol, worthy of immortalization in oil by the likes of Titian. However, Chris was quick to add, should Troy attempt to impress the gathered onlookers with his great lyrical style and golden throat, he would undoubtedly spoil the effect of his other attributes and be left dateless for the evening.

Troy, who had not failed to cruise the entire bar within thirty seconds of their entrance, loudly proclaimed that this was not a consideration as he wouldn't be caught dead dating any of the assembled patrons anyway. Chris tipped the piano player, an extremely tall, emaciated young man in leather chaps, vest, and chains who had been playing Cole Porter and Barbra Streisand medleys all night, with fifty dollars in return for his developing a sudden urge to use the men's room for the next twenty minutes or however long it took Chris to get Troy back out onto the street—whichever came first.

Eventually, Chris was able to save the ears of the recently insulted crowd by promising Troy a spending spree at both Tower Records and the Hollywood Movieland bookshop at the first available opportunity and they were able to proceed down the boulevard once again.

They ended up at Studio One, a dance bar on Robertson. Chris finally relented and permitted Troy a quick succession of straight scotches. Troy then decided to entertain the rest of the club's clientele as the belle of the ball by performing a long, seductive striptease in the middle of the dance floor while Chris remained on the sidelines, scanning the crowd.

Chris tried several times to drag Troy from the dance floor, but Troy had made the loving acquaintance of two erstwhile unknown individuals, one an attractive blond real estate salesman in a white spandex jumpsuit, the other a shirtless muscle-bound personal trainer in leather pants. Both were plying him with drinks in an effort to get him to remove the size-twenty-eight bikini underwear that barely covered his pubic area, the rest of his clothing having long since vanished.

Unwilling to cause a scene with the now totally plastered Troy, Chris fumed silently until the bar finally closed at two in the morning. As Troy, bleary-eyed, made his final swoop around the bar, loudly kissing his newfound friends goodbye, insulting his new enemies with bitchily deadly accuracy, and gathering up his stray garments from total strangers who showed various attitudes of lust, amusement, and irritation, Chris deftly liberated him from the grips of both realtor and personal trainer and led him toward the exit.

Out in the street, Chris yanked Troy into a dark cul-de-sac and began to tucking him back into his clothes. Getting him back into the tank top was no problem, but Troy continued to protest that it was too hot out for him to wear anything else. While Chris was attempting to turn Troy's ripped jeans inside out in preparation for stuffing him into them, Troy decided the neighbors could not possibly go to their graves happy unless they had heard him sing the entire score of *Cabaret* at least once.

He easily slipped out of Chris's grasp and darted across the parking lot, causing several of the departing clubgoers brief moments of dismay or delight, depending on their predilections, as the scantily-clad Troy gaily darted between the bumpers of cars lined up to leave the lot, crossed the street, ignoring traffic, and swaggered into West Hollywood Park.

Chris followed more cautiously, apologizing to irate motorists and holding up his middle finger to one particularly inebriated fellow who loudly inquired if, for fifty dollars, Chris would mind lending out Troy to serve as the entertainment for a dinner party he was hosting the following night.

Once in the park, Troy led Chris on a merry chase through the playground, up the slide, across the sandbox, and weaving in and out of the swing set before Chris finally ambushed him with a flying tackle near the teeter-totter. Clapping his hand firmly over Troy's mouth to keep him from loudly vocalizing the fate of his dear, departed girl-friend, Elsie, yet one more time, Chris none too gently crammed Troy's legs into the jeans and zipped them up, ignoring his yelp of pain when a few strands of his pubic hair were caught in the zipper.

Using his more-than-human strength, he lifted Troy over his head and slammed him down upright on his feet. Before he could recover, Chris managed to get the silk shirt back onto him by alternately flinging each of Troy's arms up into the air after the other and slipping the sleeves onto them as they came down.

With a snarl of disgust, he gave up on the footwear altogether, stuffing Troy's socks into the shoes, tying the laces together, and tossing them over his own shoulder. He completed his ministrations by cramming the fluorescent pink baseball cap firmly down on the top of Troy's head, wishing only that it would go down far enough to cover Troy's mouth as he started to protest.

Chris, once again, slapped his hand down to cover Troy's mouth and said firmly and angrily, "Look you, I have had enough. You got that? Enough!"

He removed his hand and started to stalk off across the park. Troy stood blinking for a moment, then rushed to catch up.

"I'm sorry," he mumbled.

"Sorry?" Chris roared, stopping and whirling around violently to face him. "That's it? You're sorry? We've got a killer to find and you're dancing naked in front of 200 people and all you can say is you're sorry?"

"I wasn't naked," Troy whined as they passed out of the park onto one of the residential side streets.

"Oh, no? I don't think even *I've* seen that much of you in ten years!"

"Just because you're jealous doesn't mean you have to take it out on—"

"Jealous?" Chris gasped mockingly. "Are you kidding? Jealous of the way you behaved out there like a little tramp? How could I possibly be—"

"Will you two fairies shut up?" called an angry voice. "It's two-thirty in the friggin' morning!"

Chris and Troy turned jointly to face the disembodied voice. "Fuck you!" they cried in unison.

"Oh, yeah? Well, fuck you too!" The sound of a window slamming echoed through the street.

Unbeknownst to Chris and Troy, annoyed neighbors weren't the only ones who witnessed the tiff. Rex Castillian had been lurking in the cul-de-sac off the parking lot for some time, hoping to encounter an appropriate victim as he left the club. So far, though, every man he'd seen going to a car had been in a state of inebriation. Tonight, Rex wanted his prey's mind to be crystal clear—so he would be fully aware of what Rex was doing to him.

The gods smile upon me, Rex thought. Silently, he moved closer to the vampire and his renfield, delicious frissons of anticipation coursing through his body.

Chris, still pissed off at his lover, failed to notice that the object of their evening's search was hiding in the bushes not fifty feet away. He turned his back on Troy and stomped off in anger; Troy following like a wounded puppy. They crossed the street at San Vicente and walked east without speaking to each other.

Rex kept to the shadows. Though he desperately wanted to seize the other vampire and tear him apart with his bare hands, he was not so foolish as to do so where he could be seen by the traffic on Santa Monica Boulevard.

Patience, he cautioned himself. *There's plenty of time before they'll need to retire for the day. And they have to leave the main street sometime. And,* he thought with a chuckle, *if I can't complete my work on the vampire tonight, I can always finish tomorrow night!* So intent was Rex on his prey that he failed to notice for several blocks that he was drooling.

He watched in delight as the two left the boulevard, walked a short way up Larrabee, and turned the corner into an alley. Rex quickened his pace, flexing his fingers convulsively, and bared his fangs.

Do it as quietly as possible, he reminded himself. He knew that of the two Troy was undoubtedly the noisier, and he had no wish to draw attention to his attack. While he had a general disdain for mortals en masse, he realized they could be quite dangerous. *Silence the renfield first,* he made mental note. *Then deal with the vampire.* He knew Chris would put up a fight. But Rex was much older and probably much stronger, and he relished the challenge—it would add spice to the final kill. He moved in closer.

A scant fifteen feet ahead, Chris suddenly stopped dead; Troy crashed into him from behind. Rex checked himself and ducked into a doorway. The other vampire had seen *something,* and Rex was nothing if not cautious.

"Holy shit," Chris said softly.

The alley ran behind several businesses, each with its own exit and, more important, its own trash Dumpster. There, standing beside one of the Dumpsters by the rear door of an Argentinean restaurant, was a young ghoul searching for scraps of raw or rotted meat, his head and arms almost buried in the overflowing garbage.

"I haven't seen one of them in ages," Troy said a little too loudly.

The ghoul heard him. Instantly pulling himself out of the Dumpster, he quickly looked around in fright, his gaze arrested at the sight of Chris and Troy.

"*More* bloodsuckers!" he said in dismay and, slipping on the spilled garbage, bolted off down the street.

"Did he say…?" began Troy.

"Come on!" shouted Chris, and they were off in pursuit.

Rex had his own moment of consternation. Evidently, the ghoul had at some point seen him in his travels. Annoyed at himself for his carelessness, he made a mental note to dispose of the ghoul as soon as he could—not that the timid creature would provide much sport. It wouldn't be difficult, but it was a complication, and Rex disliked complications on principal. He liked things to go the way he planned, and he felt a brief surge of rage, quickly suppressed, that the gods, who had presented him with this marvelous opportunity to eliminate his rival, suddenly seemed to be working against him.

The ghoul, unfortunately for Chris and Troy, was extremely quick on his feet—a lifetime of dodging cemetery caretakers can give a person amazing stamina. He veered right at Palm and darted halfway across the westbound lane of Santa Monica, leaping over the hood of a white Mercedes convertible as it screeched to a halt. He raced eastward down the street for several blocks, ignoring the sparse traffic, and turned north again just past City Hall. Chris and Troy followed closely behind, and Rex was forced to check himself so as to not overtake them.

So much exertion, he thought sardonically, *to prolong the inevitable.*

The ghoul darted into the side entrance of the Ramada Inn parking garage. Troy and Chris arrived a moment later, but the ghoul was nowhere to be seen.

"Where the heck did he go?" Chris murmured.

"Aruba?" Troy quipped. He was out of breath but, typically, couldn't resist the quip.

Chris shot him an irritated glance and motioned toward a row of cars to the right. Understanding, Troy moved off and, bent almost double, ran down the row his lover had indicated, hoping to catch sight of a telltale set of legs.

"You can't hide for long," Chris called out softly. He smiled as he caught sight of the ghoul crouching behind a Buick Regal. Troy had halted, panting, leaning on a white BMW parked next to the Regal. "Troy…" Chris said, pointing.

"What did I do now?" Troy asked, not understanding.

Suddenly the ghoul burst from his hiding place, shoved past the startled Troy, knocking him off his feet, and heading for the Santa Monica–side entrance. Troy emitted a little yelp of distress as his rear end impacted solidly with the concrete. He was barely able to rub at the soreness of his bruised heinie, however, before Chris grabbed his arm and, practically yanking him off his feet again, dragged him off after their escaping quarry.

Rex witnessed the entire incident from his hiding place just outside the garage. *Complete incompetence!* he thought with disgust. *Is it even worth the effort of this ridiculous chase? Even a mortal would provide more amusement.* Rex was a master at stalk-and-capture; these two bumblers wouldn't challenge him in the least. He felt his previous excitement fading. *Oh, well,* he thought, *at least the vampire's physical stamina might provide some mild entertainment. Then again, perhaps a quick kill would be best. Eliminate the competition and be done with it.* With an impatient sigh, he moved to follow the others. *Like a pathetic line of ducklings,* he thought.

On and on went the chase, down Santa Monica and up La Cienega Boulevard to Holloway. Troy had the worst time of them all as he was not only still slightly tipsy but also barefoot. He started to complain each time his feet came down on a rock, pothole, or unexpected curb. Each time however, he thought better of opening his mouth and decided to conserve his breath.

As they passed Olive Street, however, Troy stubbed his toe for the fourth time on one of the sidewalk dining tables set up outside Barney's Beanery. Loudly cursing the City of West Hollywood (for failing to repair the treacherous potholes), the owners of Barney's Beanery (for being stupid enough to put the tables there in the first place), people who thought a midnight stroll was to be conducted at twenty miles an hour, and ghouls in general, Troy followed Chris and the ghoul across the street at Flores and into the parking lot of Gelson's supermarket. What little noise Rex made following was easily masked by Troy's running commentary.

It was here that the ghoul made his first—and only—mistake. Instead of veering right and out onto Kings Road, he swerved left, hoping to find another alleyway behind the market and elude his pursuers. He drew up short when confronted by the high concrete wall backing the loading dock, his escape back along his previous path cut off by Chris's rapid approach. Cornered and in despair, he threw open the hatchway on the side of one of four large recycling bins and dove in headfirst, the little plastic door swinging closed behind him.

Chris rounded the corner seconds later and stopped. The ghoul was here; he knew it. The concrete wall was more than twelve feet high; the loading door leading to the market was chained and padlocked shut. He stood, considering.

Troy, exhausted, arrived a moment later, and in response to Chris's hand signal to remain where he was in order to block the only exit, collapsed on the ground, panting, and examined his injured feet.

Rex halted at the entry, a mere twenty or so feet behind Troy. *A dead end,* he thought. *How appropriate.*

This mad running about the city was becoming truly tiresome. Rex examined the field of battle before him critically. The ghoul was hiding in the trash container; he could hear him breathing softly even if the other vampire could not. The vampire was trapped by the high walls of the loading dock—very good! The only problem was the renfield sitting in the middle of the entrance to the driveway where he could easily be seen by neighbors or passing traffic if a commotion should ensue. Though Rex, after listening to the argument in the playground and the renfield's loud bitching, was certain he could dispatch the three without much effort, he was no longer quite so sure he would be able to do it as *quietly* as he would have liked. He looked around, considering his options, and saw a possible solution. There was a house next door, sharing a common wall with the loading dock.

Stealthily, Rex crept into the yard. The part of the lawn closest to the loading dock had been converted into a garden with trellised vines covering the wall. Rex moved toward it, mindful of not leaving footprints in the turned earth. As he drew closer to the wall, he stopped, blinking in confusion. There was a much smaller house, too tiny for human inhabitants, in the middle of the garden. He looked more carefully to see a miniature witch on a broomstick poised in midair above the little house. Closer inspection revealed dozens of happy-faced ghosts, black cats, and skeletons mounted on wooden sticks and scattered throughout the garden. A tattered windmill almost six feet high stood adjacent, with lilliputian pumpkins hanging from its arms.

Finally, there were three life-size figures closest to the wall. One was a large, square-headed green man with bolts sticking out of the sides of his neck. One resembled, as close as Rex could tell, a large dog or some kind of bear with red eyes, dressed in tattered pants and a ripped shirt. The third figure completely baffled him. It was a man in formalwear and a black cape. The hands were outstretched and the fingers hooked into claws. The hair was ridiculously styled and the face…were those *fangs* protruding from the painted snarl?

A vampire? Rex was nonplussed. The figure was such a ludicrous portrayal that he didn't know whether to be amused or offended. He passed the mannequin, resisting a juvenile urge to leer back at it, and crouched next to the wall, listening.

"We know you're here," Rex heard Chris called softly to the ghoul, his words nevertheless echoing in the quiet night. "Come on out. We won't hurt you."

The ghoul heard Chris's words, muffled through the wall of the recycling container, but was occupied with his own problems at the moment. Inadvertently, he had chosen a glass and bottle receptacle to hide in and he was desperately trying to remain still so that the glass wouldn't shift beneath him. One foot jammed into a mass of glass, sticky with the partially congealed contents of countless soft drink and juice bottles, the other thrust firmly against the side of the bin to prevent him from slipping, the ghoul grimaced in distaste as a tacky wetness began to seep through the seat of his pants and around to his crotch.

Finally, unable to stand the discomfort any longer, he slowly moved one hand down, pressing it against the one side of the bin, trying to move his body farther away from the offending liquids. The glass shifted slightly and the ghoul desperately tried to compensate, causing the bottles and jars to move even more. With a squawk and a crash, he lost his tenuous position and slipped, falling flat onto his back in the glass, the rear of his shirt instantly becoming sopping wet.

Rex seized the opportunity. He leapt upward, clawing past the vines toward the top of the wall. He realized with annoyance that large toy bats and scarecrows had been hung amid the vines, making his progress more difficult. Even so, by the time the noise of the shifting glass had ceased, he had reached the top of the high wall and was able to see clearly down into the loading dock. He crept along the wall, his footing made precarious by piles of fallen leaves. Stopping just above the vampire, he steadied himself and glanced about for a weapon. An evil, satisfied smile appeared when he saw a dead tree branch within reach, sagging under its own weight.

In the Dumpster, the little hatchway opened, piercing the dark interior of the bin with a shaft of light from an adjacent street lamp.

"Are you enjoying yourself in there?" Chris asked politely. "I should think it would be much more comfortable out here."

The ghoul reluctantly gave up and, with more shifting of glass, clambered out of the bin to stand before Chris, shoulders slumped in defeat, soaked, miserable, and reeking of stale soda pop and rancid orange juice. Neither they nor Troy heard the sharp crack of the branch as Rex, masked by the rattle of discarded bottles, stood and snapped it from the tree above them. He resumed his crouch atop the wall and examined the broken end with satisfaction. It was wickedly sharp.

Below, the ghoul glumly surveyed his clothing.

"Just look at this shirt," he wailed. "From Barneys! It's ruined!"

"You think that's bad? Take a look at your slacks," Troy called, panting heavily. "What the hell did you think we were gonna do? Rape you or something?" He rose and gingerly limped over to the other two to take a closer look at the ghoul.

The renfield moves NOW? Rex thought, silently cursing. The blond boy was standing directly in the path that Rex had planned to hurl the branch in order to impale the vampire. Strong as he was, Rex doubted he could skewer both of them with a single throw.

"Actually," Troy continued, "rape's not a bad idea."

"Hush you," said Chris. "You want to scare him off again?"

The ghoul, in fact, was quite good-looking, with creamy olive skin and big soulful brown eyes. His wavy brown hair was mussed, and he smelled rather ripe, but the wreckage of his once presentable clothing couldn't disguise the well-muscled, stocky frame underneath. His eyes brimmed with tears.

"Please," he begged in a voice barely above a whisper. "Don't hurt me."

"We're not going to hurt anyone," Chris said kindly, reaching out his hand to touch the ghoul reassuringly. The ghoul flinched and Chris withdrew the hand with a sigh.

"My name is Chris. And my friend with the healthy libido here is Troy."

Troy batted his eyelashes in what he felt was an alluring manner.

Chris and Troy, thought Rex mockingly. *How very modern!* Troy had still not moved, and Rex forced himself to remain calm. Frustration led to carelessness.

"Do you have a name?" Chris asked the ghoul gently.

"Scott," said the ghoul, bursting into tears.

For the love of all the forgotten gods! The ghoul's tears were really too much. No one had even laid a hand on him! Rex was thoroughly disgusted. *I'll make you cry, little rat,* he thought.

"What are you going to do with me?" the ghoul whined.

"We live about two blocks from here," Chris said. "The first thing we're gonna do is get you into some clean clothes."

"And for God's sake, stop crying," Troy added. "You'll ruin your mascara. You *do* have mascara on, don't you?"

The ghoul's tears ceased immediately and he bristled. "I am *not* a drag queen!"

"If those lashes are real," Troy said dubiously, "there is no God."

Rex couldn't believe what he was hearing. *They've just chased that creature half a mile…so they can chatter like magpies?* He looked heavenward and sat back on his heels. Some leaves shifted underneath him and his heel came down on a shard of broken glass. The crack was soft but audible.

Chris looked up sharply. "What was that?"

"What was what?" Troy and the ghoul asked in unison.

"Someone's watching." Chris's brow furrowed in concentration.

"A cat?" Troy suggested. The ghoul was wildly looking around for another place to hide.

"I don't think so," Chris said. "Aside from the three of us, I don't smell anything alive. And I don't hear breathing."

"It's your imagination," Troy said, dismissing Chris's concern. "Can we leave now? I'm sure Scott doesn't want to be seen in public with all those stains, even if he is a ghoul." Troy turned and flounced off toward the street.

Rex seized his chance. Springing to his feet, he took quick aim and hurled the broken tree branch at the other vampire. Chris, already alert, sensed danger, turned, and took a step toward the wall where Rex was perched. The single step saved him. Chris had an instant to take in the branch arcing through the air toward him. Before he could react, he felt a sharp pain and was knocked backward as the branch pierced through his right shoulder and emerged from his back. For a moment, his vision went black and he fell to the ground.

But Rex never saw the missile hit. In his eagerness, he'd overextended his lunge and his feet slipped on the dead leaves atop the wall. He lost his balance and reached for the tree behind him and missed. Hands grasping at air, he toppled backward off the wall and into the yard next door.

"Oh, my God!" the ghoul screamed.

Troy spun around and, horrified, watched his lover collapse to the ground. He sprang to his lover's side.

"He's dead!" the ghoul whispered in shock.

"Of course he's dead!" Troy shot back and immediately turned his attention to the body. "Chris? Honey? Can you hear me?"

Chris moaned.

"I meant, he's not breathing," the ghoul said petulantly.

Troy didn't bother to comment. "Help me," he demanded, tears staining his cheeks.

Scott paused for a second and then leaned over and slapped the semiconscious vampire across the face.

"*What are you doing?*" Troy shrieked. He threw himself protectively across Chris's prone form.

"What you're *supposed* to do!" the ghoul yelled back. "It's in all the movies. Look, it worked. He's trying to say something."

"What? Baby, what is it?" Troy asked, sobbing.

"Troy," Chris gasped. "You're crushing me. Get *off!*"

Troy realized he had thrown his full weight onto Chris's chest when he'd thought Scott was attacking him. He scrambled around behind, lifting Chris's shoulders to ease the pressure of the branch transfixing his shoulder.

"Help me up," Chris gasped.

The ghoul, now eager to assist, took hold of the protruding end of the branch and was about to use it to haul Chris to his feet.

"Don't," Troy said icily, "you dare."

Scott quickly snatched back his hand and blushed with embarrassment. Together, Troy and Scott managed to get the injured vampire upright.

"Much better," Chris winced. "Now all we have to do is get this fucking branch out of me."

The ghoul turned white.

"Don't tell me you're afraid of the sight of blood," Troy said derisively.

"Only when it's from something living," Scott confessed, ashamed.

Next door, Rex Castillian was having his own impalement problems. He'd fallen backward from a substantial height. Conscious of the lawn ornaments below him, he'd twisted frantically to avoid them and had succeeded in smashing the windmill and impaling himself through the stomach with the post from one of the scarecrows. Pieces of wood had pierced both his legs and one of his arms, and his back was covered with splinters. He grabbed onto the ersatz vampire to help himself to his feet. But the statue wasn't planted very deeply into the ground and offered little support. Rex's weight pulled it sideways, and off balance he clutched wildly for a hold. His hand caught the edge of the cape and pulled it from the figure as it toppled on top of him. A moment later, Rex was flat on his back with the snarling vampire mannequin poised as if to kiss him, the cape covering both their heads.

The physical pain was bad but bearable; the indignity was not. In any case, he was in no condition to take on another vampire, even a wounded one. Snarling at the phony vampire, he threw it to one side, noting with pleasure that he'd managed to toss it into the other two figures, upsetting them too. Then, ignoring the lights and confused shouts from the people in the house, he rose to his feet.

In time, all of you will be mine! he promised, unknowingly echoing the threat of another fictional vampire. Furious at himself and the Fates, he limped off, vanishing into the darkness.

Chris had also heard the noises of alarm from the neighbors next door. "We've got to get out of here before someone sees, Troy," he directed, "pull this thing out of me."

Troy grasped the end of the branch gingerly.

"No," Chris instructed. "One sharp pull."

"But it'll hurt!" Troy protested.

"I'll be brave, monkey." Chris smiled, then, his face set sternly, he ordered, "Just do it. *Now!*"

Troy grabbed the branch and pulled with all his might. Chris cried out in pain. Troy froze.

"What's wrong?" Scott asked.

"He's got a fucking tree through him!" Troy shouted with barely controlled hysteria.

"*Be quiet!*" Chris hissed through gritted teeth. He took a deep breath. "I think it's caught on my shoulder blade," he continued in a calmer voice. "You're going to have to wiggle it."

Troy looked at him with disbelief. "Wiggle it?"

"Troy," Chris said with as much patience as he could muster, "I know you don't want to hurt me, but there are people coming from next door. They cannot see me like this. You have to get this out of me quickly and quietly. Don't worry. I'll heal. But...*we have no time.*"

Troy set his jaw with determination, took hold of the branch, and closed his eyes. With a mighty tug, he managed to move the branch another inch or two.

"Twist it to the right," Chris instructed. "Hurry."

Chris turned even paler than usual as Troy jerked the branch around.

"It's not working," he sobbed. But just then the branch slid free with a sickening wet sound and a small gout of blood.

"Oh, shit," said Scott at the sight of the blood. He bent double and threw up. "All over my new shoes," he mourned.

Troy ignored him and threw the branch aside. He caught Chris as he collapsed forward.

"Listen carefully, monkey," Chris panted. "I may pass out. Don't leave the branch behind. It's got some of my blood on it. We need to leave now. I'll walk as well as I can but…"

"Here," Scott said, throwing Chris's uninjured arm across his shoulders. "Grab his other side."

Troy snatched up the branch and stuffed it down the front of his shorts. He took Chris's other arm, and together he and Scott managed to half drag him out of the loading dock. Once on the street, they were forced to hunker down behind some bushes when the neighbors and a rottweiler passed to investigate the noise.

"Can you stand?" Troy whispered.

"Yes," Chris replied.

"Good. We'll pretend you're drunk. I saw it in a Tony Curtis movie once."

Chris smiled wanly as he was helped upright once again.

"You know," Scott grumbled as he helped carry Chris down the street. "This was supposed to be my *vacation*!"

CHAPTER TWENTY-SEVEN

The ghoul, it turned out, preferred to be called Scotty and had come to town from Chicago. An hour later he sat, much calmer, in Chris's living room wrapped in one of Troy's less flamboyant robes, showered and dry. Troy defrosted the package of chicken he'd discovered in the freezer on the morning Becky had made her own startling discovery, and Scotty was nibbling happily at the raw, rancid fowl and sipping tea. Chris lay sprawled on the couch, pale and weak, shirtless, and with his shoulder wrapped in dozens of yards of cotton gauze and torn linens. Troy hadn't the skill of a Florence Nightingale, but he made up for it with enthusiasm. Though Chris kept assuring him that bandages were unnecessary, Troy insisted that the mummy-like wrapping was essential.

Aside from Chris's mild protests, most of Troy's doctoring was done in silence. The only exception was when Scotty got a good look at Chris's wound.

"Wow!" he breathed, impressed. "That's pretty awful looking." He looked at Chris hopefully. "If it goes to gangrene, can I have some of it? It'd be a lot better than this chicken."

Troy silenced him with a frosty glare. Chris hadn't the strength to respond. Scotty fidgeted in silence for a few moments, simply picking at his food.

"It's awfully, well, *red* in here, isn't it?" Scotty finally commented dubiously.

Troy drew himself up to his full height and commented grandly, "I did it myself."

"I dunno," Scotty said doubtfully, "looks awfully like blood to me."

Chris winced as he snickered, then wisely changed the subject. "What brings you to WeHo?"

"WeHo?"

"West Hollywood," Chris explained.

"Oh, sure. The Halloween parade." Scotty tore off another hunk of his chicken and stuffed it into his mouth, the juices dribbling down his chin. Troy looked slightly ill. "We usually go to San Francisco. This year we decided to come here instead."

"We?" Chris inquired. He shifted to get more comfortable.

"Yeah." Scotty finished the last of the chicken and held out his plate toward Troy. "Could I have some more of this?"

Troy gingerly took the plate from him and, forcing a bright hostessy smile, fled toward the kitchen.

"Some friends of mine."

"What kind of friends?"

"Oh, a couple of ghouls and an incubus from Indianapolis. Last year we ran into a couple of fur balls from Ohio, but Halloween is on a full moon this year and I've heard how they get."

"Pure myth," Chris said, dismissing the comment.

"Yeah, right," said Scotty, not believing it for a minute.

"No vampires?"

"Are you kidding? You know how your people get along with my people. We can't help it if you look dead when you're asleep. Mausoleums are dark anyway." Scotty paused as Troy came back into the room and eyed him appraisingly. "Your renfield's awfully cute, though."

Troy stopped dead. He held up the plate of chicken and then said sweetly, "Unless you want to wear this, I'll thank you to remove that word from your vocabulary while I'm around."

"What word?"

"*Renfield*," said Troy with distaste.

"Why?"

"Listen girlfriend, I normally don't like your kind either. In fact, I think your eating habits are pretty disgusting. In your case, though, I was considering making an exception. You're kind of dreamy yourself." The ghoul smiled. "*However*," continued Troy, "if you *ever* call me that again, you'll be back out with the trash cans quicker than you can say rot rat."

"I am *not* a rot rat," said Scotty, bristling.

"Ladies, ladies," said Chris sternly. "Can we please not argue for two minutes? Your voices are hurting my shoulder. Besides, we've got bigger problems here."

"How does it feel?" Troy asked, concerned.

"It's healing." Chris replied. "But it may take a while."

"I thought your kind were like Superman or something," Scotty said. "Bullets bouncing off your chests."

"Bullets aren't wood," Troy told him.

"If you carved them, they would be," Scotty pointed out helpfully.

"You may want to think before you speak," Troy shot back.

"Troy," Chris warned, "play nice." He leaned cautiously toward Scotty, testing his shoulder. Pain shot through him and, deciding to give it more time to mend, he sank back against the couch. "If I could feed," Chris told the ghoul, "I'd heal much faster. But it's close to five A.M. Not many people will be around between now and dawn. I'll sleep most of today, get an early start in the evening, and I should be completely well by midnight tomorrow."

"Cool," Scotty breathed in wonder.

"In the meantime," Chris said earnestly, "we need your help."

"Sure."

"What did you mean by *more* bloodsuckers?" asked Chris.

"The short, dark guy that's been hanging out in the parking lot behind Rage," Scotty said innocently.

"Bingo," breathed Troy.

"Tell me, Scotty. Do you think you could point him out if you saw him again?"

Scotty was puzzled. "I guess so," he said at length. "But there's two of you in the same town. Don't you know each other?"

"We tend not to be quite as chummy as you do," Chris informed him. "Ghouls tend to travel in packs. We don't."

Chris rose painfully. "Wait right here a second," he said.

"Sit down," Troy said, rising. "I'll get them."

"I am perfectly capable of walking into the next room, Troy," Chris said irritably. "I may look like something out of *Revenge of the Mummy,* but I can move just fine. Thank you for the bandages. Now, please don't mollycoddle me." He went into the bedroom.

As soon as Chris was gone, Scotty flashed Troy a dazzling smile. "Is he your lover?"

"Half a century," Troy replied.

"Gosh," mused Scotty. "And they say there's no such thing as a stable gay relationship." Troy laughed. "You ever have an affair?"

"Not with *your* kind," Troy said indignantly, and Scotty's face fell.

"What he means," said Chris, reentering the room with the file of suspects, "is that we have an arrangement."

Chris slowly lowered himself into a chair and opened the file. "He can do whatever he wants with humans, but no other undead, shape-changers, magic-users…or ghouls."

"That would be cheating," added Troy.

"What about werewolves?" Scotty asked, intrigued.

"Are you kidding?" Chris began. "He's…"

"Chris!" Troy protested in dismay.

"He's…ah…not into hairy guys." Chris smiled at Troy, who looked relieved that his lover had avoided the sensitive subject of his allergies. "He is, however, a terrible flirt."

"Why, Missy Scarlett! How you talk!"

Chris pushed the file toward Scotty. "Do you recognize any of these photos?"

Scotty picked up the three photographs.

BITE CLUB

"These are paintings," he said.

"Yes, dear, we know," said Troy patiently, as if Scotty were mentally deficient.

"Yeah, this is the guy." Scotty pushed a single photo back toward Chris.

Chris picked it up.

"Bingo?" Troy asked.

"Rex Castillian," Chris read. "First showed up around 1200 on the Iberian peninsula. Lost track of him during the Spanish Inquisition sometime after 1487. No confirmation of true death." He tossed the photo to Troy.

"Yep. I'd say it's bingo, all right."

CHAPTER TWENTY-EIGHT

Scotty spent the night at the apartment after calling his friends and filling them in on the evening's events. While Chris was on the telephone with Sylvia, Troy, at Chris's request, attempted to overcome his initial dislike of the young ghoul. After exchanging a series of witty insults and derogatory comments about each other's nature, they rapidly discovered a mutual adoration for female film stars of the '30s and '40s, and the two were soon companionably perched in front of the television set as they watched *Mildred Pierce,* silently mouthing all the best lines.

At six-thirty the next morning, Chris returned Becky's call about her discovery of the ashes. At first groggy and irritated at being awakened so early, she perked up immediately when Chris told her they'd managed to identify the rogue vampire. She arrived at the apartment forty minutes later after warning Chris to have breakfast waiting for her.

"What the hell happened to you?" she demanded, seeing Chris's bandages.

"A run-in with our murder suspect," he told her. "Either that or someone was practicing javelin throwing with trees at four in the morning."

"Let me look at that," Becky demanded.

"There's no reason..." Chris began. But Becky had taken him firmly by his uninjured arm and, with gentle pressure, forced him into a chair.

"Who did this wrap?" she muttered. "It's like untangling a Slinky." There was a crash from the kitchen. "Forget I asked."

Troy and Scotty had been prevailed upon to interrupt their screening of *The Little Foxes* in favor of making messes in the kitchen. Unfortunately for Becky, Scotty was used to consuming his food raw and preferably aged to the point of rancidity. Troy, who had never made any pretensions to Julia Child, had absolutely no idea how much food a normal person was capable of eating in one sitting. The result, when Becky arrived, was an entire package of scorched bacon (Scotty's perception of cooked meat being limited to the ability to differentiate between raw and charred), half a dozen lumpy eggs (Troy forgot to remove them from the shells before scrambling), and nine pieces of burnt yet alarmingly spongy toast (neither one had ever used a microwave, so after wondering why the bread refused to cook after ten minutes, they simply set the gas oven on broil and popped the toast in with the eggs).

"I'll stop at McDonald's on the way into the office," Becky grimaced with distaste when she saw the food. Fortunately, Troy and Scotty weren't offended as they had already removed themselves to the bathroom and were arguing about which one of them would have to strip first so they could scrub the scorched pots and pans in the shower.

"This is bad, Chris," Becky told him. "It went right through. Your shoulder's broken."

"But it missed my heart," Chris said. "In two days, you won't be able to see even a scar. I just need to take it easy for a while."

Becky looked at him dubiously.

"Trust me," Chris assured her. "I've survived much worse."

There was a crash from the bathroom that sounded alarmingly like a mirror shattering. Then the sound of the shower being turned on masked the bickering and Chris breathed a sigh of relief.

"Who's in there?" Becky asked. "I thought it was one of Troy's movies."

"A friend. He helped us get home after I was...er...impaled. They've been like that all night," he told Becky before she could ask another question. "At least we'll have a few minutes of peace." Chris handed her the file on Rex and assumed his best lecturer's manner. "I'm pretty sure this is the guy we've been looking for. One: He's old, at least 800. Two: He's good-looking enough to have attracted the victims. Three…"

"Has anyone ever told you that's a really annoying habit?"

"What?" Chris asked.

"That business with your fingers," Becky replied, mimicking him. "One: Blah, blah, blah. Two: Blah, blah, blah. I really wish you'd stop. It makes me want to break your other shoulder."

"Sorry," he said absently. "Now, where were we?" His brow furrowed for a moment. "Oh, yeah. Three."

Becky sighed in defeat.

"Three: He disappeared during the Spanish Inquisition and no one's heard from him since. And, finally, four: He's been seen in West Hollywood—recently."

"What?" Becky gasped. "Seen? You mean there's a *third* vampire in town?"

"No," Chris replied, puzzled. "How do you figure that?"

"You said you could all identify each other on sight."

"So?"

"Well, if you didn't see him, that means another vampire must've."

"Or a werewolf, or a witch, or as in this case, a ghoul."

"A ghoul?" Becky felt faint.

At this point, the object of their conversation entered the living room holding a frying pan that looked like it had been salvaged from Chernobyl.

Becky looked up. "Hello," she said and looked to Chris to make the introductions. Before Chris was able to open his mouth, Scotty screamed. Becky, startled, returned his gesture by letting out a scream of her own.

"Oh, my God!" He dropped the frying pan and darted back into the bedroom.

Unfortunately, at that moment Troy was coming through the doorway in the opposite direction carrying a casserole dish in each hand. The two met head on.

Troy went flying backward from the impact, his arms pinwheeling wildly. Both casseroles slipped from his grasp and sailed merrily across the room to smash against opposite walls. Troy lost the struggle to maintain his balance and fell backward, smashing against the coffin.

Scotty, however, managed to merely ricochet off the door frame, keeping his balance—barely—and, with a tremendous leap, clearing both Troy and the coffin, landing next to the bedroom closet. With another cry of dismay, he yanked open the closet door and dove in, slamming it shut behind him.

"*What* was that about?" asked Becky, calmer now that the initial shock had passed.

"Oh, it could be anything. His kind aren't the most stable of people. Years of hiding in graveyards, scared of every shadow." He hauled himself to his feet. "Well, let's go find out." Becky followed him into the bedroom.

Troy was lying flat on his back on the coffin, legs above his head.

"Have you noticed," Troy began, affecting an upper-class British accent, "that since we arrived on the shores of fair Los Angeles, madam has spent an increasing amount of time falling on her arse?" He rose majestically and made a show of wiping imaginary dust from his clothing.

"Pay no attention to the man behind the curtain," Chris told Becky and opened the closet door to reveal Scotty, huddled in the corner, hidden under several of the opera capes.

"What the hell is wrong with you?" Chris asked him.

"She's one of *them*!" Scotty wailed.

"I know that!" roared Chris and grimaced as his shoulder twinged.

"What's she doing here?" Scotty screamed back through his tears.

Becky, concerned, reached out a hand and gently grasped Chris's good arm. "Count to ten," she admonished him. Chris did so.

"She's a friend," he said once he'd recovered his temper.

"Are you kidding?" sniffed Scotty.

"What? You've never seen a normal before? Don't you go to work? Shopping?" Troy was amazed.

"But she's in your house," Scotty whispered as if Becky were hard of hearing. "Your home! Your lair, even!"

"It's OK. She knows about us," Chris said.

"She's the coroner," added Troy.

"Coroner?" Scotty drew one of the capes back over his head and began to weep anew.

"Oh, Jesus H. Christ!" said Chris with disgust and waded into the closet. He tried to grab Scotty and haul him out into the room, but the ghoul was flinging clothes at him, trying to get away. One of Scotty's flailing arms caught Chris on his injured side and with a cry of pain he fell to the floor. Becky rushed to his side.

"Stop it now!" Troy yelled, and Scotty froze. "Out!" Troy commanded and the ghoul meekly complied.

"I'm sorry," he whimpered. "Did I hurt you?"

"Yes," Chris said, lips tight with pain. "Can we please stop the hysterics for a moment? Or do you want to kill me and finish what the rogue started?" Scotty stood, meekly trembling as Becky helped Chris to his feet. "Well, *that* will certainly keep me off the cricket field for a few more days," he quipped.

"Can you stand without help?" Becky asked.

"Don't be foolish." Chris shook off her arm, annoyed. "I'm perfectly fine. Will everyone *please* stop treating me like a consumption victim?"

"Good. In that case, do you mind...?" Becky said, indicating the coffin. "I'm not quite used to that yet." She turned and left the bedroom.

Holding himself ramrod straight, Chris followed as Troy marched the reluctant Scotty back out into the living room and sat him down on the couch. Troy made a great show of rubbing his rear end before he sat down himself.

Once all were comfortable, Chris performed the introductions.

"Becky, this is Scotty. Scotty is a ghoul."

Becky blanched. "A ghoul?" she inquired weakly.

Troy tried to be helpful. "You know. A rot rat."

Scotty mustered what little dignity he had and shot back, "Renfield!"

Troy bristled. "Corpse chewer!"

"Bloodsucker–butt licker!"

"Carrion queen!"

"That's enough!" yelled Chris.

The two fell silent.

"Scotty is the one who spotted Rex Castillian—our killer," said Chris, determined to keep the conversation from totally falling apart. "I'm hoping he'll volunteer to help you out during the day."

"But she's a coroner!" Scotty protested.

Becky's curiosity was aroused. "So?"

"Didn't your mother ever teach you anything?" Scotty asked with disdain. "Coroners, undertakers, grave diggers, medical examiners, archaeologists—they're all the same. You know how they are. They hate the competition, trying to keep every corpse to themselves. And why, I don't know. They certainly don't use them for anything useful. Just stealing food from our table, Mama always said."

Becky felt slightly nauseated and was sorry she'd asked Scotty to explain.

"And coroners! They're the worst. They only know how to do one thing. Cut, cut, cut!" Scotty paused, then accused belligerently, "She's probably got all her scalpels in that purse right there. Just waiting to cut *me* up," then added more dubiously, "Right?"

"Good God! This is the twenty-first century! She's not going to hurt you."

"I promise." Becky gave Scotty her best smile. "All I want to do is catch whoever's been killing people."

"Oh, we never kill people," Scotty assured her earnestly. "After they're already dead it's fair game. But we never, ever kill people."

Becky looked slightly greener.

"Oh, cut it out," said Troy with exasperation. "All you people do is brag, brag, brag. When was the last time you *really* ate human flesh?"

"Please," said Becky, her voice breaking into a much higher register than normal, "don't answer that!"

Scotty began to protest, but Chris shushed him.

"Now, let's get back to the problem, can we?"

They all nodded.

"During the day, Scotty and his friends will help you scout around town. They may be able to think of some places we haven't thought of. At night, Troy and I will take over. Deal?"

"*Tomorrow* night," Troy stressed. "You need time on your back."

"Very well," Chris conceded.

"What're we looking for?" Scotty wanted to know.

Troy was pleased to show his superior knowledge of the situation. "Rex's daytime lair."

"You mean the other bloodsucker?"

"I don't mean Katharine Hepburn, Mary!"

"But I know where he lives," said Scotty.

"The prop shop on Fairfax? He's not there anymore," Becky said.

"Prop shop? What prop shop?" Scotty asked.

All three looked at him in amazement.

"You mean," said Chris slowly, "he's got *another* casket?"

"Sure," Scotty said, "I could have told you that last night if you asked me."

Chris barely refrained from slapping his palm against his forehead, cursing his stupidity.

"Where is he?" asked Troy.

"I don't know what the building's called. But it's that little brown building next to the park over by Rage. You know, the one with the blue shutters." Scotty wiped his nose.

"My God," Becky said very quietly.

"What's wrong?"

Becky looked at the other three, suddenly white-faced and shaken.

"Well...?" Chris demanded.

"You've never been there," she began, "but..." Her words trailed off. She looked at the others helplessly. "That's the morgue!" she cried. "My office!"

"Of all the unmitigated gall..." Chris breathed. "The bastard's taunting us."

"Not to mention trying to kill you," Becky pointed out.

"That clinches it," Chris resolved. "It'll be light in a little while. If we leave now, we'll make it just after he holes up for the day. It'll be the perfect opportunity to..."

"You are not honestly thinking of coming with us?" Becky interrupted, appalled.

"Yes, I am," Chris replied. "None of you has dealt with a rogue before. I have. Besides, while I can survive foreign objects trashing my body, Troy can't. He's the only one of you who has any idea of how to deal with a vampire..."

"How to deal with them...how to sleep with them...how to clean up after them...how to—"

"That will be quite enough from you, monkey," Chris cut him off. "We've got to get this guy as soon as possible—before he kills again. And Troy isn't going anywhere without me to protect him."

"You're in no condition..." Becky began.

"Nonsense," Chris said and moved toward the front door. "Let's go."

"What about the sun?" Scotty asked quietly. "It's just about dawn."

Chris stopped in his tracks.

"He's right, you know," Troy said. "You're hurt. You're tired. And you didn't have time to eat tonight. Ten minutes in the sun and you'll look like Michelle Pfeiffer in *The Witches of Eastwick*. You know, after Jack Nicholson cursed her and made her all bloated?"

"Is that true?" Becky asked. "I've seen you in the daytime."

"That was in Philadelphia," Troy told her. "It's almost always cloudy there. This is L.A."

Becky looked at Chris, expecting an answer.

"The sun burns us sometimes," Chris admitted reluctantly. "If we're hurt or hungry, it can be pretty bad."

"I am not spending the entire day rubbing aloe vera into your skin again," Troy said. "The last time he got sunburn," he told Becky, "all the satin in the coffin was slimy for weeks. At first it was kinda kinky but...he finally made me replace it."

"TMI, monkey. TMI," Chris said. "I'll manage and I'm going."

"No, you're not!" Troy snatched the car keys from the coffee table and thrust them down the front of his pants. "Come and get 'em," he taunted, "if you can."

Chris lurched across the coffee table and made a grab for Troy's crotch. He missed and fell lengthwise onto the table, landing on his injured side. Before he could try again, Troy slapped him.

"Damn it, Troy! That hurt!" Chris roared.

"Damn yourself!" Troy roared back.

"*Stop it! Both of you!*" Becky shrieked. "How much of this do you think I can take? I thought I was doing very well, dealing with dead people and..."

"I'm not dead," Scotty pointed out.

"Fine. Dealing with people who eat dead people then," Becky said snippily. "But I'm having to make a serious effort here. The least you could do would be to nix the holy martyr act."

"I am not letting Troy go out there alone," Chris insisted.

"We'll be with him," Scotty hastened to assure him.

"A fat lot of good *that* will do!" Chris huffed.

"A fat lot of good a sedative would do," Becky chimed in. "I am very tempted to indulge my curiosity and find out how much Valium it would take to knock you on your undead ass if you don't shut up."

With difficulty, Chris folded his arms and sat back on the sofa in a sulk. "We're at an impasse then."

"I still have the car keys," Troy pointed out.

"Besides," Scotty said as he pulled the blackout curtains from the window. "It's dawn."

The light streaming in wasn't very bright; the sky was barely pink. Nevertheless, as the pale light touched the back of one of Chris's hands, its effect was immediate and dramatic. The skin instantly reddened. Chris froze in shock, and before he could snatch his hand out of the beam of light blisters appeared.

"Close that, you idiot!" Troy screeched.

"Sorry," Scotty mumbled, complying. "I thought you needed help making your point."

"Let me see that hand," Becky demanded.

"Why does everyone want to kill me tonight?" Chris grumbled, cradling it against his chest.

"Now, what was that about you coming with us?" Troy asked. "I refuse to share a coffin with someone who looks like the Elephant Man."

"Look, Chris," said Becky, kneeling beside him. "We can always call Clive with an anonymous tip and…"

"No way!" yelled Scotty. "If any other normals are gonna find out about us, I'm not going." He stood, arms firmly clasped across his chest to indicate stubbornness. Only the facts that he was trembling from head to foot and starting to sweat betrayed his resolve.

"He's right," Chris mused. "Even if he's scared of his own shadow, at least he knows what we're up against. Convincing the captain would take some time." He was silent for a moment, thinking. "Very well," he conceded. "The three of you go. But—and I want to be clear about this—you'll need to follow my instructions on how to kill him exactly. If you do it wrong, he can heal and he'll go into hiding again. Then we'd be in an even worse position."

"If it's any comfort," Becky said, "I'll have my cell phone with me. If we run into trouble, I'll call. You can throw a raincoat over your head or something and come running."

"Hopefully, that won't be necessary," Chris smiled wanly. "Troy," he instructed firmly, "there's a box in the back of the hall closet. Grab some of those horrific Gothic crucifixes leftover from your decorating spree on the town house."

"I wondered where those had got to," Troy said as he moved to get them.

"Scotty." Chris turned to the ghoul. "Go into the kitchen and get some bottle or jars. If you can't find any, empty something from the fridge…"

"Not the vodka!" Troy called from the hallway.

Chris ignored him. "Make sure they're clean and fill them with water from the sink."

Scotty scampered off to comply. Becky looked at Chris askance.

"This guy was living when all the superstitions about us were accepted as fact," Chris explained. "If we're lucky, he may still believe them. If he wakes up, hold up a cross. It may help you to back him into a corner."

"What about garlic?" Becky asked.

"Maybe," Chris agreed, "but we don't have any in the house and none of the stores will be open this early."

"And the water?"

Chris grinned. "Just tell him it's holy water. He'll never know the difference." He sobered and continued. "In fact, if you throw it on him, he may blister and burn. It's psychosomatic, but the results will be the same."

Within a few minutes, Troy came back into the room with a small armful of crosses and Scotty emerged from the kitchen with several bottles of water.

"Aren't we forgetting something?" Scotty asked pointedly.

"Yes," Chris sighed. "God, I hate having to do this," he added as if to himself. He fixed Becky with a steady gaze. "Inside my coffin, the large one, you'll find a small parcel wrapped in some cloth. It's all the way down by the foot, under the lining."

Becky looked with dread at the bedroom door.

"Becky," Chris said gently, "if you can't go into an empty coffin, how do you expect…"

"I don't know *him*," Becky said irritably. "It's the thought of *you* in that thing that bothers me." She trundled into the bedroom. Seconds later, Chris heard her struggling with the coffin lid.

"What is this?" she called.

"Mallet and stake," Chris called back.

She came into the living room carrying the parcel with a look of befuddlement. "Why would you keep these in your coffin?"

"Anyone who wants to use them," Chris said seriously, "would have to get through me first."

"What if they brought their own?" Scotty asked.

Chris looked surprised. "You know, I never thought of…"

"You have a talent for saying the wrong thing at the wrong time," Troy told the ghoul.

At Troy's comment, Becky snorted, trying to muffle her laughter. But Troy was oblivious to the irony.

"Through the heart," Chris told them. "Make the first blow as hard as you can. Becky, you should probably be the one to do it. Scotty might flinch and Troy doesn't do very well with things that require precision."

"Hey!" Troy protested.

"If you don't pierce the heart with the first blow," Chris continued, "he may wake up. Do *not* look into his eyes. Some of us have the ability to mildly hypnotize normals. Troy," he turned to his lover, "if Becky freezes, you'll have to finish him off." He explained to Becky, "Troy's nature makes him slightly immune to the effect."

Becky sighed. "You know," she announced to the room at large, the stake and mallet in her hands, "this is definitely not what I had in mind when I went to med school."

"You'll do fine," Chris assured her. His tone grew grim. "You don't have any choice."

CHAPTER TWENTY-NINE

Forty-five minutes later, Troy pulled the Cabriolet to a screeching halt in front of the coroner's office. Becky uttered a silent prayer of thanks as she released her death grip on the dashboard, which was the only thing that had prevented her from bursting out of the seat belt and sailing out of the car each time Troy had rounded a corner; his driving had to be experienced to be believed. She and Scotty got out and stood watching as Troy, who had forgotten to set the parking brake, leapt back into the car and stamped down on the brake pedal to keep the car from rolling downhill onto Melrose Avenue. He quickly rejoined his companions.

"What do we do now?" Scotty asked.

"Exactly what Chris told us," Becky said firmly.

Standing outside her office, prepared to go in and do battle, Becky was having second thoughts about calling Clive. But confronted with Troy's obvious impatience to get inside (he was mentally playing the brave Scarlett O'Hara as she escaped through the flaming ruins of Atlanta) and Scotty's evident desire to bolt and hide at the least provocation (he was still not quite convinced that Becky wouldn't whip out a scalpel and attack him with it), she put her thoughts of obtaining additional help behind her and unlocked the door.

The front hallway was quiet and dimly lit, with a few shafts of sunlight streaming in through the small glass transom over the front door. The trio's footsteps echoed off the linoleum as they made their way down the hall and into Becky's office. Once inside, she closed the door and flipped on the light over her desk. She plopped down in her chair, motioning the other two to the threadbare love seat against the far wall.

"God, I'm starved." She pulled an individually wrapped cherry pie from the top desk drawer and began munching.

"Now, that's what I call nauseating," said Scotty, shuddering. "Vegetables and fruit. Eating things that grow in *dirt*. Yuck!"

Troy sat gracefully on the couch after first lifting an imaginary hoop skirt and smoothing out invisible wrinkles.

"Where do we start?" he asked, his Southern accent more pronounced than normal.

"That depends on where Scotty saw him going into the building." Becky daintily wiped cherry juice from her chin.

"The double door in the back. The beige one," said Scotty.

"That leads to the autopsy room," she mused.

"Ain't that a little bit obvious, sugar pie?" Troy asked.

"Yeah," said Becky, "Too obvious. But let's check it out anyway."

She quickly finished her pie and, grabbing another, blueberry this time, led the boys down the hall toward the autopsy room.

"Why's it so empty?" Scotty whispered as they were walking down the hall.

"Lunchtime," Becky told him sarcastically.

"Oh," Scotty said and brightened visibly. "Do you think someone's saved us a leg or something?"

"Will you cut it out already?" Becky implored, not knowing whether to be irritated or disgusted. "It's too early. No one's come in yet."

Scotty looked suitably chastised as the three stopped in front of the door to the autopsy room. In a hurried whisper, Becky warned the other two to be quiet. She slowly pushed open the doors and flipped on the overhead lights as they entered.

Scotty fidgeted uncomfortably at the sight of the stark white walls and the large stainless-steel cabinets. He gingerly reached out and touched one of the three shiny metal tables in the middle of the room, shuddering at the sight of the drains located at the base of each table.

Troy looked around in awe. "Wow!" he whispered. "How do you keep all this clean?"

"We have a straight boy who comes in twice a week to polish the silver," Becky hissed back. "Now, will you *please* keep quiet!"

She motioned toward the twelve steel doors of the large refrigerated unit set into the far wall, where her patients were usually stored. The three gathered around expectantly.

"Which one?" asked Troy.

"I don't know. One of the bottom ones probably. We never use them."

"Good," said Scotty. "How about we start at the top and work down." The other two glared at his cowardice.

Becky grasped the handle of a bottom drawer firmly, sweat beginning to trickle off her forehead. "Ready?" she whispered.

"Just a sec, Doris," said Troy. He and Scotty withdrew their crosses and held them out in front of them. Troy took the opportunity to warn Scotty. "If it's a real stiff in there, don't you go getting crazy on us or anything, you hear?"

Scotty gave him a withering glance and opened his mouth to reply. Becky slapped him gently.

"On three," she said. "One, two, three!"

She pulled the drawer open, sliding it smoothly on its rollers. The drawer was empty. Without fully realizing it, each of them breathed a sigh of relief.

"One down. Eleven to go," Becky said. Her bravado increasing with each drawer, she rapidly opened the three remaining bottom drawers. Nothing.

"Go for the gusto, I say," said Troy, and he yanked open the top left-hand drawer to reveal an elderly Asian woman, the features of her face wrenched to one side.

"She's naked," Scotty remarked as he examined the corpse closely. "What are you? A necrophiliac or something?" He pulled down the sheet before Becky could stop him. "You see!" he said, indicating the autopsy marks. "Cut, cut, cut!" He bent closer and inhaled deeply, then suddenly sneezed and wrinkled his nose in disgust. "Ugh! Formazine!"

"That's Mrs. Noguchi. Stroke."

"Yeah, and you keep your pearly whites off her," Troy said sternly.

"Puhl-e-e-eze!" said Scotty haughtily. "Look at her. Gotta be eighty if she's a day. Much too tough." He turned to Becky. "Got anything younger in here?"

Becky interrupted before the conversation could deteriorate further. "What a minute. What's she doing in number one?" She grabbed a clipboard hanging from a nail in the wall next to the refrigerator. "She should be in eight."

The trio looked at each other.

"That's this one?" Troy asked, indicating the far right center drawer. Becky nodded. With a slight curtsy and a wave of his hand, he added, "Ladies first."

Becky wrapped both hands around the handle, took a deep breath, and pulled open the door. Although they had all been prepared, each exhibited varying degrees of shock at hitting pay dirt.

There, hands crossed on his chest, lay an olive-skinned, dark-haired young man wearing black jeans and a black silk shirt.

"That's him!" whispered Scotty excitedly.

"No kidding," Becky replied sardonically. "We usually strip them before we put 'em in the fridge."

"And I thought you were a *lesbian* necrophiliac," quipped Scotty nervously.

"Nice shirt," commented Troy. "I have one like it at home."

"Don't tell me—it's red. To match the living room."

"Will you two shut up?" Becky held out her hand, waggling her fingers. "Gimme the stake."

"The stake?" asked Troy blankly.

Becky turned to look at him, expressions of horror, rage, and disbelief fighting for prominence on her face.

"The stake!" she hissed.

Troy turned accusingly to Scotty. "*You* were supposed to hang onto the stake."

"Me?" said Scotty, outraged. "I've got the holy water. *You* were supposed to take the stake."

"I've got my hands full with all this stuff!" Troy began to pull crosses and the now useless mallet from his pocket. "I'm wearing shorts. Where the fuck am I supposed to carry a stake?"

He flung one of the crosses at Scotty, who ducked.

"You left it in the car?" Becky was floored.

"*He* left it in the car." Troy pointed and threw another cross.

"I did not! It was your responsibility. You see!" said Scotty, turning to Becky for support. "You can't trust a renfield to do anything right!"

"I told you not to call me that!" Troy shrieked and let loose with a volley of crosses and small bottles of water.

"Shut up!" Becky hissed. "You want to wake the son of a bitch up?"

"Too late," said a cultured voice with a slight accent. "Much, much too late."

Arguments forgotten, the three cowered together as Rex swung his legs over the side of the drawer and stood up menacingly.

"My, my, my," he leered. "Company. If I'd only known you were coming," he shook his head in mock dismay, "I'd have baked a cake." He began to walk with measured steps toward the other three.

In a burst of desperation, Becky grabbed a jar of water from Troy's limp grip and, twisting off the top with lightning speed, flung it straight into Rex's face.

There was a shocked silence as the three waited for Rex to collapse in an agony of pain. A moment passed.

"That wasn't very nice," Rex commented absently, wiping his face with a sleeve.

"Oh, shit," said Scotty, backing behind one of the autopsy tables. "Shit. Shit. Shit." And then he added, "Shitty shit" for emphasis.

"Look," said Becky, trying to gain some control of the situation, "couldn't we all just sit down and discuss this like rational, intelligent human beings?"

"Certainly we could." Rex flashed her a charming smile. He paused as if considering and then said with great sorrow, "But that wouldn't be quite fair, would it? You are the only human being in the room. And, if you'll excuse my eavesdropping, the earlier conversation between your two friends leaves me with serious doubts as to whether they actually *are* intelligent."

"We're sorry about the stake," Becky said. "We never really wanted to hurt you. We just want you to stop killing people. If you promise to behave, maybe we can work something out."

Rex threw back his head and laughed; his laughter bounced off the high ceiling of the morgue and echoed. With each passing second, he made Scotty more and more nervous until finally the poor ghoul opened one of the glass-fronted chemical cabinets and tried to force himself inside, knocking bottles and jars to the floor.

Rex finally caught his breath and the laughter stopped. With a theatrical flourish, he wiped imaginary tears from his eyes.

"I haven't laughed like that in decades. Thank you."

"You're welcome," said Troy politely.

"But you make one mistake, young lady. I don't kill people. I kill *cattle*."

"You killed one of us," Troy protested, "and dropped off his head, and tried to kill Chris."

"Correction," said Rex sternly. "I *made* one of us for the express purpose of killing him. As for your *boyfriend*..." Rex's voice dripped with sarcasm, "he's competition. All's fair in war, as they say."

"But why?"

Rex's tone became low, hatefully intense. "It was the night I first saw you and your friend. I dislike my territory being invaded. You should have heeded the warning."

"But this is L.A.," said Becky, hoping she could appeal to Rex's reason. "There are three million people here. There's not room enough for two?"

The vampire's eyes grew cold, dead. His voice went flat. Where before he had been urbane, even witty, all traces of the civilized creature who had stood before them vanished. Now Becky could clearly see the monster behind the facade. He spoke a single, immutable word: "No."

Becky's mind was racing. She knew they were all in mortal—or immortal—danger and she also knew she wouldn't be able to count on Troy or Scotty to get them out of it. She could see that the only thing stopping Scotty from trying to make a break for the door was Rex standing in front of it. Or maybe he had gotten himself so firmly wedged into the cabinet that it would take a crowbar to get him back out.

Troy, on the other hand, was amazingly calm. So calm, in fact, that Becky feared he had gone into some kind of shock. He seemed to be either unable or unwilling to seriously consider the danger they were in; his attitude became airier and airier with each passing moment. Right now, he was looking around the room, seemingly unfocused, imagining he was God knew where else.

She tried to steady her scattered mind. *Keep him talking,* she thought. "But you killed the first ones before Chris and Troy even got here."

"Only partially correct, my dear." The sophisticated mask was back in place. "The first ones I killed died long before Chris and Troy were born." Becky opened her mouth to protest but Rex airily waved her to silence. "I know death isn't necessary, strictly speaking. But actually," he smiled evilly, "I find I enjoy it."

Becky's frantically roving gaze came to rest on the glass-fronted cabinet that Scotty had managed to vacate in favor of trying to hide under the autopsy table. She blinked. He hadn't bothered to close the door. She blinked again, mind racing even faster.

"My kind frowns on that sort of behavior. When I saw another in the street, it was obvious he was here to hunt me and try to put me down, as they say." Rex pulled out a chair and sat facing the chair back in front of the door. Becky took the opportunity to move closer to the cabinet. "I am very old, my dear. Much older than any other vampire I know of. I dislike being told what I can and cannot do by those with less experience than I." He smiled a small, private smile. "I intend to get much older. Unfortunately for you and your vampire friend, you will not." He leaned forward, and Becky managed to sneak in a few more steps, moving ever closer to the cabinet.

Rex fixed his gaze firmly on Troy. "Where is he? I want him."

"Who?" asked Troy.

"Your master, little renfield. I want him. Dead."

At the mention of the hated name, Troy's eyes blazed with anger. He tensed, launching himself at the surprised Rex. "You prick!" he yelled. "Don't you *ever* call me that!"

Troy's shoulder caught Rex in the center of the chest. The vampire toppled backward, the chair scooting out from under him as it tipped over and clattered to the floor.

Without looking at the two wrestling bodies in the center of her morgue, Becky lunged the few remaining steps to the cabinet and thrust her hands inside. Knocking even more bottles and boxes to the floor in her mad rush to discover something useful, she seized upon a bottle of hydrochloric acid and pulled off the stopper.

She turned, bottle in hand, and yelled at Scotty, "Don't just stand there! Break 'em up!"

Scotty hesitated, scooting farther back under the table. Becky grabbed a scalpel from the counter and thrust it under the table, waving it wildly back and forth in Scotty's face.

"I never liked your kind," Becky shouted. "Your mama was right!"

Scotty yelped and threw himself into the melee. Becky maneuvered for position as the tangle of arms and legs rolled across the morgue floor.

Finally, Rex landed a hefty kick to Scotty's midriff, lifting him up into the air to come crashing down on the top of one of the metal tables, his breath driven from him with a loud gasp. Rex managed to grab Troy by the back of the neck and stood, hoisting the still struggling Troy into the air, where he flailed about helplessly trying to land another punch.

Becky said a silent prayer, stepped right up to Rex, and threw half the contents of the bottle straight into his face. She backed up and stood, amazed and nauseated, as the flesh began to bubble and melt, droplets spattering to the floor.

The room became suddenly quiet; even Troy stopped struggling, watching in horror. A long moment passed, the only sound a sickening hiss as the flesh on Rex's face continued to smoke and bubble.

"That hurt," said Rex dispassionately. He shifted his grip so that both hands were wrapped around Troy's throat.

"Put down the bottle or I'll tear his head off."

Becky hesitated, uncertain.

"I mean it," he said and began to squeeze. Troy started to turn blue and make strangled little yipping sounds.

Becky slowly placed the bottle on the edge of the counter, within reach.

"That's better," said Rex and relaxed his grip. He moved toward the door.

"You tell your toothy friend that I'd like to meet him. I'll keep this one with me. Just to make sure he shows up."

"Like hell you will!" Troy shouted and began to kick again.

Rex responded by shifting his grip and casually swinging Troy around so that he connected head first with the cinder block wall. Becky gasped as Troy fell limply silent.

"Are you crazy?" Becky shrieked.

"Don't worry. I've done this enough times to know the difference between unconscious and dead. If I'd preferred the latter," he said with another of the private smiles Becky was beginning to find intensely disturbing, "you'd be scraping his brains off the ceiling."

He returned to the body drawer that he had recently vacated and removed a pair of dark blue leather gloves, a wide-brimmed hat, and a rubber Ronald Reagan Halloween mask, all of which he donned rapidly, never once taking his eyes off Becky and the ghoul. He recrossed the room and opened the door with his free hand.

"Where are you going?" Becky cried.

"I'll be sure and let you all know," said Rex pleasantly as, Troy tucked under one arm, he vanished down the hall.

CHAPTER THIRTY

Becky was devastated. As she numbly cleaned up the wreckage in the morgue, she realized she was too upset to drive. So she prevailed upon Scotty to drive her back to Chris's to tell him the news. This was a major mistake as Scotty had only minimal experience with a standard transmission. Proceeding in a series of jolting starts and jarring stops, they drove down Santa Monica accompanied by the nerve-racking sound of gears grinding together.

Scotty sensed her distress and sought to cheer her up with what he thought would be an interesting comparison of the different types of edible garbage discarded by the various four-star restaurants in Chicago. Becky was unable to pay attention, and Scotty was soon quiet, concentrating on the stick shift, which had a mind of its own.

When they arrived at the apartment, Chris met them at the door. "Where's Troy?" was his first comment.

After a series of false starts, they managed to fill him in on the morning's events. By the end of their tale, Chris was in a white-hot rage.

"I'll kill that son of a bitch!" he said as soon as Becky and Scotty stopped talking. He grabbed the car keys from where Becky had dumped them on the coffee table and headed toward the front door.

Becky quickly darted in front of him and positioned herself between Chris and the door, blocking his exit.

"You can't go out there."

"Get out of my way," he growled. "I'm warning you."

"*You're* warning *me*?" Becky asked, hurt that Chris was clearly going to walk straight through both her and the closed door if she didn't move. "Fine, asshole," she said and stepped out of the way. "But don't come running to me when they scrape what's left of you off the sidewalk. It's bright daylight out there, you idiot! Do you *want* to end up looking like the Toxic Avenger?"

Chris was brought up short, his anger evaporating abruptly as he came back into the living room and sank down into a chair, head buried in his hands. "What am I going to do?"

Becky put a comforting hand on his shoulder. "There's nothing *we* can do until *he* lets us know where he is," she said.

"That's right," added Scotty. "You can count me in too. Troy's a little flaky, but he's awfully fun to be with. I mean, for a renf...uh, well, you know. Anyway, he promised me we could watch both *Mame*s, Rosalind Russell *and* Lucille Ball. We just *have* to get him back!"

Chris looked up at Becky, ignoring Scotty's inane comments, anguish on his face. "Troy could be dead by then."

"I don't think Rex wants to kill him," Becky said. "At least not yet. We have time."

Chris looked at her, unconvinced, with such a grief-stricken expression that Becky didn't know what else to say.

"We'll need help," Chris said. He turned to Scotty. "Would your friends be willing..."

Scotty nodded eagerly. "Yeah, just let me at that guy one more time and I'll...well, I'll..."

Becky gave him a glance somewhere between disgust and amusement. "You'll hide under the table again, right?"

Scotty at least had the courtesy to look slightly ashamed as he replied defensively, "I was the one who opened the cabinet with the acid, remember?"

Becky took pity, seeing his crestfallen expression. "Yes, dear, you did."

Scotty beamed proudly.

"What if we got some of the normals involved?" Chris asked him, "and made sure they didn't know about you?"

Scotty nodded again, this time resignedly.

"Well, let's go," said Chris, picking up the phone. "I'm gonna call Sylvia first and fill her in. Then you and Scotty…"

Becky gently took the receiver from his hand and replaced it.

"There's something even more important," she said. "*You* need food."

Chris snorted impatiently. "There's no time for that. We've got to find Troy."

"Listen you," said Becky as she shoved the surprised Chris down on the couch. "You're absolutely no good to him if you turn into Johnny Torch because you're weak from hunger."

"That was a cool comic," Scotty chimed in. "The Torch guy was hot!"

Becky shot him a withering glance and turned back to Chris. "Tell me what to do."

"What do you mean, tell you what to do?" Chris looked at her, confused.

"Food! Food!" she shouted, irritated. "What do you need? Aside from blood, I mean. I assume that if it was just the blood you needed, I'd have been bringing doggy bags home from the morgue by now."

"Doggy bags?" Scotty looked at her, intrigued. "You could do that?"

"This is *not* the time, Scotty!" Becky snapped. She turned back to Chris. "Do they have to be guys? I mean, I know you're gay, but does that make a difference?"

Chris's expression showed that he still didn't get it.

"I am offering," said Becky with forced patience, "to deliver vampire takeout."

"You're out of your mind," said Chris uncertainly.

"Probably. But you need to eat. You can't go out. Domino's Pizza is obviously out of the question. So, tell me what to do."

"Well, Troy usually…" Chris's voice broke for a moment; he couldn't go on.

"Look," said Becky firmly, "you're starting to make me crazy. One minute you're rushing madly out the door, trying to turn yourself into a french fry, and the next you've already got Troy dead and buried. Now, you can sit here, pissed at Rex and feeling sorry for yourself, wasting the whole fucking day starving to death. Or we can get cracking. Which is it?"

Chris was silent for a long moment. When he finally was willing to meet Becky's gaze directly, it was with an expression of unspoken gratitude.

"They don't have to be guys, but it helps."

"Why?" she asked.

Chris looked at her dumbly. "Why?" he repeated.

"In an ideal world," Becky said, "I know I could just walk out on the street, grab some stud, and ask him if he'd mind being the main course on *Dark Shadows*. Somehow, though, I don't think I'd have many takers. If you explain why—exactly what you need—maybe it'll help me figure something out."

"You're right. It's more than just the blood," began Chris uncomfortably. "There's gotta be, well, I don't know…" He stopped a moment.

"Go on."

"This is kinda personal, you know?"

Becky waited silently.

"There's gotta be some kind of strong emotion. Fear's good. So is pain. That's what Rex probably uses. But it's also dangerous unless you kill the victim," he said grimly.

"What about friendship?" asked Becky slowly, unconsciously rubbing her throat.

Chris smiled at her. "That's very sweet." His expression grew serious. "But friendship's not strong enough. It'd be like eating Chinese food. An hour later…"

"So, it'll have to be sex?"

"It's one of the strongest emotions humans have," said Chris.

"And you like boys, to my unending dismay." She smiled.

"And the more strongly attracted I am, the stronger the response I can evoke in him."

"OK." Becky stood up, clapping her hands together sharply once. "Boys it is then. You," she indicated Chris, "wait here. And you," she commanded, "are coming with me."

Scotty blanched. "Why me?" he whined softly.

"Because, my friend, in this town you've got a better chance of bringing him breakfast in bed than I do!"

CHAPTER THIRTY-ONE

Thirty minutes later, a reluctant Scotty firmly in tow, Becky was beginning to appreciate the difficulty her gay friends had in that elusive sport known as "cruising."

First, they'd driven to the parking lot behind the Gold Coast bar, hoping to find someone looking for a little mid-morning action. They did. But the five men they encountered were all strongly vetoed by Scotty as being members of, as he so tactfully put it, "the troll patrol."

Next, they tried the Pleasure Chest. They browsed through the aisles of leather whips, harnesses, and masks, past the stacks of flavored lubricants and racks of condoms in a variety of designer colors. It proved educational, but unfortunately the only other people in the store at this time of the morning were the counter clerks. The two of them decided to hang out for a few minutes next to a display of manacles and restraints in the hope that a more easily available, preferably appetizing, gent would make an appearance.

However, after Scotty started playing with the buttons on a display of battery-operated dildos, causing them to writhe spasmodically in mechanically simulated orgasm, they started to get strange looks from the man behind the massage oil counter. Becky figured it would be better if they drew as little attention to themselves as possible and decided to leave, dragging Scotty behind her, deaf to his protests that it wasn't as if he'd *broken* anything.

They finally positioned themselves strategically in front of the plate glass window fronting the weight room of the Boys' Town Gym. Becky had unbuttoned Scotty's shirt three quarters of the way down the front and left him to "window shop" while she ran across the street to a liquor store to buy him some mint-flavored chewing gum. His breath, she had been forced to admit, left a lot to be desired. *Undoubtedly,* she thought with a shudder, *as a result of his diet.*

Feeling rather peckish herself, she purchased not only the gum but also a York peppermint patty and, in a slight assuaging of her guilt, several reduced-calorie Milky Way bars. Darting back across Santa Monica clutching the paper bag of goodies in one hand, she crammed one of the Milky Ways into her mouth and noticed with satisfaction that Scotty had taken matters into his own hands with marked success.

Not only had the ghoul removed his shirt entirely, revealing broad shoulders, a well-muscled chest, and a surprisingly small waist, but he'd also pulled the cotton slacks he'd borrowed from Troy so low around his hips that Becky could almost swear she glimpsed the beginnings of his ass crack.

And I thought he was tubby, she marveled. Stepping back on to the curb, she looked down at her rather frumpy clothing and considered her own eating habits, wondering if perhaps…and gave the idea up with a derisive snort.

Scotty was proving to be in good form, stopping every exiting athlete with a request for the time, a cigarette, or details about the gym until he'd managed to capture the continued attention of two stunning young men. In fact, she doubted that Troy, at his best, could have gathered such a remarkably good-looking duo in as short a time. She sidled up to the small crowd, not wanting to seem too obviously in Scotty's company so as to frighten away Chris's prospective lunch, wondering if she could eavesdrop and pick up a few tips to improve her own sadly deficient love life. Scotty had enmeshed the more gorgeous of the two lads, the blond, in a spirited discussion of the merits of isotonic as opposed to isometric exercise. She listened in amazement as Scotty rattled off a series of statistics, interspersed with a rather technical commentary on the kinesthetic effects of both forms of exercise. She also noted that Scotty had unbuttoned the top two buttons of the slacks, revealing a perky little curl or two of pubic hair, and the most obvious object of his attention was having a hard time concentrating on the conversation. The other boy, a short brunette with eyes so green that Becky was sure he must be wearing colored contacts, seemed intent on dragging the blond away from the conversation and edging in on Scotty himself.

Probably the lover, thought Becky. *They're both wearing identical outfits.* Squaring her shoulders, she marched past Scotty and his new friend, intentionally jostling the green-eyed boy.

"Oh, excuse me," she said, batting her eyelashes flirtatiously. "Do you belong to this gym? I'm thinking of joining."

She chose to take his grunt of response as an affirmative, and as he turned back to renew his tugging on the blond's arm, she tapped him on the shoulder. "I'm sorry?" she said. "I didn't hear you."

"I said I work there," he repeated gruffly.

Somebody up there likes us! she thought, rolling her eyes heavenward in silent thanks. "I was wondering if you knew what the price was for a year membership. It can't be more than, oh, say $1200, can it?"

Becky watched with thinly disguised delight as the green-eyed boy warred with the conflicting emotions of lust for Scotty, the desire to get his friend to leave, and greed. The employees of the Boys' Town Gym, Becky knew, worked on commission, and Becky had intentionally quoted a fee almost twice that of the normal rate.

"Maybe you could take me in and talk to me about signing up?" she hinted.

Greed finally won out and she was escorted into the club, first making sure to catch Scotty's eye as she dropped the car keys into a planter by the entrance. She had a brief second of concern as she noticed a bit of drool starting to form in the corner of Scotty's mouth as the blond removed his shirt to demonstrate the proper way to do a particular exercise.

I'm sure he won't touch him while he's still alive, she attempted to reassure herself. She could almost see the wheels turning in Scotty's head as he considered pushing the young man into passing traffic and dining on the result.

"Are you coming?" the green-eyed boy asked Becky irritably.

"I hope you have a weight-reduction program," she said hopefully as she went inside, first stopping to pull another Milky Way out of her bag.

An hour later, she managed to extricate herself from her guide. He was determined, especially since Becky had probably spoiled his relationship with the blond and any chance he may have had to shack up with Scotty, on selling her a membership—whether she wanted one or not.

Finally, after accepting a two-week free trial membership, signing a contract, and swearing she was going straight to the bank to get her host the yearly fee, in cash, she bolted out the door, relieved to see that Scotty and his friend had vanished.

She raced to the corner as fast as her legs would carry her and, digging wildly in her purse for the correct change, managed to catch the bus. Chomping into the last candy bar to fortify herself during the ride, she disembarked on the corner of Harper and Santa Monica and raced up the block to Chris's apartment building.

She burst through the front door eagerly to find Scotty seated calmly on the couch, munching contentedly on a plate of raw hamburger meat.

"Shh-h-h!" he cautioned. "He's gone. Chris is resting."

"I brought you some gum," she said for lack of anything better and tossed Scotty the pack, which he examined with distaste.

"Well?" she asked, hands firmly planted on her hips. Scotty looked up, questioning. "How the hell did you know all that?"

"All what?"

"The stuff you were spouting to that blond. That's second- or third-year med school."

"Oh, that," Scotty said blithely. "Basic anatomy."

Becky still looked confused, so he explained further. "I'm a *ghoul,*" he said proudly. "Mama was teaching me anatomy before I learned to read."

Becky refused to allow her distaste to show. "You didn't…?"

"Nah, I saved him for Chris." He bent to lick the juice from the plate. "You should've heard them in there!" He belched lightly and added, "Pity the guy won't be able to remember it."

"You're back," said Chris as he appeared in the doorway.

"How'd it go?"

"Much better," he said as he pulled the curtains aside and stood in the full onslaught of the sun with no ill effects. "I'm still a little tired, though."

"Well, you had a full meal."

"Yeah," he said and grinned. "*Full* is the word, all right."

"Did you get his number?" asked Scotty hopefully.

"Why?" Becky snapped. "In case he gets hit by a bus or something?"

Scotty looked properly chastised.

"Aren't we forgetting about someone?" she added testily. "Like Troy?"

Chris looked at her angrily. "Fuck you."

"You too, dear. Ah shit, I'm sorry. I'm just feeling a little stressed, I guess. I just spent an hour with Arnold Schwarzenegger junior and something like a thousand dollars on a membership to a gay gym."

Apologies accepted, they got down to business. After some discussion, it was agreed that Becky would take Max's photograph of the painting of Rex and speak with Clive. Scotty and his friends would spend the day searching for Rex's new lair, and Chris would stay at home, trying to get some much-needed sleep and waiting for Rex to contact him.

"Remember," Chris told them both as they left, "concentrate on public buildings and businesses. He can't enter a residence unless he's been invited."

CHAPTER THIRTY-TWO

Leaving an exhausted Chris behind, Becky dropped Scotty off at his hotel to rendezvous with his friends, stopping off at her office briefly before driving to the sheriff's station. She marched into Clive's office clutching several file folders, face set with determination, and discovered him in a meeting with a sergeant and two deputies.

"Get out," she said to the startled officers.

"What the hell do you think you're doing?" asked Clive.

"This is private. Get them out."

Clive motioned to the others to leave. He closed the door and turned to Becky. "What's going on?"

"Get Pamela over here," she commanded.

Clive bristled. "Look, you. You've been giving me nothing but attitude for the past week. Who the hell do you think you are, coming in here and…"

"I know who the killer is," said Becky softly.

Clive stopped in midstream, mouth gaping. "But how? Who?"

Becky sighed. "I've only got the strength to go through this once.

Call Pamela, but don't say anything. Just get her here and I'll tell you both at the same time."

Clive picked up the phone and called the city manager, keeping close watch on Becky as if she were an escaped lunatic, calm for now but capable of freaking out at any moment.

While they were waiting, Becky refused to talk despite Clive's questions.

"Look, Clive, I've just spent a morning that's been a cross between a day at Disneyland and a visit to Camarillo Mental Hospital. Let's wait for Pam, OK?" She sat, exhausted, in a chair. "Do you have any doughnuts?" she asked hopefully.

Clive handed his secretary a handful of change and ordered her to round up some cake or candy or something from the machines in the officers' lounge. Within minutes, she came in with a couple of packaged Danish, several candy bars, and a few packets of mixed nuts. Burman arrived less than ten minutes later as Becky was polishing off the second of three Almond Joys after having sent every available cashew, walnut, and almond on to its greater reward.

"What's so goddamn important?" she demanded, entering the room with a flurry of lime-green silk. "I've got a meeting with the chamber this afternoon on this cockamamy Halloween thing tonight and Saturday and…"

"Becky's found our killer."

Burman stopped her carefully prepared tirade, surprise rapidly giving way to relief. "Thank God," she breathed.

"I didn't say I've found him, Clive. I said I know who he is." She tossed the photo onto Clive's desk. "The name is Rex Castillian."

"Castillian? Right," said Clive, picking up the telephone. Becky leaned forward quickly and hung the phone up, taking the photo back from Clive.

"What are you doing?"

"There's something we've got to discuss first."

"Look," said Clive, "if you've violated this guy's constitutional rights or something, I don't want to hear it. Let the public defender come up with it on his own."

"It's nothing like that."

"Well, what is it?" Burman was getting annoyed.

"I have to swear both of you to absolute secrecy before you get anything out of me other than that photo and his name. And I can practically guarantee you're not gonna be able to find him or find out anything else about him. I'm willing to tell you almost everything I know, but I'm going to have to ask you not to press me on anything I can't or won't answer."

Burman glared. "How would you like to be locked up for a couple of months for withholding evidence? I'll make sure Clive gives you all the bread and water you want. You'll be looking like Donna Reed in, let's say five years."

"Fine." Becky stood up, carefully placing the remaining half of a cherry Danish on Clive's desk, and held her arms out in front of her toward him.

"Huh?" he asked.

"Cuff me. Take me away and lock me up."

"You're serious."

"Absolutely."

The other two stood poised in a tableau of uncertainty.

"Uh, Becky," Clive said, "we not only want to catch this guy, we want to put him away. We can't do that if we can't make a case to the D.A."

"Trust me, Clive," she replied, calmly resuming her assault on the Danish. "You'll never have to."

"I have had enough of this! If you think—"

"Stifle it, Pam," said Clive.

"How dare you—"

"I said, shut up!" Clive's voice was forceful, commanding. Burman, never having been spoken to by him in that way before, promptly quieted. In a more even tone, he continued, "Which do you want more, Pam? Catching this guy or yelling at Becky? I for one trust her, and for the time being I'm willing to listen." He sat behind his desk. "Before we go any further, there are a few things I have to know."

"Shoot."

"Did you do anything illegal yourself?"

"No, nothing that could get anyone in trouble. Look, Clive, I'm telling you. We can stop the killings. But this guy will never stand trial."

"Why not?"

"To stop him, we'll have to kill him."

Clive smiled tolerantly. "Becky, this is America. We can't just go around killing people who break the law, no matter how heinous their crimes are. Here," he added, handing her his handkerchief so that she could wipe her now chocolate- and cherry-covered hands.

"If you don't kill him, you won't stop him." Becky paused, carefully licking the remains of the Danish and the candy from her fingers before she used the hanky. She handed it back to him, took a deep breath, and then plunged in. "Actually, I'm hoping we *can* kill him."

Clive was uneasy. "You're not going to start with that Dracula crap again."

Becky reached down and threw the autopsy files on his desk.

Clive picked them up, puzzled. "What are these?"

"My reports."

"I've seen them already."

"No. You've seen the ones I dummied up when things got critical. These are the real ones."

"You did what?" gasped Burman, who quickly quieted at Clive's stern glance.

Clive's eyebrows inched toward his hairline as he began to read. After a moment, he closed the file and looked earnestly across the desk at Becky.

"You obviously know what's in here. What if I were to say you need a very long vacation?"

"I'd say that I've saved samples of everything and we'd better get a second opinion. I hope that's not necessary. As you can see, the fewer people who know about this, the better."

"What's in there?" Pamela wanted to know. Clive tossed her the file. She glanced at it briefly then threw it back on Clive's desk with annoyance. "Do I look like a frigging doctor? I don't understand this shit!"

"Becky seems to be trying to tell us that our killer isn't human."

"That's it!" Burman stood up. "You," she said, pointing at Becky, "are crazy! And you," she pointed at Clive, "need your head examined for even considering this shit!"

"I'm telling you I have saliva samples, Pamela. They're not human."

"Then why didn't you tell us that two weeks ago?" Burman demanded. "We could've had NASA out here already, rounding up all the little green men in town for questioning."

"I had my reasons."

"You're protecting someone," Clive said, his eyes widening with surprise.

"Yes," Becky said quietly. She looked up into Clive's eyes, "But not the killer. I swear."

Clive's gaze held hers for a long moment. Finally, he started with a realization of some kind.

"You can't mean…" he started to say. "Not…" He sat back in his chair with a tired sigh. "No wonder…" he said to himself, momentarily forgetting the presence of Pamela and Becky. Then a look of vague discomfort crossed his face and, abandoning whatever it was he had been about to say, he turned to look at Burman. "I believe her."

"Oh, great!"

"And as long as I'm captain of this station, Pamela," he said strictly, "you will do what I say. Got that?"

Burman started to protest.

"Or I will have *you* arrested. Is that clear?"

Something must have told Burman that Clive was serious. Her mouth opened and shut several times, gaping like a fish, until she finally swallowed her comments and meekly sat back down.

"Now that that's finished," said Clive, "why don't you tell us the whole story?"

Becky started speaking, filling them in on the events of the past

BITE CLUB

several weeks. Several times during the story, Burman threw up her hands, snorting in disgust and disbelief. Clive, however, was determined to hear Becky out, and each time he forced Burman to be quiet and listen.

Becky was careful not to reveal too many details. She refrained from discussing Chris's nature by passing him off as a sort of modern-day Van Helsing. Since Burman continued to be adamant in her scorn of the notion of vampires existing, it never occurred to her to ask any uncomfortable questions. Clive merely listened with a look on his face that implied he was reserving his comments.

Becky continued with her story. She left Scotty out altogether and rearranged the details of the fight in the morgue so that only she and Troy had been present. She covered the kidnapping in great detail and concocted a little white lie, telling them Chris had been so grief-stricken that she'd had to give him a heavy sedative, thereby explaining why he would be unavailable to help them out until at least early evening. It was at this point that Clive confirmed Becky's suspicion that he had seen through the weaknesses in her story and had deduced exactly who, and quite possibly what, she was protecting. He shook his head sadly and said, "Jesus, O'Brien. Can't you ever find a *normal* guy to go out with? I knew your taste in men was pretty awful, but this…"

Becky finally finished and sat, waiting for their reactions.

"This is great," said Burman. "If the press gets hold of a story like this, I can just see the headlines: 'Medical Examiner Muffs Melee with Monster in Morgue.'"

"The press is not gonna hear anything about this. Understand?" Clive was firm.

"How can you sit here and listen to this shit?" Burman asked.

Clive carefully shifted some papers on his desk so that the edges were lined up horizontally with each other. He slowly rearranged his in-box and pen holders until all was tidy and to his satisfaction. Finished, he leaned back in his chair and, to the amazement of the other two, actually propped his feet up on the desk, wrinkling and disarraying his neatly ordered papers and files.

"Becky," he said, "go out to my secretary and get me a cigarette. Get yourself some more candy if there's any left."

"But you don't smoke."

"Not in ten years. Just do it."

Becky returned in a moment with the cigarette and a lighter. Clive lit up and inhaled, coughing once. With his second drag, his face relaxed with enjoyment.

"Would you like some coffee, Pamela?"

"What Pamela would like," said Burman irritably, "is a nice stiff drink."

Clive smiled. "Compliments of the Los Angeles County Sheriff's Department." He pulled an unopened bottle of scotch out of his bottom desk drawer and poured Burman a healthy slug while she watched in shock.

"If you're drinking on city time…" she began with a threatening tone.

"Can it, Pamela. It's purely medicinal."

"Yeah. Right. Sure." She downed the liquor in one gulp, grimaced, coughed, and held out her glass to be refilled.

Becky couldn't resist. "Drinking on city time, Pam?"

"Becky…" Clive warned.

"Sorry." She stifled a small giggle and tried to look serious again.

Clive sat quietly smoking and thought for a minute. "Let me tell you both a story," he said finally and looked around for an ashtray. Becky passed him the wastebasket.

"A story? Oh, great! Just what we need," Burman sniffed. "Wait, don't tell me. It's a fairy tale, right?"

"A fairy tale? In this town, you'd be surprised?" Becky said glibly.

"No. Not a fairy tale. A true tale," Clive cut them off before they could start in on each other again. "I'll be frank. I've spent the last three weeks trying to ignore the evidence that was right in front of me." He grimaced. "Trying to bury old memories, I guess. But this…" He slapped the file. "This changes things, doesn't it?"

Neither one answered him, so he went on.

"You both know I'm originally from Louisiana?" They nodded.

"When I was a little boy, long before we moved here, I lived for a summer with my granny outside of New Orleans. Way outside New Orleans." He smiled. "In fact, she lived in the swamps."

"I can't imagine you living in a swamp. What'd Granny do? Run a dry cleaner?" Burman snorted.

"As a matter of fact, she sold moonshine. Very good moonshine, I recall."

Even Burman couldn't help matching Clive's grin.

"Oh, my granny was quite a lady, she was. She was also something of a wise woman. All her neighbors, and the nearest lived a mile or so away, would come to Granny's for herbs and love potions and such, not to mention the booze."

Slowly, Clive's voice became softer, more rhythmic, with a gentle cadence that betrayed his Louisiana upbringing.

"It was Granny's last summer—she died before fall." Clive shuddered briefly. "But I learned a lot from that woman."

"Love potions?" asked Burman sarcastically.

"Mostly willow bark and dandelion root. Granny had no secrets from me. I recall her telling me that if you make a lot of mumbo-jumbo and wear the right kind of wild costume, folks'll believe just about anything. Just make sure you don't give 'em anything harmful and their minds'll do the rest. Come to think of it," he said, looking at Pamela's outfit, "Granny used to dress a lot like you."

Burman was speechless at the insult coming from the normally deferential Clive.

"But Granny warned me about other things. Things that don't have anything to do with willow bark. Dark things." Clive became grim.

"Little footprints in the mud of the bayou, too small to be human. Will-o'-the-wisps floating out over the river. Tracks changing from man to animal and back again. I can still remember the last time…no, I am *not* gonna talk about that! Suffice to say I believe that there are more things out there than we know of."

He turned his attention to Burman. "I may be just a superstitious old fool, but Becky isn't. I've known her for nigh on five years now and I've never met anyone more levelheaded or more professional in medicine. Then again, there's that pile of dust with human bone, the coffins, the condition of the victims. I'm sorry, Pam. That's two to one. I think you've been outvoted."

Clive finished the cigarette, wistfully examining the glowing butt before crushing it out on the sole of his shoe. He dropped it into the wastebasket.

"You say it's a vampire out there? I don't want to believe you, but I'll take the chance—*after* I've seen those samples and had one of your assistants run 'em again." He paused. "I don't know what your religious beliefs are, Becky O'Brien, but you'd best say a prayer for the soul of my granny. If it weren't for her, I'd have half a mind to start measuring you for one of those little white jackets."

He gently plucked the photo from Becky's grasp.

"In the meantime, I'm going to have this copied and posted. If we do catch this guy alive, you and him are *both* going to have a lot of explaining to do."

CHAPTER THIRTY-THREE

Troy woke up disoriented—and cramped. The disorientation was caused primarily because he found himself hanging in midair, slowly swaying from side to side in what the dim lighting revealed as some kind of vertical air shaft. A series of gears and wheels gently whirled into action several feet above his head; a variety of cables hung down past his bound body to disappear into the darkness below.

The cramping was caused by the fact that his hands had been firmly tied behind his back and both legs were lashed together with heavy rope. He was suspended by a crude harness, constructed of the same rope and attached to something above him that was hidden in the murky darkness.

By far the most irritating aspect of his captivity, however, was the large foul-smelling rag that had been stuffed into his mouth, secured with electrical tape. Troy was therefore unable to talk, a situation he found intolerable, and he was limited to expressing his outrage at being trussed like a housefly in a spider's web via a series of very low grunts.

Above him, the gears and wheels increased their motion with a grinding clash, the resulting high-pitched whir drowning out the loudest of his attempts to cry for help through the gag. The cables began moving, alternately lengthening and shortening. Below him he sensed movement: A large object approached with a rush of air and a slight scraping sound.

Troy looked down, his eyes widening in fear as something moved toward him, inexorably closer and closer. Suddenly the gears and cables ceased their activity and the object halted about thirty feet below, just within the limit of Troy's sight. He started to breathe a sigh of relief, which was quickly withdrawn as, several seconds later, the object began to come toward him once again.

Fearful he was about to be crushed, he tensed his stomach muscles and drew his bound legs up against his chest. The object halted several feet below him and Troy was able to relax once again, his feet dangling just inches above the flat top of the behemoth below. Then the object began to descend.

It was at this point that Troy made two interesting discoveries. First he realized he was hanging at the top of an elevator shaft. Second, if he were willing to put a little more pressure on his already aching shoulders, he could stretch his feet just far enough for the ropes wrapped around them to make contact with one of the cables. Tightening his tummy again, he carefully lifted his legs and positioned them so that the elevator cables' motion could, with any luck, begin to saw through his bonds. For the first time in half a century, Troy Raleigh began to pray.

◊ ◊ ◊

Pamela Burman's drive home was not a pleasant one. Several times she'd been cut off by other cars in the after-work traffic, and one mentally deficient woman made an illegal left turn in front of her, almost reducing Burman's front bumper to scrap. Burman dutifully noted the license plate numbers of each of the moron motorists—on a pad she kept on top of the dashboard for that specific purpose—and smiled, anticipating the sweetness of her revenge when the unsuspecting drivers opened their mail to discover citations.

BITE CLUB

She drove northwest on Holloway, cursing both the planning and transportation commissioners as she negotiated the insanely designed intersection that would allow her to proceed north on Horn to her condo building. She made it through without further incident and, shifting into the lowest gear, proceeded up Horn, past Spago restaurant, and turned right into the driveway of Shoreham Towers.

As she waited for the valet to park her car, Burman reviewed her earlier meeting with Becky and Clive, trying to figure out what had gone wrong. Burman realized she was sometimes very difficult to deal with and that she had frequently, through sheer force of will, been able to bully Clive into complying with her wishes. This morning, though, for the first time, he'd stood up to her, yelling back and forcing her into silence. She had to admit, her admiration for the man had increased tenfold as a result.

She didn't agree with Becky and Clive's view of how to proceed; the notion that West Hollywood was beset with an actual vampire was too ludicrous to accept. Nevertheless, they obviously believed it, and in the face of Clive's threats she was forced to go along. She had no doubt that if she were to open her mouth in opposition to her colleagues' plan of action, Clive would immediately have her arrested. And Becky had assured her that if Pamela so much as thought of taking any action against them or went public in any way, she'd be waiting with the commitment papers already drawn up, ready to deny that she and Clive had ever seriously considered the notion of a vampire at all.

Turning over her car keys to the red-jacketed valet, she entered the glass double door to the building and stopped at the reception desk to pick up her mail. The top envelope contained an announcement from the West Hollywood Chamber of Commerce regarding the Halloween parade.

Pamela grimaced in distaste. In her heart of hearts, she felt that holding the Halloween festivities prior to catching the killer was a fatal mistake. But neither the mayor nor the city council nor the chamber could be prevailed upon to see it her way. She'd kept arguing until even she had run out of words, all to no avail. Tonight, the festivities would begin.

Leaving City Hall, she'd noticed the Parking Authority had already posted NO PARKING signs on the boulevard and employees of the Parks Department were standing by to erect barricades blocking the side streets and cordoning off Santa Monica between La Cienega and Robertson. The carts and booths on the median strip were already awaiting the wares of local shopkeepers, and the stage for the costume contest had already gone up at the intersection of Santa Monica and San Vicente.

Mentally cursing the foolishness of those with less vision than herself, she entered the elevator.

Maybe you're just getting old, Pammy, my girl, she thought as the doors closed for the short ride up to her penthouse unit. She sighed heavily, noting that for the past several weeks, no matter what she tried to do, she seemed to be frustrated at every turn.

Putting the debate on the wisdom of holding the celebration behind her for a moment, her thoughts moved to the more practical problems the city would face: crowd control, traffic jams, parking, and cleanup. She arrived at her floor and exited the elevator, thinking, *We're the only city in the country that can manage to clean up after 100,000 people in less than six hours and still can't manage to time walk signals so that anyone but an Olympic sprinter can get across the street before the light changes.*

Shaking her head at the perversity of running such a unique municipality, she paused in front of her door and fumbled with her keys for a moment, finally unlocking it and proceeding inside.

She closed the door behind her and stood blinking in the dimness. She had told her maid a dozen times to leave the blinds open and turn on a lamp when she left, ostensibly so that the plants would have light. In actuality, though she would never admit it, Burman's eyesight was not what it had once been, especially in the absence of sufficient light; she hated entering a dark apartment.

Although she admitted to being on "the other side of sixty," Burman had always considered herself younger than her chronological age. Over the past several years however, she found it more and more difficult to jog up the hill to her apartment upon returning

from her morning constitutional. At first she'd blamed the slight
shortness of breath and the excess of perspiration on her tennis shoes.
After irritably trying out and discarding several different brands,
she'd finally been forced to admit that at sixty-eight she wasn't quite
the athlete she'd been at fifty. Gradually, over a period of about two
years, she'd slowed down her previous attack on the hill from a rapid
trot to a brisk walk, and she now sometimes stopped at Cravings
restaurant, ostensibly for coffee but in reality as a subterfuge for
allowing her to catch her breath.

In fact, only the mayor and the city council knew her true age,
and thanks to West Hollywood's age-discrimination laws, she
would be able to hold her current position as long as she managed
to competently perform her duties and convince the city council to
renew her contract. Even Daniel Eversleigh, in the depths of their
bitterest arguments, had never dared suggest that her advanced age
made her less than capable of running the city. In fact, Daniel's
worst nightmares involved Pam's being struck by a car one morning
during her jogging expeditions, leaving him with the horrendously
terrifying task of trying to operate the city himself while searching
for her replacement.

In the darkness, however, when entering an empty room or jogging down the street in the winter predawn hush, Burman always
suffered a sense of disquiet. It was typical of her personality that she
would always fight back the rising panic, banishing thoughts of
rapists and muggers to the dim recesses of her mind, and proceed
onward, head held high, with a fearless attitude displayed to the rest
of the world.

But now, in the privacy of her own home, she gave way to the jit-
ters a little and nervously tossed her keys and purse onto the table by
the door. She removed her lilac leather driving gloves and stuffed
them into the pocket of her burnt-orange coat before taking it off
and moving into the room, tossing it over the back of an armchair.

She came fully into the living room, knocking her shin against the
corner of the coffee table. Feeling blindly about in front of her, her
hands came in contact with the shade of the floor lamp next to the

sofa. She groped for the switch and, finding it, turned on the lamp, relieved at the sudden illumination.

She turned toward the art deco cherrywood table where she kept her answering machine, preparing to retrieve any emergency messages that might have come in from the chamber, the council, or countless others.

She froze, speechless. A wave of inevitability swept over her as her greatest hidden fears were realized. There on the couch, in *her* home, was a short, muscular, dark-haired young man wearing the vilest smile she had ever seen.

Pamela started to scream but only managed to emit a small gasp. Dizziness washed over her; she couldn't believe this was actually happening. Her eyes darted to the telephone, only inches away from her hand. She moved her fingers toward it slightly.

"I wouldn't do that if I were you," commented the young man pleasantly.

He rose gracefully and began to walk toward her. Pamela fought desperately against fainting as the young man took her by the arm and forced her to sit in her favorite chair. He released her and sat back down on the couch.

"I don't believe we've been formally introduced, Miss Burman, although I know a great deal about you." His constant smile was about to drive Pamela crazy. "I'm an avid reader of *Frontiers,* the *Gazette,* and *Edge.* My admiration for you is boundless. Your name appears in print more frequently than that of the director of the Gay and Lesbian Center. A remarkable accomplishment, don't you agree?"

If this is Larsen's idea of a joke, thought Pamela, silently trying to retain her composure, *I'll kill the son of a bitch!*

"My name," the young man continued, "is Rex Castillian. Or at least that's the name you'd know me by."

"Castillian?" Burman's thoughts were awhirl. She knew she'd heard the name but was unable to still her panic enough to concentrate on where or when.

"Please, dear lady," he continued, "there's no need to be frightened. I'm afraid rape and robbery are out of the question. I'm incapable of the former and have no need of the latter."

Burman took a breath to scream.

"Ah, ah, ah," Rex cautioned, wagging a forefinger at her. "That would be an unfortunate mistake. Very unfortunate."

"How did you get in?" she finally managed to gasp.

Rex pretended surprise. "Why, you invited me, of course."

"I...invited...you?"

"At your last city council meeting, I recall. Let me see if I can remember your exact words." Rex placed one hand under his chin, feigning deep thought. "Ah, yes! I believe you said something like 'I just wish I could meet that son of a bitch once. I'd like to give that bastard a piece of my mind. I'd sit him right down in my living room and tell him what I thought of madmen who go around killing people in *my* town!' You'll forgive me if I've misquoted you slightly." Rex smiled again.

"*You!*" Pamela realized who the young man was in a flash.

"At your service." Rex made a little bow from his position on the couch.

"Now, Miss Burman," he began, "we have much to talk about." He leaned forward, the grin vanishing from his face to be replaced by an expression of serious intensity. "I understand," he continued, "that you don't believe in vampires..."

CHAPTER THIRTY-FOUR

The West Hollywood Halloween celebration was in full swing by nine-thirty Friday evening. Santa Monica Boulevard was jam-packed with people. The sidewalks were so crowded with the overflow from the bars that pedestrians were forced to walk in the street. Although only about a third of those present were in costume, it could be said that the quality of the costumes more than compensated for the number of those in street clothes.

West Hollywood's costume parade had been a tradition for many years, beginning long before the city was incorporated in 1984. What started out as a one-night opportunity for men to appear publicly in drag rapidly blossomed, with the addition of costume contests in the individual bars, into an endless promenade of people up and down the boulevard from dusk to the early morning hours.

Imelda Marcos strode regally along the median strip in her black gown, a stack of shoe boxes in each hand, while Cruella de Vil stomped down the street, shoving people out of her way and dragging a stuffed dalmatian daubed with blood-red paint on a rope behind her. Scarlett O'Hara was also present, complete with five o'clock shadow, causing not a little consternation among the masses as they were forced to duck to avoid being nailed by the curtain rods sticking out from her shoulders as she gaily pirouetted, trying to show off her dress by making it flair out attractively. And West Hollywood's Halloween parade wouldn't have been complete without the requisite number of Blue Nuns, an entire convent-full of which were reeling down the street, having liberally partaken of their namesake.

The non-drag costumes were equally original. Phileas Fogg lounged near the doorway to Rage in his balloon basket, complete with an eight-foot-diameter papier-mâché balloon overhead and a little Passepartout puppet. The Flintmobile, two lesbians in bare feet dressed as Barney and Fred, careened madly down the sidewalk, the Stone Age car forcing people farther out into the street. The Justice League of America, six stunning young men and one woman, made an appearance, but an hour later the satin-clad Batman, Superman, Wonder Woman, Flash, Green Lantern, Martian Manhunter, and Aquaman disappeared into Studio One for an evening of dancing and…whatever.

The theater and movie queens had outdone themselves this year. Liza was present in abundance—in top hat, tails, black stockings, and cabaret fringe. And a 300-pound drag queen with a microphone, red wig, and scaly green satin tail loudly proclaimed herself to be "Ethel: the Little Merman." A pink satin–clad Glinda, the Good Witch of the North, complete with a Saran Wrap bubble, majestically proceeded down the boulevard tapping people on the shoulder with her star-tipped wand and asking whether anyone had seen her lost munchkins. And Tippi Hedren, trapped in a telephone booth, fought bravely against crazed seagulls attached to the booth with wires.

The usual assortment of zombies, clowns, ghosts, ballerinas, and witches could also be spotted, but in West Hollywood such costumes were just a teeny bit brighter and more arresting than one could find anywhere else. There were dozens of people, all male, dressed as female pop stars: Madonna, Christina Aguilera, Beyonce. And every founding member of the city's chamber of commerce had conspired to march down the main thoroughfare dressed as milk cartons, with their faces protruding from the cartons' sides, whimsical descriptions of how they had been "lost" stenciled beneath in turquoise Magic Marker.

The judging of the costume contest would take place at midnight. Even at this early hour a white unicorn, several Klingons, and a group of five muscle studs wearing little more than artistically placed multicolored feathers were lined up at the raised stage on Santa Monica and San Vicente vying for a good spot in the contest lineup. The West Hollywood Cheerleaders had already assembled at the rear of the stage, ready to kick off the contest with a stunning display of gymnastic talents guaranteed to amaze and astound the crowd. Unbeknownst to the cheerleaders, the small group of leather boys gathered at the foot of the stage had not come to cheer them on to greater acrobatic feats but rather to see who would win the betting pool as to how many wigs would vacate the heads of the cheerleaders during the first five minutes of the routine.

Both Pamela Burman and Clive Anderson were slated to be judges this year, along with Daniel Eversleigh and the city council, Ed Larsen, Charles Partridge, and several other prominent business owners. The chamber of commerce, wise for once, had made certain to place Daniel Eversleigh's and Pamela Burman's chairs at opposite ends of the stage to keep them from trying to kill each other. During last year's festivities, the two city officials had been seated next to each other and had had one of their famous arguments. Pamela had triumphed after ripping a four-foot-long stuffed dildo from one of the nearby revelers' costumes and trying to bludgeon the mayor to death with it—all to the delight of a nearby *Entertainment Tonight* camera crew and to the unending chagrin of the chamber of commerce.

Becky arrived at the judges' stand at quarter to ten, relieved to find Clive already there. She'd called the sheriff's station every hour on the hour until just after quitting time, but there had been no news of either Troy or Rex Castillian. Finally, bleary-eyed from lack of sleep, she'd collapsed exhausted at her desk, finally waking up at seven to call the station for the latest report. There were no new developments.

She'd been unable to get in touch with Clive since she'd left the coroner's office at five-thirty and hoped desperately he'd have good news when he arrived at the contest. Rushing home, she'd showered, changed into her costume, and called Chris. Getting his machine, she instructed him to meet her at the stage at ten o'clock for a pow-wow. She'd tried Pamela at home also and left a duplicate message.

Fighting her way through the crowd to the stage, witch's hat askew, Becky had run into a worried looking Carlos in the guise of Shanda Leer.

"Have you heard from Ms. Burman?" he yelled over the heads of a female John Wayne and a blond-haired devil in a sequined G-string and red leather harness.

"No!" shouted Becky. "Is she here?" Becky shouldered her way through the costumed crowd toward Carlos. Her way was blocked by a group of five or six drag queens in bright pink polyester pantsuits and blond wigs carrying FOR SALE signs. One of them stopped her and thrust a pink business card into her hand. Automatically she glanced down at it and couldn't help smiling at the legend: PMS REALTY. IT'S THE RIGHT TIME OF THE MONTH TO BUY A HOUSE! By the time she looked up again, Carlos was being slowly borne away by the crowd.

"I've been trying to reach her since she left the office," he called.

"She's probably giving someone hell for watering their front lawn with a hose!" This was in reference to the West Hollywood water conservation ordinance Pam had passed during the first year of the California drought.

Carlos smiled. "Probably. See you at the contest."

A male Brunhilde in a blond fright wig and horned helmet cut off their view of one another. Becky waved anyway and moved on, clutching her broomstick.

Now at the judges' stand, Becky noted that Pamela was uncharacteristically late. She clambered up onto the platform and waited with barely controlled patience as Clive gave some last-minute instructions to one of his deputies. Finished, he turned to her with a worried expression and, taking in her costume, raised an eyebrow in query.

"The Gingerbread Witch," Becky explained. "It gives me an excuse." So saying, she plucked off one of the candy canes she'd attached to her skirt, neatly removed the cellophane wrapper, and stuck the curved end into her mouth.

"Shouldn't you have kept the cupcakes in front?" Clive asked. "You know you're gonna end up sitting on them."

"Huh?" Becky looked down at her costume. "Oh, the skirt slipped." She tugged it around so that the more fragile candies and cakes were properly in front.

"Any news?" she asked Clive once she was finished adjusting everything.

"No," Clive said. "Well, nothing good anyway."

Becky picked something up from Clive's tone. "Something's happened."

Clive removed a few specks of imaginary lint from his right sleeve and carefully adjusted his shirt cuffs before he replied, "Pamela's missing."

"What?" The candy cane fell from Becky's mouth. She deftly caught it before it hit the ground and grimaced at the stickiness. Clive, with a resigned sigh, passed her his handkerchief. Becky took it absently and wiped her hands.

"She was supposed to meet Daniel and the city council at seven-thirty to cut the ribbon starting the parade. She never showed."

"That's not like her at all."

"That's what I thought. I sent a car over to her place. She's not there. The doorman saw her come in around five-thirty, but he didn't see her leave."

"Did you check the apartment?"

"I didn't get a search warrant, if that's what you mean," said Clive huffily. "The building manager let the guys in and they sort of checked it out. You know, to make sure she wasn't lying in the tub with a broken hip or something."

"Maybe she went jogging."

"At night?"

"No, you're right," Becky mused. "She usually only goes out mornings. Are you sure they looked everywhere?"

"They didn't check under the bed or in the closets," Clive told her irritably. "She'd been home," he continued with a frown. "Her purse was on the table. But she wasn't in. Frankly, I'm a little worried." He shrugged. "But maybe she's out visiting one of her neighbors."

Becky looked up at Clive. "Pamela can't stand any of her neighbors. Maybe you should have checked the closets. And the balcony. And maybe—"

Clive's frown cut her off. "Becky…" he began patiently. "I'm sure there's a logical—"

"This is Pamela Burman we're talking about," she said, ignoring him, "Miss Polly Punctual. Did you at least put out a missing persons alert?"

"You know I need twenty-four hours for that."

"This is not a normal situation, Clive. Or did you forget about Granny?"

Clive spread his arms helplessly. "I've got someone posted in the lobby of her building. What else can I do?"

"Hello, Becky. Captain." Unnoticed, Chris had climbed up onto the platform. "Anything on Troy?" he asked, his face a picture of anguished hope.

Becky shook her head. "Have you heard anything?" she asked him.

"You mean from Scotty?" Chris shook his head. "They've been looking all day."

"Scotty who?" Clive wanted to know.

Becky reached out and touched his sleeve, leaving a smear of partially melted peppermint. "Never mind, Clive." As he started to protest she added, "I told you you'd have to trust me on some things, right?"

Clive looked at her angrily for a second. "Fine then. You two keep your little secrets. But don't think…" He ended his sentence with a snort that could have been interpreted as one of either disgust or discomfort. He turned and looked at Chris. His eyes narrowed as Chris shifted uncomfortably under his gaze.

"The expert, huh?" he murmured more to himself than to the others. "You gave him a sedative. Right. Who'd have thought it?"

"What do you mean, Clive?"

He answered her musingly. "It seems my granny might have been right after all."

"Look," said Becky, "I don't know what you're thinking…"

"Oh, I'll bet you do…"

"We don't have time for this!" She turned to Chris. "Pamela Burman's missing."

"The city manager?" He thought for a minute. "You think they're connected?"

"Young man," said Clive, "two people have vanished in twenty-four hours. I think it's fair to assume the same, ah, person is responsible. Don't you?"

"Do you have any ideas?" Becky asked Chris.

"No, I don't. He hasn't gotten in touch with me yet, but I'm hoping—" Chris stopped abruptly, staring off into the crowd behind Becky and Clive. They turned to follow his gaze.

There, about forty feet away, stood Rex Castillian wearing a green and purple jogging suit. Somehow the lopsided gray wig perched atop his head made him look more ominous than ridiculous. His grotesque resemblance to Pamela Burman was threateningly shocking.

"That's him," breathed Clive and began to motion toward one of the deputies stationed around the stage for crowd control.

"Wait," said Chris, softly but with a note of command.

The three watched as Rex, a vicious grin on his face, pointed first at himself and then held his right hand up to his ear like a telephone receiver and mimed dialing with the other. He stood for a minute, and then, with a quick bow, he vanished into the crowd.

"Does that mean what I think it does?" asked Clive quietly.

"Quick," said Becky. "Call Pamela."

CHAPTER THIRTY-FIVE

It took the three of them almost fifteen minutes to get down from the stage and across the street to the sheriff's station due to the necessity of pushing their way past assorted drag queens and costumed partiers.

"I can't believe you let your battery run down!" Becky chastised Clive for the third time.

"I don't see a cell phone in your chocolate-covered paws either, missy!" Clive shot back as he narrowly missed a collision with a boozy-smelling Marilyn Monroe.

"I told you already. No pockets, Clive! No pockets!"

"Don't look at me," Chris said, before the other two could turn accusing eyes upon him. "I barely know how to work the things."

"You're kidding," Becky said, disbelieving.

"I was born in 1750," Chris snapped at her. "I thought telephones in general were just a phase. Who knew people would want to stop writing letters?"

Finally, they cleared the crowd.

"Hurry up!" Clive urged, as they bolted through the front doors of the sheriff's station and ran down the hall to his office. Once there,

Becky pushed past him and seized the telephone, dialing rapidly.

"Come on! Come on!" Clive said urgently.

Becky forced the receiver tighter against her ear as the telephone rang for the third time. Finally, on the fourth ring, someone picked it up at the other end.

"Hello," drawled an unctuous voice.

Becky nodded, and Clive leaned over the desk to put the phone on speaker.

"Where's Pam Burman?" he demanded.

"Oh, I'm sorry. She can't come to the phone right now. She's tied up, you might say." There was a chilling giggle.

"What the hell have you done with Troy?" Chris demanded.

"Your little renfield is similarly occupied at the moment, cousin." Clive's eyebrows rose at the word "cousin."

"But I do hope the three of you will be kind enough to join us shortly. Perhaps we could all have a drink together, hmm?" Rex cackled again. "Yes, a lovely, lovely drink."

"Listen, you son of a bitch," said Chris angrily. "You hurt one hair on his head and I'll…"

"You'll what?" snapped Rex. "Kill me?" He began to laugh heartily. "Oh, I really, really can't wait until we all meet in person. Your little group is so amusing. I've had more laughs in the past few days than I've had in many years. Oh, and by the way…I must insist that only the three of you accept my invitation to come up. Do you understand me, captain? You may bring as many more of your little police people as you like, but they stay in the lobby. Or they die. It's that simple."

"You evil bastard," said Clive.

"Yes, I am, aren't I? And cousin?"

"What?" asked Chris.

"You may tell the ghoul and his friends that I'll deal with them later. I wouldn't want them to feel left out."

Clive turned to Becky at the mention of the word "ghoul"; she shook her head warningly.

"As a matter of fact," Rex continued, "I may soon be able to invite them for dinner. I'll be serving fillet of renfield. I'm sure they'll enjoy it."

"I'll kill you!" Chris shouted. "I'll rip your head off, you prick!"

"At least," said Rex with an evil chuckle, "you'll try."

There was a soft click as Rex replaced the receiver.

◊ ◊ ◊

The ropes binding Troy's feet had finally relented to the sawing action of the elevator cable. Stretching his cramped muscles for a moment, he hiked up his fanny, passing his bound hands under his rear and finally managing to get both his legs through the loop of his arms.

His bound hands now in front, he shifted his weight, swinging himself from side to side until he was able to close his knees around the moving elevator cable. With a sigh of regret for his shorts, which would soon be in ribbons, he placed the ropes binding his hands against the steel cable. He gritted his teeth against the pain caused by the elevator cable as it chafed against the inside of his thighs and began to rapidly move his hands in a sawing motion. He prayed the cable would saw through the bindings before it would be able to saw through his legs.

Within a moment or two, both his thighs and his hands were dripping blood. But the ropes, due to the added sawing motion, were quickly fraying.

◊ ◊ ◊

Clive took the corner turn into the Shoreham Towers driveway on two wheels and stomped on the brakes in anger. Chris and Becky were thrown forward by the abrupt stop. Clive leapt from the driver's seat and slammed the door of the squad car behind himself. He marched into the lobby of the building, hopping mad, without looking to see if the other two were following.

"Temper, temper," Becky said mildly to herself as she opened the rear door of the car for Chris, who was pounding on the window, frantic to get out of the car and get to Troy. He raced into the building behind Clive.

A second squad car pulled up and two armed deputies got out. Seeing Becky, they both grinned; she was an interesting sight. The witch's hat continually slipped down over her forehead, and she kept tripping over her broom handle.

Becky and the deputies reached the reception desk in time to hear Clive's final orders to the officer he'd stationed in the lobby earlier.

"And no one, that means *no one,* is to come up to the penthouse. Is that clear?"

"But officer, sir," interrupted the frightened young receptionist, "people live up there."

"Well, you just get on the house phone and get 'em all down in the lobby as soon as we've gone up." Clive turned to his officers. "And you! Make 'em stay down here until we're through."

The three deputies nodded, their heads bopping up and down like yo-yos. They'd never before seen their captain display anything other than an air of ordered calm and were uncertain how to react.

Clive turned back to the girl behind the counter. "And screw the warrant!" he roared. "Gimme the damn passkeys. Do I look like a friggin' burglar?" She meekly handed them over.

He stormed into the waiting elevator car and pressed the button for Burman's floor. A minute later, he stepped out again and stood with his hands on his hips. "Are we coming?" he asked sarcastically. Without a word, Becky and Chris joined him in the car.

As the doors shut and the elevator moved upward, Becky commented, "Could we please try to control our mood?"

"You sound like a damn nurse!" Clive was angry with good reason. At first he'd been prepared to summon all available deputies to the condo building. Chris and Becky had begged him to forgo that option; they felt the fewer people who knew what was going on, the better. Clive had finally seen the wisdom of their words, but he was far from happy about it. A compromise had been reached; one car would accompany them to keep residents from getting off on the top floor of the building and to maintain order in the lobby. The three would go up to face Rex Castillian alone.

Clive pulled his gun from its holster and checked to make sure it was fully loaded.

"Fat lot of help that'll be," commented Chris. Clive simply glared at him.

"I suppose we should've stopped by Irvine Ranch for some garlic first?" Clive's sarcasm was impossible to miss.

"We were gonna try that in the morgue," Becky said. "Chris said it wouldn't work."

"Well, just what the hell are we supposed to do then?" Clive demanded.

"I'll think of something," said Chris.

"Oh, great! *Now* I feel better! I'm about to be bat bait and I've got Casper and Wendy to help!"

"Just remember, if we can get Troy and Pamela into one of the other apartments, he can't get in without an invitation."

"And how the hell are you supposed to get in?" Clive demanded. Chris looked at him, slightly startled.

"Christ, give me some credit," Becky said. "*I'll* invite him."

The doors opened and they got out.

They walked down the hall on tiptoe. Becky stumbled over the broomstick again but Chris caught her before she could fall. When they reached Burman's door, Clive pushed them flat against the wall on either side of the doorway and prepared to knock.

Before he could lift his knuckles to rap, however, Becky pounded the broomstick on the door. At Clive's look of shock, she said, "What? You think maybe he's got a gun?" She tried the handle and, finding the door unlocked, opened it. The three of them froze for a moment as screams echoed from somewhere inside the apartment. Without a word, Becky dashed inside.

Clive looked at Chris. "He's killing her," the Captain gasped in disbelief.

"No…" said Chris thoughtfully. "I don't think so."

For the first time a look of doubt showed on Clive's face. "Maybe we should have…" He stopped and looked at Chris again. "Would *silver* bullets—" he began.

"Werewolves," said Chris, abruptly dismissing the question. He turned to follow Becky and stopped in the entryway, unable to go any farther. He turned to Clive sheepishly. "Uh, there seems to be a problem."

Clive shook his head in amazement and entered the apartment. He motioned for Chris to follow.

Becky stood in the center of the living room, frozen. At first Chris thought she'd been rooted to the spot in terror, but as he came closer he saw she was trying very hard not to laugh.

"What's so funny?" he whispered angrily.

"Can't you hear that?" she gasped. "In the bedroom."

And they suddenly could. What they had at first taken for Pamela Burman's screams of agony resolved into words. Intent on deciphering the screams and shouts, neither of them noticed Chris as he suddenly stiffened and bolted back out the front door into the hallway.

"No, *you* listen to *me*, you bloodsucking bastard!"

"Madam, please…"

"Don't you 'madam' me, you prick! How dare you come into *my* town…"

"I'm warning you, Ms. Burman. Either you'll be quiet immediately or I'll replace the gag."

"I'm warning *you!*" Pamela screamed. "You put that fucking thing in my mouth again and I swear to God, I'll rip your goddamn balls off with my bare hands!"

The two remaining in the living room heard a crash.

"You bastard!" yelled Burman in the other room. "Look what you made me do! That was my mother's!"

There was another crash.

Becky and Clive poked their heads around the doorjamb to witness an amazing sight. Pamela Burman was partially tied to her vanity chair. She had managed to work her legs free and was hobbling around the room, bent halfway over, the chair attached to her back and arms as if she were giving it a piggyback ride. Rex Castillian was attempting to catch her and sit her back down.

As they watched, Rex caught up with her. He grabbed her arm, but Burman lashed out with one leg, catching Castillian in the shin with one of her wooden platform heels. With a small yelp of pain, he leaped away, circling around once again to try and attack her from behind.

"So! You don't like wood, huh?" Burman snarled. "Just let me get loose for two seconds and I'll give you a wooden enema you'll never forget!" Her right leg lashed out and she smiled as Rex yelped again and leaped out of the way. "By the time I'm done with you, you son of a bitch, you'll have my fucking dining room table shoved up your ass!"

Clive stepped out into the center of the doorway, gun raised and pointed at Rex. "Stop right there!" he ordered.

"Oh," commented Rex, rubbing his bruised shin, "such drama."

"It's about time you two bozos got here," said Burman.

"It is indeed," said Rex, who slowly began to advance on Clive.

"I'm warning you, I'll shoot!" said Clive.

"Oh?" asked Rex. "Here, let me help." He reached up and ripped his shirt open, baring his chest. With one fingernail, he slashed a small circle in the skin around his left nipple. "Let's see if you can hit the bull's-eye." He came forward menacingly.

Without hesitation, Clive fired. The gunshot, tremendously loud, startled Becky and Burman into producing small shrieks of surprise.

Clive was a remarkably good shot. The bullet caught Castillian in the dead center of the circle he'd drawn, flinging him backward as it passed through his body and hit the sliding glass doors that opened on the balcony behind him. The glass shattered with a tremendous crash as Rex toppled to the floor with a look of surprise.

"Goddamn it!" yelled Burman. "They'll assess me for that!"

Clive lost his temper. "What the hell did you expect me to do, Pam? I'm saving your life, for chrissake!"

"Next time could you try to save it without costing me a fortune in plate glass?" she growled back.

Clive bent to untie her. "Sit down and let me get these ropes, will ya?" Burman sat.

"Clive?" began Becky, her voice tinged with horror.

"What is it now?" He was absorbed with a particularly difficult knot. "Vampires!" he snorted. "Y'all really had me going there for a while." The knot came loose. "I've had grandmothers fussing over traffic tickets who were tougher to take down than that guy. I can't believe I actually fell for that crap."

"Uh, Clive?" Becky said again.

"You'll never take him alive," he mimicked. "God, you and your weirdo boyfriends!"

Burman stood up. She looked past Clive's shoulder ready to blast Becky for the whole Count Dracula thing when her eyes suddenly grew as large as dinner plates.

"Clive?" Pamela said.

"What?" he snapped.

"I think you'd better pay attention to what Becky's trying to tell you."

"What the hell is it?" he demanded, whirling around to face Becky. His view was blocked however.

Rex Castillian had gotten to his feet. He was standing in the center of the broken glass, grinning. His shirt was still open, the back of it hanging in tatters. The skin on his chest was smooth and unmarked.

"Now," he said, "let's have some fun."

◊ ◊ ◊

As soon as Chris had realized Burman was alive and obviously unhurt, his thoughts turned to Troy. He knew Becky and the others were in mortal danger, but Troy was his primary concern. The thought of going through even one day without Troy's effervescent smile and outrageous campiness filled him with a feeling of unbounded loss.

He knew Troy was still alive—he sensed it—but in what condition, he couldn't tell. From the moment they'd entered the building, he had the feeling Troy was near. But where? He wasn't in Burman's apartment: Chris had been certain of that as soon as they'd entered. The intensity of the feeling had decreased when he'd walked through the door. But he *knew* Troy was close by.

As Becky and Clive left the living room for the bedroom, Chris ran out of the apartment through the front door. The feeling got stronger. God, where was he? Close, oh so close. In fact, Chris could almost smell him. If only he could still the panic that threatened to overwhelm him and think!

Wait a minute…smell him…smell him…

Good god! thought Chris as the scent of Troy's blood finally fully penetrated his conscious mind. *I can smell him!*

Knowing Troy was nearby and bleeding, Chris began following his scent like a bloodhound. It seemed to be strongest near the elevator. With a cry of panic, using all of his unnatural strength, he forced the elevator doors open and leaned out over the empty shaft.

The smell grew much stronger. As he took a second whiff, something wet hit him on the top of the head. He wiped the dampness away absently and stopped, looking at his hand in amazement— blood. He tasted it. With a pang of horror, he realized the blood was unmistakably Troy's.

Behind him, he heard a gunshot followed by the crash of glass shattering. He debated for a split second. Then, frightened for Troy's safety, he leaped out into the shaft, grasped the cable, and began to climb.

He got only six feet up the cable when he collided with something soft in the darkness. He reached up and a volley of legs began kicking him in the head.

"Go away!" Troy shrieked. "You get away from me! You touch me and my lover'll stake your ass so hard…"

"Monkey!" said Chris, irritation mingled with relief. "It's me! Stop kicking!"

"Chris!" Troy's voice was joyful. Chris climbed up past him and took him in his arms, the two of them dangling fourteen stories above ground, lips plastered together. Troy finally broke the clinch, childishly eager to tell his story.

"I saw the light when the doors opened," Troy said. "I thought it was him."

"Are you all right?" Chris demanded. "My God, Troy! If he's hurt you, I swear I'll—"

"Look," said Troy happily, holding out his bleeding wrists. "I used the elevator cable. I cut my leg pretty bad, though." He looked down. "And my shorts are a total loss."

Chris, without a word, kissed Troy again long and deep. A moment later, Troy came up for air.

"Hey, I keep telling you. One of us still has to breathe here."

"Let's get you down." Chris swarmed up the cable to the machinery above. By pulling the rope attached to Troy's harness, he was able to haul Troy up to one of the metal beams crossing the elevator shaft. In moments, the rope harness followed Troy's other bindings down into the darkness below.

"Where's Becky?" Troy asked.

"Good God!" Chris exclaimed. "I almost forgot. They're in the apartment! With him!" He turned to Troy. "Can you make it down the cable?"

"Just go," said Troy. "I'll be right behind."

CHAPTER THIRTY-SIX

ex was enjoying himself immensely. He took great satisfaction in positioning himself in front of a different item of furniture every time Clive was ready to pull the trigger. So far, the bullets had passed completely through his body each time to totally demolish the television, an antique armoire, a glass and brass shelf unit, and Pamela Burman's signed limited-edition David Hockney lithograph—among other things.

Between Clive's frustration, Burman's howls of protest at the destruction of her property, and Becky's terror, Rex reflected that he'd rarely been able to cause such an emotional upset in a group of normals without resorting to at least *some* physical force on his part. It was almost worth being knocked off his feet with the impact of every bullet. But the gun would shortly be empty, he mused, and then...!

As this thought crossed his mind, the hammer of Clive's pistol clicked down on an empty chamber. Clive stared at it, an expression of disbelief on his face, and then in a burst of frustration he hurled the empty pistol at Rex's head. Rex dodged it easily and it sailed across to room to land on the crystal decanter of brandy that Burman kept on her bedside table. The reek of spirits filled the air.

"That was antique Waterford," Burman snarled. "Somebody's gonna pay for this!"

"Get out!" Clive hissed at her.

"What?" she asked. "How dare you…"

"Just take Becky and get out!" He pulled the passkeys out of his jacket pocket. "Get into another apartment."

"I don't think it would be wise to try *that*," said Rex mildly. He crossed to Clive and caught hold of his arm as Clive drew it back to toss the keys to Burman. "That won't do at all." Slowly, inexorably, he covered Clive's hand with his own and began to squeeze.

Through her fog of panic, Becky heard the bones in Clive's hand shatter as Clive sank to his knees with a bellow of pain.

Rex released him and the keys dropped to the floor. He picked them up and Clive scuttled away, clutching his mangled hand.

"We won't be needing these," he commented and, without looking, tossed them over his shoulder and through the shattered glass doors where they sailed over the balcony to plummet to the pavement fourteen floors below. "And come to think of it," Rex continued, "we won't be needing you either. At least not all of you." He smiled.

"What…what do you mean?" Clive moaned.

Rex crossed to Clive's huddled form and reached down to grasp his shirtfront. Hauling him into the air with one hand, he said, "I only need one worm for the fish I mean to catch, and I doubt you'd be the most effective bait." Rex slowly raised his other hand toward Clive's face, fingers spread. Placing his thumb and little fingers on opposite temples, he squeezed gently. Clive screamed in agony.

"Now," he said to Pam and Becky, "I haven't done this in a very long time but…" He squeezed again, harder. "If you do it just right," he frowned in concentration, "the eyes will come clean out of the skull." Clive shrieked.

"That will be *enough*." Chris's voice was forceful but calm. He stood in the doorway to the bedroom.

"Ah," said Rex, with an overly polite little bow, "my final guest."

"Put him down."

"Certainly," said Rex and effortlessly tossed Clive across the room, where his body impacted with the sole surviving intact item of furniture, Pamela's art nouveau dressing table, reducing it to splinters. Pamela rushed to Clive's side.

"Why are you doing this?" Chris begged.

"Simple, my young friend. As I explained to this dear young lady…" He reached out and grabbed Becky, whirling her around so that she was facing away from him, the broomstick flying out of her hand through the remains of the glass doors to clatter to rest on the balcony. "I dislike being told how to live my life." He pulled her closer and her hat was knocked to the floor. "I especially dislike competition."

He unsheathed one long fingernail and held it to Becky's throat, drawing a small droplet of blood. He daintily licked his finger. "Delicious," he drawled.

"I noticed you in town last week, my friend," he continued pleasantly. "You should be pleased I recognized you. Although I've managed to withdraw from society for a while, I make it a point to keep my ears open. Christopher Driscoll, isn't it? Born in the mid 1700s? I understand you have quite a reputation for, what's that word you all use? Ah, yes, 'putting down' our more voracious relatives." His voice lost all pretense of politeness. "As if we were rabid animals!" he spat. "No, my dear Christopher," he said mockingly, indicating the others in the room, "*these* are the animals! Cattle to be used at our pleasure. Now," he went on in a falsely civil tone, "you will be so kind as to go over there to that broken table and find a piece of wood. A long, sturdy piece of wood."

"What do you think you're doing?" Chris asked defiantly.

"Why, instructing you in the art of suicide."

"What makes you think I'll do it?"

Rex thrust his finger a full quarter inch into the flesh of Becky's throat.

"So what?" said Chris nonchalantly. "She'll be dead in twenty or thirty years anyway. What's to stop me from just walking out?"

Chris was desperately trying to keep Rex's attention. He could see over Rex's shoulder and the sight filled him with dismay. Troy was clambering onto the bedroom balcony. He spotted Chris and smiled brightly. He pointed toward the living room, obviously pleased with himself.

Chris realized with horror that Troy must have gone out the doors in the living room, onto the balcony and, Chris shuddered at the thought, *jumped* across to the adjacent terrace outside the bedroom. Chris fought against trying to signal him to go back where he came from. If Rex had the slightest inkling Troy was standing behind him, Chris knew he'd abandon or kill Becky in favor of Troy as a better hostage.

Rex began to laugh. "Your reputation as a *human*itarian, your penchant for putting down rogues, the knowledge that I make an extremely patient enemy. Any one of a dozen things."

Rex's gaze became steely, like a serpent about to strike. "And the knowledge that I will slowly, oh so slowly, crush the life from your dear friend. Your lover, I believe?" he asked with distaste.

"Where is he?" Chris shouted unnecessarily. Burman had finally seen Troy on the balcony. Chris hoped his outburst had covered her gasp of shock. Fortunately the night was windy and the open air rushing past the open doors would prevent Rex from smelling Troy's bleeding wrists and thighs. At least, Chris hoped it would.

But Rex was enjoying himself far too much to notice either Burman's stifled gasp or the faint smell of Troy's blood. "Oh, he's hanging around. Somewhere." Rex giggled.

On the balcony, Troy was looking for a weapon. At first pleased with himself for thinking to leap from one balcony to the other, he was now seething with frustration that he hadn't thought to carry anything with him.

He considered one of Pamela's lounge chairs momentarily and discarded the idea when he realized he'd never be able to move them quietly enough so that Rex wouldn't hear. Anyway, they were plastic, not wood. He brightened at the sight of a dying ficus tree in a large clay pot. If he could stun Rex with it—maybe hit him over the head—Chris might be able to finish him off.

Troy had absolutely no doubt that Chris would save the day. He just needed a little help. If only there weren't so many normals in the room.

Troy picked up a heavy ceramic ashtray, hefted it with satisfaction, and moved toward the room, hoisting it over his head to strike.

"No!" Chris yelled, his control slipping for a moment when he saw what Troy had in mind. He barely recovered by pretending his outburst had been aimed at Rex. "You'd better tell me where he is," he demanded.

"Or what?" asked Rex.

"Or…or…" Chris's mind was racing. Suddenly he had an inspiration. "Or I'll stake you so hard, we won't be able to *sweep* up the dust."

What is he talking about? Troy wondered. Then he saw Becky's wooden witch's broom, lying in clear view at the balcony entrance. Taking it up quietly, he smiled.

Becky's thoughts were in turmoil. She was terrified, and her throat was starting to hurt, but there was something she was sure she'd missed. Something they'd seen when they entered the bedroom. She mentally ran over the scene they'd been greeted with.

Pam was tied to the chair and she was yelling. Nothing odd there; Pam was usually yelling. Rex was threatening to gag her. Well, couldn't really blame him for trying…Wait a minute, she thought. *Why couldn't he manage to get the gag into her mouth?*

Pamela kept kicking him, but Becky couldn't see how a creature that could take six bullets and barely flinch could be put off by an irate Burman in platform heels. And hadn't Pamela said something about her dining room table? Just what the hell had she been talking about?

Stake! her thoughts cried out. *A wooden stake! And Pamela's platform shoes have wooden heels!*

Unable either to look down to check or to remember which pair of black pumps she'd put on when she'd changed, Becky took a deep breath, said a silent prayer, and slowly lifted her right foot.

Poised to thrust with the broom handle, Troy stopped in dismay. The end of the handle was blunt. Maybe Chris had the strength to drive it through Rex's chest, but Troy certainly didn't. He reconsidered.

"Enough chatter," Rex said. "Either you pick up one of those table legs and place it against your chest or the mortal bitch dies. Now."

In exasperation, Chris watched Troy's confusion on the balcony. "Please, God," he prayed, "just this once, let him use his head."

Slowly, Chris moved over to the wrecked vanity table and picked up one of the wooden legs. Hoping Troy would get the idea, Chris brought the table leg down sharply across his knee, breaking it into two halves with wickedly jagged ends.

Out on the balcony, Troy finally saw the light and began to look around for something he could use to break the broom handle.

"Lest you think you can manage to use that thing on me," Rex continued inside, "remember, there's someone who's come between us." He carefully maneuvered so that Becky was between his own body and the table leg. "Now," he continued, "open your shirt and place the wood over your heart."

Chris slowly unbuttoned his shirt. He reversed his grip on the shaft of wood and positioned the jagged edge against the left side of his chest, feeling the slight pricks of discomfort as the splinters bit gently into his skin.

"More toward the center," Rex spat nastily. "Don't play games with me. I've seen enough innards to know where the heart is."

Chris sighed and moved the table leg so that it was directly over his heart. "Fat lot of good medical school did me," he murmured.

"That's better," said Rex with satisfaction. "Now, you will fall forward, and it will be *I* who will sweep *you* up." The tension in the room was almost a physical presence.

Troy's frustration was boundless. He didn't have the strength to break the broom; besides, Rex would hear the crack. But with Chris standing there about to skewer himself, Troy knew he could wait no longer. Raising the broomstick over his head, he silently crept into the room.

No one was prepared for Rex's curse of pain as Becky brought her heel down sharply on his instep with all of her strength. His grip loosened for a moment as she twisted almost fully out of his grasp.

"Bitch!" he shrieked, and as he made a grab for her throat Troy rushed up behind him and clobbered him over the head with the broomstick so soundly that it snapped clean in half.

Rex wobbled slightly, his hand going to clutch at the lump on his head. He lost his grasp on Becky altogether and she slipped away.

Troy stood frozen, looking with astonishment at the jagged end of the broom he held clutched in his hand. "Now, why didn't I think of that sooner?" he asked.

"Hit the dirt!" Chris yelled to the coroner, at which point both Becky and Troy dropped to the floor.

Chris reversed the chair leg and lunged. At the last second Rex twisted to the side, and the wooden spear, instead of striking him in the heart, pierced his left shoulder, running clear through his body, the point emerging from his back.

Rex let out a roar of pain and grabbed the chair leg with both hands. Cursing, he started to pull it from his body.

Chris lost no time. He stooped, stumbling over Becky's prone body, and grabbed the broken broom handle from Troy. He stood brandishing it like a spear.

Rex smiled evilly through the pain. "Not so easy to kill, am I?" With a final grimace, he yanked the chair leg from his body and hurled it at Chris.

Surprised, Chris instinctively batted it away with the handle of the broom as Rex attacked, fingers contorted like claws, reaching for Chris's throat. Chris hurriedly swung the broom handle back around and watched with a cringe as Rex, unable to check his forward rush in time, impaled himself upon it. Unfortunately, the handle had penetrated Rex's body too low to be fatal. Wounded, Rex was likely to become even more dangerous.

A jet of blood shot from his stomach and Rex sank to the floor, clutching at the broomstick. His hands scrabbled futilely on the blood-slicked wood of the broom.

"Not so easy..." he breathed, then grinned and began to try to stand up.

From the corner, unnoticed by any of the others, Burman stood up, picking up the other half of the broom from where it had fallen near her. As Rex finally struggled to his feet, Burman moved forward and with all her strength shoved the wooden spar into the center of Rex's back. Chris watched Rex's eyes widen in shock as the tip of Burman's makeshift spear passed through his heart and emerged from the front of his chest.

"Funny," she remarked, "I always thought the heart was on the left too."

The eyes of the two vampires met. Chris's gaze was filled with unutterable sorrow; Rex Castillian's eyes were filled with something else.

"So long..." he gasped. "So many years..."

He collapsed to the floor. Turning his head to meet Chris's eyes one final time, he breathed, "At last..." His eyes closed.

Suddenly, there was a rush of air as if the room had been invaded by a Kansas tornado. Becky, Pamela, and Troy shielded their eyes from the wind; even Chris was forced to blink.

A moment later, the windstorm ceased as abruptly as it had began. The two halves of the broken broomstick clattered to the floor.

There, where Rex had been lying seconds before, was just a pile of dust, already disturbed by the breeze from the broken glass door, and the clothes Rex had been wearing. Of his body, there was no sign.

"Well," said Burman with satisfaction as she went over to Rex's remains and kicked at them, scattering the dust even more, "that'll teach him to fuck with Pamela Burman!"

She picked up one half of the broomstick and stood, her eyes surveying the wreckage of the room. Finally, her gaze came to rest sternly on Chris, who was standing over Becky's and Troy's still prostrate forms.

"What I want to know now is," she said, brandishing the broken broomstick threateningly, "which one of you three bozos is gonna pay for my stuff?"

CHAPTER THIRTY-SEVEN

Two weeks had passed; it was mid November. Troy had shown up at the morgue several days earlier, interrupting Becky's autopsy of a young woman who had been a member of a film crew shooting scenes for the remake of *Bringing Up Baby* on location in West Hollywood Park. The deceased, one Sheryl "Duke" Ambrose had been one of the leopard wranglers on the set, enticing the leopard up a flight of stairs so that the director, a gruff-voiced Italian who was already three weeks and several millions of dollars over-budget, could get a particularly difficult shot—the camera having been hidden in one of the stair risers in order to shoot the leopard's underbelly as it went up the stairs.

The leopard, a gentle creature affectionately dubbed "Penny" by the film crew, refused to be enticed, preferring to lounge at the foot of the stairs, soaking up the late-fall sun. The film crew had tried everything; Penny merely glanced disdainfully at the choice hunks of raw meat being waved at her by them. Finally, the unfortunate wrangler had put her shoulder to Penny's hindquarters and began to shove her up the wooden stairway.

As Penny's paws hit the first set of stairs, she changed her mind, deciding that sunbathing opportunities might be better at the top of the stairway after all. She suddenly bounded up the stairs, taking everyone by surprise. The startled Ms. Ambrose had grabbed onto Penny's tail and had been hauled up the steps after her. At the top, disoriented from banging her head repeatedly against several of the stair treads, Ambrose relaxed her grip and fell.

The unit nurse examined her and discovered a broken leg, a dislocated shoulder, and a possible concussion. The ambulance had been summoned and Ms. Ambrose was loaded onto the gurney by the paramedics in preparation for going to Cedars-Sinai. Unfortunately, however, the paramedics had difficulty with the rear ambulance doors; they refused to open.

Leaving their patient strapped to the gurney by the curb on San Vicente Boulevard, both attendants began to haul on the doors. The doors flew open, spilling one of the paramedics onto the curbside grass and sending the other backward to slam against the gurney. The wheel locks on the gurney failed and, still bearing the unfortunate Ms. Ambrose, it sailed into the middle of San Vicente Boulevard without warning.

Surprised motorists swerved to avoid it as it raced south down the gently sloping street, past the Pacific Design Center, and soared toward the intersection at Melrose. By rolling her body from side to side and shifting her weight, the resourceful Ms. Ambrose was able to direct the escaping gurney off to the side of the road and toward a business specializing in ornamental ironwork. Zooming up the driveway with barely slackened speed, the gurney burst through the glass doors of the shop and raced across the showroom floor as the sales clerks looked on helplessly.

The gurney finally came to rest, slamming against a decorative iron gate with a distinctive art deco lily pattern that had been hung on the far wall of the showroom. The shop's employees raced to the aid of the screaming Ms. Ambrose, but they stopped as the loud groan of tortured metal filled the air. Slowly, the weight of the gate pulled the nails upon which it was hung from the wall. Everyone watched in horror, none more so than Ms. Ambrose, as the gate came crashing down, obliterating both the gurney and its occupant.

Ms. Ambrose had been brought in to Becky DOA with the imprint of a calla lily still visible in the middle of her forehead.

The film company was suing both Penny's owner and the paramedics. The paramedics were suing the ambulance company. The ironworks was suing the film company, the paramedics, the City of West Hollywood, and Ms. Ambrose's estate. The city was suing the film company. And Ms. Ambrose's eighty-five-year-old mother was suing everyone.

Troy burst into the morgue as Becky was just finishing up with a plaster cast of the offending lily. He hoisted himself up onto the adjoining table and, swinging his legs back and forth like a small child, watched Becky's actions with interest.

"What happened to her?" he asked, curious.

"It's a long story. Almost three blocks long. What's up?"

"I need your help," Troy said.

Becky almost dropped the plaster cast.

"No way!" she said. "There is *no way* I'm gonna get involved with any more vampires, ghouls, or...or...whatever!" She placed the plaster cast carefully on the counter. "Every time I pass so much as a palm reader, I get chills up and down my spine."

"But Becky..."

"No buts about it! Clive Anderson is still in a cast, we had to rebuild the front entrance to City Hall, and Pamela Burman is fighting with her insurance company, trying to explain how her apartment got trashed. Apparently," she said dryly, "insane vampire killers are exempt under the Acts of God clause in her policy."

"It's nothing like that."

"It better not be," she said sternly.

"It's Chris."

"What's wrong?" Becky was suddenly concerned.

"Well, nothing," Troy replied. "Well, if you call turning 240-something 'nothing.' "

"His birthday?" Becky asked.

"Yeah, I want to give him a surprise party before we go back to Philly next week." Troy made a face of disgust. "Philly! Yuck! I've been trying to get him to stay, but you know how he is. Do you think you could…?" He stopped, looking at her, measuring her probable response. "No, I guess not. After all, he's only known *you* ten years. If *I* can't…"

"Is that what you came here to talk about?" Becky asked, hoping he would come to the point quickly so she could finish work and get to lunch.

"No," he conceded and cleared his throat in preparation for his sales pitch. "It's just that, well, since Scotty and all went back to Chicago, we don't know many people out here. Except for my tricks, I mean, and I really couldn't invite any of them."

Troy picked up one of Becky's clamps to get a better view and began opening it and closing it in fascination.

"What's this for?" he asked.

"Not for you." Becky gently removed it from his inquisitive little hands.

"Well, *excuse* me, Miss Thing!" said Troy saucily and went on. "Anyway, would you, ah…I mean…do you think the police guy and the old lady would mind coming?"

"If you call her an old lady to her face, she'll mind." Becky picked up a scalpel and turned back to her work. "I'll ask. Now, shoo!"

The party on the fifteenth was sparsely attended but very successful. The guest list was not limited to Burman, Clive, Becky, and Troy. Hanna and Gustav had also shown up; Hanna had spent two days in her kitchen in preparation and stood by the dining room table in Chris's apartment beaming with pride as the three normals complimented her on her culinary expertise.

Becky, seeing the huge dining room table laden with food, including some orgasmic looking pastries, felt as if she'd died and gone to heaven. She judiciously sampled the salads and main dishes Hanna had prepared and then shamelessly loaded her plate with luscious-looking desserts and dove in.

Troy had managed to keep Chris ignorant of the party by turning the stereo up and climbing into the coffin with him until he was certain that the guests had all arrived. Chris emerged from the bedroom, showered and dressed this time, to be greeted by an enormous sheet cake bearing so many candles that Troy would later spend an entire afternoon getting the smoke stains off the living room ceiling and the wax out of the carpet.

All of the guests had taken undue care in their choice of gifts. Hanna and Gustav gave him a small oil painting of a young, muscular Moses leading the Israelites out of Egypt. "It's a Botticelli," Gustav explained. "We bought it from Sylvia. It reminded Hanna and I of when we first met you."

Chris, who was so touched he would have wept had he been able to do so, immediately sent Troy to fetch a hammer and nail and hung it directly over the sofa in a place of honor.

From Clive, he got a little fourteen-carat-gold stake on a chain to hang around his neck. "I started out looking for a silver bullet," Clive offered shyly, "but I remembered in time."

Burman offered him a long, flat package wrapped in bright red and silver paper. "Sorry about the color," she grumbled, "I had no idea it was gonna clash with your decor." Troy shot her an irritated glance that she pointedly ignored.

Chris unwrapped it to reveal a framed lobby card from the Broadway production of *Dracula* starring Frank Langella. So as not to show favoritism, he hung it next to the Botticelli.

"Now mine!" said Troy with barely concealed excitement. He scuttled under the cloth covering the dining room table and emerged tugging at a large crate.

"Gimme some help here," he complained. Gustav and Becky moved to assist him. "I got a crowbar too," he said proudly.

After much effort and several splinters, the gift was uncrated to reveal a gorgeously lacquered antique coffin.

"I got the idea from Becky and the loan from Sylvia," said Troy. "It's the one from the museum. Bela Lugosi used it on Broadway. I had it refinished and relined." He flung open the lid to reveal a spanking-new scarlet satin lining.

"What is this with him and red?" Burman asked Clive sotto voce.

Finally, Becky approached Chris with a plain heavy cardboard box. She handed it to him with a serious look in her eyes. "I had no idea what to get you," she said. "But I wanted it to be something, you know, meaningful."

Chris opened the lid. The box contained moist black soil with a few small pieces of rock. He looked at her, a question unspoken on his face.

"It's from West Hollywood Park," Becky said. "I've been educating myself. I hope, in time, it will be as kind to you as the other." She opened the antique coffin and folded back the lining covering its bottom. Reaching into the cardboard box, she withdrew a heaping handful of earth and spread it out, mixing it in with the Massachusetts soil that was already there. She turned to look at Chris once again. "Do you understand?" she asked softly.

Chris nodded as the others, one by one, Clive first, followed by Hanna and Gustav and, finally, Burman, silently took a handful of soil from the box and added it to the bottom of the coffin.

"Well," said Troy, barely restraining his happiness as he added his own handful of earth to the casket, "I always knew she'd come through if I asked."

Becky's eyes never left Chris's, and although she knew it was impossible she would almost have sworn that in the corner of his right eye she saw a small, red-tinged tear.